Iron Heart

by

Gini Rifkin

Iron Heart

COPYRIGHT © 2011 by Gini Rifkin

Cover Art by *Nicola Martinez*

The Wild Rose Press
PO Box 708
Adams Basin, NY 14410-0706
Visit us at www.thewildrosepress.com

Publishing History
First English Tea Rose Edition, 2011
Print ISBN 1-60154-892-3

Published in the United States of America

Faran, the Iron Heart.

It was a name that set one's mind to wondering. Did he pride himself on disallowing any woman to touch his cold hard heart? Did he woo ladies into love trysts with promises of treasure and pleasure only to tragically desert them?

For certes he was unlike anyone Leanora had ever known. He approached life fearlessly, as if he dared anyone to cross his path, his mood, or the territory he called his own. And his generous mouth was an unbidden fascination. It could accommodate a childlike smile, tempering all the fierceness he worked so hard to portray. Or it could accommodate a reassuring smile, making her believe everything in her troubled world would be all right.

He was handsome to be sure—with a rock hard body, images of which occupied her thoughts much too often. And his mind was also intriguing. As strikingly developed as his form, it was a quality Leanora truly admired. Knowledge could be a powerful weapon, and Faran appeared well armed.

To her benefit, he seemed preoccupied with the present and not with prying into her past. Nor did he threaten to rule her future. He treated her differently, he treated her like...a friend. The idea stunned her. Life had never afforded her the opportunity to know or cherish another person in such a manner. Another new experience.

Then a spark of yearning for more than mere friendship flickered inside of her. *You can never trust a man,* she chastised, *you can only believe in yourself.* Unyielding logic cooled the fiery ember of need, but not before it claimed the barren part of her never before touched by warmth or light.

Dedication

Another one for Gary—gone but never forgotten.
Until we meet again, the song will go unsung,
the poem remains unspoken.

Gratefully dedicated to the voices in the night.
You shared the pain and kept me sane.
Always keep in mind I love you.
Special thanks to The Wild Rose Press
and Amanda Barnett—maker of dreams.

*The days on earth for every one of us are numbered;
he who may should win renown before his death; that
is a warrior's best memorial when he has departed
from this world.*

~The Beowulf

Chapter One

The Farne Islands, September 879 A.D.

They had stolen his past. And he was about to
lose his future.

Faran wrestled for control of the steerboard. He
had never fought harder, not even at the shieldwall.
Yet, try as he might to guide his small ship to safety,
the storm howling down from the north thwarted his
every move. Deadly rocks ringed the shore—looming
dangerously close.

He hazarded a glance at his three stalwart
companions. Heads down, they strained at the oars,
and while their loyalty and courage nourished his
soul, he knew in his heart their attempt was futile.

Who had conjured this pernicious maelstrom?
Only moments ago, the sky had been blue and the
sea calm. This raging tempest, wielded by a
merciless hand, threatened to destroy his ship, his
companions, and his hope for redemption. The gods
had forsaken him yet once again.

****

Exhausted, Faran lay prone upon the cold wet
shore, his head turned to one side, the sand grating
against his cheek. He groaned and willed himself to
turn over, but muscle and sinew refused to follow
where his mind desperately tried to lead.

Resigned to immobility, he studied the area
within his scope of vision. Where were his hearth-
mates? Did they live? Were they nearby, possibly in

need of his help? These thoughts pounded through his brain even as the surf pounded the craggy coastline.

A piece of flotsam washed up on the beach, and an inquisitive gull swooped down to inspect this treasure newly relinquished from the sea. The runes etched upon the smooth wooden surface were familiar to him—the board had once been part of his sailing vessel. But his ship had gone down—along with his good intentions.

He closed his eyes and recalled the rasping sound of wood scraping rock. A mountainous wave had swallowed his ship, and he had been catapulted body and soul into the sea. Then along with the other aquatic grist, the ocean had chewed him up well and good, only to regurgitate him upon the shore like an unsavory bit of shell.

At the memory of the underwater horror, his eyes snapped opened, and he sucked in a lungful of air. Surely the gods had made a mistake. He was Tyne Faran Kilbraun, the Iron Heart. Seventh son of the man who ruled the Storm Geats, seventh son of the woman who belonged to the tribe of the Wulfingas. He was keeper of the Word and protector of the sacred relics. Were these facts of no consequence to the deities who ruled the heavens and the earth?

Anger flooded his senses, renewing his resolve to live, renewing his hunger for revenge. Once he had known the love of his family and the pride of his countrymen. Now he was a man alone and disillusioned. And like a withered old crone, he lay in a heap, unable to move or even call out for help. But he refused to draw his last breath on this godforsaken jumble of rock. Not here—with no one in attendance but the crabs who would come to pick clean his bones. He could not leave this mortal coil without reclaiming his honor. If he were to die now, his parents would live out their lives in shame, and the history of his people would be lost forever.

In painful confusion, his mind wandered between the world of light and the domain of darkness. Yet, regardless of which realm he traveled, each was filled with nightmarish images—visions he could neither battle nor escape.

Time, indifferent to his suffering, traveled onward and with a final caress, the soft rays of the setting sun stroked his exposed skin. Small consolation for his bruised and battered flesh, still he gratefully accepted the warmth. Come the gloaming, even this comfort would be taken from him, and he would be left to languish in the cold arms of the night.

As the sphere of shadows crept closer, a fiery image of Lord Gorham blazed across his mind. That murderous bastard and his depraved sister, Romaine, were responsible for what had befallen his people. Although in truth, there was blame enough to share.

He gritted his teeth and sought to raise his hand to implore the Fates to deliver him from this tragedy. But he no longer possessed the strength to lift his arms, and he no longer possessed the naïve spirit of youth to challenge the judgment of the gods.

****

Leanora tapped her foot with impatience. Would the sun never set? Thank goodness, the autumnal equinox would soon be upon them. After Mabon, the hours of brightness, stretching into forever, would wane even more to her advantage. Until then, wait she must, for it was no longer safe to venture out along the shoreline in the light of day. Of late, there had been an increase in the number of ships passing by. And although no one had yet to come ashore on her tiny isle, they might if they saw her.

Like silent demons, the wretched ships

appeared without warning. Their wickedly graceful, serpentine prows gliding out of the sea mist—mighty beasts, unstoppable and terrifying in their splendor. At the very sight of them her heart raced with fear, and it did not calm again until the ships were reduced to harmless blurs upon the horizon. Yes, it was safer to wait until nightfall.

As darkness subdued even the memory of the sun, she grabbed up a large basket and drew aside the ragged piece of cloth hanging across the cottage door. She liked to think of her habitat as a cottage, although in truth she knew it only merited to be called a hut. Woven of sticks and branches, it listed in the direction of the prevailing winds. She had lived in a real house once. A home of timbered halls carved from towering oaks. Woven tapestries warmed the walls, but those who dwelled within had been wrapped in cold cruelty. Thank the Lord those days were over. She was safe now. Was it worth the price of living like a peasant, with threadbare clothes and no well-tended hearth? She had to believe it was so.

Turning her back on her thoughts and the hut, she stepped through the doorway. The sand, still warm from the day's heat, comforted her bare feet, and threading her way between the huge boulders, she glanced at the troubled night sky. The stars refused to shine, and high-riding clouds obliterated the full moon. There would be no helpful illumination to guide her to the nets along the shore. No matter, she knew the way by heart, and the use of a torch might attract more than moths in her direction.

At the breakers, she paused and listened to the ocean's never ending song. Tonight the tune seemed filled with lament. There was no gurgle of happiness where the waves lapped at the rocks, and no sigh of contentment as the receding waters rushed back to the sea. Perhaps the elements regretted their earlier behavior of today when the wind had terrified the air and the waves had battered the island. For a moment she had feared for her life, but the storm had soon passed. Like people, the wind and the water were fickle and not to be trusted. Yet on occasion, the sea could be benevolent, and she gave thanks for the fish and crab it provided. Together with foraged berries and the eggs from the chickens, her meals were healthy and varied. Not grand fare, but good enough for now.

Angling to the left, she abandoned the shelter of the rocks and headed across the slope of open beach. A sharp wind teased her ankles, buffeting her from behind. It felt as if another storm approached. Or did the cold herald more than a change in weather?

In answer to her unspoken question, she tripped over something where nothing should be. Her skirt tangled about her legs, and she pitched headfirst over the unexpected obstacle. The basket flew from her grasp as she landed with a thud in the sand. A cross between a growl and a groan came from the mound that had caused her fall.

On hands and knees she scurried to one side. Then leaning forward, she peered through the darkness trying to determine what lay before her. Was it a scaly monstrous thing from the sea? Or worse yet, a human? Instinctively she unsheathed the long-bladed dagger hanging at her waist.

The *thing* groaned again, and uttered several words in a language unknown to her.

Holy Savior, it was a man. She prayed he had not been sent to find her. Her mouth went dry, her throat constricted. She tightened her grip on the hilt of the knife. "I will kill you before I let you take me back," she threatened, not caring if he understood her Saxon words.

He made no response in sound or movement.

What should she do? *Drive the knife swiftly into his heart,* instinct urged. Weapon at the ready, she awkwardly crawled forward on both knees and one free hand. She was glad for the darkness hiding his features. A faceless enemy was so much easier to hate and deliver unto God.

Drawing closer, she realized the man lay upon his stomach. In ire, she jammed the knife into its rawhide case. Reaching across his broad shoulders, she gripped the remnant of his tunic, and using her body as a counterweight, leaned backward. The stranger rolled toward her. She scrambled out of the way as he settled onto his back. A rush of air escaped his mouth.

"Thank you," he whispered, through lips that sounded stiff and parched. This time the words he uttered were in Saxon English. He may be the master of two languages, but he was a fool to thank her for helping him.

She knelt once more at his side, and again took up the blade. Like a pagan priestess about to perform a sacrifice, she raised the knife high overhead and tensed for the downward thrust. Then the horrible truth of what she was about to do hit her full force and her resolve faltered. The moon broke through the clouds casting an ethereal brightness upon the man's face and chest. He gazed up at her with an expression as startled and questioning as a child's.

She swallowed hard, shocked by the manner of brutality that had come so easily to her. The pain and suffering she had seen and endured did not give her free reign to become as merciless and savage as her tormentors. Still, she must protect herself.

Leanora glared down at the man. His straight nose and the planes of his cheeks were highlighted by moon-glow, and the same celestial light turned his shoulder-length hair into a mantle of silver. Her gaze drifted lower.

He labored for each breath, and through the rips in his tunic a wet glittering iridescence reflected off his powerful chest and well muscled abdomen. The arm rings he wore and the scars that he bore proclaimed him a warrior, a man who had faced many enemies, a man who had won the day.

Captivated by these thoughts, she remained unmoving. The rough pebbles dug into her knees, and her arms ached from holding the knife on high. A decision must be made. But she was more familiar with taking orders than making far-reaching resolutions.

"Half the treasure will be yours," the man croaked, "if you let me live."

Treasure? There were not enough riches in the world to prompt her to risk her freedom.

She brought the knife down with all her might, burying it to the hilt in the sand beside the stranger's right ear. "You owe me your life, warrior." She spat out the words like bitter fruit tart upon her tongue. The man's eyelids drooped, and his head lolled to one side.

Leanora rocked back on her haunches. Then she began to shake, not out of dread for what she had almost done, but out of fear for what she had not been able to do.

Desperately she prayed her compassion would not also prove to be her undoing.

Chapter Two

The piercing sound of a cock's crow catapulted Faran to consciousness. By the gods he felt awful. His entire body was one giant throbbing ache. He could not determine where one pain stopped and another began. As the raucous noise shattered the silence for a second time, he cringed and opened his eyes.

Sunlight speared through a gap in the vine-covered roof and clawed a path to the far reaches of his brain. Fragmented recollections tumbled through his mind—his vessel, the reef, the rocky shore. Even now, the smell of the ocean hung in the air, but he was not at sea, the familiar pitch and roll of his ship was blatant in its absence. How had he endured the night? And how had he reached this place of shelter?

He swallowed, and then grimaced. His throat felt lined with thistle, and his stomach was queasy with having held a barrel of seawater. He tried to turn on his side, but could not move.

Alarm accompanied his pain. It was not lack of strength staying his actions. His arms, chest, and thighs were tightly bound to the raised pallet upon which he lay. Sweat sprung to his brow as he struggled to free himself, but the more he fought the ropes, the more constricting was their grasp. Numbness crept down one leg where the cord cut off his circulation.

Resisting the urge to continue thrashing about, he tried to calm his panic and reason out his situation. Then a merciless throbbing seized his head—the pain increasing with his efforts to think in too great a detail.

He had never been held captive, and to be rendered meek and defenseless was a fearful thing. His method of warring was to meet his enemy face to face. This was a new experience, one he did not favor. He willed himself to take a full calming breath, but the bindings were so restrictive he could barely breathe at all—let alone deeply.

Cautiously, he angled his head to one side and glanced around. Where were his companions? Guilt overtook all other emotions as he realized misfortune had again befallen those around him, those he loved and sought to protect.

Clinging to resolve rather than recrimination, he studied his place of imprisonment. The walls of the hut were crude, made of branches and sticks, and the floor was a mixture of dirt and sand. Bunches of sea grass were tied in the rafters, and the only favorable comment the shabby accommodation could inspire, was one in praise of its cleanliness.

He shifted his gaze and his vision blurred, doubling his nausea. But as he concentrated on the far wall, the world slid back into focus. Near the open doorway, a basket and a shabby cloak hung from fish-bone hooks. A walking staff leaned against a corner post. Stumps and planking served as furniture—some pieces requiring assistance from one's imagination. A meager habitat by any standard, unadorned except for one small well-turned coffer, oddly out of place.

A shadow fell across the threshold. He feigned sleep and heard someone enter. They drew near and stopped by his side, tugging at the ropes as if checking to see they remained secure. Then the person retreated.

Unable to curb his curiosity, he opened his eyes and caught sight of a woman dressed in a white nightshift. In bright contrast, her waist-length red hair fluttered about in disarray. She glanced to the side, and her profile sparked a vivid image from the night before. The female had thought to kill him. His pulse quickened, and he prayed the young woman's mood had improved with the coming of the dawn.

She untied the neck of her chemise and eased it down off her shoulders. The loose fabric caressed shapely hips, and his trepidation warmed to a hotter more basic emotion.

Supple charm graced her movements as she poured water from a bucket to the indentation of a flat stone serving as a basin. And although her mantle of russet hair obscured her nakedness, he could still see the sweet gentle curve at the small of her back.

More of her comely form was exposed as she retrieved a drying cloth and placed it at the ready. Her breasts were small, and in the chill morning air, her shell-pink nipples were erect and inviting. Pleasure streaked through his loins, and he grew hard with imaginings. Then he writhed in misery as the needful ache added to the pain already haranguing his body. Still, it was reassuring to know at least part of his anatomy had not succumbed to injury.

The woman hesitated and darted a glance in his direction. He closed his eyes, hoping he had not been caught looking. When she did not speak nor approach his pallet, he dared to watch once more.

She was sleek as a red deer in spring, but as she lifted her arms and gathered her hair into a thick knot, his lusty daydreams faded. With her tresses swept aside, he could see dark streaks upon her back. At first he did not recognize the marks, then he clenched his jaw. They were the healed wounds of the whip. He had rarely seen a man so scarred, and never a woman. The wretch who had beaten her must have been cruel indeed, with a vile temper and a heavy hand. What fortitude it must have taken to survive such an ordeal.

She leaned over and washed her face, and his gaze slid lower. The thin muslin stretched taut to reveal every curve of her nicely rounded bottom. The hemline shifted upward, exposing shapely ankles and calves. A long-legged wench she was.

Her ablution finished, she tugged on a linen smock, a forest green skirt, and a short over-tunic. Then using a comb whittled from wood, she unsnarled her hair, plaited it into two thick braids, and tied the ends with bits of colored cloth. Securing a rawhide-encased dagger at her waist, she appeared ready to face the day.

As he thought to speak, she grabbed up a leather bag familiar to him. Taken by surprise, Faran held his words. The pouch had been tied at his waist when his ship had gone down. It contained his most precious keepsakes. He was glad it had been salvaged, but was not pleased this stranger poked about his personal effects without his leave.

The woman nimbly untied the sack, drew forth the vellum map, and studied it from various angles. Her curiosity short lived, she set the rendering aside and next retrieved his talisman. Admiring the iron heart, cross-wrapped in wires of gold, she traced her finger across the runes etched upon the stalwart piece of metal. Hefting it several times, as if trying to determine its worth by its weight, she discovered it possessed a hollow center with something hidden inside and she shook the amulet beside her ear.

To see his cherished talisman clutched in the hands of another made his blood run hot. It was more than just a fetish with which she toyed. It was his essence, his spirit.

Unable to force open the heart to reveal its contents, she snatched a large stone from the floor and raised the rock on high.

"The tooth of the boar resides within," he called, phrasing his words in the language she had used the previous night.

She spun around, lips parted in surprise, but gave no verbal response as her eyes narrowed and her gaze swept the length of his body.

"You are finally awake," she retorted as if accusing him of oversleeping. "I thought mayhap my prayers would be answered and you would succumb to your injuries."

"Sorry to disappoint you. Now untie me."

She dropped the rock and tossed his amulet onto the "table." "I think you are fine as you are," she replied, her hands on her hips, her head tilted defiantly.

"You have no reason to bind me like an animal," he argued. "I mean you no harm."

"Regarding your intentions, only time will tell," she countered, "and I would sooner trust an animal than a man."

The woman fought well with words, but he was in no mood for sparring. Hopefully, she was practical as well as clever. "I must relieve myself. I thought you would prefer I do so outside. The choice is yours."

She frowned as if she had not considered this possibility. Then she crossed the hut, grabbed a length of seal-hide rope, and took a tentative step in his direction. "Hold forth your hands," she ordered.

When he complied, she warily touched his forearm then jerked away as if his flesh burned her fingertips. Why did she approach him as if he were a mad hound?

Compressing her lips into a determined line, she converged upon him again. This time, without hesitation, she tied his wrists together. Employing a much longer length of rope, she attached one end to his right ankle and the other end to a corner post of the hut. After loosening the restraints binding his body, she drew her knife and stepped back, motioning for him to go about his business.

Exuberant at being released, he levered upright onto the edge of the pallet. The blood drain from his head, and the room spun at an alarming angle. He hunched forward and took a deep breath. From the corner of his eye, he saw the girl reach out as if to steady him. Then she hesitated and retreated farther away from his side.

He gathered his strength, tensing and flexing his muscles in random order. His body felt shattered into pieces more plentiful than the stars, but he did not think he had suffered any broken bones. Slowly and carefully, he raised his head and glanced out the open door. There were no other huts in sight. "Are you here alone?"

The girl stiffened and tightened her grip upon the knife. "That would be foolish of me."

"Yes," he agreed, "foolish indeed." Thoughts of his comrades again came to mind, and he opened his mouth to inquire as to their whereabouts. Then he reconsidered. What if they were safely entrenched in the surrounding hills? She may not know of their existence, and an ill chosen word on his part might cause them discovery or worse.

"How many came with you?" she asked.

The question took him by surprise. Then foreboding sprang to life in his stomach and spiraled through his guts. "I came alone," he lied.

"So far, I know of three others," she quietly revealed.

The Valkyrie take him, she had found them all. He bowed his head, and clung to the meager hope and comfort uncertainty offered. Then he could wait no longer to know the truth. "Are they alive or dead?"

"Dead," she whispered, and that one word, spoken so softly, cut him more deeply than had she wielded her dagger.

He recalled the uncommon fierceness the female had displayed last evening, and red flags of fury unfurled in his mind pushing aside sorrow. Had she been responsible for the death of his friends? He slid from the pallet. "What happened to them?" he shouted, as he wrestled with the ropes binding his wrists. "Where are they?"

Her eyes widened in alarm. "There was nothing I could do." She sidled away. "When I came upon them this morning they were already dead—already unsouled." Sympathy shimmered in her vivid blue eyes—genuine enough to convince him she told the truth.

"There are no others?" she finally asked.

"No, there are no others." He glanced away and hobbled toward the door, the rope-leash dragged behind him as if he were some unfortunate slave. Overcome with the need to appear strong before his captor, he straightened his protesting body to its full height and stepped out into the light.

The glare of day sent him reeling, as did the knowledge his friends were dead. Now he suffered in spirit as well as in body. Ascending a small hill, he halted beside a tree. How could they be dead and gone forever? Yet what else should he have expected on this accursed venture. Three more deaths were now added to the trove of regret and sorrow he carried. It would have been a kinder fate to have died along with them. But once again, like in his village, he had been spared while others had perished.

Hampered by the cords around his wrists he clumsily reached under his tunic to free himself, then he glanced over his shoulder. To his annoyance the girl stood in the doorway. "This will take all day if you watch," he called in irritation.

She moved away from the entrance of the hut. With a sigh of relief, he pissed into the underbrush and slumped into a more tolerable stance. After readjusting his clothing, he rested his shoulder against the trunk of the tree, and stared out at the unrelenting sea.

In the blink of an eye, everything had changed. For his three childhood friends, their first sojourn would be their last. Their bright journey to adventure, now a somber portage through Death's door. It seemed like only yesterday they were all high-spirited lads yearning to go a-voyaging, wishing to fight their way to glory, to earn honor and acclaim. Cloaked in youthful optimism and girded with unbound exuberance, they had thought themselves invincible. But mortal frailty was like clay in the hands of Fate—meanly twisted and reshaped for no more valid purpose than the amusement of the gods.

Grief knotted in his chest and tears bit at his eyes. "I promise you this, my friends," he vowed, "you shall have a proper burial and be remembered for the heroes you became."

Turning away, he vowed another oath. For the sake of his people and the memory of his companions, he would continue this quest to its inevitable end. Only now he would go forth alone— the way in which he should have begun.

Weary from his short foray, he shuffled back toward the hut. He had enough aches and pains to thoroughly torment two bone-houses, and he felt light headed again. What he needed was food, then he would see to his comrades.

He flexed his shoulders trying to work out the stiffness, and for the first time, he noticed the cuts and bruises on his hands and forearms had been treated with a balm he did not recognize. How curious the woman had ministered to him with such care after threatening to take his life. At least she had not stolen his arm rings.

He reached again under his tunic. The ointment had also been applied to the wounds on his abdomen and groin. She had not only tended him well but without reserve. A ball of warmth collected in the pit of his stomach, and he wondered if she liked what she had seen. She was not an unappealing bit of softness. But her temper seemed harsh and most unpredictable.

Working his way down the hill, he studied the lay of the land. A blanket tied to a rope of braided vines lay abandoned in the shade. A smooth indentation in the sand led from the rope to the shore. So that is how she moved him from the water's edge. She had dragged him a goodly distance using a tree trunk as a pivot point. Quite the clever notion—for a female. He must have walked from there to the bed, although he could not recall doing so.

He trudged on. The fire pit, ringed with rocks, seemed small and not suited for more than one or two people. Only one cloak had hung beside the door of the hut, and the enclosure offered but the one sleeping pallet. He paused and glanced around in every direction. Could it be possible she really was here alone. But why? He recalled the marks upon her back. She could be a runaway slave. He gave a snort of amusement. She did not speak nor act like one.

Entering the shelter, he eased his tortured body down upon a stump. "What is your name?" he asked.

Mutely she dismissed the question as she went about shortening the rope running between his ankle and the corner post.

"I am Faran Kilbraun, the Iron Heart." He nodded toward the heart-shaped amulet lying next to his bag on the crooked table.

"Where is the treasure you promised?" she demanded, ignoring his introduction.

"What treasure?"

At her murderous expression, another piece of last night flashed through his mind. He recalled offering her half of his treasure in return for his life. It had seemed a good idea at the time.

"Well, I do not have it on my person," he said.

"It was on your ship?"

"No...it was not on my ship," he answered, truthfully. "I haven't, ah, exactly found it yet."

"I knew I should not trust you," she shouted.

He jumped at her outburst and watched in silence as she stormed about the restricted confines of the hut.

"I should have left you in the hands of the Lord Savior. The ravens would have been even more delighted with four bodies upon which to feast."

He grimaced at the image her words conjured. "Your God is supposed to be merciful," he chided.

"It is not always so." She halted across the room from him. "Sometimes, regardless of which deity one petitions, the neediest of prayers go unanswered."

It sounded as if she spoke from experience. Suddenly the woman appeared exhausted, and for a moment, he thought her chin trembled. She turned away and cradled her head in her hands as if she pondered what to do next and he almost felt sorry for her. Then he glanced down at his bound wrists and remembered he played the prisoner.

"I am hungry," he announced.

"Well find something to eat," she snapped, over her shoulder. "I found you on the beach. I did not give birth to you."

"Thank the gods for small favors," he muttered,

"your kind probably eat their young." She spun around to face him, and her tight-lipped expression made him rue his hasty retort. Issuing insults would not aid his cause. He must treat her like the women he so easily seduced at home.

"Free my hands," he coaxed.

"No," came the adamant reply, "they remain tied."

"Then I am somewhat at a disadvantage in tending to my own needs." With all the charm and guile he could muster, he offered her his most winning smile.

"Oh, by the Rood," she swore. "Stay put and I will fetch you something." Grabbing up a small wooden bucket, she stalked from the hut.

In her absence, he removed the rope from around his ankle and took the opportunity to nose around the pitiful dwelling. Everything he came upon seemed for practical use, giving him no insight into the personal life of the girl who thought she held him prisoner.

With a chuckle he studied the rope still wound about his wrists. It was already coming loose. It would take little effort to shed the flimsy shackle, but for now he would let it be. She seemed sorely frightened of him, and unless she came at him again with ill intent, he would play her game a while longer. To gain her cooperation freely would be his preference, although if necessary, he had no qualms about wringing it from her.

He picked up his amulet, slipped the thick leather band over his head, and wedged the heart beneath the neck of his tattered tunic. The cold metal settled with a familiar feel upon his bare chest, the weight of it reassuring, the power of it renewing to his purpose and strength. He gave thanks it had not been lost to the sea. He should never have removed it in the first place, and he would never do so in the future.

Ignoring the map, he delved into the pouch and retrieved the items she had yet to examine. Except for the small bag of silver, the two remaining articles were of importance only to him. The amber brooch, belonging to his mother, he fastened to the band of his amulet. The bronze dagger, belonging to his father, he slipped under his leather belt far off to one side.

At the sound of rustling, he hurried back to the sleeping-pallet to assume his role as captive.

"You will have to be satisfied with berries and dried fish," she handed him the container.

"It sounds most nourishing," he said cheerfully. His good humor seemed to aggravate her. Too bad he couldn't find the proper enthusiasm for the sport. With his bleak circumstances overshadowing his mood, he ate in silence.

The girl roamed about the room, putting things in order although none of the rough-hewn furnishings seemed truly out of place. "Might I have some water?" he asked around a mouthful of dried fish.

"No. 'Tis hard to come by on the island"

"Do you always treat your guests so unsympathetically?" he challenged, wondering how such a contrary spirit could be housed in such a compelling frame.

"Guests come by request," she pointed out. "You just happened by. You should take what you are given and be happy." She strode over to the leather bag and rummaged again inside. Then her head snapped up and she stared at his chest—focusing on the bulge formed by the heart amulet.

He popped another piece of fish into his mouth, and smiled at her heated glare. To his relief, she did not pursue the issue as she fingered the small bag of silver coins.

"Did anything else wash up upon the beach?" he asked and savored the last handful of sweet, refreshing berries.

"Not as yet, but the tide will turn again midday. Something may come ashore then."

With renewed interest she studied the map. "Where were you bound?"

"One or two days' sea journey to the north," he said and set aside the empty wooden pail.

She gave a little shudder as if the destination, or traveling upon the whale-road, did not appeal to her. "The fortune is there?" she asked.

"Most probably." Faran was not accustomed to answering other people's questions or obeying their commands, but he supposed it mattered little if she knew of the treasure and his destination. It was possible she could somehow aid his cause, or at least help him off of the island—although, how a mere woman could do either eluded him. He knew of no females possessing enough common sense or fortitude to go adventuring.

She stepped into a shaft of sunlight to aid her in interpreting the map. "And if the riches are not there?" she asked, facing away from him.

"Then I will seek them elsewhere."

Weary of dancing to her melody of questions, Faran decided it was time he called the tune. Slipping free of his bonds, he silently sneaked up behind the woman. Nothing must stay him from his purpose. Not his enemies, not the Fates, and certainly not this wisp of a female.

Chapter Three

A shiver snaked across Leanora's shoulders.

She turned—it was too late. He was nearly upon her, his expression fierce, his hands no longer bound. She threw the map at him and drew her knife. The warrior stood his ground and eyed her with an expression of wariness mingled with confusion. Crouched low she awaited the attack.

"Give me the knife," he ordered. "I will not hurt you."

Not hurt her! He was mad if he thought she would believe such a lie. And if he wanted her weapon, he would have it, blade first. She slashed out with the dagger and nicked his arm.

"You bloodthirsty wench," he growled and clamped a hand over the cut. "What drives you to such madness?"

She didn't answer, her only concern escaping. But his imposing figure blocked the path to the door. If she could push past him, and gain the shelter of the hills, she might find safety there—at least for a little while.

Seeking room to maneuver, she stepped back and tangled one foot in the gnarled bush recently sprouted up in the middle of the dirt floor. She hadn't had the heart to rip it out, just as she hadn't had the heart to kill the man who now threatened her existence. On both accounts, her compassion was returned with treachery.

Floundering, she tripped sideways. The warrior

snared her left forearm, his grip unyielding. The knife flew from her grasp, and as her legs buckled beneath her, he eased her to the ground.

Wrenching free, she crawled about seeking her weapon. He saw the blade first and kicked it beyond her reach. Out of options, she cowered in the nearest corner, her arms covering her head. A sob escaped her lips, and as fortitude slipped from her soul, despair sprang to life in its place.

The warrior drew closer, his form obliterating the sunlight streaming in through the doorway. She huddled coldly in his shadow, every muscle tensed in anticipation of the pain to come. But nothing happened. Why did he not strike her? Through a veil of tears she stared up at him. Legs braced wide, he towered over her—his stance one of strength barely held in check.

Anger bred from desperation conquered her fear and like a huge bubble, the feeling welled up in her chest. With newfound abandon, she released all the pent up fury she felt for the world. She struck out with her fists, daring to pummel the legs of the giant. Strong as an ancient oak, time tested and tempered by the elements, not a move did he make— nor did he retaliate.

Physically exhausted, she ceased the attack and sagged closer to the ground, chastising herself for being weak of form as well as spirit. She should have been strong last night. Instead she had surrendered her bed to this marauding devil, rubbing his body when he shivered, giving him valuable water when he licked his lips in thirst.

He bent down, his face so close she could feel his breath. Then he grasped her by the shoulders and hauled her to her feet. Her tears distorted his image, save for the brilliance of his light green eyes. Their intense hue reminded her of the jungle cat she had seen in a traveling caravan. And just like that ferocious cat, this man could eat her alive.

Fighting for her life, she cursed the white God as well as the gods of her ancestors. Damn all the Deities. None of them showed mercy to a woman alone.

"Stop crying," he commanded and shook her near senseless. Her knees went weak, but he held her fast, keeping her on her feet. "What is your name?" he demanded.

She started at his question, and then laughter spilled from her lips. Again he wanted to know her name. How polite. Most men raped and pillaged with far less formality. She gasped for air, near giddy with the lack of it. He swept her off her feet, crushed her to his chest, and carried her toward the bed. Her crazed laughter slid sideways into a scream.

"I should have killed you last night," she shrieked and kicked out with her feet. "I should have left you to die, you treacherous Dane."

He stopped dead in his tracks. "I am a Geat not a Scylding," he shouted at her as if it made some great difference to him. It certainly made no difference to her.

The muscles of his arms and chest bunched and flexed as she strained against him, and his man scent filled her nostrils. He continued onward, and locked within his fearsome grip, she felt as fragile as last year's willows. With nary an effort he could crush the life from her body, yet as they reached the bed, he laid her down with surprising gentleness. She clenched her eyes shut and pushed at his hands, but instead of tearing at her clothes, he covered her up.

"By the gods, calm yourself," he ordered. "I told you before, I will not harm you."

She squinted up at him. He just stood there, staring down at her. She choked back a whimper and trapped her lower lip between her teeth to keep it from trembling. Did he toy with her like a cat with a mouse, gaining her confidence only to later pounce upon her unannounced?

His tawny brown hair was in wild disarray and he raked it back from his face with both hands. The mane of a lion surrounded his green tiger-eyes.

"Do it and be done with it," she sobbed and stared up at the ceiling.

"Do it?" He gave a bark of laughter. "The women I make love to do not have snot running out there noses, nor do they shriek with terror. They often moan with pleasure, of course, but that is a different matter altogether."

She wiped her hand across her nose and mouth. What was wrong with him? Was this his first time marauding? Did he not know the rewards due the conquering hero?

"You are not going to beat me and have your way with me?"

"It would be poor repayment for your saving my life, even if you were compelled to do so out of greed."

"Then you are different from every other man," she accused, still not believing him. She drew the covers up to her chin as if they would protect her should he change his mind.

"I war only with men," he said scornfully. "And I have yet to find it necessary to force myself upon a woman. They generally come to me quite willingly." His crooked smile revealed even white teeth, and a touch of pride mingled with his last words. "But I do not favor being tied up," he added, the ferocity returning to his features. "And I will not tolerate being questioned and ordered about. You have nothing to fear from me as long as you tell me the truth."

With a shuddering breath Leanora tried to quiet her pounding heart. The truth was the last thing he would wring from her.

"Tell me your name," he ordered for the third time.

"No." She snuffed her runny nose and hiccupped. This man had blundered onto her island uninvited, and now he intimidated her with his superior strength. If nothing else, she would safeguard her name and purpose here.

Anger flared in his eyes, and an exasperated growl escaped his lips. Leanora clenched her fists and set her jaw. She did not care if he hollered and yelled or threatened to beat her from now until the Summer Solstice she would not tell him her name.

"I owe you my life," he admitted, "and although it took some bargaining to attain your help, I will not forget what you have done." With a weary sigh, he dragged a stump closer and sat down. "It is most difficult to properly thank someone when you do not know their name."

She remained silent, and the passing of time felt as if it echoed around and within her. She peered at him more closely. Last night, as he slept, this man's expression had held a gentle strength, more attractive than frightening. And when not grimacing in pain, his lips were soft and tempting with no sign of practiced cruelty. No sign of brutality hovered there now. He merely appeared concerned as he returned her stare.

"You are here alone, are you not?" It was more a statement than a question.

"Yes," she finally admitted, seeing no point in lying any longer about the obvious.

"How did you get here? Did you crash upon the rocks as did we?"

Under the covers, Leanora crossed the first and second fingers of both her hands. "Yes," she answered. Yet, she had not been marooned here. Her boat was hidden in a cove on the far side of the island. She had purposely landed here with four chickens, a rooster, one small coffer, and a slim hope for survival.

"Lucky for you, your chickens knew how to swim," he said, the doubt obvious in his voice.

"Yes, it was most clever of them."

"And everyone else with you died?"

"Everyone else? Oh, yes," again she lied. "Now please, no more questions. I do not favor them any more than you." She uncrossed her fingers to grip the edge of the covers.

"I have only one more."

"Oh blessed be. What is it?"

"Has no one come close enough to the shore that you might signal them for help?"

She was afraid to answer. How could she explain to him she did not wish to be rescued? "The ships passing by are few, and I have not tried to attract their attention," she confessed. "Here I am safe. A rescue by the Danes could leave me in more dire straights than I face now." She studied his features as he considered her response.

"Yes, I can see where falling into the hands of the Scyldings could prove most unfavorable." Thoughtfully he rubbed his knuckles along his jaw. "They are a dangerous lot, equally skilled as traders and traitors. And no doubt the Swedes are skulking about as well. They are worse than the Danes. But I am with you now," he added brightly, as if this made an important difference in her condition. "And I do not propose to stay here, nice as the accommodations might be." He rolled his eyes, and Leanora's ire rekindled.

How dare he criticize the way she ran things. This was her island, her home now. "I do not wish to leave," she blurted, not missing his raised brow of surprise. "And" she added, "there is nothing wrong with this hut that a little honest work will not put to right. It is only slightly sagging after yesterday's fit of bad weather."

He had no right to issue orders and delve into the reason as to why she was here. Trading away the entire outside world for safety and solitude had been her only choice. So what if life passed her by at a distance, silent as the ships she so dreaded? It was not a situation easily explained. And better he think her crazed or a liar, for if he knew the truth, he could use the information for his own gain.

Faran scrutinized her face. His pale emerald eyes seemed to hold the memories of a thousand years, and they compelled and frightened her with equal intensity. Her heart raced. Did he read her soul? No one must know her darkest secrets.

"I should collect the rainwater from the storm," she said breaking the spell of his unwavering stare. "Upon my return, we can bury your comrades." She slid from the pallet on the far side and hurried beyond his reach. Being near the warrior unsettled both her mind and body—in ways she had not anticipated.

He twisted around on the stump to face her. "I would prefer to bury my friends first. You can fetch the water later."

"If I do not go now, the water will be lost to the heat of the day. Let your friends feel the warmth of the sun a little longer. It will not touch them again for all eternity."

He gritted his teeth as if to stave off the sadness shadowing his eyes, then he nodded. "I could help you haul the water," he offered, rising.

She stiffened and stood taller. Was he really trying to help? Or did he only wish to know from where the water came? "No." The word came out more harshly than intended. "You must rest," she added to cover her unease.

He cocked his head to one side and perused her

from head to toe. "What should I call you?" he mused. His voice was soft, almost crooning, as if he sought to gentle a woodland creature.

It had been many weeks since she'd studied her reflection in a wavering puddle. Did she resemble a frightened rabbit, or some other wary forest animal? She tugged back a stray lock of hair, and one small bit of her wished desperately to be found attractive. Another more practical part, remembered beauty was no blessing. It was best to keep a safe distance from this or any man. Hopefully her unruly appearance and odd notion of staying here would help hold this stranger at bay.

"You may call me whatever suits your fancy," she answered, refusing to give ground concerning her name. Her obstinacy appeared to amuse him.

"Perhaps I shall call you Egbert or Horatio."

She fought back a smile. Did the warrior possess a sense of humor? "If that is what you wish." This man may command superior strength, but he would not triumph over her in a game of will.

He said no more, and to her surprise, helped gather the sheep-bladder containers. Suspicion rose again about his intentions. Her father and brothers would never have lifted a hand to help her or her poor mother. They ate, drank, and slept for only one purpose—warring. It had been hard growing up in a world where brute strength and even cruelty were the characteristics most likely to win respect and admiration. And it was hard to imagine Faran's world had been different.

He stepped closer, his arm brushing her shoulder, and again she felt small and fragile compared to his imposing size and obvious strength. Jerking away, she clutched the containers against her chest, grabbed her walking staff, and hurried out the door of the hut.

Wrapped in the comforting arms of the fresh air

and sunlight, she breathed deep—hoping to calm her pounding heart and tattered nerves. Then she studied the broken shells at her feet, and a lump of sorrow knotted in her throat. Her dreams of sanctuary had been shattered into just as many pieces. The warrior had ruined everything by coming here. By purpose or by chance, Faran Kilbraun had discovered her safe haven—the only place she had ever known peace and solitude. She hated him for that.

Quick on the heels of her sorrow came panic. What would become of her now? She could never go back. An image of the brutish husband she had cowered beneath flashed through her mind, and although the day had grown warm, she shivered with dread. Her back tingled at the memory of his whip, and a sickness that always accompanied thoughts of him gripped her stomach. He had fractured her spirit, making her dread to live to see another day. The wretch was dead now, but having been charged with his murder, he threatened her life from the grave.

Tightening her grip on the walking staff, she shoved the remnants of her past to a dark corner of her mind where they were rendered into oblivion. Then concentrating on keeping her footing, she traversed the rocky terrain lying between her shack and the precious water supply.

By accident she had discovered the natural reservoir, and although not spring fed, the pond collected the frequent rains. After lining the bottom of the shallow pool with smooth pebbles, the silt had been eliminated, leaving the water clear enough to drink. Would the limited source support the needs of two people?

She hurried along. Then something moved in the underbrush. Instinctively, she reached for her weapon only to grasp the empty sheath. She had forgotten the dropped dagger. A small furry culprit peeked from the bushes, and with a friendly squeak, scurried away. It was only a vole, yet the feeling of vulnerability persisted. She turned back to retrieve her knife, then stopped. Why bother. The only thing on the island she truly need fear was the warrior.

Continuing on, she shook her head, trying to clear her mind. Her emotions were running rampant. Without forewarning, a spark of womanly interest flared within her, illuminating a tiny forgotten corner of her soul. Before she could stop it, a girlish thought slipped free into that brightness. Faran...It seemed a comforting name. And he was easy to look upon. She was drawn to his light green eyes, yet it was disconcerting when his gaze pinned her in place, numbing her mind even as it scorched her flesh.

Oh, by the saints, what foolishness was this? It mattered little what he called himself, or whether his name flowed easily from her lips. He was a man, he was here, and he could not be trusted, that is what mattered. Stabbing her walking stick into the ground, she marched on.

At the pool, she knelt by the edge and fished out the leaves and other debris deposited by the recent storm. Then pretending each receptacle represented Faran's head, she soundly shoved it under the water, held it down, and watched the bubbles gurgle up to the surface.

Why had the Lord seen fit to burden her in this manner? For heaven's sake, the man was a pagan. His heart amulet was decorated with mystic runes and Woden's symbol. Although in truth, she could not hold his belief in the old gods against him. Only recently had she and her family accepted Christianity—baptized more in the name of politics than piousness. Many clans had done so to pacify the priests sent by Aelfred, the king of Wessex. She had best be careful. With one such as Faran close at hand, and Brother Thomas no longer at her side, she could easily slip back into the old ways.

The bladders filled and properly tied off, she threaded the loops of twine onto the ends of her walking stick. Then positioning the staff across her back, she headed home.

As she ambled along, the hide containers swung to and fro, calming her thoughts until Faran again came to mind. The man appeared educated and not accustomed to doing the bidding of others. And if he truly were a Storm Geat, it was unlikely he had been sent from her dead husband's tribe.

She had never met anyone from Faran's clan. They lived far to the south, many of them inhabiting the isle known as Gullin, in Bracklesham Bay. Faran had traveled many leagues seeking the treasure he promised. If indeed a treasure did exist. More likely he had made the story up to save his life. Had she shown him mercy only because of the promise of riches? That was a concern. Surely there was still some bit of kindness and charity buried deep within her.

One thing was for certain, his desperation to leave the island was going to be a problem. What would he do if he found the little boat she had hidden? At best he would steal it and leave her stranded here. At worst he might force her to go with him.

Entering the hut, Leanora hastily stowed the water. Where was he? And where was her knife? In search of both, she rounded the corner of the shack and tripped. Strong arms cushioned the fall and held her in place.

Sprawled in the shade, Faran sat sharpening her blade. His outstretched legs had caused her upset, landing her unceremoniously in his lap. Her skirt bunched up around her thighs, and her cheeks grew hot with embarrassment. She struggled to cover herself. But the more she wiggled, the higher her skirt rose, and the more heated grew his gaze.

She placed one hand on his thigh and pushed against him in order to rise up and free her skirt. Then her hand slid sideways into his crotch, and he gasped and grabbed her wrist. The veiled look in his eyes indicated neither hurt nor anger. He released her wrist and glided his fingertips upward along her arm. When the back of his hand grazed the tip of one of her braids, he seized the ends and rubbed them between thumb and fingers as if savoring a cut of fine silk.

Her breath caught in her throat. She sat unmoving, captivated by the nearness of this man, this stranger, this foreign warrior whose gaze ignited a fire in her belly both frightening and pleasing.

With an odd smile, he studied her bare thighs. Her skin tingled, as if he had touched her there not just looked. Then he stared once more into her eyes, and a warm drizzly feeling seeped through her midsection, pooling between her legs—a part of her body familiar only with pain.

Her braid forgotten, he reached up to stroke her cheek. She eased forward, knowing she should not, but this newfound sensation coursed through her body like life-blood, leaving her lightheaded.

Faran leaned sideways, taking her along with him until they lay side by side and face to face. He drew closer, his mouth but a breath away from hers. She wanted to breach the small distance, to taste him, to surrender to the sudden need smothering fear and logic and all other emotions.

Just as her wayward wish was to become reality, he withdrew slightly and grinned. Then before her brain could reason what was happening, he gained his feet with an agility not expected for his size. Instinctively, she grabbed the hand he offered, and he pulled her upright before him.

Disappointment nearly rocked her off her feet. Then embarrassment and rejection tore into her. She had been found wanting. She should consider such a condition a blessing, but truth be told, she felt foolish. He had tricked her. What else was he capable of? She balled her hands into fists, and glanced at her knife where it lay on the ground between them.

Faran followed her line of sight and quickly retrieved the weapon. He held the knife loosely in one hand, his body relaxed yet poised on the brink of action. "I thought to hone this for you before your return." He wangled the blade back and forth. "It sorely needed work," he chided. "There is nothing worse than being pierced with a dull blade."

"Give it back," she demanded, "and we shall put your words to the test."

His expression of teasing transformed into concern. "Maybe I should keep this a while longer."

Their prior moment of playfulness took flight and she stepped backward. Distrustful strangers once again, neither was sure of what the other might do.

Faran raised his hand and the sun glinted off the blade. Would she never learn? How pitiful to think she could die of wounds inflicted by her own dagger.

She turned to run. Faran grabbed her arm and held her in place. Then he flipped the knife around and offered it to her hilt first. "I will tell you but one more time. I will not hurt you. I trust I can expect the same in return."

With a shaking hand, she accepted the knife, and the heat and strength of him warmed her fingers where they brushed across his palm. Why did he trust her, she certainly held no such feeling for him? She could not. He was a man. Or was it still a game he played?

"I must see to my friends," he said, and turning away, he headed toward the beach.

"Wait, please." She contemplated apologizing, but if he played her false it would only add to his amusement. She must show her willingness to cooperate in a less obvious way. "We should collect wild berry sprigs to adorn their final place of rest."

He hesitated, and then returned to her side.

"Do you believe in the Cross?" she asked.

"I believe in myself," he answered defiantly.

Lord above, he truly was a heathen.

"And," he added, "in earning the honor and valor in this life necessary to procure a place of glory in the hereafter." He stared at the beach. "For their sakes," he added, "I hope good intentions are justly counted—for my comrades had little time for anything else in a life-web spun in such short measure."

The bitterness in Faran's voice surprised Leanora. His green eyes darkened to the shade of the North Sea in winter, and his expression was just as cold. It seemed something more then the death of his friends weigh upon his mind. His resentment appeared older and more practiced, as if something plagued him of a magnitude over and above this recent happening. Without thinking, she reached out and rested her hand upon one of his arms. Her touch seemed to draw him back from wherever his mind had wandered.

"Gather your blossoms and branches," he said. "I would not deny my friends your thoughtfulness. If only we had their battle gear to accompany them on their way. Now they must make their final journey unarmed and without riches. It is unfortunate," he added, "that there is neither wood at the ready for a suitable pyre, nor boats available to properly send them forth to Valhalla."

Beneath her fingertips she felt the corded muscles of his forearm. They professed the prowess of his form, but she thought right now his spirit was as fragile as a babe's.

"We could bury each with a skin of water," she suggested. "It's the most precious thing on the island. Who knows," she pondered, "the road to eternity may be long and dusty. And wherever you go, from this day forth, you shall remember them when you drink a cup of clear bright water."

"You are given to fanciful thinking," he said.

At first she thought he criticized her. Then he placed his hand over hers where it still rested on his forearm. "The water would be appreciated."

She gathered the boughs of flowering berries, and grabbing the water-hides, they walked to the beach. When she knew he was not looking, she nervously scanned the horizon. The boat she had seen at dawn was long since gone, but she was watching, always watching, for the ships.

****

A shady spot on a small rise was chosen to serve as the gravesites, and using the edges of flat rocks, she and Faran arduously dug the three graves. As she toiled in the heat of the day, sweat dripped from her face into the partially dug hole. Her muscles screamed in rebellion and the rough stone tore at her fingertips rendering them raw and near bleeding.

About to beg for a respite, thoughts of the three men they buried silenced the plea. With the patience of the dead, they had awaited their final repose. Never again would their finely muscled bodies feel the simple joy of movement, nor would their lungs expand with breath or mirth. She could endure a little longer.

Showing extraordinary strength, especially after

what he had suffered at the hands of the sea, Faran dug two of the graves before she finished the one. He seemed to attack the sandy ground with unabated anger, as if the earth had caused the death of his friends, or as if the pain he suffered while he labored was a penance because they had died and he still lived.

In silence, they returned to the beach to retrieve his comrades. At dawn, Leanora had wrapped each man in the cloak he wore, covering their sightless eyes and expressionless faces. No animals had disturbed their solitude, and they were just as she had left them.

Together, she and Faran struggled to carry the stalwart warriors one at a time to their final resting. A container of water was placed beside each man, and Faran removed three of his most finely wrought silver arm rings, placing one on the chest of each friend. The graves were filled, and the branches of flowering currants placed carefully upon the newly turned earth.

Leanora bowed her head in prayer. Whether they be Christians or pagan, she implored her God to take the three strangers into His fold.

Faran chanted his own prayers, and imbedded the rune-carved wooden panel from his ship in the ground as a grave marker.

"What does it say?" she asked.

"Valor, Honor, Glory," he said coldly. "That is for what we searched. But there is another panel," he added and stared out across the water, "and although it may lie at the bottom of the sea, it shall mark my course and temper my resolve."

"It is scribed as this one?"

"No." Faran's gaze turned resolute. "It bears but one word and one cause—revenge."

Lenora could not help but wonder if the revenge he sought would end up in death for the warrior.

Chapter Four

Faran notched the tree at his side, marking off another sunrise. He prayed his fifth day upon the island would not be as mind numbingly boring as the prior four. If he were forced to stay much longer on this isle of deadly tedium, he feared to lose himself to raving madness.

Shoving the dagger under his belt, he wandered down to the beach not paying attention to the path. By now he knew the craggy shore like an old friend. And while it felt good to be near the water, it would feel better to be upon it. With each passing day, the trail he followed grew colder and his need for vengeance burned hotter.

He glanced at the large trees growing up in the hills. He might try building a boat or raft. But even if the wood were of the correct type, without the proper tools, it would take him many months. That was not the answer. Why had Destiny bid him perform a task of redemption only to abandon him in this forsaken place?

He paused and kicked at the logs and tinder now laying ready for a signal fire. He wondered how long the female had lived here, and how she had endured the sameness with no one to talk to other than her chickens and the stars.

Legs braced wide, hands clasped behind his back, he studied the waves and the dark expanse of the sea. The watery realm held many a mystery as it stretched into forever. It reduced a man to raw elements as it tested his courage, his endurance, and his standing with the gods. Of late, he questioned his ranking in any of these categories. Then he studied the horizon. During his time at the watch he had seen only two ships, both at very far distances. And the woman denied seeing any at all. Did she tell the truth? It seemed safe to assume she harbored more secrets besides her name.

With a sigh of resignation, he flexed and stretched in the morning sun and absently noted the dark rich color of his arms and chest. Living half-naked in the wild was a different experience for him. At home, he generally occupied his time retelling the history of his people, interpreting dreams and visions, or wandering the dense woods—activities offering him little prolonged contact with the sun. And although he also trained daily and rigorously upon the practice field, his regular duties required more brain than brawn. The truth be known, he'd won his arm rings defending their island, this was his first sea voyage, and so far it was not at all what he had envisioned. He missed his family, and he mourned the loss of his companions, and nothing seemed to be going as planned.

Did the woman miss her family as well? She seemed surprisingly comfortable with her isolation. He shuddered at the memory of the whip marks on her back. It was sad to think this lonely existence proved preferable to the life she had led before coming here. Still they all bore scars wielded by life's cruel whip—either on their bodies or their souls. And hiding away on a deserted island hardly seemed the remedy.

Again he wondered what her name might be. Her refusal to tell him was a condition he found both vexing and entertaining. *Gillyflower*, the name he had chosen for her, seemed fitting enough. It was a bloom he had always favored.

He glanced inland. There she was now, carrying a large cloth bag. Gracefully she picked her way along the rocky shore, but when she spotted him, she stumbled. His presence seemed to cast an odd spell upon her, causing her feet to tangle with whatever was near at hand, or simply with one another.

She offered a nod of acknowledgement but did not venture closer. After placing the bundle by the water's edge, she began washing what few bits of clothing she possessed. As she waded into the shallows, the breeze flattened her tunic against her torso and hips, outlining her tempting figure.

Thankfully, she finally seemed convinced he did not harbor a sinister plan to pounce upon her in a lustful frenzy. It had offended his sense of honor that she thought him prone to such acts. It also mystified him as to why she did not find him irresistible. Having six older brothers and no sisters, Faran had little experience with the logic of females. He knew well and good how to make love to them, but the concept of simply being friends with a woman was beyond his ken.

As tiny waves lapped at Gillyflower's feet, she raised her skirt above her ankles, and tucked the fold of fabric under the leather belt knotted around her waist. With the unwitting help of the wind, her skirt billowed about and he caught a glimpse of slender thighs. A charming image of her frolicking naked in the waves stole into his mind, and he wondered what it would take to breach the battlement of fear guarding her warmest treasures.

She was an odd mosaic, tough yet comely. And outspoken—more so than any female he had ever known. And while she intrigued his mind, it was the fact that she inflamed his loins that occupied his thoughts. There must be some way to entice her willingly to his bed. It seemed a worthy goal upon which to labor. He had always fancied a good riddle, and Gillyflower was fast becoming a puzzle worth the effort of solving. Leaning back against a rocky outcropping, he observed her as she awkwardly waded in the shoals. She never ventured far, and if a wave of the slightest proportion curled in her direction, she quickly scurried from its path. She seemed to fear the water as well as the outside world.

With an exclamation of delight, she interrupted her chores to retrieve a large pink shell. Bright-eyed with curiosity, she studied it, then gently returned it to the sea. She did not carelessly cast it aside— rather she carefully set it back as if she regretted having disturbed it in the first place. She afforded this unmoving breathless conch more sympathy and concern than she showed to him. His Gillyflower was a strange and rare blossom indeed.

Finished with her task, she stuffed the last piece of clothing back into the bag and carried the dripping mass inland. The braided grass-rope, now tied between two trees, served as a drying line. Disenchanted with watching the never changing horizon, he decided to help hang the cumbersome articles.

"I thought to lend a hand," he explained at her questioning look.

Her eyes narrowed slightly, as if she sought to discern some other meaning to his words. "I see," she replied, not thanking him.

The front of her over-blouse was damp and clingy, outlining her breasts in glorious detail. Covertly, he watched the tantalizing display—each rhythmic rise and fall of her chest a fascination.

"No ships this morning?" she asked.

"Only at a far distance," he answered distractedly. As if in relief, her shoulders relaxed and the neckline of her top gapped to reveal a provocative hint of cleavage. Faran felt himself growing rigid, and only with dogged determination did he shift his concentration from her breasts to the job at hand.

As she struggled to lift a wet cape to the line, he stepped closer to help. The tail-end of the dripping material flipped backwards and slapped him in the face. He gasped as cold water ran down his cheek onto his chest. With her hand midway to her open mouth, she stared at him in horror, then cringed as if in fear of a reprisal for the accident.

Faran sputtered, laughed, and wiped his face with the back of his hand. "One near drowning per annum is enough, thank you." When her grim expression turned to a tentative smile, he decided to pursue the opportunity for mischief.

Grabbing up the next item, he held it over her head and wrung the water from it. She squealed and ran from his side, but he had no intention of giving up the game so easily. He chased her around the bushes and trees getting more of the remaining water on himself than her. Quick as a cony she ran, escaping through spaces between trees and plants too small to accommodate his shoulders. But her speed did not compensate for his agility and cunning, and as she skittered around the far side of the hut, she crashed right into him.

He wrapped his arms around her—the wash forgotten. Exhausted from running, her breath came in fits and gasps. With her sodden top now a flimsy barrier, the softness of her breasts and their nubby centers teased his bare chest.

Gliding his hands upward, he tangled his fingers in the burnished locks. And as his yearning turned full-blown and blazing, he dipped his head and stole a kiss. Her full pink lips seemed to welcome his. They were soft, slightly parted, and just as savory as he had imagined. But when he tightened his embrace, she turned unyielding, cold and hard as a poorly tanned buskin.

"Please, stop. Let me go."

The alarm in her voice convinced him she did not play at wanting her freedom. As bidden, he released her. She took a step back. A frown puckered her brow as if she were surprised at his compliance.

"'Twas just a kiss, Gillyflower, and as sweet as the blossom for which you are named." At his teasing, the frown disappeared and what might pass for amusement flickered in her remarkable blue eyes.

Before she could protest or dwell upon what had happened, he grabbed the dropped garment, took her by the hand, and led her back toward the shack. "Come. Let me help with what is left." She did not pull away from his gentle grasp.

What a pity; every time they fell into an easy camaraderie, something scared her back into the silent world of mistrust. It did not seem she had been around men very often. Or perhaps she had been around them too much.

As they finished the work in silence, she moved carefully and precisely so not even their hands accidentally brushed together. Again he wondered what made her so skittish. Having successfully avoided all of his questions, her past remained untold. Which was probably just as well, as he had little desire to trade histories. His past was best left to the shadows as well.

Their task finished, he thought to grant her some solitude. "I'm going for a walk-about," he informed her. Not waiting for a response, he ambled down the beach, heading north into the trees and across to the other side of the island. It was the last bit of territory he had yet to explore, and quickening his pace, he scaled the rugged terrain.

The wind blew more purposeful on the up-slope. He should have worn the tunic recently washed ashore. Except for his spear, and a few items of clothing, nothing else of consequence had survived the sinking of his ship. It was as if the vessel had never been, or had existed only in a dream. And it left him stranded in a netherworld, caught between the past he wished to exonerate, and the future seemingly beyond his grasp.

Like a cold black stone, a feeling of dread sat upon his stomach, and loneliness shrouded his spirit. What if he were abandoned here for years, or even the rest of his life? His family would think him dead, his covenant of revenge and redemption would go unfulfilled, and he would go to his grave a coward. And until that time, he was trapped here, tormented by lusty desires for a maiden who feared his slightest touch. By the gods, the Fates did find humor in twisting the lives of mortals.

Gaining the far side of the island, he wandered along the water's edge, his boots making a scrunching sound in the wet, hard-packed sand. The cove before him, offered a calm surf but few trees and little shelter.

As he sought a likely spot for a respite, he spied a clump of brush near the water's edge. Seeking the shade projected by the jumble, he dropped to the ground, plucked a piece of sea grass, and idly chewed upon its stem. As he leaned backward, the mound gave way and he nearly fell over.

Scrambling to his feet, he shoved aside the tangle of brush and stood awed by his discovery. It was a boat. Little, to be sure, but a boat.

He rejoiced in his good fortune, and running his hands over the rough planking, he peeled the stray sticks and leaves from the pitch and tar caulking the seams. Accept for the missing steer-board, the vessel appeared intact. Nothing else seemed amiss. Nothing else indicated it would not be seaworthy.

He let loose with his best war cry. He could

leave tomorrow. Wait until he told the girl. Laughing out loud, he fell to his knees and threw back his head. "Thank you, Woden," he prayed, arms extended skyward. "You have given me another chance."

Gaining his feet, he stepped aside to admire the small craft. Something had been etched upon the wooden prow. He grabbed up a handful of sand and rubbed at the boards to displace the caked on dirt. The image of a cross and a small bird was revealed—not symbols for a pagan wayfarer.

With only one sail and limited freeboard, the craft would be barely large enough for two people. He tossed aside the folded sea-garment lying in the hull of the boat. A wooden crate was revealed. Chicken feathers were stuck to the knotty wood and a broken eggshell lay in the bottom of the boat.

A long delicate hair, snagged upon the gunwales, fluttered in the breeze. A reddish-gold pennon, it declared much, even as it taunted him with several unanswered questions.

Chapter Five

Leanora sat quietly in her hut, sorting and de-stemming currant berries. A smile captured her lips as well as her mood.

The warrior's playfulness had been akin to fun, a feeling for which she had long ago abandoned hope. And his teasing kiss had been tempting. She had pushed him away out of habit rather than a true fear for survival. Without fail, he kept his promise to treat her with respect. And after her tirade following the killing of one of her chickens, he had even agreed not to slaughter anymore of her pets for food.

In the future, however, she must insist he wear his tunic when in her presence. It was wicked and heathen for a man to go about near naked, even if he did possess a form most pleasing to gaze upon.

Her hands stilled as she recalled how the most appealing trappings often hid the ugliest of intentions. Her husband, believed by many to be quite handsome, had been mean as a starving wolf. And when she had sought refuge from him with his rune-counselor, the holy man's beautiful bright robes had concealed a darkness called greed. A condition rewarded by her husband when she was quickly returned into his cruel keeping.

Was Faran any different? It was all so confusing. He incited myriad desires in her body, new longings that fought with the old despairs of her heart. Reliving how it felt to be held captive in Faran's arms, she crossed and uncrossed her legs and moved restlessly upon her chair. Sometimes his presence magnified the emptiness inside of her. This made no sense at all. And the truth be known, she was beginning to feel safer on the island since his unceremonious arrival.

Her hand tightened around the berries, and the juice bled onto the rough tabletop creating a reddish blotch on the pale slab of wood. Damn Faran anyway. Before his arrival she had successfully ignored the loneliness of her self-imposed isolation. But with each passing day she felt less guarded around him, and now she knew not what she feared most—his staying or his leaving.

She licked the fruit juice from her fingers, and the smile returned to her face. Gillyflower, what a ridiculous name he had chosen for her. All her life she had been treated as a prickly gorse bush, a thorny nettle that inconvenienced her father, irritated her brothers, and displeased her late husband. Kicked at and unwanted, she had never been made to feel pretty, and never looked upon as a delicate pink blossom. Faran had quite an imagination, and he appeared to be on friendly terms with words and phrases.

She rubbed a chapped hand against the dry skin of her cheek. She was fortunate he did not call her Swamp Myrtle. No doubt that was what she more closely resembled. The seawater was most unkind to one's skin. And the rainwater was too precious to use in its place. Could this be the true reason the warrior did not force her to his bed? Was she too hideous to be desired? It seemed a more likely reason than to be spared out of kindness. Or was something wrong with him? A birthing injury or a battle wound. A tingling teased through her as she recalled the night she had tripped over Faran on the beach. Ministering to his cuts and bruises she had seen no signs his manly prowess had been adversely affected. His well-muscled form appeared bold and properly developed in all respects.

At least the warrior was uplifting to be around, his mood generally of good humor. How unlike her father and brothers. They were always grousing about something: the food, the weather, the fact they must go to war, or the fact there was no war to fight. They were never happy.

Faran's whistling snagged her attention. It would seem he had enjoyed his walk.

"Ah, there you are," he said brightly. "I have found the most curious thing upon the shore."

"Do tell." She set the bucket of currants aside to give him her full attention.

"'Twas huge and lumbering," he began, "and crouched in the brush." As he spoke, he bent over and crept along before her, one hand contorted like a claw poised before him. "Silently it sat, waiting for me to uncover its hiding place." Although he did not sing the words, he had the talent of bard or scop as he performed his dramatic re-enactment.

"Where did you find such a thing?" she asked with naïve enthusiasm.

"On the far side of the island. Large and mottled brown it was, nested in a gathering of bracken."

The tone of his voice changed, and anger now flavored his words. He straightened to his full height. A shiver convulsed through her. Something boded ill here. He stepped forward and planted the palms of his hands flat upon the little table standing between them.

"What was it?" she asked, dreading the answer she suspected was to come.

"It seemed more suited to the water," he goaded, "although it lay abandoned upon the inlet. And it bore the sign of a cross and bird upon its bow."

"No," she cried and leapt to her feet.

They faced one another like two startled roe in a

thicket.

"Why did you not tell me of the boat?" he asked, his face pale with his fury.

"It is mine. I had the right to decide when to tell you—or not to tell you at all."

"Did you fear I would take it from you?"

"Yes. No. I do not know what I feared. I just was not ready to trust you. And now, I suppose you will prove me right by stealing it from me."

"I will purchase it."

"It is not for trade. It is my only means off this island."

"You will never leave here, you are afraid of your own shadow. I can see it in your eyes each time I speak of being rescued. I am surprise you had enough fortitude to find your way here in the first place."

Faran's words wounded her deeply. It had taken all the courage she possessed to leave her mother and Brother Thomas and journey to the island, and she would not be forced to return to the deadly peril awaiting her.

"I must leave as soon as possible," he argued. "Give the boat to me. I will come back for you when my quest has been fulfilled."

"I do not believe you. Why should you come back?"

"Because I said I would."

"No," she cried, adamant in her decision. "The boat and I are as one. We stay here together or leave together. There is no other way."

"Then come with me."

Go with him? But he could drown her when they were out at sea, or abandon her at the first port. She could not go with him.

"Or I could kill you now," he said, a knowing look in his eyes, "but I will not. Instead I am begging you to help me. I must be away from here."

"Your circumstances do not concern me"

"There you are wrong," he replied with conviction. "By the hand of Fate, or Woden, or even your own God's direction, I was delivered unto you. My people are suffering, but you can change all that. Please, they will perish without your help. You do them a great injustice by ignoring their impasse."

"And you do me a great injustice by playing upon my sympathies. You do not know what you ask. And you do not know of my suffering."

"What I seek outweighs the mere needs or desires of either you or me. I cannot let anything or anyone interfere with my purpose." Iron resolve glinted in his eyes. "Half of the treasure can still be yours," he added.

The treasure...How could she have forgotten about the treasure? If she could gain a goodly fortune, she might buy freedom from her past, and security for her future. She would no longer be forced to live in exile. She could go back and rescue her mother from the dire straights in which she no doubt languished.

"If you surrender the craft to me," he coaxed, "I will still make good the promise I made to you on the first evening we met."

"And you will break your promise if I do not?" she asked in disbelief. "That hardly encourages me to commend myself into your keeping."

"But you thought to kill me that night," he said in defense of their original covenant. "I was bargaining for my life, and half delirious. I almost told you about the sword."

"The sword? What sword?" So, here was another thread with which he wove his tapestry of tall tales. "Why are you silent?" she taunted. "Do you fear to trust me?"

Still he hesitated. Evidently while he expected unquestioning faith from her, he would not risk the same himself. "Tell me of the sword," she insisted, "or I will not even consider your plight."

Faran clenched his jaw and stared at her as if judging her worthiness. She squirmed uncomfortably under his heavy scrutiny.

"You are correct," he conceded. "I cannot ask more of you than I am willing to give in return. Sit and I shall tell you of the sword."

She hesitated, afraid now for the opposite reason. He was putting his trust in her, something she would be hard pressed to reciprocate. And what responsibility might accompany the information he would impart? Finally, with reservation, she took a seat.

Faran paced about, his long strides eating up the limited space in the hut. Rubbing a hand across the back of his neck, he seemed to be carefully organizing his thoughts.

Abruptly he came to a halt before her. "I am the seventh son of Aris," he claimed with obvious pride. "He is a much honored man amongst the Storm Geats. And we are a brave and daring race, come from Jutland far across the North Sea." He stood tall, his face taking on a noble countenance missing until now.

"The blood of heroes runs in our veins," he added matter-of-factly rather than vaingloriously. "I uphold the old ways. And my sacred duty is to guard the heritage of my people. I protect the memories and teachings of our ancestors, preserving them for the children of the future."

Larger than life, Faran stood before her. And as he shook his tawny hair back from his face, she noticed for the first time, it possessed a slight curl. In fables of old, lions with curly manes were peaceful and helpful. Did the same logic hold true for men cast in the image of lions?

"There are three sacred artifacts," he continued,

jolting her out of her musings, "and they represent the spirit of my kinsmen. Together they symbolize our past, even as they herald our future. And their safekeeping is...was...my responsibility." At this last declaration, his shoulders slumped and for a moment he appeared most distressed.

The wind outside sprang up, and the mournful howl added to the forlorn atmosphere cast upon the room by his image. For a breathless moment, Faran remained silent. She had the urge to prompt him, but the sadness in his eyes stayed her words. What dreadful thing had happened to cause him such sorrow? Now he trod upon her ground, for that was a feeling she knew all too well.

"Please," she finally whispered, eager to hear more of the legend, "go on."

He started, as if surprised by her presence, then a smile curved his lips and his eyes warmed to a vision only he could see. "There are three treasures, and they are magnificent. The first is a scabbard encrusted with jewels. Made in a time before our reckoning, the wealth of the stones is impossible to calculate. It represents glory, the prize we must merit to insure the story of our life will live on after our passing.

"The second is the shield of honor." He spread his arms high and wide as if offering praise. "Wrought from precious metals, it was forged in fires burning in caverns far beneath the surface of the earth. The shield offers protection against man or beast, and it possesses the power to momentarily confuse an opponent when facing an enemy.

"And finally," he said, reverently lowering his arms to his side, "there is the sword, Neagling. Once, long ago, in a battle with a fire-breathing beast, it was shattered to pieces. But by magic known only to Weland, it was reborn. It can hew a tree with one blow, and when danger is nigh, it shows the position

51

of one's enemies. The sword stands for valor, of which I have none." The last he added quietly, his hands clenched into fists.

Leanora tried to understand Faran's fervor, but it seemed these objects held too much importance—nay, power—over him. He worshipped them as gods.

"Do you not see?" he demanded. "The three symbols are as one, for a man must possess valor, to fight with honor, to achieve glory. But now the sword and shield are gone, and the scabbard lies empty. No glow issues forth from the precious stones surrounding it. My homeland is barren, newborn babes do not thrive, and the old are heartsick with no desire to go on." The wind rocked the hut with a fearful blast, reinforcing the importance of his words. "It will be our doom."

Three symbols honored as one—a trinity of sorts. It brought to mind what Brother Thomas had taught her regarding the Father, Son, and Holy Ghost.

"But how were the sword and shield lost?" she asked wanting to know more. Then she hugged herself to ward off the chill now invading the hut.

"Suffice it to say they are gone," he replied woodenly, "along with two coffers. One houses the gold, and the other is a casket of jewels." He returned to pacing, and a vague expression slipped across his face. He was lost to a memory again.

Leanora was intrigued by his story. It sounded like a childhood tale of fantasy, a fable to be sure. It even included reference to a dragon. She studied Faran, and although this saga seemed unbelievable, it was obvious his anguish was genuine. She should try to help him.

An unfamiliar sense of importance gripped her. Did she really have the power to improve the lot of an entire group of people? She had once thought to aid her own clan by becoming a peace-weaver, and she had later tried to ease the burdens of those ruled by her husband. But these efforts had been unsuccessful—garnering more misery for herself and those she thought to defend. This time, the price of her involvement would be the loss of her safe-haven and her peace of mind. And it would require blind trust in a man she hardly knew, and belief in the promise of a treasure she had yet to see.

The fear in her heart sparked anger in her soul. These Storm Geats were nothing to her, she owed them no fealty. Besides, she felt there was more to this tale than had been revealed. Faran was not being completely honest with her.

Abruptly she stood. As her gaze tangled with Faran's, her logic and resolution began to surrender to the despair in his eyes. He was reaching out for help. And if what he professed were true, turning her back on him would put her one step closer to becoming as hard and evil as those from whom she hid. Of course, other than Thomas the monk, no one had ever bothered to give her a helping hand.

Pondering what to do, she took her turn at pacing. Unmoving as a temple carving, Faran awaited her decision. The wind found renewed enthusiasm for gusting and blowing, and as it whistled and lamented through the hut, her thoughts swirled in confusion. She wanted to believe Faran, but she had been played false too many times.

As his expression chipped away at her, she realized she could not choose freely while in his presence. Like it or not, he possessed the power to govern her mind by swaying her heart. "I must consider all you have told me." She grabbed her worn woolen cape. "Alone," she added over her shoulder.

Outside the hut, the chickens gathered around her feet. The hens pecked teasingly at her toes and clucked and scurried about in their usual greeting ritual. Except for the one Faran had eaten, the happy little brood had survived quite well upon the island. She supposed they would continue to thrive without her—should she decide to leave.

She shooed them aside and bent into the wind. It screamed down from the hills, and only with a supreme effort did she reach the shelter of the nearby trees. Roiling clouds darkened the sky, and the surf crashed upon the shore matching the turmoil within her mind. She drew her cloak more closely about her shoulders. Even the elements seemed to urge her to take her leave. And in truth, if this was autumn's offering, she might not wish to experience winter.

Tears ran down her cheeks, but not because the sand-filled air buffeted her from all sides. She cried because she was tired, and afraid, and so lonely it manifested into a physical pain. To preserve her life, she had left all behind and sought this island. But was life worth living if not shared or filled with purpose? How was she to decide what to do? If she left this haven and fell into the hands of her dead husband's tribe, her life would be at risk. If she stayed, she took the chance of missing out on life altogether.

The wind increased to a fevered pitch, yet Faran stood there solid as a rock, unbending in the onslaught of nature. His hair blew back from his solemn face and she knew he watched her. As if sensing her distress, he ambled away giving her every opportunity to make her decision without his influence.

Surrounded by the familiar stones and trees, Leanora's sorrow grew in equal measure to her anxiety. This was the only place in which she had ever known peace. Putting an arm around the tree at her side, she held on tight to its girth, as well as to her broken dreams.

She felt so alone. There was no one to help her decide or to tell her what to do. She should put her fate in the hands of the Lord. Of course, he too was a man. Still, she needed strength and wisdom beyond her own reasoning. "Please, God," she prayed, staring once more at the hut. "Give me a sign."

Before her words were lost to the wind, her plea was answered. The shack swayed and shuddered, and with a tormented groan, it collapsed flat to the ground. Nothing remained standing. Then the wind stopped and the dust cleared. It was as if her "cottage" had never existed and the days she had spent here were just an illusion, a temporary respite to strengthen her for what was to come.

****

Leanora crawled beneath the makeshift lean-to Faran had constructed. This would be her last evening on the island, and lying there in the dark, stiff with fear and worry, the sound of Faran's even breathing was somehow reassuring.

He had been joyful at her decision to relinquish the boat and travel with him, but she was terrified. She was also of a practical mind. If Faran had landed here by chance, than someone else could also, and she dare not take that risk. She had to seek the treasure, had to gain the power to shape her own destiny. This was a turning point in her life. She must leave the sanctuary of her island and reaffirm herself as a living breathing part of Mankind.

"Faran, are you awake?"

A drowsy mumble was his only response before he rolled away from her and seemingly went back to sleep.

"My name is Leanora," she declared to the dark night, "Leanora Wrenn. And although I am sorely afraid, I must face the world again."

She heard Faran's sharp intake of breath. He

hadn't been asleep after all—but her words had been meant only for the moon and stars.

He turned onto his back. Their shoulders touched, and in contrast to the cool night air, the warmth of his body was an unexpected comfort. Her heart pounded in her chest.

"Sleep well, Leanora Wrenn," he said softly. "Whatever is to come, we shall face it together."

****

Brother Thomas gently tossed the last shovelful of dirt onto the grave. Then he sank to his knees to pray beside the freshly turned soil.

"Dear Lord, let there be a place among your flock for this kind woman. Although she was a Christian but for a short while, she did cleave to your teachings more ardently than many who are born to it. In the face of daunting opposition she fought for peace in this war-torn land, and she took your words to heart and encouraged others to follow your path. Have mercy upon her soul."

Using the shovel for support, the old monk gained his feet and shook his head in sadness. He thought about constructing a cross to mark the resting place, but that might lead to the desecration of the unguarded grave. God would know where to find Ageetha Wrenn, and in the end, he supposed that was all that truly mattered.

He leaned against a tree to catch his breath and renew his strength. Digging a grave was a heavy task for an old body and a weary spirit. But it was the least he could do for her. They had been through much together. He had ordained the wedding that sent her daughter, Leanora, into the hands of their enemy—all in the hopes of ending a lifelong war. And he had helped her to break the law to save that same daughter when the peace they sought was defiled by men with greed in their hearts and blood upon their hands.

He glanced around and wondered what had become of Ageetha's husband and sons? All dead, he knew, but in what unconsecrated soil did they repose? He should say prayers for them as well, even though they had taken the cross only to placate the king of Wessex and not the King of Man.

At times he worried that the world suffered under a madness where only the sword was worshiped and not the word of God—or for that matter words of any kind. He treasured the gift of reading and writing, and on occasion had to curb his pride in knowing both. Most people were ignorant of such skills, and saw little value in learning either. When he offered to teach them, they sneered at his attempts, pointing out neither accomplishment was likely to put food on the table or keep the Danes from killing their families and robbing them blind. When a man toiled from sunup to sunset, there was little room in his day or his heart for learning. But such thinking precluded enlightenment, condemning Mankind to living more like the animals he tended, rather than like the children of Christ.

With a sigh, he made his way over to the donkey patiently awaiting him. He tied the shovel to the pack and untied the tether from the tree. "Come, my long-eared friend," he coaxed as they struck out toward the windswept coast. "I'm afraid I must barter you for a boat, and go to find Leanora. Much has changed since she sought shelter on her island."

Chapter Six

Come the morning, they hauled food and water, and their few possessions, from the camp to the boat. Leanora retrieved the steerboard from where it was hidden, and after quickly mending a small tear in the sailcloth, they were ready to leave.

As the tide came in, they pushed the little ship to free water and climbed aboard. The happiness in Faran's face equaled the sadness dwelling in Leanora's heart, but she felt better when he flashed her a reassuring smile. Such enthusiasm was difficult to resist, and as the sun shone brightly and the water remained placid, it added to the hope that she had chosen wisely.

"Make watch off the bow, and alert me of impending rocks," Faran ordered.

Well, that had not taken long. Apparently he thought himself the leader of their complement of two. Rather than argue, she did his bidding. The truth be known, she was not good at steering.

Hour after hour they made their way northward. The sea ran swift beneath their prow, the day slipped away, and soon it was near eventide. "There is an island to starboard." She pointed out the location.

"According to the map, it's the Holy Island," Faran replied.

"Castle Lindisfarne stands there," she called over the wind now sprung to life. "Are we to make port?" she asked, as a queasiness twisted through her stomach.

"I would rather not. If we stay well out in the whale-road, and drift tonight with the prevailing wind and current, we should reach our destination by tomorrow morning."

With a groan Leanora turned her back to Faran. She knew it made more sense to keep going, but as she hunkered down low in the boat, logic was replaced by an unexpected sickness.

As the daylight disappeared and true darkness fell, the wind continued to rock the small craft with enthusiasm. She sat rigid and stared at her feet, trying to ignore the churning in her stomach and the whirling in her head. Cautiously she reached for a skin of water then hesitated. It seemed unlikely anything would remain long in her belly. She should never have left the island.

Her symptoms did not improve with the coming of the chill night air, nor with the sight of Faran eagerly consuming boiled eggs and salted fish.

"Sure you do not want this last fish?" He held it up for display. That did the trick. Hanging over the side of the boat, Leanora vomited. She wished to die rather than spend another moment on this boat. The thought of jumping overboard even crossed her mind.

"What are you doing?" he asked stupidly.

"The sea does not agree with me." She grimaced and fell back onto the floor of the boat.

Tying off the sail and steerboard, Faran moved closer and crouched at her side. "You are as green as your skirt," he said his eyes wide with amazement. "Why did you not tell me you suffered from seasickness?"

"I did not know. It is my first time so far out on the water. Is it fatal?" she asked hopefully.

"No, it only makes one wish to die. I am sorry to see you suffer so," he added sympathetically and stroked her arm. "We could try to reach the shore in the dark," he offered, bolstering her into a more upright position. "But it would be risky, with a grounding upon the rocks a likely conclusion. And from personal experience, I can advise against such an undertaking. Besides, you will probably feel just as bad tomorrow when we again take to the water."

With a sad little groan she tried to appreciate his honesty. "Keep going," she relented, "and let us be done with it. I do not wish to prolong this agony."

Crawling to the side, she again wretched and gagged. To her embarrassment, Faran kept to her side. She turned her head, not wishing him to see her in such a state. But not chastising or teasing, he gathered her hair back from her face and held it thus until the spell passed.

Leaning sideways, he snagged a piece of bedding, dipped the cloth in the cold seawater, and wiped her face. Then he turned her around, and they both slouched down into a sitting position.

In the dark, Faran's eyes appeared black. And the moon, breaking the horizon, reflected hazily off the angles of his cheeks and the strong bridge of his nose. She did not resist as he slipped his arm around her shoulders, cushioning her against the hard wooden struts. Through the fog of her distress she felt a light-headedness—it came from Faran's gentle touch rather than the brutal hand of the sea. But the feeling dissolved away as another wave of nausea gripped her.

Desperately, she clutched at the front of his tunic. "Is there no cure for this?"

"Well," he said hesitantly. "I know of a few things said to relieve such a condition."

The ship caught another wave and slid down the swell. In an attempt to steady herself, she leaned into Faran, her breasts pressed up against his chest. He shifted about to accommodate her. His face loomed close, and his solid form offered warmth and support.

"For heaven sakes," she pleaded, "tell me what to do."

Still holding the cloth, he used the tip to slowly trace the outline of her lips. "I have heard," he crooned, "the surest and most pleasurable way to remedy your plight is to make love—slowly and repeatedly—all night long."

****

"You foul beast." Leanora groaned and weakly shoved at him. "'Tis no jesting matter."

"Truly, I heard it to be so." In all honesty he had been told making love worked in dispelling seasickness. He had only wished to test the theory. It never hurt to ask.

Another wave of distress washed over her. The icy glare melted, and with a miserable whimper she drew her knees to her chest and rested her forehead upon them.

"Poor little Gillyflower." He patted her back. "I have never before seen anyone the hue of pea-and-lentil soup."

"What is the next choice in cures?" she demanded, her words muffled by her skirt.

"A second method? Oh yes, it is most improbable."

"Trust me," she retorted, "nothing is more unlikely than your first suggestion."

"I believe you," he reassured. He was in trouble now, for he knew of no other remedy. Yet he had to offer something lest she think him completely heartless.

"You must sleep with tiger whiskers beneath your pillow," he said, concocting the most incredible story possible. He waited for the suggestion to bring more ire, instead an expression of relief crossed her face.

"Why did you not say so in the first place," she admonished.

Moving carefully, as if to maintain an even keel, she crawled over to her small personal coffer, rummaged about, and to his amazement produced a wooden box containing three large thick whiskers. They were as long as the span of his hand. The wide end black and the tapered end white. Scooting closer, he examined them.

"By the gods, where did you acquire these?" Gingerly, he touched one. They were brittle, yet flexible, and judging by their size, the animal from whence they had come must have been glorious in both stature and power.

"I saw a jungle cat and lion in a traveling fair," she stated proudly, the glow on her face momentarily overshadowing the green tinge. "They were magnificent. Yet their eyes held a near tangible sorrow. I do not think they tolerated well their confinement. They wished desperately for their freedom, I could tell, for at the time so did I."

"But how did you come by the whiskers? Do not tell me you casually plucked them from the mouth of the creatures."

"No," she admitted with a smile. "The man in the turban who governed the beasts gave them to me. May I leave them in the box for sleeping?" she asked, still taking him seriously.

How extraordinary. She actually accepted his improbable tale as truth—but what else should he expect from a girl who included tiger whiskers amongst her most prized possessions? "Of course," he reassured. "I do not see that it would hurt."

Piling their cloaks into a heap in the prow of the ship, his Gillyflower curled up in the woolen nest and slipped the box under what served as her pillow.

"Good night, Faran. Thank you for the advice. I feel better already. And you are truly a generous person to stand watch alone all tonight."

Stand watch all night? When had he offered to do that? He gave a chuckle as he realized the little minx had outsmarted him. He stood and glanced down at her. She was so small she barely made a bump beneath the covers. He had an urge to reach over and tuck her in, but he balled both hands into fists and forced the thought from his mind.

"Tiger whiskers have many uses," she added with a sleepy drawl. "The man in the traveling show said, in India, if a married woman seeks to become a widow, she grinds up tiger whiskers and puts them in her husband's food. Soon after her wish comes true."

That gave him pause. Surely she was joking, repaying him with a tall tale of her own. Still the very idea made him feel as if a hedgehog were wedged in his throat. He swallowed hard. "Remind me to do all of the cooking if ever you are in an ill humor."

"I never revealed that part of the tiger's magic to my husband," she added before burrowing deeper into the bedding.

"Your husband!" A tightness gripped his stomach, and now he was the one who felt sick. Woden help him. All he needed was a jealous husband hounding his trail. He glanced over his shoulder, half expecting the man to materialize up from the watery depths.

"Do not worry, he is dead."

"Dead?"

"Yes, dead. No longer among the living, and I pity the other souls in hell since his arrival." Her words were stone cold, implying much, yet telling him little. "Do not ask me more," she added, as he opened his mouth to speak.

She closed her eyes, leaving him to wonder how many tiger whiskers she had originally been given.

****

All through the night, Faran monitored the movement of the stars and kept watch over the young woman who continued to sleep peacefully. What was it about Gillyflower that so captured his interest? Sometimes she was childishly innocent, wide-eyed at the smallest of wonders. And at other times, she was wise beyond her years, like a crone who had seen too much of the world's misery and injustice. She was a child/woman, unknowingly toying with his emotions. At least he thought she did so unknowingly. That she had been married came as a surprise and curiosity. She was certainly not the virgin he had envisioned.

While the stars changed partners and danced across the sky, images of a naked Leanora danced through his thoughts. He had not been with a woman in a good long while. Not since the day before his village had been attacked. Not since the day before he had lost his honor and the relics. He wanted to touch Leanora and be touched by her, yet he knew any attempt at bedding her would be met with rejection. She was just beginning to trust him, an act that did not seem to come easily to her. It would be lowly of him to fracture that fragile feeling of faith. But someday she would change her mind, and he would be waiting.

He shifted his position to ease the ache stirring in his loins. Then he shifted his thoughts to ease his conscience.

****

Morning slipped over them clear and calm. Once during the night Faran had dozed off. Luckily, he had tied the steerboard in place, and showing an unusual modicum of pity, the gods had guided the boat safely through the deepest water and along the proper course.

The unintentional respite invigorated his mind

and body, and with the dawn, came another chance for him to succeed in his quest. He must cleave to such a possibility, because there were only two ways in which he could return home—a vindicated warrior or a dead one. Some members of his tribe had forgiven him for being young and foolish, but others had not—especially the king. And although it was not Faran's fault the battle had started, it was his fault he had misinterpreted the counsel of a dream, a vision that distracted him from keeping watch over the heirlooms.

Leanora stirred, interrupting his thoughts. She struggled to shed the allure of sleep, and like a contented cat, she stretched luxuriously, then curled back up into a ball.

During the night, he had decided the best way to keep peace with her and his manhood, was to treat her as any other comrade-in-arms. He would advise her of his mission, at least as much as he dare, and ask for her opinion on matters affecting them both. It sounded like a plan that could not fail.

The sleep still in her eyes, she sat up in earnest and glanced around. This morning the color in Leanora's cheeks was much improved. Apparently her confidence in the ridiculous remedy held more power than the remedy itself. But faith was a tricky sentiment, it could encourage men to travel down roads best avoided, and it offered men reasons to endure suffering without question or recompense.

"Good morning, Gillyflower," he called to her.

Stifling a yawn she returned his greeting with a limp little wave, crawled over to the side of the ship, and made a rather feeble attempt at washing her hands and face. It seemed safe to assume the morning did not inspire her to immediate action. Sitting as if dazed, she stared off to the left and watched the shoreline slipping by.

"Are we almost there?" She squinted up at the

sky to check the position of the sun.

"Almost," he replied, smiling at her question. She sounded like a halfling badgering her parents on the way to the fair. "According to the map," he added, "we have only a short distance to go."

"Is there anything left to eat?"

Here was a surprise. "A few currant berries and two boiled eggs."

"Good. Thanks to you, I am starving."

"I am glad," he said with a slight pang of guilt. What could it hurt for her to believe in the magic of exotic animals from strange lands? Her own God seemed reluctant to bestow upon her any good fortune in exchange for her praise and worship.

"Do you wish me to steer so you might take a rest?" she asked as she pulled the meager offerings from the pouch designated as their larder.

"If you could but see to it while I...ah...whistle in the wind, I would appreciate it."

"Oh, I see," she said with a knowing smile. "I wish it were so easy for a woman."

"Women were not supposed to be on ships," he countered, "or provisions would have been made. Can you wait until we go ashore? We could drop sail and you could hang overboard," he offered at her silence. "Or you could take to the water. Although the sea is very cold and the waves are still running high."

"NO," she said vehemently crossing her legs. "I'll wait."

He stepped to the far side of the sail, somewhat mystified by her abrupt response to his sensible suggestions. "I am at the mercy of your discretion," he called to her.

"I shall not look," she promised.

At her words, he suffered a twinge of disappointment, then he faced downwind and relieved himself. Returning to her side, he offered her the map. "I believe we are here," he said pointing to an area well past Lindisfarne and just before the Firth of Forth. She slid the vellum from his hand, and he grabbed the steerboard.

"But that is Lothian," she declared, her brow knitted in distress. "I did not know that was to be our destination. Lord Gorham rules there, he is a cruel master. Many go to visit his land but few return."

"We go to the Isle of May, off the coast of Lothian," he reassured. "At least that is the plan for now."

"That eases my concern but little," she replied and searched the map for the tiny speck of an island. "Gorham's sister, Romaine, rules there. She is more cruel than Gorham. And the last I heard, a heathen in the worst sense. Oh, sorry," she quickly added.

"How soon they forget." He mildly chastised her criticism of a religion she had only recently abandoned. "Besides, Gorham and Romaine are evil by heritage and choice, not because of the gods they profess to honor. And I hear, even they have recently bowed to the cross."

"That comes as a surprise. And at times, I too cling to the old ways," she admitted. "This new religion thrust upon us, is difficult to understand. But as King Aelfred seeks to unite this land, he demands fealty to this Christian God."

"I would not worry overmuch regarding who rules the country," he pointed out. "We are not likely to break bread with King Aelfred anytime soon. And you should believe in whatever you wish. It cannot hurt to have all deities available for help on this venture."

Again, she studied the map. "As a woman, I suppose it is foolish of me to fear Romaine. I hear it is only men for whom she has an unnatural fondness."

67

His hand tightened over the steerboard until his fingers ached. "All should fear Romaine," he growled, "man, woman, or child. She is a black-hearted bitch and to gain power and wealth she will kill anyone who stands in her way."

Rage boiled up in him. "My father knew her father, and my grandfather her grandfather, and so on back to the beginning of both our people's history. Always we have fought, even in the old country, but never before has either tribe disgraced itself by stealing sacred relics."

She stared at him, and the morning glow washed from her cheeks. "She is of the tribe who stole your treasure? This changes much," she added.

"Well, it's your boat," he said gruffly. "If you do not wish to put in there, you can set me ashore and keep going. I told you I would not force myself nor my quest upon you."

"You promised we were in this together," she retorted, her eyes darkening to a smoldering blue. "Do not attempt to abandon me so readily. I never said I would not go. I just was not aware of our precise destination."

"Well, now you know."

"Am I to expect this reaction every time we do not see eye to eye?" she asked in a huff. "Should I hold my tongue, and not point out a rock if the boat does head toward one, lest you think my suggestion to change course seems contrary or disagreeable?"

"Are you quite finished?" he asked, his gaze locking horns with hers.

"Yes," she replied, "now answer my questions." With a surprising amount of dignity she smoothed out her skirt and sat down.

His mind was made hazy by the flurry of her words, and it took him a moment to remember what her questions had been. As it came to him, he relaxed his expression. "You may speak freely to me of anything at anytime," he promised. "And while I cannot assure you I will never get angry, I will at least listen to what you have to say."

"I intend to hold you to those words." Her expression did not soften, as she pinned him with a steadfast gaze. "By the way," she added, "we head for a large rock on the offhand side."

Faran threw all of his weight against the steerboard. "Take in the sail," he hollered.

She stood with her hands upon her hips, making no move to follow his order. "Are we partners?" she demanded.

"Yes," he shouted.

"To the end?" she pressed.

"Yes. For pity's sake, mind the sail."

She ran to the mast, caught up the rope holding the crossbeam, and with the expertise of a veteran seaman, she trimmed the sail neat as could be. The ship yawed to one side—missing the rock by a mere arm's length.

Leanora threw him a devilish smile. "Praise the Lord," she shouted over the wind.

Clinging to the mast, she faced into the wind. The breeze kissed her cheeks and renewed their color as it blew her ginger hair back from her brow. Ensconced in wild abandon, and outlined against the far horizon, she resembled a carved figurehead upon the prow of a Viking ship. She also appeared a lustier pagan then he could ever hope to be.

He cursed under his breath. The woman must have Frankish blood for she was stubborn to a fault as well as proficient. With a shake of his head, he maneuvered them toward the Isle of May. "Put us to half sail...please." He added the last for good measure. "Where did you learn about ships and sails?" he asked as they came about.

"I have been observing you since we left the island. And growing up on Ridley harbor, I often watched the ships from the window in my room."

"What else did you see from your window, Gillyflower?"

In place of an answer, she gave him a wistful smile. Then she turned away as if such memories were too painful to contemplate. Chin high and back stiff, she stared out to sea, and he knew it was useless to pursue the subject.

His gaze drifted lower to her tiny waist and nicely rounded bottom, and his resolve to treat his shipmate as a man wavered. What had seemed an easy solution in the dark of night lost its credence by the light of day. He yearned to slip his arm around her and offer consolation from the world of which she seemed reluctant to speak about. But it was hardly the time or place for such notions.

Fast approaching the rocky shore, he concentrated on steering the boat around the island. "I would prefer to land on the far shore," he said, "where we can hide the boat. But you will have to go forward to watch for shoals and reefs. Does that suit you?"

She gazed at him thoughtfully. "Yes," she agreed, "it seems a good plan. And hiding the boat is a wise idea. I have the feeling we shall be leaving the Isle of May with even greater haste than in which we arrive."

Chapter Seven

Faran angled the boat between two rocks, Leanora furled the sail, and their forward momentum carried them gently aground.

Clambering over the side, she landed in ankle-deep freezing cold water increasing her already urgent need to pee. They muscled the craft farther onto the beach, then side by side, grappled across the wet sand. Preoccupied with locating a suitable bush, she tripped on a clump of sea grass. Faran casually reached out and grabbed her arm, keeping her upright. She could not fathom why, but falling down in Faran's presence had become a predictable occurrence.

"Thank you," she murmured, and shrugging free of his grip, she veered off toward the trees. "I can wait no longer," she added over her shoulder.

He gave a nod of understanding then turned his back. She squatted down behind the nearest thicket. The grass prickled her bare bottom but she did not care. Stomping the area flat first would have taken too much precious time.

A wave of relief washed over her. By the Rood, it felt good to be once more upon solid ground. Hunkered down, she watched a column of ants marching along between tiny colonnades of nettles and clover, a bee hummed merrily nearby and the warmth of the sun comforted her backside. She felt almost happy, and once again harbored the belief that leaving her sanctuary had been the correct

71

choice after all.

Returning to the shore, she watched Faran rummage about in the bottom of the boat. At her approach he straightened. "If by chance we do not make it back, it would be advisable to take everything of importance with you now."

Her bravado faded, and her hand stopped mid-stroke as she dusted off the back of her skirt. "What do you mean not make it back?"

"Well it is always a possibility," he said, and gathered underbrush and small branches.

His words rekindled her fears, and spurred by panic, she scrambled back onto the boat. What should she take? Everything on the craft was of importance or she would not have brought it along in the first place. As she pawed through bags and pouches, a tightness constricted her chest, and her insecurities screamed out in demand for first one item and then another. She must have her tiger whiskers and the tattered piece of silk belonging to her mother and clean clothes and a few cooking utensils and...

"Perhaps you should just wait here," Faran said as he eyed the mountain of articles she had accumulated into a pile.

He was correct. She could not possibly take all of these items along. Leaving the safety of her island had obviously taken a toll on her senses. And now the thought of losing her few remaining possessions was precluding clear thinking altogether.

Faran continued to cover the boat with branches. He moved leisurely, and his easy manner and the mundane task calmed her. He slapped another branch over the hull closing off more of the sunlight, and a shiver of excitement sprouted up deep inside of her. She preferred that feeling to fear, although at times the two were hard to tell apart.

Why did she worry so? They would be safe.

Faran had probably been on many a bold adventure. He would not lead them into danger with no means of escape.

She shoved her two small wooden boxes into a bag, tied them securely, and crawled through the opening left to accommodate her. Then she arranged the brush to cover the gap, and cloak in hand, hurried to catch up.

Faran was already several strides into the woods, heading toward the inhabited side of the island. As she reached him, a new worry crept forward to badger her thoughts. How would they find their way back to the boat? She turned around and stared at the beach and the hump of bracken. Periodically she repeated this action, trying to commit to memory a picture in reverse. Soon every tree looked the same, and with each backward glance, a different vista greeted her. Her shoulders slumped, and she sighed in frustration. She would never recognize the trail upon which to return.

Faran came to her side. "Why do you stop, always looking back?"

"I am afraid we will never find the path to return to the boat."

He stood behind her and placed one hand upon her shoulder. "Do not look at the ground," he instructed, "but study the horizon beyond the island. On the far coastline of County Lothian, two dark mountaintops dominate the view. If you walk always in the middle of those peaks you will find your way back."

She concentrated hard, trying to make sense of Faran's words, but his nearness overwhelmed her senses, and the heat of his body enveloped her like the finest woolen garment. When he turned, and headed deeper into the forest, the warmth dissolved away, leaving her breathless and shivering.

"But what guides us at night or on a foggy day?"

She asked and scurried to catch up. "You trust too much in Fate."

"And you trust not enough."

How was it Faran could be so daring? He seemed ready to challenge the world with little more than what he carried upon his back. She, on the other hand, fretted over everything. Would they get lost, where would their next meal come from, would the people of the town be friendly, what if they were robbed, what if someone stole their boat? What if they were separated?

Faran scowled down at her. "There is little purpose to put so much thought into worrying about tomorrow when we may not live past today."

"God's bones," she swore under her breath. This Geat was as crazy as he was fair of face. Half an arm's length taller than she, he walked straight as the staff he carried. And although she thought of herself as hearty and fit, she could barely keep up with his long-legged steps. He seemed to approach life fearlessly, like the jungle cat to which she compared him. His stride was bold, as if he dared anyone to cross his path, his mood, or the territory he called his own.

She glanced again at her comrade-in-arms. Sunlight flashed off the amulet he wore. Faran, the Iron Heart. It was a name that set one's mind to wondering. Did he pride himself on disallowing any woman to touch his cold hard heart? Did he woo ladies into love trysts with promises of treasure and pleasure only to tragically desert them?

For certes he was unlike anyone she had ever known. Handsome to be sure—with a rock hard body, images of which occupied her thoughts much too often. And his generous mouth was an unbidden fascination. It could accommodate a childlike smile, tempering all the fierceness he worked so hard to portray. Or it could accommodate a reassuring smile, making her believe everything in her troubled world would be all right.

And his mind was also intriguing. As strikingly developed as his form, it was a quality she truly admired in him. Along with religion, Brother Thomas had taught her about foreign methods of reasoning and the use of logic different from her own. Knowledge could be a powerful weapon, and Faran appeared well armed.

To her benefit, he seemed preoccupied with the present and not with prying into her past, nor did he threaten to rule her future. He treated her differently, he treated her like...a friend. The idea stunned her. Life had never afforded her the opportunity to know or cherish another person in such a manner. Another new experience. Then a spark of yearning for more than mere friendship flickered inside of her. *You can never trust a man*, she chastised, *you can only believe in yourself.* Unyielding logic cooled the fiery ember of need, but not before it claimed a barren part of her never before touched by warmth or light.

"When we reach the outskirts of town," Faran advised, startling her back to the present, "we must be cautious and not attract attention. I propose we enter quietly but with confidence, as if we have nothing to hide. Then we will mingle with the milling throng. What think you?"

"Yes, as you say," she quietly agreed.

This was the second time he had asked for her opinion. Wishing to seize such a rare opportunity, she tried in vain to think of something worthy to add to his statement. Nothing came to mind. She had little practice in offering advice or expressing ideas. Other than the audacious act of fleeing to her island, the events in her life had always been governed by the whim and will of others. Giving voice to thoughts and desires seemed as foreign to her as learning to fly. Foreign, yet exhilarating.

The forest thinned, and a formidable stonewall rose up before them. Unassailable, the grand obstacle seemed worthy of keeping people in as well as out. They skirted the perimeter of the bastion, and as the sun clung to the pinnacle of the sky, the sound of village life filtered through to them.

Faran slowed his step. She did the same. The resounding ring of the smithy's hammer drifted on the breeze. Merchants hawked their wares, the venders repeating their invitations to buy in several languages. Apparently the Isle of May saw a variety of visitors, and the tradesmen were not about to lose a profit because their words were not understood.

"Put on your cloak and cover your head," Faran instructed.

"Why should I?" She balked at the idea. "I am warm now from walking." *And from carrying this heavy bag,* she thought irritably.

"You will invite trouble," he pointed out. "You are fair to gaze upon and your hair attracts attention."

She was pleased Faran found her comely, but bundled up in the heat of the day she would feel like a leper. He stopped and held her back until she relented. In no time at all, her hair was stuck uncomfortably to her cheeks and forehead, and her face felt flushed with the heat. Then, as they entered the main gate, the bright colors and boisterous activities overshadowed her cross mood.

A juggler, standing on an upturned crate, performed for coins and trinkets. Beside him, a man with a dancing monkey vied for their attention.

The smell of food, both familiar and foreign, set her stomach to growling and mouth to watering. So loud did her hunger make itself known, Faran liberated a silver coin from the pouch he carried, and purchased two roasted turkey legs. At least one of her many worries was dispelled, she would not starve to death—today.

The grumbling in her belly was silenced, but a river of noise and merriment continued to flow around them. On her left, an argument broke out between two men. It appeared they both sought to purchase the same fine silver fibula. As the bargaining price went higher and higher, so did their tempers. Like an angry bull, the larger of the two men charged the other. Grappling in a tangle of arms and legs, they fell to the ground, scuffling first one way and then the other. The bystanders retreated to allow them room to fight. Before she could do the same, one man rolled too close. She gave a small yelp and jostled sideways into Faran. He thrust his walking stick and the remainder of his food into her hands, and with a feral growl, strode forward.

Grabbing the offending ruffian by the scruff of his tunic, he jerked the burly peasant off the ground, and tossed him aside. The fellow cursed and rolled to his feet, intent upon continuing the brawl. Faran stood waiting, legs braced wide, the muscles of his arms and thighs bunched and begging for release.

An expression of caution wiped the sneer from his opponent's mouth, and after a moment of contemplation, the man backed away. Disappointed the fight should end so quickly, the crowd dispersed.

"It was not my fault," Leanora defended, as Faran returned to her side. Her hood had fallen back and her mass of loose hair had already drawn several stares.

"I know," he said, as he drew the hood back over her head. No anger sounded in his voice, and his eyes seemed to question her defensive words. "You are unharmed?" he asked as he took back his food and staff.

"Yes. I am fine," she whispered, coaxing the

answer out around a fluttering in her chest. No one had ever bothered to worry about her safety. Why did he? She hoped he would not grow tired of such a burden.

They ate in silence, tossed the bones to a waiting hound, and wandered about the streets. Several women glanced seductively at Faran, and he openly grinned back at them. Leanora could not blame the females for their prurient interest, but she also did not like it. With a frown, she trailed along and questioned the possessiveness pricking at her humor. Faran was her partner, nothing more. And once they had found the treasure, they would go their separate ways. She had no right to covet him or give a care as to whom he found attractive.

As Faran halted dead in his tracks, she bumped into him. His expression turned menacing, and shifting her gaze, she discovered the reason.

Across the village was a grand house, a miniature palace, and upon the parapet stood a woman who seemed to stare directly at them. Black as soot, her hair hung down past her shoulders, and even at this distance, Leanora could see the garments she wore clung tightly to her shapely form. The woman turned and clapped her hands, and a large man, bald as a melon, appeared at her side. Was this a eunuch? She had heard such men attended the rich. The female spoke, waved him away, and retreated from the rampart.

"Was that Romaine?" Leanora asked.

"Yes," Faran ground out the answer, his mouth contorted in a sneer.

"She seemed interested in us. Or at least in you."

"It must be your imagination," he reassured, but the lack of conviction in his tone belied the words. "Come," he urged, "let us continue exploring."

They meandered about in what appeared to be a

random pattern, but it did not escape her attention that they drew ever closer to "Romaine's Domain," as she had dubbed the royal residence. With a sinking feeling she realized Faran sought an encounter with the lecherous woman who ruled the island.

Many unpleasant legends surrounded the Queen of the May. She lusted after men, enjoying them in every carnal manner possible. And later, when her lovers disappointed her, or she grew tired of them, she coldheartedly made sure no other woman partook of what had once been hers. Sometimes she put them to death. Sometimes she only removed the part of them that made them men.

"You seek the she-devil who commands this city," she accused, in a hushed tone.

"Yes," Faran admitted. "Though you be but a girl, you are not easily fooled."

"Do you fancy girls are born without brains?"

"The thought has occurred to me on occasion." His look of innocence softened the jest.

"Well, I am not so afflicted, so do not try to deceive me." She halted and tugged at his arm to draw his attention to her next question. "Are you sure Romaine has the treasure and the heirlooms for which you seek?"

"No, not really. But she at least has knowledge of their whereabouts."

"How do you know this?"

"After my people were attacked, objects were left behind to make us believe the Saxons were at fault. But as my comrades and I followed the horde, we caught an injured enemy warrior trailing behind the retreating forces.

"We recovered the scabbard from him, and with encouragement, the man confessed to being part of Romaine's army. Before he died he also explained how another group of men, dressed as Geats, were to attack the mainland Saxons throwing blame on my tribe."

"But why would Romaine's people trouble to play you false with such deception?"

"They do not wish us to live in peace. Or for that matter, in any other condition. Now they have our relics and the treasure and none of the burden nor expense of war. At their leisure, they can delight in their ill-gotten gains while the Saxons do them the favor of trying to kill us."

"Gorham and Romaine—to what tribe do they show allegiance?"

"They claim to be the children of giants and the descendents of Cain."

"Then they are the enemies of both the Geats and the Saxons."

"Lifelong enemies of the Geats, recent enemies of the Saxons. And the ever treacherous Danes," he put in, "are the enemies of all."

"Can you not find other relics?" she urged.

Faran look of exasperation and shock spoke volumes. She had not thought it such a remote idea, and again she had the distinct impression there were parts to this story yet to be revealed.

"No," he said harshly. "And I cannot tell you more."

"Well it was just a simple question," she said, feeling unjustly set upon. "I am only trying to do my part to help."

The flint-hard look in his eyes softened, and for a moment, she thought he was going to add something important. But he remained silent, and signaled for her to follow as he worked his way around to the back of Romaine's imperial hall.

They paused beside a rock wall running the length of the building. Oddly, no guards were in sight. In her omnipotence, Romaine seemed overly confident. Faran put a finger to his lips, and led her farther down the alleyway to a circular stairwell which led to the top-floor accommodations.

"If I do not return in a reasonable amount of time," he began, relinquishing his walking stick into her care, "you are to save yourself and make for the boat in all haste."

"I will not," she exclaimed. The prospect of being left alone horrified her, as did the idea of abandoning him to his fate. "I'm coming with you. We are partners."

"Yes, we are partners. And partners look after one another. That is why you will stay here." He lightly touched her cheek, then turned and bounded up the steps. Open mouthed, she stared after him and reached for his shadow as it disappeared around the first curve of the stairway.

"How long should I wait?" she squeaked in a voice strained thin by fear. She took a step forward to follow. It was too late. He was gone. Alone and vulnerable, she hunkered down beside the stonewall.

****

The evening shadows lengthened and fused into solid blackness and the damp air, ushered in on the wings of darkness, chilled her to the bone.

What was that sound?

"Faran?" she whispered. Cold silence was the only reply. In the distance, a dog barked and somewhere a baby cried, otherwise the little town slept peacefully while she sat abandoned in a land governed by a madwoman.

Tired and hungry, she gathered her cape closer and hugged herself for warmth. As her eyes grew accustomed to the dimness, she fought the tears threatening, gained her feet, and peered around in all directions. How could he do this to her? Was it really for her safety he left her here alone in the dark? What if he had already recovered the treasure and relics and left by another exit. And all the while she sat here like a simpleton wondering how long she should continue to wait.

She glanced at the village. The lights there burned with a welcoming glow. But above in Romaine's Domain, the dim illumination appeared secretive. Suddenly, brazen sounds of perverse gaiety oozed out of the open doors and windows—the merriment at the palace had begun. Playful shouts of men and the rippling laughter of women hung in the night air, dripping over the balcony and raining down upon her like a cold spring shower.

Off to her left, something moved in the rubbish pile. She reached for her dagger. Venturing out into the world had not seemed so frightening with Faran at her side. Now alone in the dark, she was intimidated by every noise—imagined or real. The intruder gave a disinterested meow, and with its tail in the air, the cat disappeared into the shadows. Her back to the wall, she sighed in relief.

By the saints, what was taking him so long? Maybe he had been caught.

Another bout of laughter erupted overhead, and the heat of anger burned upon her cheeks. Or maybe he was up there enjoying lascivious pleasures in warmth and splendor while she waited down here in cold discomfort.

What should she do? How long had she waited? The passage of time was devious and hard to measure. Moments of dread lingered forever, while joy was fleeting and soon but a memory. Should she return to the boat without Faran? That seemed complete folly. Besides, she was not about to so easily give up her share of the treasure. She had forfeited much for the promise of that wealth. Riches, she reminded herself, she had yet to see. If Faran deceived her, and Romaine did not torture him to death, he may wish she had.

Another raucous outburst spilled down from above. Then a shriek split the night, bristling the hair on the back of her neck. Clutching her bag to her chest, she reached for the solid support of the wall. Going back to the boat was beginning to sound better and better. But could she find the ship in the dark, and if so, could she push it to free water at low tide? She had never sailed at night, and she had nowhere to go. And what if he needed her help?

Rooted by indecision and worry she stared up at the palace. Then a realization gripped her with sickening and painful clarity. Faran would not be returning from this hideous woman's lair, not without assistance.

Her heart tripped forward at a furious pace as she crept closer to the stairway winding upward into the smoky darkness. Partners took care of one another. Faran had said so.

Chapter Eight

Faran gave another yank against the chain attached to his left wrist. Then he slumped back upon the soft pallet and let his arm fall slack at his side. Waking up restrained in unfamiliar beds was becoming a recurring pattern in his life, or perhaps this was to be expected when one went adventuring.

The last thing he recalled was being in a brawl with four soldiers. They had intercepted him as soon as he had reached the upper level of the palace—and they had apparently won the field. So much for stealth and cunning.

Where was Leanora? His heart raced until he remembered *suggesting* she wait for him in the walkway behind the palace. Hopefully, she was still there and out of harm's way. How could he have let this happen? If she were hurt it would be his fault, and although his body remained basically sound, what little pride he had left could not withstand another beating.

Again his plans had gone awry. Again the Fates laughed rather than smiling down upon him. Did he not deserve better? Earning back the respect of the gods was proving more difficult than he had imagined.

The large pallet, to which he was bound, was unusually tall, affording a sweeping view of the room. Without doubt this was Romaine's gilded lair. Never in his life had he seen such shameless opulence. Numerous golden sconces lent an ethereal glow to the tapestries clinging to the walls. Persian rugs, thick as ermine pelts in winter, covered the floor. Ornately carved tables held goblets, flagons, and plates—all of bright silver and all studded with jewels. The splendor of the room was grotesque, and he wagered the grandeur had been bought with the blood and suffering of others.

An eerie sense of being watched tugged at him and he gazed upward. The panels in the overhead archways were painted with very beautiful, very naked women. Framed in gold-leaf, the nubile females depicted all manner of carnal desire as they mated with men as well as one another. Their red lips smiled temptingly, their kohl-rimmed eyes were veiled with sensual delight. And although Faran considered himself well rounded in the field of making love, some of the activities they performed had never occurred to him. Traveling truly did broaden one's education.

The females in the murals were of every size and color, offering a bevy of firm thighs and nicely rounded breasts. Each was tinted in a different hue, ranging from delicate pink to exquisite sable brown. The well-muscled men, however, were all fair-skinned and flaxen-haired, and oddly, their expressions seemed tortured rather than pleased. There was pity in their eyes.

A chill gripped his mind and then his body. He was clothed in nothing but a loincloth and his amulet. He felt totally defenseless. Jaw clenched, he strained once more against the binding chains.

"'Tis futile to resist the irons. Just as it is futile to resist the desires of Romaine."

He peered in the direction of the throaty female voice. There she was, the bitch who had destroyed his life. She leaned seductively against the doorway, sleek as a wolf and no doubt just as predatory. Her hair, black as sin, tumbled wildly about her head and shoulders. A sly smile curved her lips. She wet them with the tip of her tongue as if in anticipation of a well-cooked meal.

Raising a golden chalice, she drank deeply and slowly, then savoring the contents she peered at him over the rim of the cup. A shiver convulsed through her body, and her dark eyes glowed like hot embers raked from the fires of the underworld.

She slid one hand down the front of her body, her fingers gliding smoothly over the silk tunic scantily covering her robust form. The thin cloth clung to her like the soft skin of a ripe peach, revealing every detail of her female form.

"So you are Romaine," he acknowledged, pretending not to know who she was.

"Yes," she purred. "And you are my captive."

Did she realize he was a Storm Geat? "Release me. I have no quarrel with you," he lied.

She glided forward to stand at his shoulder. He forced his gaze from the V of her thighs up to her face. Eyes—the deepest brown he had ever seen—stared back at him. The black centers were so enlarged they appeared bottomless, and there was an emptiness about them that did not set well with him. "What do you want?" he asked.

An aroma of exotic fragrances, pungent and sweet, clung to the air around Romaine, and while the hand she rested upon his bare chest was warm enough, her long red fingernails dug into his flesh with cold certainty.

"I want pleasure," she said.

"And what if I am not in the mood for the games you wish to play?"

"No one has yet to deny me," she bragged. "And when I am through preparing you, you will want it as much as I."

She dragged one claw-like nail across his chest, then down to his stomach. He shrank back from her touch. She laughed and reached sideways to retrieve a small scimitar lying upon the table at his feet.

Woden help him. Did she think to kill him? Or worse yet leave him alive but maimed?

The curved blade of the menacing weapon gleamed wickedly in the candlelight. His panic increased as Romaine slipped the cold metal beneath the linen. He sucked in his belly and held his breath, afraid to move. With one quick motion, she sliced through the cloth and liberated him from the meager wraps. Her eyes widened with delight, and her lips parted in appreciation as she assessed what lie beneath the rent fabric.

"It has been a long time since I have had a man such as you," she said with a sigh. "You will please me well."

Exhaling, Faran struggled to free himself. The woman was mad. She had helped to plan the destruction of his village, and even if that were not true, he did not think he could bolster his manhood under circumstances such as these.

She smiled, evil and sly, a she-cat ready to consume him whole. This did not inspire him to passion. Neither did being tied spread-eagle upon a sacrificial bed. The vulnerability of his position caused his panic to rise but nothing more.

Tossing the blade upon the table, she stepped to the head of the bed, leaned over, and roughly kissed him. When he did not respond, she poured some of the liquid from the cup she held into his mouth. Taken off guard, he coughed and sputtered and unintentionally swallowed the bitter brew. A feeling of warmth flashed through his body, settling hotly between his legs.

Romaine lapped up the nectar running down his cheek. "'Tis too good to waste," she purred in his ear. "I fear you could do with a little more."

She held his nose, and when he gasped for

breath, she forced more of the potion past his lips. Then shifting her hand to cover his mouth, she made sure he could not spit out the strange concoction. After choking down the second dose, he found it difficult to think clearly.

The colors in the room seemed to grow brighter, and the girls in the overhead pictures appeared to come alive. They laughed down at him as they squirmed and twisted in pursuit of their sexual fantasies. And although he willed against it, he grew full and hard.

"Take enjoyment in what is to be." Romaine caressed his chest and shoulders. "You cannot stop it."

She kissed him deeply, forcing her tongue between his lips. She tasted the same as the exotic drink, and Faran's mind could no longer conquer the desire coursing through his veins. Logic and purpose had been betrayed, and relying only upon instinct, he tried to repel the kiss. Then, the woman who ruled the Isle of May began to torture him.

Without pity, she swept a large feather over the length of his body. Gently, repeatedly, she dragged it back and forth between his toes, between his thighs, around the part of him that ached and throbbed with a horrifying need. Long delicate strokes, teasing every inch of his skin, arousing him beyond anything in recent memory. He groaned and nearly begged for the female body hovering so near yet just out of reach.

Romaine drank more of the potion, and poured another dollop into his mouth. Again, taken off guard, he choked down the mind-twisting concoction.

Throwing aside the feather, Romaine ripped apart the neckline of her tunic and pushed the torn fabric down over her shoulders. Roughly, she fondled her exposed breasts, moaning at the self-induced delight.

Fascinated, he watched as she drew lazy circles around her dark nipples bringing them to hard peaks. Twisting closer, she pressed one breast to his mouth, her left hand cradled his head against her warm succulent flesh.

"I will release your leg-irons if you promise to be good," she offered. She eased back, but tightened her fingers in his hair as she awaited his nod of cooperation.

"Yes," Faran lied "it would help me to please you all the more."

"Good answer, my pet. I shall hold you to your word." Taking up the key hanging from a silver chain around her neck, she unlocked the manacles on his ankles. He gasped in surprise and his mind reeled as she raked her fingernails upward along the inside of his thighs. For a moment, he could not recall where he was or why he had come here.

Romaine screeched and howled like a vixen on the prowl. Then she rent the remainder of her tattered garment to the hem. The discarded remnants fluttered to the floor in silken elegance, only to be crushed underfoot as she clawed her way up onto the bed.

"You are mine now," she said, straddling his hips. And after being with Romaine, you will never want another."

Retrieving a vile from the table, she pulled the stopper free with her teeth and dripped golden oil, thick as honey, onto the front of her body. Forming a tiny stream, it ran down between her breasts and onto her abdomen. She poured what was left across his chest, spit out the cork, and threw the bottle aside.

With practiced hands, she massaged the balm into his skin, enlivening every fiber of his being. Faran cursed the fates that allowed him to become this woman's captive. He hated what she was making his body do. She was his sworn enemy, and making love to her was the last thing he had in mind for this black-haired whore.

He had to resist, had to get away from her. He tried once more to break free of the manacles shackling his arms. They held fast, but as the metal bit into his skin, the stab of pain seemed to work as an antidote to the potion. He struggled harder. Blood showed on his wrists, still they would not release. Fighting to recover control of his mind and body, he breathed deep and slow and like a misty fog, the cloak of illusion began to evaporate.

Quickly, he must gain the needed information before Romaine realized he had no intention of gratifying her sordid needs. "Have you led many battles?" he crooned. "I am partial to women of guile and strength." The words upon his tongue felt as caustic as the bitch's brew.

"Yes, my love, I have done so." She leaned forward and bit painfully at his neck and shoulder.

"Tell me of your most recent victory," he goaded, hoping to arouse her vanity rather than her sexual desires.

"I have fooled the Geats and blamed all on another," she proudly stated. Then she snarled, victory glittering in her eyes. "The Storm Geats think 'twas the Saxons who did the deed." She threw back her head and laughed.

He trapped her between his thighs trying to still her gyrations. "Most ingenious," he said, nearly choking on the false praise. "And what of your bounty?"

"I took the coffers, and my brother, mawkish goat that he is, settled for their old sword and shield. He is more sentimental, where I am practical. But we both share an equal hatred for the Geats."

Faran gritted his teeth in anger. The silly bitch did not even care about the worth of the relics.

"Do not speak of foolish things," she gasped. "Make love to me, make me feel like the beautiful queen I am."

Having determined the location of the relics, his disgust for Romaine overruled caution. "Sheep will fly, and the stars grow dim, before a Geat warrior pleasures a sea cow such as you." As the reckless words left his mouth, he knew they sealed his fate.

When the meaning of his statement became clear, the lust faded from Romaine's eyes and a look of fury moved in to take its place. She pummeled his chest and pulled his hair.

He bucked upward trying to unseat the crazed hag, but she rode him like a seasoned warrior, a twisted smile distorting her lips.

"You will die for this, Storm Geat," she spat. "And not quickly or pleasantly." She balled one hand into a fist and drew back her arm. He gritted his teeth as she delivered the first blow. She took aim again, but stopped in mid-swing. Her eyes turned dull and unfocused, and she slumped forward. The air whooshed from his lungs as she lay there unmoving, dead weight upon his chest.

By the gods she was heavy.

Chapter Nine

"Is she dead?" Leanora asked, and carefully set aside the dented silver serving bowl.

"I think she lives," Faran gasped from beneath the royal fleshpot sprawled upon his body. "Retrieve the key from around her neck and unlock the chains binding my wrists."

Leanora stood her ground, arms folded across her chest. Romaine's exotic beauty made her feel painfully thin and pale. "My but you are most fickle," she accused. "Do you tire so readily of your new playmate?"

"What?" Faran's brow furrowed in confusion.

"Until the very end you did not seem unduly distressed with the lady's attention. What did you say to make her so angry?"

"How long were you watching?" he asked, ignoring her question.

"Long enough. You owe me your life twice now."

"How is it you reckon that tally?" he sputtered. "It's true you tended me on the island, but I doubt I would have died from having too good of a...."

"Never mind," she interrupted, "you know what I mean."

The truth be told, Leanora had been captivated by the display she had witnessed. Apparently Romaine did not conduct her life based upon the rules set down by men. The Queen of the May had been the one demanding pleasure, not Faran. Grudgingly she admired the woman for that. It had never occurred to her a female might enjoy coupling, or seek such amusement without concern for the man. In her world it was the man's desires that must be accommodated. Blessedly brief, was the only good thing she could think to attribute to her late husband's rough demands. She had complied out of fear and duty, but never once had his brutish touch pleased her. That it might be otherwise was an intriguing prospect.

"Did you learn anything useful?" she asked. "From where I hid it was hard to make out your words."

"Yes, to be sure," Faran acknowledged. "I for one thought Romaine's feather torture particularly worthy of remembrance. But she did not divulge the ingredients contained in the lotion she so lavishly spread upon my body."

"I was referring to the relics and treasure, you toad."

"Oh, the treasure. I could tell you more easily if I could but breathe. Get this female baggage off of me."

She prodded Romaine to make sure she had not awakened, then like a sack of meal, she rolled her to the far side of the bed. The woman landed with a dull thud, coming to rest upon her back.

Eyes wide, Leanora stared at Faran's unclad form, and a hot desire to try what she had interrupted streaked through her. Instead, she dragged her gaze upward to his face.

"If you please." Raising his arms he shook the manacles.

Trying to reach Romaine's key, she leaned across Faran, and the point where their bodies touched glowed and tingled. The aroma of the fragrant oil wove a spell that tantalized her senses making her dizzy.

Halfheartedly she searched for the silver chain.

Then the warmth of Faran's breath upon her cheek drew her attention. She turned her head to gaze into his eye. "Why did you not please her as she wished?" she dared to ask, made bold by curiosity and his captive condition. "It may have gained you your freedom."

Faran contorted his face as if he tasted gall. "Romaine's lust is fearsome and suffocating. She is driven with no more logic than the ocean crashing upon the shore. And she has even less compassion for what lies in her path.

"Besides," he added his features relaxing, "making love is not a weapon to smite down an enemy. It is a gift between two people to be shared and enjoyed." He stared at her lips. "I would not tarnish my extraordinary ability of delighting women by indulging in false practices."

"I think the potion still distorts your mind." She laughed. "You are so full of yourself you will not need to eat for a fortnight."

"Hunger comes in many forms." His smile turned seductive, and the color of his eyes darkened to a warm sea green. "At present," he added, "food is the furthest thing from my mind."

Knowing Faran was partially restrained, she savored his nearness and their wayward conversation. But his close proximity affected her oddly. Her heart pounded too quickly, why, it even skipped a beat, and her breathing was irregular and much too rapid. Wild, delicious sensations teased her from the inside out, spawning urges she had only known in musings and dreams.

Faran pressed his bare chest upward. The heat radiating from his muscled form penetrated even the thick linen she wore, and a fiery craving pulsed through her body and weakened her knees.

Unintentionally, her fingers found the silver necklace. With a sharp tug, she broke the chain and slid it free from around Romaine's neck. Faran's mouth curved into a knowing smile, and he watched her so intently her hands trembled as she unlocked the wrist irons.

Naked as a babe, he rose to stand at her side. She tried not to look at him, but not too successfully. Totally uninhibited, her warrior casually stretched and glanced around. "Do you see my boots or garments anywhere?" If she did not know better she would think he purposely strutted his magnificent body before her.

Thankful for an excuse to busy herself, she turned away and spied his belongings on a nearby trunk. "I have them," she called. Gathering them up, she tossed them in his general direction not daring to partake again in the sight of his fully revealed form. Seeing him naked made her most uncomfortably warm.

As Faran dressed, Leanora dragged Romaine's body to the center of the pallet and slipped the cruel manacles around the queen's arms and legs. It would not hurt the woman to have a taste of her own medicine. And it might buy them time once the harpy awakened.

"What about the treasure?" she asked for the second time.

"The coffers are here," Faran reassured, "but the sword and shield are with Gorham, in Lothian."

Lothian... The Saints preserve her. "Does this mean you now head to the north?"

"Yes. Up the coast but a short distance, then inland to the city of Gylfi."

A groan escaped her. What was she to do now? Staying on the Isle of May was out of the question. But a trip to the heart of the most dismal county in the North Country did not sound much better.

"We can trade the boat for horses when we reach the shores of Lothian," he added enthusiastically.

"Just a moment, if you please." As she turned to face him, the old sensation of having her life controlled by another reared its ugly head. Part of the treasure was hers, and she would do as she pleased, not as Faran so ordered. "I have little choice but to flee this island with you. But I do not wish to sell my boat, and I do not wish to remain a moment longer than necessary in the wretched land to which we travel. Spend part of your recovered wealth on a horse. The boat is mine."

Heaven above, what was she saying? She did not really wish to part Faran's company. On the contrary, she would do anything to stay by his side. This thing called freedom was as intoxicating as the brew Faran had been forced to drink, and it made senseless words fly out of her mouth.

At his crestfallen expression, she wished she could take back her words. "Oh, why must you go to Gylfi? Is not the treasure enough?"

"I wish it could be so, Gillyflower, but to my people the sword and buckler are more valuable than a thousand treasures."

Leanora turned back toward the pallet, but not before she caught the fierce, haunted look in Faran's eyes. It was that damnable all consuming do-or-die expression she was coming to know so well. It made him appear invincible, like a warrior on a mission divinely inspired by some powerful ancient calling. Yet at other times, she had witnessed the little boy in him drawn to the wonder and beauty of the world around him. It seemed the heart of the warrior beat beside the soul of a poet, and both traits aroused feelings to frighten as well as excite her.

Her fingers twitched with the urge to touch Faran, and her cheeks grew hot as she vividly remembered the more interesting parts of him now properly clothed. These urges confounded logic and waged a war deep inside of her—she was losing the battle against them.

As Romaine's head lolled to one side, Leanora jumped and stared down at her. Now in repose, the woman appeared much younger, even vulnerable. A single tear, blackened with kohl, slipped from beneath the queen's lashes. It ran down her flawless cheek, leaving a dark streak across her face—a grotesque crack in an otherwise perfectly sculpted mask.

"I am sorry, Father," Romaine murmured, "please do not beat me. Please do not send me to his room tonight."

Was it possible Romaine rode the Night Mare too? A small grain of pity chafed at Leanora's conscience. She grabbed a coverlet and tossed it over the woman's naked form, but her compassion was short-lived. Even if they fought similar demons in life, Romaine chose to battle them by embracing wickedness, fighting evil with evil. And while Romaine had survived to rule her own realm, the power gained left her greedy and cruel.

"She does not deserve your sympathy," Faran stepped to her side. "She deserves the sharp edge of this." He held his dagger at Romaine's throat.

"Wait," Leanora exclaimed, as she reached out to stay his hand. "You cannot kill her in cold blood."

"Why not?" His hand tightened upon the hilt. "I seek no quarter and I give none. She would do the same to you or me without a second thought."

Faran had every right to seek retribution for the foul acts Romaine had committed, but might he not later regret such a deed? She did not believe deep down inside he could do such a thing without it weighing upon his conscience.

"There is no glory in it," she pointed out, trying to sway him from his intent.

This seemed to give him pause. Then to her horror, Faran slashed the blade anyway. But rather than cutting Romaine's silken throat, he liberated a large hank of hair at the temple above her right ear. He shaved it off at the roots, leaving a round red patch glistening like a burn. The odd styling would needle Romaine's vanity for many months to come, even for the rest of her life if the hair did not grow back.

Faran threw the fistful of black curls aside as if they scorched his flesh. "She's a man-eater and a woman-hater," he said, "and she has caused the death and destruction of many of my people. If we meet again, I will not stay my weapon."

Leanora secretly rejoiced at Faran's show of compassion, but she was leery of acknowledging his actions too heartily. Some men saw mercy as a weakness. "You did the right thing," she said, treading lightly. "Sometimes it takes more courage and strength to hold back the sword than to wield it."

"I know, I know. Praise the Lord and turn the other cheek. You Christians are brimming with righteous parables and verse but that did not save your Christ from the cross, and it will not save us from the queen's wrath and fury once she awakens."

Retrieving the feather used to torture his body, Faran shoved the quill beneath his leather hair-tie. The plume hung down his back like a banner of conquest

"Come, we must leave before we are discovered." He gripped her arm, led her across the room, and threw back the lids on two small coffers. "Here is the treasure I sought...I mean, we sought," he corrected.

She gasped in awe. There it was, the reason for which she had risked everything. Faran had not lied. The bounty was near unimaginable.

"We should put everything in one trunk," he suggested, breaking her spell of fascination. "We will have only one chance to escape. There will be no coming back for seconds."

They transferred the jewels to the chest holding the coins, and struggling with her end of the heavy burden, she grimaced and shuffled along trying to keep pace. At the door, when Faran halted to peer out into the hall, she groaned in relief and set down her side.

"The way is clear," he whispered. "But we must hurry. Dawn will soon be upon us."

"We should use the back stairs, and leave by the alleyway," she suggested.

"Agreed." He nodded. "Hopefully we will be well into the woods before true daylight breaks."

She gritted her teeth and tried to keep up, but her arm and shoulder soon ached, and the feather sticking out of Faran's hair began to irritate her to no end. It bobbed and fluttered about when he spoke, and as he turned his head to check the passageway at their back, the damnable thing slapped her in the face. Crushing a wicked impulse to tear loose the ratty plumage, she remained silent and trudged on.

Undetected, they labored their way to the first floor. Only one guard did they pass. The sentry snored heavily and blissfully in his chair. A flagon of brew was on the floor at his side, and a sleeping, half-clothed girl was draped over his lap. It would seem last night, debauchery and merrymaking abounded in all the ranks.

As the thin pastel fingers of dawn reached out to paint the far horizon, they slipped silently through a side entrance.

Trying to ignore the burning pain in her shoulder, Leonora concentrated on what the treasure would buy for her and her mother. She even promised to tithe a goodly amount to Brother Thomas in payment for his helping her to escape to her island. *Just get us to the boat*, she prayed as she forced near-lifeless fingers to grip the strap and her feet to match Faran's long stride.

Finally gaining the cover of the woods she demanded a rest. "I can go no farther," she hissed. Dropping her side of the trunk caused Faran to halt in his tracks. Did he not realize she could not bear such a weight? He treated her like a brawny lad rather than a girl.

Exhausted and hot, even in the chill morning air, she unlatched her cape hook and threw the garment to the ground. In her other hand, she still toted the leather bag containing her two wooden boxes.

"I cannot carry this cumbersome casket all the way to the boat," she declared.

"Then what do you suggest?" Faran asked, irritably. It appeared his sleepless night and the waning effects of Romaine's happy brew were taking a toll on his mood. "I cannot convey it alone," he needlessly pointed out. "I could manage half the weight by myself, but I am afraid it would be your half left behind."

"Why you wily weasel, you promised me an equal share."

"And so you shall have it. Here is your allotment." As he spoke, Faran opened the trunk and divvied up the treasure. She clenched her fists in anger and watched in amazement as he dumped her portion onto her cloak. "There," he said, "now all you need to do is transport it to the boat."

"And so I shall, you mangy dog," she snapped back, her mood as surly as his.

She grabbed two sticks, arranged the straight branches beside her cloak, and using the knife he had sharpened for her, cut several strips from her leather bag. With one piece she tied the two sticks together at one end. Folding the cape into a pouch, she secured it between the branches and then added her leather sack to the bounty tucked away in the folds of wool.

Without a word she snatched up the tied end of the travois and marched off, dragging the conveyance between the trees and over the low bracken. A little smile tugged at her lips. She did not have to look back to know Faran stared after her in open-mouthed wonder.

Battling alone to carry the half-empty, yet heavy wooden coffer, Faran crashed through the woods behind her. And based upon the heated phrases he uttered, it seemed he did so with a lack of ceremony and good humor.

To her fortune, the sky was clear and she easily followed the landmarks he had pointed out to her yesterday. Soon the distance between them increased, and the sound of his fitful progress grew indistinct.

At the shore, she removed the brush covering the boat, dismantled her carryall, and stowed her cape and treasure aboard. Then she sat down upon a large boulder to await Faran's arrival.

Before long he stumbled into view, groaning under the weight of his burden and gasping for breath. He dropped the trunk onto the ground at her feet and glanced at her as if he expected her to jump up and assist him. But she smiled sweetly, folded her hands in her lap, and remained seated. Realizing he was on his own, he struggled to retrieve the coffer from the dirt and clumsily hoisted it into the boat. A tired and worn demeanor etched lines into his face, and she did not have the heart to tell him he had lost the ridiculous feather from his hair.

"I am sorry," he apologized. "That noxious potion has put me out of sorts."

His apology and pathetic expression wore down her resolve and she gained her feet to fetch him a gourd of water.

Collapsed on the ground beside the boat, he

drank greedily, half of the liquid running down his chin and onto his chest. Morning sunlight sparkled off his wet skin where it showed through the V in his tunic, and images of his naked body skittered through her mind. She sat beside him on the large rock, and halfheartedly tried to think of something more edifying.

As she watched the forest for signs they had been followed, it fully dawned on her she was a very rich woman. She had more coinage and jewels than she could use in a lifetime. She could return home, and although not responsible for her husband's death, she could still offer wergild. Then the false charge of murder would be lifted and she could live out her days in peace and comfort.

She glanced down at Faran. He sat with his eyes closed, his head tilted back against the hull of the boat, one arm resting on his bent knee. A shadow of a beard, usually scraped clean each morning, accentuated the planes of his cheeks, lending a roguish toughness to his appearance.

There seemed much contrast between the rough nature of questing and this man's true countenance. And although he was resolute, at times he did not seem the sort to enjoy adventuring. Perhaps he had been on so many sojourns he wearied of them.

Faran's breath now came more easily, yet he still appeared fatigued. His strength had been sapped by the concoction he had been forced to drink, and by the debauched treatment of the depraved harlot who had administered the draught.

She sighed. Resting silently beside Faran, their bodies only inches apart, Leanora felt as if she had known him for years. And more and more she yearned for the closeness she knew he would offer beyond mere companionship. Yet years of hiding her emotions stopped her from making such a wish come true. They might share the treasure, but it was safer not to share dreams or desires.

Twisting slightly on the boulder, she reached over to touch a lock of Faran's hair. He shifted his weight and his shoulder brushed against her thigh. She jerked her hand away, and then felt silly for doing so. Why did she fear him? He had kept all his promises to her. Something no one else had ever done.

"Thank you," she said the words barely more than a whisper.

"For what?" he asked languidly, his eyes still closed.

"For keeping your vow to share the treasure."

"You are most welcome, Gillyflower," he replied and smiled.

And thank you, she silently added, *for not being like all the rest.*

****

"Faran, wake up."

She had let him sleep for a few moments hoping it would restore his vigor, but now the sun burned bright and they should be on their way.

"What—I'm awake." Faran sprang to his feet.

Towering over her, he glanced around, his shoulders squared, his legs braced wide, ready for battle. What would it be like to face him in true combat? It was a chilling thought, and she realized there were many sides to the man who stood before her.

Seeing no danger, he relaxed his stance and reached out to stroke her cheek. How could such gentleness be contained in a hand so strong? A hand she imagined caressing her throat, caressing her...

Abruptly she stood. Faran grasped her shoulders, and with a hooded expression studied her lips. It was a look reminiscent of that special day on her island, that day he had kissed her. It seemed a lifetime ago. And now the thought of Faran wanting her was exciting rather than frightening. But she would be risking much if she crossed the boundary of friendship into that unknown world.

She eased from his grasp. "We must be going," she reminded. "We dare not tarry any longer." Seeking action to cover her confusion, she hurried to the far side of the ungainly craft, threw the water-gourd aboard, and helped Faran push the boat to open water.

****

The sun was near full zenith when they touched the shores of Lothian, yet the atmosphere surrounding the North Berwick seaport was dismal and uninviting.

A fetid breeze crawled out of the dank woods, ushering along a foreboding chill. To the north, the ominous saw-toothed mountains were shrouded in patches of shaggy gray fog.

Something sinister clutched this land in talons of icy indifference, and the grim vision sent a shiver slinking down Leanora's spine. She stepped from the boat and shrugged her cloak more tightly around her shoulders. The sooner she left this place the better.

"As soon as I have retrieved my belongings, I will see you off," Faran said as if he understood her longing to be on her way. His somber eyes revealed no particular emotion.

A deep sadness overtook her. Did he part from her so easily? To aid his cause, she had loaned him her boat and forfeited the safety of her island. Side by side, and shoulder to shoulder, they had outwitted Romaine and recovered the valuables. How could the time they had spent together mean nothing to him?

Twice now she had rescued him, and half of the treasure seemed cold repayment for so personal an act. Would things just go back to the way they were before Faran, the Iron Heart had come along to turn her world upside down? She would be alone, albeit rich, and she would be bored. Just now, at this very moment, she realized how pointless and uninteresting her life had been. Of course that was the lot of most people, but now she had been afforded a taste of adventuring, and she wanted more of the same.

"I am grateful for your help." Faran reached over the freeboard to grab another bag. "And although the quest is but half done, you have every right to abandon me here all alone, left to my own devices. You should feel no compulsion to see the journey to its end."

Why did he make it sound as if she were deserting him? "Do you wish me to remain with you?" she asked and searched his face for a sign it was so.

He shrugged. "I wish you to do what will make you happy," he countered, giving her an answer neither binding nor setting her free.

Again, as when they left the island, he made it strictly her decision, no threats or coercion. There was no logical reason why she should travel with him. Yet if she did not continue on with Faran, exactly where would she go? Back to seek her mother of course. But then what?

She gazed at the faces of the people on the wharf. Their eyes were cold, and their expressions unfriendly. She did not wish to join their order. Their wraps drawn tight around thin, dejected shoulders, they seemed huddled in lonely isolation against not only the wind but also one another. She needed a new stage upon which to play out her new life. Not the place where she had grown up, and not back to the isolated island to which she had retreated.

"Of course," he added, "without your counsel, I will probably fall prey to all manner of sin and heathen temptation. But that is not your concern either. What be the loss of one more lowly pagan soul to your God?"

Now here was a reason to stay she could readily accept. A reason missionary in nature rather than personal. Mercy, he was giving her an excuse, shifting the blame to God's shoulders if things did not work out. Truly Faran was a word-weaver, a master at compelling people to support his needs and causes.

She had to admit it was a comfort being near him. But the feelings tempting her to stay also urged her to run away as fast as possible.

"I cannot have your eternal damnation upon my head," she blurted before she could change her mind. What did she have to lose? Choosing the safe path had not helped her in the past. "As your comrade-in-arms, I will stay with you a while longer."

Faran's smile filled her with delight. But her joy swiftly fled as she gazed inland toward their destination. Like a living breathing entity, the terrain before them seemed to groan in pain and pulse with dark secrets.

Chapter Ten

With a twinge of sorrow, Leanora stood by her decision and helped to unload the last of their cargo. Poor little boat. It would not be easy to part with it. The vessel had served her well, carrying her hopes and dreams to safety as well her personal effects. But that was the past, and she must look to the future. Besides, there was no turning back now.

Employing his gift of charm, Faran bargained away her ship and managed to acquire not only two riding horses in the trade, but a small parcel of food and a few items of clothing. Or what clinched the deal could be his imposing size and air of authority. Compared to Faran, the local clientele appeared withered and drab in both spirit and form.

She glanced at the horse—the idea she owned livestock was uplifting. Yet before reality came to full bloom, a flock of needless worries spiraled down upon her. Horses needed to be fed and stabled. They could become injured or sick and eventually they would grow old and die. A boat had none of those cares.

"A boat will not help us to cross the valley," Faran said as if privy to her list of worries.

She gave him a halfhearted smile and nodded. Then embarrassed, she swiped at the unexpected tear running down her cheek. Faran turned away to evenly distribute the load on the animal he was to ride.

"You are too sentimental," he gently chided and

helped her to mount. "It is a disadvantage in so cruel a world."

"Someone must keep alive foolish fancies," she countered with a wistful smile, "and the belief in wonderment."

He gave a snort of amusement, patted her knee, and mounted his own animal.

For the first few miles they traveled at a brisk walk, and Leanora concentrated her efforts on remaining upright on the spirited creature rocking beneath her. She had no experience with horses, but in deference to her plight, at least she did not suffer from seasickness. Of course the possibility of being pitched headfirst from the beast seemed a worthy concern.

Gripping the horse tightly with her legs, she dared to study her surroundings. What she saw did little to mend her worries or brighten her spirits. Deeper into the forest, the ancient oaks became more numerous, and she felt like an interloper in the midst of a battalion of watchful wooden sentries. Thick cluster of leaves and mistletoe clung to the top branches nearly blocking out the light. And unlike the Isle of May, a pall of sorrow hung in the air, almost tangible in its presence.

She shivered and prayed all of county Lothian did not labor under such misery.

****

Above the canopy of trees, the color of the sky appeared odd to Faran. It was a murky gray-blue, the same hue as a well-tempered blade, and it hung just as heavily overhead. In the forest, no birds twittered and no animals scurried about, and the unnatural silence increased his concern.

Flexing his shoulders as if he could shrug off the oppressive gloom, he turned and glanced back at Leanora. She too seemed uncomfortable in their strange surroundings. Her smile was tentative as she clung to the mane of her horse with both hands. He waved encouragingly then faced forward.

The girl's decision to travel with him to Gylfi had pleased him beyond measure. He was rather proud of himself for having convinced her to do so, and he refused to believe she relented only for the purpose of saving his soul. Then again, he could be wrong. Gillyflower was the first woman he had ever known as a hearth-mate, and the experience continued to confound him. True, he was becoming a bit more adept at divining what she was thinking, still the logic behind those thoughts generally defied reason.

Thank the gods her conversation was sparse in dosage, and more interesting than most female's. She did not drone on and on about clothes or food, nor complain there was too little of either.

This fierce Saxon girl, with copper-colored curls, had burst upon his life so unexpectedly. She aroused his curiosity as well as his manhood, and admiring her from afar was becoming a hellish torture.

This morning, before they had left the Isle of May, he had desired her with a need barely able to be contained. The rush of remembrance set his cock throbbing and he shifted uncomfortably. How he wished to savor her shell pink lips once again, and he wanted to taste that smooth, milky skin so soft and delicate. Perhaps he only wanted what he knew he could not have. Time would tell. He had yet to meet the woman he could not charm.

He chuckled and recalled the conveyance she had constructed to transport her share of the fortune to the boat. He had expected her to start crying at his unintentional contrariness. Whether she realized it or not, Gillyflower was a survivor. Her jealousy of Romaine had amused him as well, but she needn't have worried. Just the thought of that diabolical she-devil made him shrivel like a spider on a hot rock. Not since Beowulf had fought Grendel's mother had a man crossed paths with such a wretched female.

Romaine inspired tales of horror. More fodder to add to the horrible dreams that harried him. In the dead of night or in the bright light of day, haunting visions of his failure to his king and his people hounded him. Surely more joyous times would prevail once the relics were restored.

The relics. Was it his imagination or could he feel their power as he drew ever nearer to them? He had not told Leanora the complete story of the sword and shield. He had not told her to whom the antiquities had once belonged, or that they held an enchantment born of another time and place. And he had especially avoided telling her how their loss riddled his soul with shame.

An icy chill seeped through the thick layer of his cloak, and his thoughts spun back around to the present. It felt as if the forest exhaled a long frigid breath. Warily he glanced around, expecting to see something sinister crouched in readiness. He reined in his horse and motioned Leanora forward.

She halted at his side. Both horses nervously browsed upon the foliage, eating frugally as if the grass tasted peculiar and not to their liking. Their ears twitched, and occasionally their heads snapped up in reaction to sounds he could not hear.

"I do not like this land," he said and retrieved the map from the pack tied to his mount.

"I feel it too," she agreed. Her voice was hushed as if she hesitated to break the heavy silence permeating the air. "Is there another route to Gylfi we might follow?"

He studied the map. "Not an agreeable one. The mountains bar hope of passage to the north. And I doubt the forest on the south side of the ridge is any more hospitable than this one. I say keep going on this road, but you have a right to speak as well."

She stared at him, and again he found her sapphire eyes a fascination. What thoughts lived behind their blue brilliance? There was an innocence about her that was dangerous, and her unpretentious manner was more deadly to his sensibilities than Romaine's well-practiced seduction. It touched a place in his soul that made him wish to spend many a night with her—not just one.

She eased back the hood of her cloak, setting free an avalanche of gleaming red tresses. In the dimness surrounding them, hers was an ethereal brightness, and he yearned to weave his fingers in the silky fire shimmering about her head and shoulders.

As she slid the map from his grip, her delicate hand brushed his, but she did not shy away from the unintentional touching. This budding trust bolstered his flagging pride. It also scared him. If she placed her faith in him, the burden would be heavy.

His shoulders sagged in relief as she turned her gaze to the map, releasing him from her scrutiny. Brow furrowed, she carefully considered the situation. "I agree," she said and handed back the rendering. "We keep to this road. It appears the shortest route, and the sooner we pass through this woodland the better. Although," she added, "I fear this melancholy is not peculiar to the forest, rather it sits upon the entire dominion. What tragedy did so strike this realm?"

"I have heard tales as to what so cripples the land and people," he admitted and tucked away the vellum, "but I do not know if the legends be truth or fancy. And I am not sure I wish to find out."

The dread he felt was reflected in her eyes. "Come." He nodded toward a little meadow off to the right. "If you like, we could rest for a while and take nourishment. Whether we delay or not makes no difference," he added at her hesitation. "Regardless of the pace we set, we shall not reach Gylfi by sundown. We will have to spend the night in these woods."

"Then let us rest," she agreed, weariness heavy in her voice. "To have my feet once more upon solid ground sounds even more inviting than the food. I do not know which is worse," she confessed, "sailing in a ship or riding upon a horse."

"Soon, you will have the chance to experience the two as one."

"What?" Her back went rigid and her movements stilled. "How can this be?"

Avoiding her question, he helped her to dismount, all the time wanting to call back his words. Damn, he should have waited to tell her. If she knew what was to come, she would no doubt worry the rest of the day and all of the night. Avoiding her question, he turned and busied himself securing the horses.

"Faran," she prodded, "what mean you by that remark"

"A river lies between here and the city of Gylfi," he reluctantly answered. "The map shows fords but no bridges. And according to the man to whom we traded the boat, the rivers are near torrents with late summer runoff."

She visibly shivered as if struck by a cold wind. "Can horses swim?" she asked, and grabbed his arm.

"Yes," he reassured, "even better than chickens."

Ignoring his jest, she released her death grip on his arm, but her cheeks grew ashen. It was not the first time she had shown a fear of water, and Faran wondered why she should dread such a crossing. Before he could ask, she turned away to fetch their food.

Deciding it was best to let the matter lie, he

cradled her elbow in his hand and ushered her toward the remains of a fallen tree. "Here is a suitable log for my lady's repast," he said brightly, trying to dispel her concerns and the sullen surroundings.

The color in her cheeks seemed to improve as they sat and shared the crusty bread, a bit of honey, and a generous hunk of hard yellow cheese. As they ate in silence, he studied the ground at his feet. So that was what made Lothian so peculiar. He held out his hand and moved it back and forth. In this kingdom, where gloom and dreariness reigned unchallenged, there existed no shadows. With a shuddered, he gained his feet.

"What is wrong?" Leanora asked and gathered the remnants of their meal.

"Oh, nothing." He forced a lightness to his words he did not feel. "I thought to walk off some of this stiffness." He stretched and wandered off studying his surroundings with fresh insight.

What if there was no true morning or night, only this continual murkiness? Without the reliable rising and setting of the sun, and the phases of the moon and stars, how was he to mark the passage of time or calculate the distance they traveled. Navigating this countryside had suddenly become even more difficult as well as sinister.

He glanced at the horizon. Thank the gods the mountains remained constant. The ancient peaks seemed to rise above the tribulation gripping the rest of the land. That thought was reassuring. If he kept the craggy snow-capped pinnacles to his right, which was north, he would know they were steadily heading to the west.

Retracing his steps, he spied Leanora. She remained seated upon the log, elbows upon her knees, her chin resting in her cupped hands. She seemed to be studying the patches of blossoms dotting the glen. Had she noticed all the blooms were pearly gray and spiritless? Life here seemed but a worn dream, with the earth denouncing all color so as not to shatter the fragile illusion.

Unaware that he watched, she stood and stretched her arms skyward. What a willowy embrace those limbs could offer. Then a vision of her shapely legs burst upon his mind as he recalled the time on her island when she had raised her skirt while washing clothes in the surf. More hot coals were added to the smoldering embers gnawing at his belly.

He did have a penchant for women. All women, except of course Romaine. Women were to life, as a proper mead was to a meal. Neither was necessary for survival, but oh, how much more palatable they made the world. He could not recall a time when he had not found females enchanting. Even as a lad, he favored their company, a condition incurring endless teasing, nay, ridicule, from his six older brothers. On occasion, when the rousting and fighting was done for the day, he sought the telling of tales, and the interpreting of dreams, activities much appreciated by young women. That is when his brothers had constructed the amulet, calling him Iron Heart as a jest, because he loved all women, and would give his heart to none.

To this day, he would much rather breach the silken walls that housed a woman's treasure than the keep of any castle. And although many women had tried, none had found the secret to winning his real heart or the iron heart he wore.

But Gillyflower was exasperatingly different. For reasons unknown, she did not find him irresistible. Had her husband been so cruel as to forever ruin her need and desire for a man's touch? Knowing she had belonged to another galled his sensibilities and unleashed a new emotion. He wanted to protect her, and walk beside her into the future, regardless of what it might bring. Thoughts such as these came unbidden, and they disturbed him much.

"We had best resume our journey," he called more sternly than intended.

Confused by his curt manner, she hurried forward, her steps made quick by the practiced fear always shrouding her when she thought he was angry. He regretted his terseness, but was too tired to offer an explanation or an apology for his mood.

Again, he helped her to mount. When she was properly seated, he slowly slid his hand from her waist to her thigh. Her firm muscles tensed beneath his fingers and her lips parted in surprise, but her eyes did not freeze to blue ice—rather they warmed to the color of forget-me-nots.

With a little smile, he turned to mount his own horse. Surely it was only a matter of time.

****

The eerie light in the sky lessened, and Faran reckoned it must be well into evening. Through the gathering gloom, he peered back at Leonora. She appeared half asleep as she swayed along with the rhythm of the horse. Spying a sheltered glade, he guided them off the trail and into the secluded nook. Before he could dismount and reach her side, Leonora slid to the ground.

"Oh merciful heaven," she exclaimed as she took a tentative step. "My legs are as if carved of wood, with no memory of how to walk."

Faran's own legs ached, and his backside felt numb. He had not ridden a full day's worth in a long while. Unfortunately, he knew they would be more stiff come morning, but he saw not reason to impart this information.

"I will see to the animals and start a fire, if you would gather wood."

"A fire and a hot meal sounds wonderful," she agreed and began her search for logs and branches.

Before long, a formidable mound of wood materialized at his side, and she sallied forth with yet another armload. "There is plenty here now," he laughed, working with flint-rock and metal. "We plan to stay but the night, not the fall season."

He bent to blow on the small hopeful flame. She dropped the last of the kindling onto the pile, and wandered off.

With a little coaxing the fire roared, and although the heat seemed strangely minimal, the vision helped to brighten their dismal surroundings. He cut up turnips and potatoes and set them to boiling, then glanced around for Leanora. She was nowhere to be seen. An unreasonable panic twisted through him. It seemed colder and darker without her by his side, and the odd feeling he had misplaced something important tugged at him.

"Leanora," he called through cupped hands as he searched for her in earnest.

"Over here," she answered cheerily.

He scrambled through the bracken toward the sound of her voice. So that is what she had been up to. Using their cloaks as blankets, she had constructed a cozy bed. A pile of bracken served as the mattress, and a covering of evergreens, hand-woven into a canopy, would shelter them from any wind and rain.

"It is for the both of us?" he asked, his hope rising as quickly as the bulge below his waistline.

"Yes," she replied evenly. "'Twas not practical to make two and we shall be warmer this way. But you must behave yourself," she added as she gained her feet and dusted her hands together.

"Yes. Partners only," he promised, squelching the disappointment he felt before it reached his voice.

They ate sparingly, hardly able to detect the flavor of the food. It seemed hollow and without substance. Then as the night grew older, the fragile atmosphere grew blearier, and the remnants of the day seemed to be stretched even thinner.

"I am for bed," Leanora said stifling a yawn. She rose, rubbed her backside, and limped off toward their bed. "Good night, Faran," she called over her shoulder.

At her words, his heart lurched. He longed to run after her, to sweep her up into his arms, to carry her the short distance to the waiting bower where the heat of his lovemaking would drive away the cold and gloom. But she was not ready.

"Good eventide," he called as she disappeared from sight.

He paced about for a moment, trying to stave off the torture that would surely come if he dared to lie down at her side. Then he wandered closer and peeked at her through the lacy boughs of the trees. Head bowed, she knelt in prayer. Her faith in this Christian Being intrigued him. Faran had come across his share of monks and priests and heard their story, still he did not understand why so many people believed in a God who had led no famous battles, or why they followed a man who had not been mighty enough to avoid being caught and crucified.

From what he had been told, this Savior had lived like a peasant, and only peace and happiness were promised in the next lifetime. Where was the reputation and glory a man needed by which to be remembered? Where was the glory indeed?

He returned to the fire and threw on another chunk of wood. As the log hit the bed of coals, it sent sparks shooting up into the air. They danced about like fireflies, merrily spinning to a tune only they could hear.

Soon the fire waned to dark embers, and his body cried for sleep. He could no longer delay seeking the warmth and softness awaiting. Picking a path through the bracken to Leanora's side, he eased under the cover.

She reposed upon her back, and her slow even breathing, assured him she slept soundly. Edging closer, he studied her profile. The urge to touch the tip of her nose near overwhelmed him. Even in sleep her lips were tempting, and the curve of her chin showed a gentle strength.

She sighed and turned away from him. He curled in the same direction, inching closer. Without warning, she pressed her hips back against his, stepping up his heartbeat tenfold. He bit back a groan and returned the pressure with the part of his body now aroused and hard. Slipping one arm over her, he settled his hand lightly upon one breast. Through her soft shift, he traced the erect and full outline of her nipple. The cadence of his breathing increased and he kissed the nape of her neck. Leanora's only response was a small mewing sound. Then she turned again to settle onto her stomach.

Gently, he rubbed her back, gradually sliding his hand downward to the rise of her bottom. His mind conjured detailed visions of the body he touched, sending his craving to dangerous heights. He could barely breathe for the need welling in his chest. He had never gone this long without a woman, and he had never been this close to a woman who did not desire him. With a shuddering gasp he rolled away and stumbled to his feet.

Growling in the night like an angry beast, he sought something to fight other than this unquenchable lust. But there wasn't anything. In frustration, he grabbed up a horse blanket, wrapped it around his body, and stalked away to sleep by the dying fire.

The cold ground chilled his bones but not his desire, and alone in the night he questioned his courage and resolve as he fought the old demons and now this new one.

****

Beneath the glow of the moon, Romaine stood on the shore of the Isle of May. Idly, she twirled the white feather around and around in her fingers as she glared at the far away mountains. No doubt it was to the shores of County Lothian to which her reluctant lover had fled. In the morning she would follow. The journey to Gylfi was long and arduous, and she was too tired to put to sea tonight.

She might have made an early start, but it had taken several hours before she had gained release from the manacles. At first, all about the castle had assumed her screams for help were the normal sounds issuing forth from her love chamber—and they had not dared to interfere. Only when her eunuch had arrived with her regular afternoon sustenance, had her predicament been realized and she had been freed.

And even had this not been the case, her head ached most dreadfully, and she was not in the mood to endure the chastisement her brother was bound to ladle out in generous portion upon her arrival.

He would delight in mocking her for being duped, but eventually Gorham would also help her exact retribution. The blood they spilled, and the blood they shared, was thicker than water. It was the only drink to quench their thirst for power and fortune. So it had always been since the day they had sworn the covenant. They would always save each other's neck, and watch each other's back.

She gave a cruel laugh, setting the raw area on her scalp to throbbing. Then a menacing snarl clawed its way from her throat to her lips. Never in her life had she suffered so painful a betrayal and humiliation. The Storm Geat bastard had insulted her three times over. He had refused to make love to her, had stolen her treasure, and had disfigured her beauty.

Snapping the feather in half, she threw the pieces to the ground. The warrior would pay dearly for this. When next they met, hot pokers and cold steel would caress his skin—not lustful strokes and perfumed oils. She would eat his heart raw. And that simpering flame-haired bitch riding with him would watch.

Pivoting toward her waiting soldiers, she made sure the toe of her boot ground the bright plume into the dirt.

Chapter Eleven

Leanora squinted opened her eyes. Why was she was sleeping under a tree? Finally, recalling the reason, she sneaked a peek sideways. The rest of the bed was cold and empty, the nettles only slightly disturbed. Faran had not slept beside her.

It was important she do her fair share on this journey, and last evening, constructing the bower had been the only thing she could think to contribute. Offering to prepare meals was certainly no option. When her mother had tried to teach her the art of cooking, she had always made herself scarce. She had hoped by lacking such a skill, her father could not sell her off as a desirable wife. Too late, she realized cooking did not rank terribly high on a future husband's priority list. Later she used her lack of talent as retaliation to sorely irritate her spouse. Three times a day she had assaulted him with the most frightful meals possible. Faran deserved better.

With a sigh, she sat up and coughed. Breathing came as a surprising disappointment in County Lothian. The air was thin and unfriendly as if someone or something had already used it all up. Dismissing the odd notion, she rummaged around beneath the covers, located her clothes, and slid them on.

The snap of a twig sent her to her feet, an action immediately regretted. Although it seemed impossible, her stiffness had grown worse overnight.

"Another day upon that boney beast will be the death of me," she muttered crossly as Faran approached

"Well, good morning to you too, Gillyflower." His words were cheerful enough but it did not appear he fared much better. He moved cautiously, and there were circles beneath his eyes as if sleep had eluded him.

She retrieved his cloak from the bed and shook the twigs from it—her body rebelling with each jarring movement. With a chuckle, she handed him the cape.

"Pray what could possibly be funny at this hour and in this place?" he asked.

"Your hair," she said. "It sticks up in a most riotous manner. You look like a baby chick after a spring rain." She lifted her arm, yearning to reach out and smooth down the unruly thatch of lion's mane. As she hesitated, Faran captured her wrist and drew her closer.

"And you look like a silky, bright-eyed vixen, red-furred and full of mischief."

His lips were dangerously close. What did he taste like? The one and only time they had kissed, she had been too frightened to notice. She held her breath waiting for, hoping for, another chance to find out.

He leaned forward, then spun her around, and gave her a playful whack upon her bruised rump. "See to your morning duties," he teasingly ordered, "and I will find us something to break our fast. Warm water awaits by the fire."

Faran turned and strode toward the horses, leaving her teetering off balance in both thought and motion. Well, she had no one to blame other than herself. She had been the one to insist he keep his distance. Still his manner left her unsettled. In truth it was becoming downright annoying. Part of her yearned desperately for his touch. But part still feared being intimate with him. Her body was scarred. He might turn away when he saw her back. And the act of coupling had always been a frightful ordeal for her. Would it truly be different with Faran? She pondered these concerns as she headed for the bushes.

Upon returning to camp, she gratefully accepted the currant berries and slice of dried meat Faran offered. The horses, packed and ready for traveling, indicated there would be no lingering over the morning meal. She was glad. This dusky clime did not lend itself to leisurely respites or peaceful daydreams.

****

Bouncing painfully along atop her horse, Leanora leaned over to peer at the ground. The trail was becoming more and more obscure, and she hoped they were still headed in the proper direction. Then the unmistakable sound of rushing water drew her attention. She jerked upright, and all concerns for the path disappeared posthaste.

How could she have forgotten today's river crossing? With each plodding step, the horse delivered her closer to the edge of her worst fear.

The trees thinned, and a grassy slope ushered her to the banks of the torrent. Her stomach heaved, and the memories engulfing her were more riotous than the water raging before her.

The river was angry and unsympathetic and it churned with the mud and sand kicked up by the current. She would be just another piece of flotsam carelessly tossed about and washed downstream. She would fall off and drown, and she did not wish to die in this dark godforsaken land. Dread encircled her, growing ever tighter, squeezing the breath from her lungs.

"I will go first," Faran shouted over the sound of

the water and her pounding heart. "When I am safely across you will follow. Agreed?"

She stared back at him as if he spoke in a foreign tongue. She could not do this. Crossing water in a nice safe boat was one thing, but trusting to a horse and her ability to stay on its back was completely another matter.

She glanced over her shoulder, considering the path they had traversed. But to her surprise, the thought of going back and being separated from Faran scared her almost as much as the thought of crossing the river.

"Leanora?" Faran grabbed her arm and shook her. The action shattered the chrysalis of terror sheathing her mind.

"What?" she asked, not remembering a word he had spoken.

"I will go first," he repeated slowly. "You will follow after I am across."

"Yes, I understand...no, I cannot do this. You must go on without me."

"I cannot leave you here." He seemed appalled at the idea. "Do not worry. It will be over in but a moment."

Oh, sweet Savior! Leanora pressed her lips together to stop the scream rising in her throat. Those were the same words her wretched husband had spoken before he had thought to drown her. Truly, she could not do this.

She jerked on the reins and tried to turn her horse around, but Faran grabbed the halter. "There is no turning back," he said, "we must go forward."

His words rang true in more ways than one. She could not forever hide from her fears and run away to an island every time she became frightened. But it would be a shame to die now, just when she had hopes of gaining her freedom.

"I'll not allow any harm to come to you," Faran

said more gently. "We shall tie a rope to your waist," he explained, "and I will carry the other end across. Once I am on the far shore I will secure it to that large oak tree. Then, if your horse stumbles or you fall off, the rope will keep you safe."

If her horse stumbled? Damnation, she hadn't even considered that. Here was yet another spear to add to the armament of concerns she carried. Still, Faran's idea about using the rope was reassuring.

He looped her cape up over her shoulders so it would not trail in the water, then he handed her one end of the braided hemp.

She snaked it around her midsection, brought it full circle, and worked at tying a knot. But her hands shook, foiling her attempt. Taking up the rope, Faran tied it for her, and gave it a tug to make sure it held.

He shifted his hands from her waist to her shoulders and without warning, leaned forward and kissed her cheek. "For luck," he grinned. Surprise and the heat of his touch momentarily dispelled her glacial fear.

With the end of the rope wrapped over his forearm and tightly gripped in his left hand, he kicked the sides of his mount. The animal gave a snort and sprang into action—and horse and rider plunged into the foaming water.

Whooping and yelling, Faran was like a child at play. He enjoyed the thrill of challenging sound logic. How did one learn to be so brave and free spirited? For her, danger was to be avoided at all cost. For him, it was sought after with relish.

He safely reached the halfway point, and she could tell his horse no longer touched the rocky bed of the river. The beast swam for its life, then found his footing, and scrambled up the slippery shore on the far side. With a raised fist, her warrior taunted the river. "You could not stop Tyne Faran Kilbraun, the Iron Heart," he shouted as he leapt from his horse. The animal at his side shook like a big dog, sending water spraying in every direction. Then it bucked a few times and whinnied as if it too felt a cockiness born of accomplishment. The image of Faran, brave and triumphant, and the words he spoke were seared into her memory.

As promised, he tied the rope to the tree and motioned for her to come ahead.

"You can do it," he shouted encouragingly.

Transfixed, she stared wide-eyed at the hypnotic flow of water and her fear bound her in place.

"Romaine would not be afraid," Faran taunted.

At his words, her eyes narrowed and her courage bobbed to the surface. Why did he think of that black-haired witch at a time such as this? Not willing to be found lacking in comparison, she gritted her teeth and dug her heels into the sides of the horse. The animal danced sideways then lunged forward.

Freezing water wrapped icy fingers around her legs. She shivered so violently she could barely breathe. Even her eyeballs shook, blurring her vision. Blood roared in her ears, and her heart pounded much too fast. Tearing her gaze from the water, she glanced up at Faran, and the hot rush of excitement engulfed her.

He stood on the shore, one hand grasping the rope, the other outstretched and reaching in her direction. His expression seemed filled with pride, and that thought sent a thrill to the very core of her being. She was no longer afraid; she felt invincible.

Then, just as she dared to hope for success, the expression on Faran's face turned to one of alarm. She glanced upstream and gasped. A huge tree rushed toward her at ramming speed. The tangled roots, wicked and pointed, sliced through the water like the claws of a giant beast. She urged the horse to swim faster, but nothing could save them from the behemoth bearing down upon them.

Her mount tossed its head, the whites of his eyes bright beacons of fear. The tumbling oak hit him in the hindquarters, and with a pitiful neigh he went under. She lost her grip, pitched forward, and flailed helplessly about. The monstrous tree careened by, less than a hand's breadth away, dingy foam churning in its wake.

She screamed, giving voice to her terror, but only a gurgling sound came out as dirty water filled her mouth.

Her sodden cape and clothing grew heavier and heavier—dragging her deeper into the watery arms of a fatal embrace. She should forfeit the weighty cloak to the river, but to loosen the clasp she must let go of the rope, and what if it were to come untied. The rope was her lifeline. She would die without the rope, for in truth, she could not swim a stroke.

With unseen fists, the rocks beneath the water battered her body. Her lungs burned with the need for air, and she prayed for a quick deliverance straight into heaven. Then her feet touched bottom and her head broke the surface of the water. Fighting to gain purchase, she scraped along the shore as Faran reeled her in like a hooked fish. On the bank she rolled to a stop, collapsed in a heap, and burst into tears. Her horse came ashore farther down stream.

Faran knelt at her side and cradled her in his arms. "You are safe now, no need to cry. You did it, you crossed the river."

He peeled off her wet cape and rubbed her back and shoulders, driving the chill from her body. She peered at his smiling face and wrapped her arms around his neck. Having safely reached dry land, the excitement of conquering the river surged through her veins like liquid fire. She had experienced a similar headiness watching Romaine and Faran. It seemed danger and coupling fed the same desires. No wonder men courted peril with as much enthusiasm as they courted women.

"Thank you for saving me," she whispered and nestled against his broad chest.

"I did but little. But now I only owe you one rescue to pay back my debt."

Her smile faltered. Did he only wish to keep her near until he could fulfill some honor-bound obligation? She struggled to her feet, and her triumphant crossing lost some of its glow.

Faran rose to stand at her side, his expression unreadable.

"Do you feel able to travel a while longer today?"

"Yes." She nodded. "If the horse is unhurt, I would distance myself from this river as quickly as possible."

"Good." He wrung the water from her cape and hung it across his mount. Then he snuggled his dry cloak about her shoulders. The soft wool smelled like him, manly and musky, with the fresh scent of pine needles still upon it. She drank in the fragrance, not caring if its intoxication turned her mind once more to thoughts definitely leaping beyond the boundaries she fought to maintain.

Faran retrieved her skittish animal, and with a practiced touch, he ran his hands over the legs and flanks of the horse. Satisfied, he assisted her to mount.

"We laughed in the face of danger today," he said, "and do not tell me you did not enjoy it."

"Yes," she admitted, realizing it was not easy to abandon the glorious feeling of having cheated death. "I did. A little. But I am glad the worst of our journey is over."

Faran's features remained impassive but a muscle twitched in his cheek.

"Please tell me the worst is over."

"Worst is a term dependant upon one's point of view," he hedged.

"What lies ahead? Tell me quick and be done with it." She held her breath, waiting for him to speak. Then he flashed that reckless one-dimpled smile—the one that could melt resolution carved in stone.

"Not to worry," he cheerfully informed her. "It's only the serpent tower of Ella."

Chapter Twelve

"The serpent tower of Ella?"

Leanora gripped the folds of her damp skirt so tightly, water oozed from between her fingers. God's teeth, she had thought the place a legend—a story of make-believe to frighten little children and timid adults. "It truly exists?"

"It is real enough to have killed the mighty Viking, Ragnar Lodbrok." Faran seemed impressed, nay, pleased, with this dreadful fact. Then his expression turned thoughtful. "Of course, there is still some confusion as to whether the pit within the tower was filled with adders or conger eels at the time."

"Well I hardly think the difference of much importance." She shuddered as a detailed image of conger eels formed in her mind. Fright alone would kill her if she were thrown into a den of those horrible creatures. Pale brown along their top and grayish-white along their belly, they were ten feet long, with gaping jaws and needle sharp teeth.

"How are we to survive what a Viking warrior could not conquer?"

"I was hoping you might have a suggestion," he answered brightly. "You are most resourceful."

"Flattery and your confidence will be cold comfort to me as I lay moldering in my grave." Stomach churning, she wished for a chamomile infusion.

"You cannot triumph over adversity if you

forever hide from it," Faran chided. He tightened a loose strap on his mount's halter then climbed aboard. "How a man is remembered is his only reward. I would be remembered for my courage in all matters and for my loyalty to my people and our heritage."

"But you race headlong to meet this catastrophe," she accused, "another calamity fate has tossed so casually in our path."

"There is much for which I must atone," he added and nudged his horse forward. "I grow no younger, disallowing for the luxury of caution."

Faran's quest seemed a matter of life and death, and again she wondered what drove him to such daring. What relics could be worth tempting such peril and hazard?

Regardless, she supposed she might as well hear the details surrounding their newest dilemma. "Tell me all regarding this wretched tower," she relented, guiding her horse up alongside his. "Forewarned is forearmed."

"That's the spirit." Faran smiled, and even the corners of his eyes crinkled with warmth. "A lowly serpent's keep cannot hinder the likes of us."

She rolled her eyes at his enthusiasm, and while her gaze was heavenward, offered a prayer he was correct.

"From what I have been told," he began, "if the hoary beasts are asleep or well fed, one finds the path through Ella of little consequence. But if the creatures seek food or amusement, all is lost. Then whoever dares to pass through the tower is doomed."

He gave her a sideways glance as if to check her level of hysteria, and she fought to school her expression into one of indifference.

"In the middle of the winding passageway," he continued, "off to one side, there is a set of doors, stately in nature and grandly carved. They lead to the room containing the pit. Should they open as you pass, a voice known only to you in your dreams will beckon you forward to a deadly fate. No one may hear the utterance and survive."

"But it is permitted to gaze upon the demons and still live?" she asked. God forbid she should misunderstand the rules governing their ordeal.

"I believe it to be so."

"And the horses will not be bothered by the voices?"

"The serpents have grown particular over the years. Now they seek only human flesh."

That revelation near damped down what little optimism remained, but a seed of an idea was already taking root in her mind.

"When do we reach this horror?" she asked as they rode onward.

"It lies beyond the next hill."

"Well, nothing like waiting until the last moment to acquaint me with our next disaster." Before her ire could reach full potential, they faced the hellish keep.

The dank, crumbling walls rose up before them, a hulking sentry, blocking all forward progress. A vile liquid, dark and red as blood, oozed and sweated from the main archway. And a putrid odor, drifting from the fortification, stung her nostrils and brought tears to her eyes.

She studied the surrounding terrain, but the jagged mountains flanking the citadel crushed all thoughts of an alternative route. No wonder few travelers returned from this realm. The land of Lothian defied the natural order of existence. The forest, the river, the very air—all were threatening in their own way.

She dismounted and led her horse off the trail and to a nearby clearing. Faran followed her lead. "If you would kindle a small fire," she requested, "I have a plan that might help our cause."

Without question, he set about the task.

Retrieving the last bit of honeycomb from the food pouch, she drained the golden syrup onto a crust of bread and handed it to Faran. With childlike enthusiasm, he ate the sweet morsel and licked his fingers. She dropped the waxy remains into a small copper pot, then added a bit of sappy resin collected from a nearby fir tree. Laying out the details of her plan, she placed the tiny cauldron near the fire and they waited for the contents to melt and mingle.

"Are you sure you wish to go through with this?" she asked. If her scheme failed, they would both die. On the brighter side, there would be little time to wallow in guilt, or garner lengthy recrimination.

"I am not afraid," Faran said. "I trust you."

The confidence in his eyes made her palms sweat. "Well, you should not," she said, her words sharp with irritation. "I haven't the slightest idea what I'm doing. Besides, this is your quest not mine and I shouldn't have to be responsible for its success."

"When the gods saw fit to tear me from the shieldwall of my companions, they also saw fit to deliver me into your hands. You shall help me achieve what three stalwart men could not. I feel this in my heart and I have seen it in my dreams."

"Seen it in your dreams?"

"Yes. On occasion I have visions that come to pass."

Heavenly Father, now he claimed the art of prophecy. Their gazes clashed head-on, and although she wished to look away, she could not. "What if I do not possess the courage needed to champion your cause? And what if your visions are distorted in this realm of confusion?"

He offered no answer, and even as she said the words she did not believe them. Something special lived in Faran's soul. At least it seemed that way to her. His green eyes, the color of spring, reflected a truth and wisdom built upon a foundation of memories older than his years.

"I have faith in you," he said quietly, "more than you have in yourself."

"More than you should have in any mortal," she warned.

"You can never trust too much."

"But you can trust unwisely."

The melted honeycomb sputtered, and she turned to fetch it. None of this would matter if they did not survive the tower. Tending the mixture, she stirred the contents with a dry twig. "The wax is near ready. Is there anything else we should discuss?"

"Yes," he said, "you shall go first this time, and I will follow. If anything unexpected happens, you must flee onward through the passageway. Promise you will not wait, or come back for me."

"And if something happens to me you will do the same," she challenged.

"Yes, of course."

How easily he lied. He would not leave her behind, and her heart gladdened at the realization.

"Promise you will go on without me," he insisted as he sat upon a nearby stump.

"I promise," she lied as well. She would not abandon him either, and such loyalty came as a surprise.

Gathering the folds of her skirt to protect her hand, she gripped the handle of the little pot and dribbled a bit of waxy liquid onto her forearm. The mixture was free-flowing but not so hot as to burn them. Capturing a small puddle in the palm of her hand, she returned the pot to the fireside. As the mixture cooled, it became opaque and more solid. She kneaded it and pinched it, and worked it into a small tapered tube.

Faran tilted his head and she inserted the warm wax into his ear, smoothing it into place, completely sealing the opening. Periodically she studied his face to assure he suffered no pain from the heat of the wax. With his one ear attended to, she repeated the same on the other.

Motioning for him to stand, she hollered out his name. He shrugged his shoulders and indicated he could not hear her. She clapped her hands and called out once more, but again he shook his head.

"It has done the trick," he shouted in too loud a voice. She nodded, excited her idea might work.

Taking her turn, she sat upon the stump, submitting to Faran's clumsy attempt to brush aside her hair. His strong hands, so sure at tying a knot or lifting a great weight, seemed awkward at this task. Yet, she savored the sensation of his fingers as they grazed across her temple. Brazenly she leaned forward allowing her thigh to brush against his legs.

It felt good to be near him. Her heart beat faster, and that strange feeling of hunger and yearning slipped over her.

As the second glob of waxy resin obliterated all sound from her world, Faran reached for her hand and pulled her to her feet. His mouth moved but she heard no words, and she shrugged her shoulders to indicate such. He nodded in approval, handed her the little copper pot, and turned to stamp out the fire.

She stowed their gear and mounted her horse. Each time she swallowed, her ears crackled, and she glanced around uneasily. Being rendered deaf made her nervous as well as light-headed.

Faran nodded for her to take the lead. She nudged her horse into a walk, and felt rather than heard his hoofs strike the cobbles. Near the portal, the frightened beast balked and shook his head. He sniffed the air, and only with encouragement advanced

On the far side of the dripping archway, a void of boundless black awaited. The horse's steps faltered as if he pushed through deep snow or mud. So complete was the enveloping darkness, Leanora thought to reach out and part it like the folds of a black tapestry. She had to force herself to breathe the foul ether, and the damp atmosphere seemed to turn to liquid in her lungs, leaving her gasping for more air.

Panic began to set in. Maybe they should turn back. Then she rounded a slight turn, and a burst of light beckoned. It came from the far side of the tunnel. Bolstered by the brightness, she rejoiced at having progressed so far.

The horse advanced more willingly, then skittered to one side bringing her square on with the before mentioned wooden doors. They swung inward, revealing a magnificent chamber, and unable to look away, she stared into the cavernous room.

The walls were shot through with streaks of silver and gold, and all manner of treasure lay in careless heaps upon the floor. In the center of the room was the huge pit. An ethereal glow filled the chamber, and like shooting stars, colors of every hue raced toward her. The pinpoints of light careened off the walls and through the doorway, bouncing down the passageway. The fascinating display made her forget the rancid smell assailing her nostrils and the damp cold shrouding her body. Then the lights faded, and the first terrifying eel appeared.

He peeked up over the edge of the pit and studied her with his serpent eyes—black as obsidian, hard and lifeless. Then his entire head was visible, including a slavering mouth. From the depths of the abyss, the hideous creature uncurled. Its glistening head and rippling neck ascending higher and higher until it brushed the arched ceiling.

Several more undulating congers joined the first forming a towering bouquet of wangling eel heads. They waffled to and fro and grinned down at her, their wavering shadows dancing upon the walls. One serpent bent forward and sniffed. Instinctively she drew back. The other eels followed, but their extended heads stopped just shy of the portal. They could not pass beyond the boundaries of the room.

Taking turns they leered out at her, their mouths snapping open and shut in anticipation of her mortal flesh. She recalled the times she had eaten eels, 'twas most unsettling to be on the other end of the trencher and knife with one.

They drew back, as if making room for her. Their mouths curved into harmless inviting smiles and they no longer seemed threatening. What could it hurt just to touch one? Resisting the urge, she tightened her grip upon the reins until her fingernails dug into the flesh of her palms. Still, one part of her wanted to surrender to the ugly beasts in the enchanted chamber. Leaning forward, she reached out to them. She wanted to hear the voices of her dreams. She wanted to hear her own screams.

The horse made to step forward, but Faran grabbed the halter and turned the animal aside.

She jerked on the reins, fighting his intentions.

"Let me go to them," she cried, looking back at the captivating eels. The words echoed only in her mind, and by sheer brute strength, Faran muscled her horse onward. His hand came down hard upon the rump of the animal, and as if freed from a spell of immobility, the horse leapt forward. His hoofs skidded upon the moss-covered stones, then he gained his footing and ran full-tilt down the corridor. Farther from the chamber, her senses cleared and she gave the beast his head and clung to his back. The terrified horse fled through the far archway into the waiting meadow. Seemingly exhausted, he stopped of his own accord, hung his head, and stood trembling.

The deadly craving to sacrifice herself to the monstrous eels ebbed away, and Leanora felt weak with the knowledge of what she had almost done. She would not have made it without Faran.

As she turned to look for him, he careened to a halt at her side, and clawed at his ears to remove the wax. She did the same.

"We have done it again, Gillyflower," Faran crowed. Then a serious expression crushed the mirth from his face. "I thought for a moment I had lost you."

"I don't know what possessed me," she gasped, still unnerved by how close she had come to surrendering to the eels. "I was driven to act beyond common sense. You saved me again, Faran. We are even now. You owe me nothing."

"Our journey is not yet over. We had best leave the final tallying until then." Mischief sounded in his words.

"Sometimes I think you maddish," she declared.

"I have been accused of such before," he openly admitted.

Was he aware the path they traveled was harried by mythical misadventure? She did not remember seeing the serpent tower noted upon the map.

"Was Ella marked upon the vellum?" she asked, her suspicions peaked.

"Well, not exactly," Faran admitted, "I saw no need to complicate the rendering by pointing out every potential disaster."

"I see. And what other unmarked wonders stand between us and your sword and shield?"

"None. Truly."

To her practiced ears, his guileless tone sounded

more like a trumpet of alarm. "I don't believe you," she said. "Where feats of daring are concerned, you know no fear and I know nothing else. It is safe to say we measure foolhardiness upon different scales, mine the more easily tipped. What else lies before us?"

"Well," he finally conceded, "some may view Black Rain Lake as a hindrance."

"Go on," she prompted.

"It acts as a giant moat, ringing Gorham's castle. The town of Gylfi lies beside it."

"That is the same lake known as the Mere of Sleeping Misery?"

"I believe some call it such."

Her pulse hammered in her temples, but this time, blatant excitement outweighed fear. She stared at Faran. Heaven help her, his audacity was contagious. She was ready to charge headfirst into this next adventure, ready to feel the thrill of danger coursing through her veins. Yet she must not admit to this revelation too easily.

"I think I might include the mere as a possible impediment," she maintained.

"But it has been years since anyone has died in the black waters," Faran protested. "Why nowadays, there is even a ferry that crosses it with praiseworthy reliability. How could one small lake possibly cause us hardship?"

How indeed. She had a feeling she would be finding out firsthand and all too soon.

Chapter Thirteen

"Well, are you coming?" Faran prodded.

Pondering her decision, Leanora nibbled her lower lip, a lip he found particularly exciting. A rosebud mouth not available to him. And that hair, so full of fire, was like the desire burning in his belly for her. Why could he not let the matter rest? Somehow, it had become his personal challenge to have her come willing to his bed.

"Lead on," she said, breaking his reverie. "Sometimes I think you seek to kill me off that you may take back my half of the treasure."

He started at her words. Then noticed her sarcastic smile and relaxed. Of late, he leapt to the defense of his honor too quickly. It was not logical, but it was also not without reason.

Reaching forward, he worked at untangling a lock of her hair caught in the clasp of her cloak. She sat unmoving and unafraid, a condition becoming more commonplace. They were familiar with one another now, and it was hard to imagine his world without her. Never before had he known the daily routine of a woman, but he knew Gillyflower's likes and dislikes. First in the morning she washed her face, before she combed her hair. And she drank her herbal infusions hot and dark, without honey. And while she possessed the curiosity of a cat wanting to explore the world, she also harbored the timidity of a mouse who sought the security of a dark snug nest. They spoke of everyday matters, and although he had shared many things with the previous females in his life, he had never conceived of discussing the mundane or the personal.

The strands of hair loosened. As he captured and gently twisted them around his fingers, he realized what made her different. She never expected him to be anyone other than himself. And it mattered not to her who his father might be, or what his past had been. Of course, she did not know how miserably he had failed himself and his people.

The silken locks slipped free, and he lowered his hand. Too bad his life could not be so easily untangled.

They rode along in silence, but he was ever conscious of Leanora's presence at his back. It would have been a lonely journey without her, and he thought she was secretly beginning to enjoy their trek across the north of England. She seemed happier now than when first they had met.

A rare stab of guilt reminded him he had played upon her sympathies to gain the use of her boat, and he still sought her body as sport. And other than friendship, what could possibly come of their being together? They were complete opposites. She sought the wings of freedom, and he sought the binding chains of vengeance. They did not even have a religion in common. By the gods, what was this? Did the feelings of a female cause him concern? This too had never happened before.

****

Lothian's perpetual gloom waned darker, and Faran pushed the horses even harder. Since crossing through the Tower of Ella, a tangible unease and dreariness hovered ever closer, and he wished to reach Gylfi before it became necessary to spend another night on the open road—unprotected. A decent meal, a lively mead, and a warm bed also sounded good.

The forest thinned, and the lights of the city twinkled upon the horizon. In the dull, sullen atmosphere, the pinpoints of illumination seemed cold and unfriendly, rather than warm and inviting.

Pausing on a small rise, they studied the town and ebony tarn. Black Rain Lake was both the bane and lifeblood of Gylfi. It offered up the strange black salt—the town's only commodity—and it kept safe their ruler and oppressor. The sooty lake also surrounded the malevolent island upon which Lord Gorham's castle roosted like a boney vulture. The sinister image did not encourage exploration of either the water or the island. Yet that was where they must go.

With a lordly gesture, Faran bowed. "Welcome to the fair city of Gylfi, Lady Leanora." He tried his best to sound cheerful, but instinct warned him sadness was a way of life here.

Skepticism shadowed Leanora's sideways glance as if she suspect the hardest part of their quest still lay ahead.

"I propose we bury our treasure here," she suggested out of the blue. "Then we shall not have to constantly worry over it while we are in the city."

He cocked his head and considered the idea. She gave a shy smile and shrugged her shoulders as if in retrospect she thought she should not have spoken. She had such little confidence in herself, when truly she was quick witted, and at times, filled with the most inspired notions.

"A grand idea," he reassured. "Choose a spot."

Her smile deepened and she sat taller. Faran wished he could more frequently draw that reaction from her.

They dismounted, and she led him to the tree that would serve as the marker for their buried treasure. Again he realized how their perception of the world differed. Like the tower of Beowulf, he

142

would have picked the tallest most impressive fir, but Leanora chose the tiniest pine. Her choice made the most sense. No one would even notice the sickly little tree, let alone imagine it guarded a hoard of gold and jewels.

Employing a couple of stout sticks, they dug a hole and lay to rest her two small boxes and the thick leather pouch now holding their combined treasure. After carefully redistributing the fresh turned earth, he stepped back to get his bearings and memorize the area. Then he patted the purse tied at his waist. The few coins within should easily sustain them over the next day or two. At least that was the plan.

As they picked their way back through the tall pale grass, he reached out and took her hand. "In case you trip," he said as she hesitated. He enjoyed the feel of her tiny hand in his. She remained silent, but tightened her grip.

When they reached the horses, he helped her to mount.

"Something is wrong?" she asked staring down at him.

Nothing a long night wrapped in your arms would not cure, he thought and slid his hands from her body. "Are you sure you wish to ride with me to Gylfi?" he asked. "Gorham will not easily surrender the sword and shield, and even now Romaine most assuredly hounds our trail."

Leanora's gaze skimmed across his face, and her eyes held a faint flicker of concern. "We are partners," she reminded, "until the end."

Until the end. That phrase allowed for ominous conclusions as well as happy ones. Danger brooded all around and he had goaded this girl into following his path. Now he was responsible for her safety. Once again, too late, he realized he should have come alone.

****

As quietly as possible, Faran and Leanora entered the bleak town. Gray thatch-roofed cottages lined the street, their windows shuttered for the evening. No sounds of gaiety or brawling broke the silence of the night and the town seemed more dead than asleep.

They meandered about to get a feel for the village, there was a distinct lack of establishments offering victuals and accommodations. Thankfully, near the wharf, he spied a large lumbering brute of a building hunkered down beside the water's edge. The sign out front, hanging motionless in the stagnant air, promised livery, lodging, and simple fare.

Reaching the stable without incident, they secured the horses for the night and cautiously entered the old timbered hall. He halted just inside the door and glanced around the dimly lit chamber. The eyes peering back from dark corners glinted with a mixture of curiosity and meanness.

"'Tis cold out, Faran," Leanora complained, pushing into the room to stand at his side.

A murmuring broke the silence, and the watching eyes turned leering. He grabbed Leanora's arm with one hand, and rested the other upon the hilt of his dagger. Then urging her to keep in step, he strode calmly but purposefully over to the proprietor.

"Eventide," the old man grumbled out a greeting. "What can we be doin' for ye."

"Two rooms please," Leanora said.

"One room," Faran corrected, "and livery for two horses." Still holding her arm, he jerked her into silence as she made to protest his request.

"The only lodging left is in the rafter space," the man informed him. "But I'll only charge you half the fee. Stayin' long?" he asked eying them with curiosity.

"How long we tarry is not our choice," Faran replied. "The room will suffice." He tossed two coins on the counter. "We need food as well."

Leanora's scowl hung like a pall over them as they waited for the man to procure a trencher of cold meat and cheese and a skin of mead. Following the innkeeper up the rickety ladder to the loft, they crossed the rough-hewn planking to the far end of the building. Located over the kitchens, the room smelled sour, and the thatched roof rained down bits of dirt and dust as two pigeons, taken by surprise, sought more peaceful residence. Faran glanced out of the one tiny window. It offered a hazy view of the lake and his enemy's castle.

The squat little man set the food down and lit the lantern, and after pointing out the bed and the garderobe bucket, he took his leave.

"Why did we not seek another inn?" Leanora demanded. "One with more rooms available?"

"I saw no other inns. And it would make no difference. Had there been one hundred inns and one hundred rooms available, you would not sleep alone tonight."

Her eyes widened in surprise.

"Do not worry," he reassured. "I thought to defend your honor, not take it." Although, on second thought, it was possible their circumstances could work to his advantage. "Nothing happens here tonight not by your decree."

"You truly thought to protect me?"

"Of course."

The doubt ebbed from Leanora's eyes. "Forgive me," she apologized. "I thought you finally showed your leopard spots by wishing to compromise me."

"Did you not see the men downstairs drooling at the sight of you? How could I let you fend for yourself in a room of your own? I would not have anything happen to you." The fierceness with which he brandished his words surprised even him.

"Thank you," she said, her warm gaze locked and held his.

"You can trust me," he defended. "You should know that by now."

"I am afraid," she admitted.

"Of what, Leanora, me or yourself?"

"Both," she whispered. "And so many other things."

"You needn't be. I promise."

"In my life, promises have always been broken."

"Than start your life anew, right here and right now. We should all be given second chances," he added, and prayed it was so. For if ever a tortured soul needed an opportunity for redemption it was his.

She appeared so forlorn, and her sigh sounded more like a sob. Boldly he reached for her. She stepped closer.

"It would be easy to succumb to your charms, Faran. But when you are gone, then I shall miss you all the more."

"Gone? Do you foresee something that I do not?"

"No," she admitted with a sad little smile. "The only things I see in the future are the remnants of the past."

"Then again, look only at the here and now. Look at me." Arms held wide, he offered shelter and comfort.

A dreamy-eyed expression softened her features, and she melted into his embrace, her sweet mouth but a breath away. And as their lips lightly touched, she slipped her arms around his neck. He had done it. He had won. She was ready to yield to him.

A spear point of remorse pricked at his conscience. She gave herself honestly, but he took her as first prize in a game he played against himself. Who cared? She was in his arms. That was all that mattered.

He teased her lips with gentle kisses. She hesitated. "Be easy, Gillyflower," he reassured and stroked her hair. Soft as moonlight, her tresses glided through his fingers.

"I think you want me," he challenged. "I feel it in your touch and I see it in your eyes." She leaned closer, her body molding to his, making it yearn all the more for hers. "Let me show you that being with a man can be the greatest adventure of all."

She gazed up at him, lips parted in an invitation for him to continue. He moved his hands to frame her face and captured her mouth with his. She offered no resistance, and he eased his tongue past the soft lips he had coveted for so long. Lips he had tasted once before, and dreamt of one thousand times over. She seemed awkward but not fearful as she followed his lead, deepening their kiss, silently asking for more.

He shrugged out of his cloak, she slid free of her cape and wrapped in single-minded purpose, he eased her down upon the sleeping pallet.

His heart raced, he was ready for her now—too ready. He gritted his teeth. If he didn't concentrate on something else, it might all be over before it began. As he nipped at her neck, she shivered and arched against him driving his passion again too high, too fast. He wished to tear at her clothes and enter her now, drowning in her body, never coming up for air. He should go slow, but at any moment she might change her mind.

With a determined touch, he worked at her heavy linen top. When the fabric fought his intentions, he slipped one hand beneath it to caress her breasts. Through the lighter fabric of her shift, he felt her nipples pucker. Her breath came in soft, quick puffs against his neck. He imagined tonguing those firm buds—teasing, demanding, suckling. He ached with the need to stroke her silky body and fully explore every part of her with his hands and his mouth. He sat up, pulling Leanora along with him.

She shivered as he tugged at the edge of her over-blouse, and eyes wide, she glanced around as if considering a means of retreat. But she held her ground, and he realized how much courage it took for her to offer herself to him. Without asking, he knew her husband had been cruel. The scars he had covertly seen upon her back bore proof of the punishment meted out upon her body. But what horror had been inflicted upon her spirit and mind?

Feeling suddenly callous, he held back. She had surrendered. He was the victor. But in winning he had lost. He could not make love to her as if she were just a common meal to satisfy his hunger for a woman's thighs. She was a feast to be celebrated, at the right time and place, but not here—her soft white skin touching the filthy pallet, fetid air filling his nostrils rather than her scent, the sounds of drunken chaos mingling with and defiling her cries of pleasure. He gathered her into his arms and hugged her to his chest, rocking her to and fro.

With one moment of pure trust, she had captured and held him more completely than a hundred years of bondage could claim. He would not betray that trust. His valor was tarnished enough as it was, and such action was unbefitting the man he sought to be.

"I did something wrong?" she whispered.

"No, Leanora. You did everything right." He eased her away from his chest and studied her face. Because he had won her for the wrong reasons, he would sacrifice what he wanted so badly...at least for tonight. "You mean more to me than just the release of this rutting hunger you kindle in me. Do you understand what I am telling you?" he asked, his voice thick with the unspent passion still coursing through his body.

"Yes, I think so." She reached up to touch the corner of his mouth. Her eyes were filled with tears and her breathing was still too rapid.

He smiled at her. She didn't have an idea in Hades what he was talking about—he barely understood it himself. Yet she believed in him and granted him her faith.

Previously in his life, many women had accosted him with carnal game playing, trying to bind him to their side. And although he freely took what they offered, his iron heart had always remained untouched. He had promised them only the complete fulfillment of their needs, and a trinket or two, and that had been enough. But with Leanora it was different. She had forged a fire within him mighty enough to melt an entire treasure trove of well-tempered iron hearts.

She strained upward and pressed a tiny kiss upon his cheek. His resolve wavered. "Not tonight," he said in a strained voice, his face turned skyward, "not tonight." There would be another time—a more fitting time—for them to become lovers.

With the pad of his thumb, he gently erased the tears glistening on her cheeks. "Go to sleep," he urged. She opened her mouth to speak, but he silenced her with a finger across her lips, and without question she closed her eyes. Again they lay side by side, and Faran held her close until she slumbered peacefully.

"Dear little Gillyflower," he murmured, "I promise you our time will come."

****

Off the northern shores of England, Aelfred, king of all Wessex, stood on the deck of his new ship. Night had fallen and the sea was calm. For several days there had been no sign of the avaricious Danes.

Gazing at the rugged coastline, he felt a surge of deep devotion for the country he sought to unite and govern. Since the battle of Ethandun there was tentative peace. The foreign invaders had finally withdrawn from Wessex, and even though Danelaw now encompassed Northumbria, Mercia, and East Anglia, there had been less warring along the northern realms. Still, he did not trust this concord would last indefinitely. The Danes would not overlook a good opportunity to sally forth with ill intent. It was just in their nature, and just a matter of time.

They were fierce warriors, these Scyldings, and they no longer came to England to merely raid and run. They had settlements now, and they wintered here as well. Proficient at forced marches, they were also surprisingly capable when mounted—thus becoming a more dangerous threat with each passing season. And they were pagans, a condition he found most unsettling. Many had submitted to baptism, mainly because it was forced upon them, or because they thought to lull him into thinking they were cooperating—when in fact they were plotting trouble. He could only hope someday they would see the true path and follow the Christ.

Still, he must properly give thanks to the Lord for this reprieve from conflict

"Send for Brother Thomas," he ordered. "I would see him before I retire." As he waited for his command to be carried out, the king smiled at his choice in clerics.

There were many holy men at his beck and call, priests who tripped over one another to be by his side. But oft times, those men seemed motivated by the desire for wealth and status unbefitting their calling. On the contrary, this old monk seemed guileless. His well-worn clothing and lack of possessions indicated worldly goods held little attraction for him, and this quality was reassuring.

Aelfred glanced up as Brother Thomas hurried to his side. "Yes, your grace," the monk began, "what might I do for you this evening?"

"There are several correspondences to be written," he instructed. "And I would hear the scriptures this evening. However, I will need your assistance in these matters, Brother Thomas. I am tired and my illness plagues me mightily."

"Yes, my lord. I regret you are unwell, but it is always my pleasure to serve you in any way I can."

They entered the king's private cordoned-off area of the ship. Aelfred paced about, stopping periodically when the griping pains came upon him. He had suffered this agony over most of his twenty-nine years, and unfortunately they were not something to which one grew accustomed. Thomas proceeded to the small makeshift table holding vellum, ink, and quill.

"Wait," Alfred ordered as the monk reached to light the cresset lamp. "Use the candle instead. It is of my own invention," he stated proudly. "I have been working many months on its creation. It is a method of measuring time," he added at the monk's questioning look. "However long it takes to burn the wax between the marks, is the time it takes for one hour to pass. And if constructed in the correct proportions, and burned in an atmosphere of calm, it is surprisingly accurate."

"Quite ingenious my lord," the monk acknowledged, the awe evident in his voice.

Aelfred smiled. The world held so many marvels in both form and idea. Then he frowned because it quite saddened him that England, the country he loved so dearly, was replete of accomplishments seen in many civilized nations. He had been to Rome more than once, and had observed firsthand what mankind could achieve. He often wondered if it were the lack of religion holding back the people here. The church could make a grand difference on this wayward island. An all encompassing entity, it could tie together the Saxon kingdoms. It also offered education, and the only hope for England to become the magnificent country he dreamed it could be.

Thoughts of religion and travels abroad brought Bishop Swithun to mind. His childhood tutor and friend had been such an inspiration in his life, and the man's death grieved him still. He glanced up and studied Brother Thomas. Surely it was a sign from above to have crossed paths with this unlikely man on the feast day of Saint Swithun.

When the dictation was finally completed, the king took to his pallet. Brother Thomas offered him an herbal mixture to soothe his stomach, then drew up a chair to commence reading.

"Here," Aelfred offered, "use this." He handed the monk a beautiful aestel book pointer. It was crafted of gold and cloisonné enamel and covered with a transparent piece of rock crystal. He enjoyed seeing it in the hands of someone who cherished books. With wide eyes and a shaking hand, the monk accepted the use of the marker.

"I am grateful you travel with us," Alfred said, when the monk paused following a particularly long passage. "I believe God sent you to me to help bring the message of Christianity to this land."

"I owe you my life, my lord," the monk replied, casting his gaze downward. "I am honored to travel with you and to be at your command."

"That answer pleases me, and I have a special mission for you Brother Thomas. Have you heard of County Lothian?"

The monk nodded slowly and without enthusiasm.

"Yes," Alfred agreed, "just to think about such a

place gives one pause. Still I wish you to go there as my emissary." He heard the monk's sharp intake of breath, but the brave little man issued no protest or complaint. "The ruler there has been baptized. But I fear this was a ceremonial gesture only. And the holy man I previously sent to instruct his people in the way of the Lord seems to have disappeared. I believe you would make a worthy replacement. You must teach the people of Gylfi to read and write, Thomas. That is the most valuable gift one man can bestow upon another."

A look of astonishment transformed the monk's usually peaceful expression. Was it due to the praise offered, or did the thought of traveling to Lothian render the man speechless.

"Speak up, Brother Thomas. Do you not wish to travel as the king's man to this heathen land?"

"You...you do me untold honor in asking," the monk stammered. "I question if I am up to such a task, but I accept it with sincere humility and enthusiasm."

"That is the answer I had hoped for and expected," the king said. "I must sleep now. We shall escort you to the nearest port navigable by our ships. I don't dare set you adrift on your own again," he added with a chuckle.

The monk stood, and gently set aside the book still cradled in his arms. Then with a small bow, he made to return the aestel.

"You may keep the book pointer," Alfred said.

At the very idea, the monk took a step backward. "It is much too grand a gift for a man like me, my lord. Would it not better serve to be donated to the poor or..."

"No," Alfred interrupted. "It is for you and you must keep it always. It will remind you that knowledge is the greatest wealth of all, and you must endeavor to increase your wisdom until one day it is equal to the worth of that which you hold in your hands."

****

Thomas left the king's private area and stood on the deck of the ship. He gulped in the cold night air hoping it would clear his thinking. Moonlight gleamed off the unexpected treasure, and he marveled at the value of the beautiful object he'd been given. On occasion Alfred presented such items to his bishops, but to bestow such a gift upon a lowly monk was extraordinary.

Of course, over the last few weeks, his life seemed to have been fraught with extraordinary events. After burying Ageetha Wrenn, he had set off in search of Leanora, to tell her what had become of her family and to rescue her from her self-imposed exile. But he had found no trace of the girl on the island. Then while trying to return to the mainland, an unexpected gust of wind had torn his sail asunder, and his tiny ship had been set adrift—left to the mercy of the sea.

Helplessly floating beyond sight of land and hope of rescue, he had prayed for strength and forgiveness for his sins. And when an impenetrable fog gathered, and the tremendous storm clouds threatened, he thought to meet his Lord that very day.

Then out of the sea mist, the royal fleet had appeared. He had watched in awe as they spotted him and drew near. Bobbing along side one of the grand ships, he near fainted with surprise when the king peered down at him and gave the order he should be taken onboard.

As his feet touched the deck, the thunderclouds had thinned. The sun had come out, and the fog had been blown away as if by the breath of God. The men on the vessel appeared awed by the transformation in the weather, and when the king pointed out it was the feast day of Saint Swithun, they all crossed themselves repeatedly as if witnessing a miracle. Then they chanted the childhood ditty associated with the revered man.

St. Swithun's day if thou dost rain
For forty days it will remain:
St. Swithun's day if thou be fair
For forty days 'twill rain na mair—

Such portents still held much weight amongst the common man, especially sailors, and they took consolation in finding reasons for why Nature or the world around them acted as it did. Far be it for him to question their reasoning or take from them this small comfort. There were many things in life that defied understanding.

Besides, he had to admit it was quite an auspicious coincidence, and it had wrought a significant change in his own life. A change which might lead to the ending of his life—if things did not go well in County Lothian. He shuddered at the thought of meeting Lord Gorham. The man ruled his small kingdom with a heavy hand, and it was common knowledge the land and his people suffered much beneath his cruelty.

And what of Leanora? Where had she gone? Now his search for her would be woefully delayed.

Chapter Fourteen

Leanora lay beside Faran, listening to his slow even breathing, and thoughts of last night tiptoed through her mind.

Blinding, deafening rapture had slid over her like a silken nightrail, and the evening would have ended quite differently had Faran not interrupted their touching and kissing. Surrendering to him had seemed right, but she was so travel worn, and the bed was dirty, and it just was not what she had envisioned as their first time together.

Somehow he had realized all this, and there could be no doubt now he had procured only one room in order to protect her. He had not forced the situation, and he could have. Rather he had held her innocently and protectively until she had fallen asleep, and the recollection of his embrace left her near breathless. Never before had she known how wonderful it felt just to be comforted and to feel completely safe.

She had also never felt so alive, an experience to savor. It was as if a dam had burst within her and she had been washed clean and carried beyond her old memories, her old miseries.

She studied Faran's face. Last night, the need between them had crackled like the air in a thunderstorm. He had wanted her most urgently, but there had been a sharing in his eyes rather than a taking. He was different—he had to be—because she thought loving him would be a wondrous thing.

And although the thought of giving her heart to another was a terrifying prospect, for a few glorious moments she had been happy.

Moving slowly as thickened whey, she slid off the pallet and gained her feet. Faran remained sleeping peacefully. As she gazed at him, the gnawing inside of her intensified. His kindness was chipping away at the defenses she had labored a lifetime to build. But she must not forget it was dangerous to need someone. His winsome features and her lusty feelings for him were overruling logic. Or was logic sorely overrated as well? If she were to begin her life over, as he suggested, that too should be left behind. She smiled. At least she had not recently fallen down in front of him.

Stepping away from the bed, she breathed a little easier. They had only been together for a short time, yet it seemed a lifetime ago she had found him lying upon the shore of her little island. So much had changed since then. She was free now to do as she pleased. But what pleased her heart worried her soul. Reckless abandon was not a mantle she had worn before, and choosing wisely was not as easy as she had imagined.

Padding quietly across the room, she peered out the window. Sweet Savior. In the dull glow of a Lothian morning, the ominous lake and castle were almost painful to behold. She gripped the rough-hewn windowsill and leaned forward to study the dismal scene. The water in the lake, black as the outside of a cook kettle, appeared thick and sluggish. Patches of foul-colored mist curled up from it in a ponderous mucky cloud.

"Forbidding sight is it not?"

She jumped, hitting her forehead on the window casement. Rubbing the spot, she turned around. "Most assuredly." She searched Faran's face to determine his mood.

A lazy smile curved his mouth and his gaze turned heated as it meandered the length of her body. Guessing he relived the intimate moments they had shared, a hot blush warmed her cheeks.

"Are you as hungry as I?" he asked nonchalantly.

"Starving." For much more than food, the unspoken words tripped through her mind. And by the expression in Faran's eyes, he felt the same. At least it pleased her to think it might be so.

Retrieving his cloak from where it hung from a rafter in the middle of the room, he gathered the remnants of last night's repast hidden in the folds of fabric. The food had escaped being ravaged by insects and rodents and they sat and made short work of it.

"I drank all the mead," he said with a sheepish grin. "I was hard pressed to fall asleep last night after we almost...."

As his meaning became clear, Leanora nearly choked on a piece of dry bread. "I understand," she acknowledged. Other words and phrases flew through her mind but halted short of her mouth. She wanted to say more, wanted to tell him how much it meant to her that he had treated her with such respect and thoughtfulness. But she had never discussed such intimate matters with anyone, let alone with a man. "Have you a plan for crossing the lake and gaining entrance to the castle?" she asked, changing the subject

"Yes...no...well, sort of."

That did not sound reassuring.

"I thought I would linger about the wharf. Surely help of some sort is needed dockside. Or I could stow away on the ferry taking supplies to the island."

"I see." She tried to appear enthusiastic but his ideas seemed a bit ill conceived.

"Well if need be, I will swim there," he stubbornly proclaimed, "it's not all that far." As if to check the distance, he gained his feet, strode to the window, and peered out.

Swim! A wave of nausea welled up in Leanora. Lord above. To her, purposely going into that black water was unthinkable. Their ordeal of crossing the river on horseback had nearly killed her with fright, and the distance to the island was much farther than the width of the river.

She glanced at Faran. Apparently, the thought caused him no concern. But then what did? "It's a positively frightful notion," she countered, and once again rued the tribal heirlooms he sought. She was jealous of the hold they had over him. They drove him to defy danger, and they threatened to take him away from her—perhaps forever. "You risk all in what you prepare to do," she argued. "That will not help your people."

"There is no other path for me, the relics are very old."

"Old? You are ready to trade your life for something because it is old?"

"Everything in life is a trade, Leanora. To experience the thrill of adventuring you must relinquish the need for security. A lesson you have learned quite well," he praised. "And to liberate your heart from loneliness," he added, absently touching the iron fetish he wore, "you must hazard the risk of breaking it."

She stared at Faran. His words were edged with emotion and wisdom. He definitely possessed the nature of a word-weaver housed in the frame of a warrior. But his idea of sacrificing himself for the heirlooms still seemed foolish.

"A pretty speech indeed, and possibly true. But when all is said and done, that for which you are willing to die are still just old weapons of war."

"They are the weapons of our most revered leader," he said. "Have you not guessed by now to whom they once belonged? They are the sword and shield of Beowulf."

Beowulf... Even she had heard of this ancient hero. No wonder the artifacts were deemed important. Would she not show the same devotion and fervor if she sought the relics of a saint, or a piece of the Rood?

"Beowulf is near as hallowed to us as Woden." Faran added. "His sword, straight and true. His shield surrounded by the symbol of the Geats. Both are worth one hundred times my pitiful hide."

"Not to me," Leonora breathed softly and gained her feet. She yearned to reach out to him, but had little practice in giving or receiving consolation or reassurance. Faran might push her away, and she could not abide his rejection. But that was selfish thinking. His soul cried out for tenderness and healing.

Daring to draw closer, she slipped her hand in his and nestled her head upon his shoulder. He leaned toward her, not away, and her trepidation faded. "Is there no other way for you?" she asked gazing up at him.

"No." His voice was adamant, and his thirst for justice once more stood between them. "I was not there when the battle began," he added, anguish evident in his voice, "but I shall be there at the finish. The dead must be vindicated and the living reborn. And this treachery must be brought to an end."

"But why must you accomplish this undertaking on your own?"

"I am not alone, Gillyflower. I have you." A winsome smile softened his determined expression. "Come. I will tell you all." As he spoke, Faran drew her over to the sleeping pallet and tugged her down to sit at his side. Finally, the missing pieces to the tale he told were to be revealed.

"The day of the battle dawned peaceful and clear," he began, and cradled her hand in his lap. "There was nothing to portend the attack, and it seemed inconceivable danger lurked cloaked within such a glorious horizon.

"The night before, I had a dream. It lingered in the light of day—vivid and powerful. In the vision I saw a glorious stag, the span of his antlers near precluding him from passing between the trees in the forest. The magnificent heath-walker was grayish-silver, and his eyes glowed with the life spark of the land.

"All morning, as if under a spell, I wandered the nearby forest, pursuing the nonexistent stag. And driven by this all-consuming madness, I left the treasures far behind. I chased fantasies, and imagined magnificent tales ripe for the telling. And all the while, my people spilled their blood and felt the bite of our enemy's sword."

"But you did not know," she defended.

"It was my duty. I should have been there." He clenched both of his into fists.

"At dusk, the spell lifted. I saw smoke above the village, and realizing it boded ill, I ran back as fast as I could. When I arrived, the fighting was nearly over, but the dying and the screaming continued. I joined in what remained of the battle. The enemy, driven back, fled to their ships—the relics in their possession."

She slid her hands around his fists, and he glanced at her, his expression etched in dark remorse.

"What happened next?" She stroked his hands trying to soothe his pain.

"I was stunned and sickened to witness what had taken place in my absence. Night fell, and like a rogue wolf, I circled the town in the dark. Then I sought my parents. Thinking I had been injured or killed in the melee, they were overjoyed to see me. I told them I had gone hunting, following a buck far into the forest. My mother assured me my presence would not have altered the outcome. The temple housing the relics was totally destroyed, and all who defended it were slain. One more person would not have made any difference.

"They did not condemn me, but I could not forgive myself. Many of my friends lay dead, and one of my brothers was seriously wounded. Had I been there, I might have vanquished at least one mortal blow. That would have been enough."

"You also most assuredly would have been killed," she pointed out.

Faran slipped free of her hands and leapt to his feet. "A warrior always faces the possibility of death. Such thoughts would not have stayed me from my duty. It is better to die in battle with glory than to live safely as a coward."

She rose to stand before him. "You are not cowardly," she declared, speaking with the assurance and authority beyond her ken. "You were drawn away from that battle for a purpose. It is why you had the dream. You were meant to survive."

An odd expression flickered across Faran's face as if he had not considered such a possibility. "Perhaps," she added as words winged their way from her heart to her lips, "perhaps your task is to recover that which has been stolen, and to preserve the side of life that balances the brutality of war. That is also a noble aspiration and can require as much from a man as any battle of the flesh. What you shall accomplish in your lifetime will live on in history forever. It will live beyond the memory of that battle, or even the memory of your own name."

Suddenly a withering fatigue claimed her, and

her bones felt soft and wobbly. Faran gathered her into his arms, keeping her upright. Why had she said those things? One moment she had been praying to God to help her know what to say, and the next moment those words had burst out of her mouth. But they rang with truth. Faran was special, and not just to her.

She realized now he had to follow his quest. There was no other way to ease his pain—no other way to erase the memory of the day causing him so much suffering. "How can I help you regain the sword and shield?"

He smoothed the hair back from her brow. "You are to do nothing, and you are to stay here." The gruffness of his voice indicated his concern for her. "Your belief in me is enough, and I will not have your death or injury on my conscience as well."

"But you cannot leave me here."

Faran turned away and paced the room, running his fingers through his long mane of hair. Indecision clouded his face. Pausing before her, he rested his hands upon her shoulders. "You are right," he admitted. "And I must apologize, Leanora, for I have led you a perilous dance. We shall have to stay together, taking our chances as they come."

She smiled eagerly. He seized her upper arms as if to drive home his next point. "We must keep our own counsel," he warned. "And you must not stray from my side for a heartbeat."

Not for a heartbeat, she silently repeated.

****

Faran bound his hair in a leather cord, then they left the inn and headed for Black Rain Lake.

Usually a wharf boasted a flurry of activity and the crisp smell of freshwater breezes. But the atmosphere at the Gylfi dock was layered with sullen unrest, and the odor clinging to the air was of something dead or dying.

There was no hustle or bustle. Workers performed their tasks with somber expressions and sluggish movements. Even the children stared back at her with dull eyes and little curiosity, their empty faces the most haunting of all. These poor villagers lived within the clutches of a dark secret.

"There is a sadness here defying my understanding," she whispered.

"It is as if they have no will of their own, and no hope," he agreed. "It is much the same with my people now."

"To be exact," a voice echoed from behind them, "they have no spirit."

In unison, Leanora and Faran spun around. A young man of Faran's height returned their stare. Although slight of build, he was fair to look upon, with soulful brown eyes and sable-colored hair. He seemed more animated than the other inhabitants of the town.

"I am Cynric," he offered. "Bard to the king, but puppet to no man." As he spoke, he patted the beaver-skin covered harp slung across his back, then the knife sheathed at his hip. "You are not from around here." His statement held equal measures of curiosity and envy.

"We come from many leagues to the south," Faran replied, not offering the stranger their names. "What did you mean about these people having no spirit?"

"That is how Lord Gorham rules them so effectively," Cynric explained. "They have no desire to rebel or to leave. They have no spirit."

Leanora recognized such despair. It could eat away at the core of one's being, devouring the inner beauty that made each person a reflection of the Creator. It left only an empty shell and a sad recollection of what might have been. "Has it always been so?" she asked.

"It has been thus since before my lifetime," Cynric answered bitterly.

"The elders of my tribe recounted grisly tales of the evil dwelling within this county," Faran admitted. "But I did not realize its talons gripped the land and the people with such assuredness. How did this come to pass?"

Cynric studied both of them as if gauging their trustworthiness. "My songs and stories usually come at a price," he said without embarrassment.

Faran liberated a coin from the money purse and offered it to the scop, this bard, this teller of tales.

Cynric readily accepted the token and escorted them to a more private area beneath a large tree. He glanced around, as if making sure they would not be overhead. "Many years ago," he began, "Lord Gorham's father bargained away his soul and those of his descendents. In return, he received powers no mortal man should possess. This prior king ruled the realm without mercy, thwarted only by the Shadow Spirit of Gylfi. The Shadow Spirit protected the people and gave them the desire to persevere and hope.

"For years, the king and this ancient female warrior fought, and their powers being equal, no one ever won or lost. Then Gorham's father learned the secret of deception. He tricked the Spirit Warrior to a cave where she saw an image of herself asleep upon a sarcophagus. When she touched the effigy she became one with it. Before the Shadow Spirit could save herself, the monarch flooded the lake and sealed the cave with the black waters of sleep. To this day the beautiful maiden slumbers in the caves beneath the surface of this ebony pool." Cynric gave a nod toward Black Rain Lake. "Now shadows no longer exist in this realm, and the spirit of the land and the people rests with the faerie warrior."

"And Gorham's father still lives?" Leanora asked.

"No," Cynric said. "The spell of deception cost him much. Day by day, he grew thinner and more pale until he reached the point of nothingness and disappeared. But his hideous offspring have rallied to his cause, taking over where he left off. Gorham and Romaine are more savage than their father ever dreamed of being. And as they split the power, they also split the consequences, so both survive."

Faran's eyes narrowed with suspicion. "How is it you are not burdened by this mournful spell?"

A smile, wistful yet genuine, played upon Cynric's mouth. "Some of us are born with a caul, the veil of protection. It is a mixed blessing. We are not afflicted by Gorham's evil, but we are doomed to helplessly watch the suffering of those we love."

The bard grew silent and stared at Leonora. So keen was his gaze, she took a step closer to Faran.

"What is your name, lady?" the stranger asked.

She glanced at Faran. Was it wise to confide such information? He nodded his consent.

"I am Leanora," she said.

Cynric's bold stare did not lessen, and he seemed especially captivated by her eyes. "Forgive me," he apologized, "I have rarely seen eyes of such a joyous hue."

"But they are blue," she said. "The color of the sky."

"Not this sky," he pointed out, "at least not for many generations."

Her gaze flickered upward, then back to his face. Everyone in Gylfi had brown eyes framed by black or brown hair. And the clothes of the villagers were shapeless and drab, stark black, dingy white, or some other somber shade.

"What do you here?" the minstrel boldly asked. "I think there is the seed of a good ballad waiting to spring to life in the wake of your footsteps." This time the smile curving the scop's mouth also brightened his eyes.

"I am Faran Kilbraun, and I wish to gain entrance to Gorham's castle. He holds, without ransom, that which belongs to me."

The frankness of Faran's statement startled Leanora. Cynric also raised a brow of surprise. Then the minstrel and warrior took one another's measure.

"*We* wish to gain entrance there," Leanora corrected. She was not about to be left standing dockside. Both men glanced down at her as if they had just remembered her presence.

"It is possible I could help you," Cynric offered, watching them with the bright eye of a curious sparrow.

"Why do you not leave this place?" Faran asked.

"For the same reason you ventured to come here."

Wariness sharpened Faran's expression.

"I too seek something precious Gorham has stolen," Cynric explained. "And like you, Faran, I will leave only after I have recovered what belongs to me."

"What did the king thieve from you?" Leanora asked. At her words, the sadness in his eyes intensified.

"He took the song from the heart of the woman I love, and the joy from her face. Her name is Kayden," he explained. "We grew up together and fell in love, promising to marry when we were old enough. But she is not like me. The misery of the land seeped into her soul, smothering the light of love that once shown in her eyes. Now she is like the others, with little enthusiasm for life, let alone for me."

"You speak as if you think to win her back. Is

there a way to break through this dismal canopy of anguish?" At the thought of being part of such a miracle, a tingling coursed through Leanora's veins. More and more, she was beginning to like adventuring.

"There is a way," he acknowledged. "But it is dangerous, and anyone who aids me or my companions runs the risk of Gorham's retribution."

"Why have you not done something before now?" Faran asked.

"The dream of reclaiming the land has lain in wait for many decades. But men like me—born with the veil—are not common in Gylfi or anywhere in Lothian. Only now are there enough of us to garner a fighting chance against Gorham. We could use one more in our rank and file, especially a warrior such as you."

To her surprise, Faran remained silent. Why did he not offer to join them? She caught his attention, and with a nod of her head and the sideways cast of her eyes, she urged him to offer Cynric their help. Instead, Faran gripped her arm and dragged her aside. "I suppose you wish me to champion this stranger and his cause," he challenged, his mouth a flat line of protest. She gave him a weak smile and a little shrug.

"I do not think it wise for us to become embroiled in this local rebellion. We know nothing of this man or his comrades, and we have our own purpose here."

"I knew nothing of you, but I came to your aid," she replied stubbornly. "You cannot go storming through life expecting help from everyone else without giving it in return."

Faran remained silent, and since saving an entire county from a curse eons old did seem a bit overwhelming, she decided to try a less formidable approach. "We would be helping two people in love.

What could be a more worthy mission?"

Faran gave a snort of sarcasm. "You follow fanciful whims and romantic notions again, Gillyflower." He studied her face. "Very well," he finally relented, "I cannot deny the bondage of the people and this land is a trespass against nature, and a sin in the eyes of anyone's god."

His arm across her shoulder, he escorted her back toward Cynric. "We are willing to assist you," Faran said, "but not at the jeopardy of our own quest."

A feathery lightness fluttered in her chest. He did this for her. She prayed it was a wise decision as well as a kindhearted one.

"It could put you in grave danger," Cynric bluntly pointed out.

"I have a feeling danger will know us regardless of whose purpose we follow," Faran replied with a half-hearted grin. "What is your plan?"

"First," Cynric explained, "those who work at the castle must be liberated. My Kayden labors in the palace kitchens. I will lead them to the west side of the island where two boats are hidden. We will use them to cross the lake, and with the aid of rope ladders, climb over the wall of the dyke. Then, once everyone is safely away, the water will be drained from the mere. But this can only be done on the Autumnal Equinox, the day marking the balance of light and dark. It is the day the sun rises due east, a time of wonder, a time of thanksgiving. It is also the same day the Spirit Warrior met her doom. It must be the same day she returns to her people and the land."

"And what of those at the castle who do not follow you?" Faran asked.

"To leave or stay is their decision. Those who oppose us, or who do not believe we can succeed, will be left to their own devices."

"Can you win?" Faran asked.

"Not if we do not try," came Cynric's heated reply.

Faran would respect that answer, but it did little to console the doubts crying for attention in the back of her mind.

"If you gain us passage to the island," Faran promised, "I will aid you in saving your woman and releasing the water. But it would be most helpful if we could recover our property before you unleash your plan."

"We will try to accommodate you," Cynric agreed. "But the day soon approaches. And if we miss the appointed time, unlike Persephone, the Spirit of the Mere will not be given even a partial reprieve from her dark underworld."

In a show of fealty, the men grasped one another's forearm, and as they started for the dock, she quickened her pace to keep up with them.

"We must hurry," Cynric advised. "The last ferry leaves shortly. No one will brave passage across the lake come the gloaming."

"What is the reason for this?" Faran asked, voicing the question clamoring in her mind.

"A hellish creature lives in the lake, its disposition as black as the water. It keeps Gorham safe and the people frightened. It also guards the cavern where the fey spirit sleeps."

Leanora's step faltered. If what found asylum in this lake was fearsome enough to quell the hearts of full grown men, she might want to reconsider venturing out upon its domain. Then she felt the reassuring touch of Faran's hand at her elbow. He would protect her—and to be separated from him now was unthinkable.

They reached the ramp leading to the guardhouse. Cynric paused. "Explaining Leanora's presence to the sentries should be no problem," he reassured. "Dancing girls are frequently transported to and from the island. You, on the other hand, present more of a challenge." He glanced thoughtfully at Faran. "We might prevail upon them to believe you are a juggler seeking employ. Just do not offer to perform for them."

"They will not be suspicious of you going to the citadel?"

"I do not think so," Cynric said, "I visit there often. Sometimes by request, and sometimes out of sheer boredom."

They trudged up the gangway to the heavily guarded portal leading to the ferry. Beneath their combined weight, the narrow plank swayed unsteadily. Faran adjusted her hood to cover her hair and slid his hand to the small of her back.

Cynric flashed them a warning glance and held one finger to his lips. "Let me do the talking. Good day, friends," he greeted the guards. "Room for three more on the last tow over?"

"Who be with you today, Cynric," one soldier asked. He perused them with a critical eye, and Leanora shrank back from his penetrating stare.

"Both are amusement for the king," the minstrel explained. "The big, ugly one juggles and performs feats of strength. And it takes little imagination to guess what talents the young lady possesses."

The guards guffawed at Cynric's suggestive remark, but made no attempt to stop them as they ambled forward through the gatehouse and onto the ferry. Scanning the deck of the dilapidated hulk, she saw they were the only passengers.

"Hurry along," the ferryman fussed, "we be late already." He stared apprehensively at the sky, then the water, and cast off the stern line.

Leanora peered around in sudden alarm. The ferry was awfully small, with no walls nor railings, not even a rope to prevent one from falling overboard. She fled toward the heap of cargo haphazardly stacked in the center. Gingerly, she sat down upon an upright barrel and latched onto the hemp that bound a nearby trunk. Faran positioned himself nearby.

The ferryman took up the towrope, and as they shoved off into open water, the three guards unexpectedly leapt aboard.

One man boldly strode up to her and pulled down the hood of her cape. "Let's have a look at the king's latest morsel."

Leanora's breath caught in her throat. She saw Faran tense, and heard his stifled growl. Willing Faran to hold his ground, she forced herself to smile up at the soldier. He seemed in awe of her long red hair.

"More burnished gold to add to Gorham's treasury," another man said, licking his lips. The third sentry was silent as he reached down to adjust himself under his tunic. If they accosted her, Faran was sure to come to her defense, and he would be sorely outnumbered.

"How about a song, lads?" Cynric offered as he drew the chant-wood from its fur pouch. Silently, she thanked him for distracting the men.

He adjusted the willow pegs of the worn maple harp, quickly tuning the six-string instrument. Then, he sang a lively ballad about Gylfi, and the brave soldiers who guarded her.

She averted her face to hide her smile. She was aware Cynric was not sincere in his praise of the guards, but they were not, and the soldiers lapped up the compliments like kittens in the creamery.

Wandering slowly away from her, Cynric drew the men to the other side of the ferry. As they cheered and laughed, the barge reached the deepest part of the lake. Praise be, they were halfway to the castle. Was it possible they could make passage without incident? She relaxed back against the crates and blocks of black salt. Then the tune ended.

"I could do with a bit of jugglin' now," one soldier insisted.

From an open barrel, he grabbed three pale apples and tossed them in Faran's direction. Taken by surprise, Faran dropped the first one then fumbled around with the other two.

She caught her breath.

"Stop the ferry," one sentry ordered and they lurched to a halt.

"He ain't built like no juggler I ever seen," another man said. "He seems more suited to warring and trouble-making."

Faran held his position, neither denying nor agreeing to their claims.

"Where'd you get so many battle scars?" the surliest of the three asked.

"Learning to juggle daggers and spears," Faran said evenly.

The men sneered as they circled him. She made to rise, but Cynric slipped silently to her side and held her back.

"He didn't get them arm rings jugglin'," another man put in.

Before she could blink an eye, the three soldiers rushed forward and shoved Faran backward off of the ferry.

She screamed and ran to the edge of the raft. It jerked back into motion and she nearly tumbled over the edge after him. Heart pounding, her breath coming in fits and starts, she dropped to her knees and stared into the murky depths of the black water. Where was he? Why did he not come to the surface?

Chapter Fifteen

Water, cold and black, forced its way into Faran's nose and mouth. Which way was up? So complete was the darkness it was impossible to guess.

Panicked, he fought the watery arms of death—arms that held him to its bosom and sought to squeeze the last breath of life from his lungs. He unclasped his weighty cloak, sacrificing it to the lake, and with a supreme effort willed himself to immobility. Almost immediately he began to rise, and drifting in the silent ebon womb, an odd languid peacefulness threatened to lull him into acceptance of his fate. Then instinct took hold, sending him kicking and clawing upward. Lungs burning, heart thumping, pulse bounding.

He wasn't going to make it. The effort had come too late. Remember Beowulf and Breca, he told himself. Remember the legend—how they floated together for five nights in the open sea, five nights until the tide tore them apart. Inspired by the familiar litany, he coaxed the last bit of energy from his exhausted muscles, and sputtering and cursing, he broke the surface of the lake.

Treading water, he glanced around. Damn the bastards, they had a peculiar way of resolving differences in Gylfi. Where was the ferry, where was Leanora? A dark veil burned his eyes, obscuring his vision. He ran one hand across his face and up over his head and looked again. He could see the barge now, heading toward the island. And there was Leanora, leaning over the side, searching for him in the wrong direction.

She appeared safe enough, and the thickheaded soldiers seemed unaware they were comrades. What would happen if their relationship came to light? And what might lie ahead for her now that she was on her own? Hopefully Cynric would watch her back. At least he damn well better or he would wish he had.

Leanora turned and spotted him. Before he could motion for her to stay put, she gained her feet and rushed toward the stern. Then she tripped over a thick coil of rope and sprawled onto the deck in a heap. Seemingly uninjured she raised one arm and reached out to him. Again he marveled how her brain and her feet could live in such opposition to one another.

Before he could grant her a reassuring nod, his own plight took president. Something scaly and dreadfully large rippled past his legs. He gritted his teeth, afraid to move. Then he paddled faster, and although the effort might be futile, he drew his knees up closer to his body.

Buffeted by the creature's wake, he fought to maintain his head above the water as a vision of behemoth-sized jaws, lined with sharp white teeth, flashed through his mind. If he did not return quickly to the dock or the nearby beach, he would become dinner for what lived in this dark soup. Again, thoughts of Beowulf bolstered his courage. The hero of long ago had fought many a scaly water-monster—refusing to be eaten limb by limb, refusing to become a banquet on the bottom of the sea. He must do the same.

As the soldiers added their brawn to the ferryman's efforts, the image of the raft grew rapidly smaller. After one last look at Leanora's forlorn figure, he turned and swam for his life.

****

Leanora lay upon the deck, her bruised body throbbing unmercifully, yet she hardly noticed the pain. Faran, poor Faran, and there was nothing she could do to help him. She willed the rhythm of her heart to slow as she fought to take deep breaths and recover her composure. She mustn't let the guards discover a connection between herself and the man they had cast overboard. That would aid neither of them. Heartsick and seasick, she stared at the putrid liquid bubbling up behind the ferry. Then with a shudder, she crawled away from the edge.

The ferry plowed swiftly onward, and although she could barely make out his image, she saw Faran reach land and struggled free of the black mere. Thank the Lord he was safe. Safe—and very far away. As the seriousness of her situation sank in, her heart again raced.

Being separated from Faran was like severing part of her body. She felt empty when not by his side, and her desire for adventuring did not fill the void.

The transport jerked and ground to a halt. Cynric crept to her side, eased her to her feet, and ushered her forward. An angry bruise on his left cheek indicated his payment for a remark he had made to the soldiers.

"Please," she begged the ferryman, "I no longer wish to go to the castle. You must take me back to the city, immediately."

"There be no more crossings 'til, morning," the old man said, his eyes wide with wonder as if he thought her crazed for even suggesting such a thing. "You'll have to wait until sunup." He tied off the ferry and threw out the plank. "Oh, my yes," he clucked. "You'll have to wait until that cavorting beastie is sleeping soundly once again."

Shoving Cynric aside, one of the guards came to stand before her. "Change of heart so soon?" he mocked. "And you have not even met Lord Gorham. Do not be so quick to depart, mayhap you will like how he treats his women—though if you do, you will be the first." He laughed down at her and patted her cheek sympathetically. "I hope there is some fight left in you when he tires of your company and gives you to us."

Rooted in fear she stood before him. Cynric grasped her arm and hurried her off the ferry and onto dry land. Before they could talk privately, a woman the size of a small ox came to claim her. She studied Leanora with a critical eye. "Well ain't you the pretty one with all that coppery hair and skin so fair. You won't be needing this." She snatched Leanora's dagger and slid it beneath her own belt. "About time we had more kitchen help," she added resting her hands on her overflowing hips.

Leanora pondered the remark. She mustn't be assigned to the kitchen. That position would not afford her a chance to explore Gorham's inner sanctum. "But you are mistaken," she lied. "I am Lord Gorham's dancing girl."

The woman took momentary pause at her statement. "Dancin' girl my arse," she hooted. "That's what they all calls themselves. And you'll dance all right—on your backside—as the master calls the tune." She gave another mean laugh. "Call it what you will, it won't be long until you're beggin' to scrub the pots and pans."

Seeking an alternative to this grim scenario, she tried to edge around the lumbering woman and closer to Cynric.

"Not so fast, dancin' girl." The burly female scruffed Leanora by the neck of her tunic. "The women's quarters is this way."

Cynric stepped forward. Then all Leanora saw

were the backs of the three guards as they placed themselves between her and any assistance Cynric might have been able to offer. Yanking Leonora through a door in the bailey wall, the woman dragged her down a dark passageway.

"You'll need a good scrubbin' down, and then a perfumin', before the king will have you," the matron said. "Pity I be so belabored or I'd see to you personally." A sly expression crept across the big woman's round face. She slid her free hand sideways and rubbed it roughly across Leonora's breasts. "Pity indeed."

Leonora's skin crawled, and she clamped her mouth shut to keep the nasty retort trapped harmlessly inside. She struggled to free herself, but the woman's iron grip rendered the attempt useless. Besides, there was little point in fighting to escape. If she gained her freedom, what then? There was no ferry back to the city until tomorrow, which meant she would have to spend the night on the island without shelter or food, and there might be wild animals here and where would she find water and...Merciful Lord, she was doing it again. Worrying over everything that might happen instead of concentrating on what was happening.

She fought to collect her thoughts. What would Faran do? Probably try to win this woman over with a wink and a knowing smile. That thought led to a disturbing image. She best bide her time and work out a sensible plan.

Maintaining her death grip, the dreadful hag marched her through another portal and into an open courtyard. Dull-eyed servants interrupted their chores to glance in her direction. Disinterested, they returned to their labors cultivating a small patch of straggly pale green herbs and vegetables.

Forced through the main part of the stronghold, Leonora concentrated on taking note of the twisting path. They crossed through the cool damp butlery and she saw huge casks standing along all the available wall space. Gorham would not run low on wine or mead.

Something scurried across their path. She dug in her heels and hung back.

"No dawdlin' now," the woman hissed. "It's only a rat and a small one at that."

Small—it was the size of a cat.

"Come along, I say. I got other duties needin' my attention. I can't spend all day on the likes of you, even if you are a sweet young thing."

The woman came to an abrupt halt. Leanora bounced off the unshakable bulk as if she'd hit a tree. Taking no notice, the woman selected a large iron key from the collection hanging suspended on a chain at her waist. She unlocked and opened the door, shoved Leanora inside and slammed it shut. The rasp of the lock sounded with finality as it fell back into place.

Saints above, why did that horrid woman lock her in? There was no place for her to run.

Stepping closer to the door, she pounded on the sturdy oak and clawed at the lock, but it was a worthy barrier and her efforts were fruitless. Fighting back tears, she stood on tiptoes and peered out the tiny window cut into the thick door. The hall was dark and deserted.

Angry and frightened, she rocked back down flat onto her feet and leaned her forehead against the wood. It was stifling in the misty, humid chamber, the weak breath of air trickling in through the high small opening only a slight comfort.

Her hair grew damp and curled around her cheeks and temples and she grabbed at the neck of her over-blouse and tried to alleviate the overpowering warmth. As she gathered her thick mantle of tresses to one side, a shadow fell across her from behind.

Fists clenched and ready to fight, she turned to face what lurked at her back. Four pair of eyes ringed with kohl, returned her stare. It was a gaggle of young girls, all dark-haired and dark-eyed. But unlike the rest of the people here, they possessed a bounty of energy, and their clothes were brightly colored and decorated with pearls and strands of gold. They drew closer, their vermillion stained lips widening into smiles.

"We did not expect you for two more weeks," one of them chirped.

"Where are you from?" another asked.

"What is your name?"

"Why is your hair like polished copper?"

Leanora glanced from one girl to the next, unable to answer one question before another was asked. "Please," she petitioned, "I must leave here immediately and return to Gylfi. Do you possess a key to the door?"

All four girls giggled as they reached out to take her hands and gently guide her farther into the room. As they seemed to harbor her no ill intent, she cautiously followed through an archway and down several steps into a smaller chamber. The walls of this secluded nook were covered from floor to ceiling with tiles of blue. Woven mats and plump multicolored pillows lay strewn around the edges of the room. Fluted columns supported a latticework overhead. But the most remarkable feature of the alcove was the small sunken pool in the middle.

Boughs of fragrant herbs and flowers were woven into the overhead lattice, and like long supple arms, the blossoming tendrils draped down from above trailing leafy fingertips in the sparkling water. A brazier burned in each corner spewing out exotic and hypnotic aromas.

The scene, tranquil and reassuring, brought an

unusual peacefulness to Leanora. Her eyelids felt heavy, and the drowsiness spilling over her chased away her fears. She did not even resist as the four handmaidens began to undress her.

"First you must bathe," the shortest girl crooned as she untied Leanora's belt. So light was their touch as they stripped her naked, she felt as if she had been delivered into the hands of cherubs.

Now unclothed as well, the four girls escorted her into the pool. The bottom of the steaming pond was carved of smooth wood. Indentations and outcroppings of various dimensions lined the sides. They settled her into one conforming to her size and shape, and in the back of her mind, a nagging thought of danger kept fighting its way to the surface. But she could no longer remember where she was or who might be trying to harm her. How could anything be amiss when she felt so contented?

She reclined, and dreamily watched the young girls as each performed a special task. One added fragrant salts and rose hips to the bath. Another offered her a goblet of wine. Red as wild raspberries, it tasted good but odd, not bitter and not sweet. The third girl washed Leanora's hair with extracts of lavender and balsam. The fourth gently cleansed her body from forehead to toes. They filled her cup with more wine and fed her fruits and sweet cakes. It was all she could do to keep her eyes open.

"Come, lady," they called in unison and urged her to rise. Why were they treating her so royally? She could not recall. She could not think a proper thought.

Drifting over to a padded table, she climbed atop it and stretched out on her back, surrendering once more to the ministrations of the four handmaidens. They dried her hair and untangled it with a jewel-studded comb. Then they massaged and oiled her body, every single inch.

Thick, fragrant lotion was poured across her breasts and stomach, over her shoulders and down her arms. They rubbed it across her thighs and between her legs, and an image of Faran broke through her consciousness. Faran, dear Faran. He had made her feel this way too, all warm and tingly.

Where was he? She wanted him, needed him. The more they touched her the more she craved him. Eyes closed, she saw his light green ones veiled with passion, and she felt his strong hands caressing her willing flesh. An unstoppable pleasure tunneled through her, and she reached out for him, but cold nothingness was all she embraced.

She gasped and opened her eyes, pushing at the hands touching her so intimately. The girls twittered and helped her to sit upright.

With care and attention, they painted her eyes and lips, and dressed her in a flowing white gown girdled in gold. As if in a dream, she stared at her reflection in a mirror of polished metal. She looked like a princess. Would Faran think her beautiful? "Faran..." As she whispered his name, the desire for him spiraled deeper.

"Now you are ready for Lord Gorham," they declared.

Gorham? What were these dear ones carrying on about? She forced herself to concentrate. Gorham? The name sparked an unpleasant feeling. But she could not remember why.

Dread niggled at her, and like a lump of old pease porridge, a knot formed in the pit of her stomach. Her thoughts would not stand still, they swirled about, hinting at logic, then escaping without making sense. "Who is Gorham?" she whispered in confusion.

"Who is Gorham?" They laughed merrily, and led her toward the door. "He is the ruler of all Lothian. And he will not be denied."

Chapter Sixteen

"Stay away," Leanora warned, and aimed another apple at Lord Gorham's head. Fright had counteracted the soporific spell, and now fully awake, she had no intentions of playing the docile sheep led willingly to the king's bed.

Lofting a handful of figs in his direction, she gathered another armful of projectiles off the serving table and sidled toward the door. She had only been in the sovereign's chamber a few moments, but already the wall behind him appeared as if it had been struck by a runaway fruit vendor's cart.

Holding her ground, she sized him up. The saints preserve her, he was positively the tallest man she had ever seen. And dressed in a black robe, and a mantle of fur, he was a towering specter of malevolence.

"The door is locked," he growled impatiently, and ducked to avoid the orange she hurled at him. "There is no escape. Why do you not calm yourself and we can discuss your situation."

"They told me you desired a dancing girl," she railed back at him. "Not a...a..."

"Whore?" He finished the sentence for her. "You may dance if you wish, but your most important consideration will be pleasing me in a more personal way. When, where, and how I desire." His cold calculating gaze was near palpable, and it left her feeling naked and shivering.

Where was Faran? Where was Cynric? She was

furious at having been abandoned to face this royal demon on her own. All men, in all realms, were treacherous swine, and she wished she had never agreed to come here.

White-hot anger guided her aim as she launched another pelting of fruit at the man who ruled this dreadful land. With his huge hands and little effort, he easily deflected the barrage, then he studied her with a piercing gaze that harbored a wolfish quality. The furry covering draped around Gorham's neck and shoulders seemed to bristle, and a menacing laugh erupted from somewhere deep inside of him. He appeared barely human. Flickering candlelight created eerie shadows, and an unholy aura contorted his features into a doglike image, matching his golden eyes. As his haunting howl echoed around the cavernous room, she felt more and more like helpless prey.

Lurid and penetrating, his gaze settled upon her breasts. She glanced down at the gossamer low-cut gown. It hid little from view, and each labored breath she took thrust her womanly attributes forward for his inspection. With a lascivious grin, he advanced one menacing step, then another and another. Her crop of ammunition depleted, she had nothing left to throw at him. Desperate, she darted sideways putting the width of a massive table between them.

Gorham chuckled, and flung the furniture aside as if it were made of kindling. Her eyes widened in alarm, and she backed up against the wall.

"I only wish to gaze upon you," he said in a coaxing voice as he edged closer.

The expanse of his broad shoulders filled her entire field of vision. Then her gaze crept higher until she could see each hair composing the short black beard and mustache guarding his features.

"Once there were flowers here the color of your

eyes," he said, "Are you afraid me?" he asked. What passed for a smile altered his mouth, but his gaze remained hard and mirthless.

Afraid? She was scared spitless, which was why she could neither answer him nor swallow. She pressed harder against the wall to keep from shaking, and her neck cramped with the effort of peering up at him.

His smile contorted into a sneer and his left hand snaked out to grasp the hair at the nape of her neck. "You should be afraid," he warned.

Locked in his grip, her heart beating wildly, Leanora raised her fists to strike him. Deftly, he seized both wrists in his free hand and savagely twisted her hair. "Resistance will be punished tenfold," he threatened. She stopped struggling, knowing it would make little difference. Like all men, in the end he would have what he wanted.

He released her hair, slid his hand around to her throat, and loomed over her. She squeezed her eyes shut tight not daring to move.

"You learn quickly," he said and rubbed his abrasive beard against her cheek. His hot breath was like a cloud of vapors smothering her and panic rose in her chest. Setting free her wrists, he dragged his hand downward to grip the curve of her bottom— roughly caressing and meanly pinching. Eyes now wide open, she whimpered in pain. Gorham groaned with pleasure.

Pinned against the wall, she could not retreat as he rammed up against her, grinding his hips into hers. The gown she wore was so thin, and his robe so light, she could feel the full hard length of him as distinctly as if they were both naked. Now a new dread commanded her attention. This bulging male part of him was as grossly oversized as the rest of his body. This realization conjured frightful images, but as he sank his teeth into her shoulder, the visions were stricken from her mind. Like a wild animal, he bit and sucked at her flesh.

Forsaking his threat of punishment for resistance, Leanora kicked and screamed with all her might. He was mad, and she was going to die.

Without warning, the king shoved her toward the middle of the room. "Dance," he ordered. "Tempt me tonight with your fleshy delights. Whet my appetite for what I will soon taste and devour."

Unable to move, she mutely stared back at him.

"Why are you really here?" he snarled and stalked closer. "The new concubine will not arrive for another fortnight. You are an imposter," he shouted, "and not of this realm."

He had been toying with her, knowing all along she was not the girl he awaited. Leanora was so frightened she thought she might faint, or throw up, possibly both. She gripped the back of a nearby chair with one hand and jammed her other fist against her mouth.

Gorham crossed his arms over his chest, awaiting her answer. Her blood glistened on his mouth. "I like the taste of red-haired women," he said and licked his lips. "Why are you here?" he repeated.

She inhaled deeply through her nose, trying to counteract her lightheadedness. She could not best this man with brawn, and he seemed too demented to accept reason. She must use her wits. What would he least expect her to say?

"I came to plunder your gold and jewels," she declared. "I heard you employed dancing girls and thought it a means of gaining entrance to your stronghold." Standing taller, she perused him with what she hoped was a disdainful glare. "I suppose the treasure is a myth," she scorned knowing a man's pride in his wealth was as precious a target as his pride in what hung between his legs.

He threw back his head and laughed. "There is treasure here you may be sure," he arrogantly boasted, "but instead of stealing it you shall become a part of it. I have never had a red headed beauty at my beck and call. In all of Lothian such coloring is most rare."

His gaze raked her body, its intensity compelling her to take a step backward. "Uncommon objects are meant to be savored fully and frequently," he said, dragging the back of his hand across his mouth. "And I may never get my fill of you."

As Gorham lunged for her, his foot slipped on the smashed fruit littering the floor. She ducked to one side. He sailed past, hitting his head on the leg of the upturned table. With a sickening thud, he collapsed upon the floor—his face as white as the Crookhamshire salt marsh.

She crept closer. Bright red blood seeped from the gash on Gorham's head. It spread freely and mingled with the berry-juice already staining the floor.

Dear Lord, she'd killed the king.

****

By the light of the moon, Faran bathed for a third time. The woodland stream was surprisingly warm, which helped to liberate another layer of black goo from his skin. The devilish substance floated down the creek in a dark swirling ribbon, and dark tormented thoughts twisted through his mind.

What had befallen Leanora? He must get back across the lake. He needed to see her again, hold her in his arms, assure himself no harm had come to her. But the night yielded not one person in the city of Gylfi with enough fortitude to aid him in his cause. Fear of Lord Gorham, and the water surrounding his citadel, shackled the minds of the villagers as surely as the unwholesome Lothian air crippled their bodies.

Scooping up big handfuls of water, he doused his head again and again until his hair rinsed clean and his thoughts ran clear. He had thought to steal a boat, but the few that existed were heavily guarded. He supposed there was no other way for it. He must wait until dawn.

Resigned to such a fate, he gained his feet and scrambled up the low bank on the near side of the creek. Excess water trickled softly across his bare shoulders and down his naked torso. The sensuous feeling invigorated his body, sending images of Leanora arcing through his mind. If anything happened to her, he would skin Cynric alive.

It was an idle threat, and not from the heart, but it made him feel better to aim his frustration at someone other than himself. He paced back and forth in the sparse grass. Then grabbed up his tunic, dried his face with the fabric, and jerked the shirt on over his head. In truth, Leanora's predicament was his fault. Again, he had failed, and now she was in imminent danger.

Breechcloth in place, he stretched out upon the cloak he'd purchased from an old man he'd met wandering along the shore. The light evening breeze dried the remaining moisture on his skin and hair, but as he visualized Leanora's face and womanly form, the chill air seemed to disappear and a wave of heat blazed through him. He burned hotter and grew hard remembering last night. He should not have abandoned the opportunity to make love to her. It would have been a glorious memory to cling to on this lonely night. Yet it had seemed meaningful to her that they had not followed through with their desires. Had it been any other woman, he would have persisted—regardless of the time and place. But Leanora had altered the normal course of his life.

Jaw clenched, he tried to concentrate on something else, it was either that or he must find another stream, one where the water ran cold. Still the image of her was more tenacious than the black water of this lake and he could not purge her from his mind. Dear Gillyflower. Night or day she occupied his thoughts, and not only in a lustful way. Although small and timid, she found the courage to stand up to him, especially when her sense of fair play was threatened. And while she no longer abided by his religion, she helped him find the relics of his people, believing if not in his gods, at least in him. Resourceful without being vainglorious, she had so much potential, limited only by her own horizons.

He couldn't suppress a laugh. For one so sleek and romantic in thought, she was also clumsy as a spring foal. He wondered if she tended to fall down all the time, or only in his presence.

Easing upward onto one elbow, he plucked at the grass. Then he clenched his fist and smashed it into the ground. Maybe he should risk swimming to the island. But what if the *thing* came after him again? Or what if the beast he had encountered was like Grendel, merely the offspring of an even more grisly horror living in those dark depths? Dead, he would be of no use to anyone, least of all Leanora.

He was not sure what to do. His thoughts raged back and forth between logic and rash action, and the line between courage and foolhardiness seemed thin indeed.

Abruptly he stood, jammed his feet into his buskins, and cross-gartered them.

This waiting was a hellish task. It drove one's mind to all manner of foul imaginings. He had to keep moving. Flanked by frustration and wounded pride, he paced beside the stream and begged the dawn to hasten its arrival.

****

Gorham moaned and jerked his right arm. Leanora started and jumped backward. The progeny of Satan still lived. As she watched, a smile twitched on her lips. It had been a refreshing sight to see someone other than herself pitch headfirst to the floor.

At Gorham's second moan, she fully recovered her senses. She must leave swiftly, before he regained consciousness. Shivering with fear and the chill night air, she grabbed a blue embroidered tablecloth from the floor. Wrapped in the fine linen, she studied the room for a means of escape. All of the windows were set high up in the wall. Reaching them would take a feat of daring—and what peril might lie beyond? There must be another way.

Once more, her glance swept the room. The inside of Gorham's castle was as brightly decorated and uplifting as the outside was somber and depressing. It was as if the king had leeched all the color and happiness from the realm and infused it within his keep. She touched the wound on her shoulder. He was a predatory beast. She could almost believe the wretch fed upon the blood of young women as he savaged the domain.

Her gaze fell upon the only door in the room. Gorham had told her repeatedly it was locked, but hoping against hope, she ran to the portal, yanked upon the brass handle, and stumbled backward as the door swung inwards. Another lie in the midst of many.

She rushed down the dark hallway to her right, then recalled this path led to the room with the steaming pool, and as far as she could remember, nothing else. Ruing her knack for wrong choices, she stopped short and retraced her steps, tiptoeing past the door leading to Gorham's chamber. Caution to the wind, she fled along the musty corridor, down a winding staircase, and across an enclosed courtyard.

This was more like it. Surely the door before her would lead to freedom and the safety of the night.

She shoved it open and charged forward.

The hall within was overflowing with boisterous young soldiers, all in various states of dress and disarray. Some ate and drank, some played board games, others talked and joked in small groups. Startled eyes turned in her direction, and a wave of silence washed the room. Then a din of voices erupted.

The nearest man grabbed her, and yanked her down onto his lap. He laughed with glee as he pawed at her breasts and pressed wet kisses to her throat.

Several more soldiers advanced—their hands all reaching in her direction.

"Hold on, lads," one man ordered. It was one of the soldiers who had been on the ferry. "That be the king's new woman."

The guard restraining her reared back and cocked his head to one side. "Then why ain't she with the king?"

Chapter Seventeen

The Lothian excuse for a sunrise was accompanied by dark clouds. They boiled up against a gray sky, a stiff wind at their back.

Faran's heart was as desolate as the landscape, his soul as unsettled, but at least the longest night of his life was finally over.

Being torn from Leanora's side for just one evening had been an experience he did not wish to suffer again. It left him feeling more forlorn then when he had departed his home to begin this quest.

As the overloaded supply barge upon which he rode lumbered across Black Rain Lake, he peered into the dismal water and touched the runes on the amulet he wore. Did the sea demon of yesterday now sleep in its lair? Deadly strength and cold indifference had surrounded that creature, and the memory of the hideous beast had won a high ranking in his inventory of nightmares.

Seeing no signs of the dreaded fish, he willed himself to relax, but his calm was short lived as forked lightning split the sky and thunder tore through the air. Far behind them, sheets of rain pelted down, and the city of Gylfi became a fuzzy blur. The squall headed in their direction, and he doubted the ferry would make land on Gorham's island before the downpour caught up with them.

Drawing ever closer, the deluge touched the edge of the lake, and the rain turned black, creating a dark veil closing out the world behind it. He rubbed his eyes in disbelief and peered again at the unnatural sight. Now the downpour was directly overhead. The ferry scraped to a halt on the isle, and he leaped ashore and sought shelter beneath a buttress.

The black rain drenched everything in its path, depositing another layer of darkness upon all it touched. Like watery soot thrown from an unseen hand, it spattered against the castle walls—their original hue of white now long forgotten. Dripping down the sides of the citadel, the foul water soaked into the dingy soil, and soon, sluggish ebon rivulets ran along the cobbled walkway beneath his feet.

The tempest moved on, crossing once again beyond the boundary of the lake, and he watched transfixed as the black rain transformed back to crystal clear. He shuddered. The curse upon this entire county was most peculiar, but here upon the island it was even more sinister. Something unholy prowled unfettered here, something that should be stopped.

"You there, get to work," the bargeman ordered. "Ain't you never seen rain before?"

Faran nodded obediently and began unloading cargo. The man overseeing the barge was a surly brute, and not wishing to garner undue attention, Faran put his back to it. Traveling on the supply raft had been his only alternative to the passenger ferry where surely he would have been recognized. As the man turned away to engage in conversation, Faran sneaked off in the direction of the castle kitchens.

Around the back of the building, he found Cynric sitting dejectedly upon an unused baking kiln.

"Where is Leanora?" he demanded, startling the bard to his feet.

Cynric spun around, his right hand upon the hilt of his dagger. "God's teeth, you scared a year's life from me."

"The girl, where is she?" Faran repeated.

"I am sorry," Cynric admitted, "but I have not seen her since our arrival yesterday. And there is a rumor ripe this morning that the king's russet-haired mistress tried to kill him last night. Do you think they speak of Leanora?"

"Without doubt," Faran groaned. Anger and frustration again rode him a dark race. "What exactly did you hear?"

"Only that she was taken to the king's chamber last evening and escaped soon after, leaving Lord Gorham with a head wound keeping him abed the rest of the night." Cynric hung his head. "We were separated as we came ashore. I could not help her."

"That is of no consequence now," Faran said. "Where is she being held?"

"I am not sure. I searched all night in near every part of the castle, but I found not a trace of her."

Faran noticed the livid bruise on the man's drawn face and the dark circles beneath his eyes. He thought Cynric's efforts to locate Leanora had been genuine enough, but he had obviously overlooked something.

"Think, man," Faran ordered. "She has to be here somewhere."

"There are only three places I have not tried—the treasury, the old dungeon, and Gorham's bed."

Gorham's bed...Every muscle in Faran's body tensed, and he took a menacing step forward. Blind rage obscured reason as he thought of Leanora at the king's mercy. His Gillyflower beneath the rutting loins of the mad monarch.

He gritted his teeth to stifle an angry retort, reminding himself it was not Cynric's fault she was in danger. "If Leanora tried to kill the king last night," he reasoned, "I doubt she is still between his blankets this morning. Where is the old dungeon?"

"Across the bailey, to the north." Cynric pointed out the direction to take. "But it is not in use these days."

"For Leanora, they may have revived old customs."

Cynric made ready to join Faran, then the scop hesitated and glanced over his shoulder at the kitchens.

"Where is your woman?" Faran asked.

"I saw Kayden only briefly," Cynric answered, his tone downhearted. "But by nightfall, no matter what, she leaves the island along with all who choose to do so."

Faran studied the bard's forlorn expression. Did his own appear as hopeless and female smitten. "How is it a mere woman can so easily reduce a full-grown man to the image of an abandoned child?" he asked.

"A female can inspire a man to his best achievements or his worst," Cynric pointed out.

"Aye," Faran agreed. "Stay and wait for Kayden," he advised. Relief washed over the scop's face. "I will find Leanora. And if we are not at the boats when it is time to leave, you are to go without us."

Faran raised a hand, silencing Cynric's protest, then he gripped the slighter man's shoulder in a brotherly manner. "You have long awaited this battle for freedom," he said. "If you and the rebels are to liberate Gylfi and County Lothian, you must keep to your plan or tempt the Fates to failure. Neither I nor Leanora would wish to cause your defeat."

Cynric wavered only a moment. "We will leave as arranged," he agreed, "and wait as long as possible before draining the lake."

Faran knew this last concession meant possible jeopardy to their strategy. The rebels could only hold off Gorham's army for a short while, and they dare not miss their window of opportunity as far as setting free the Mistress of Black Rain Lake.

"You do not owe me this," Faran said, "I have not aided your cause in any manner."

"Oh, but you have," Cynric said. "With the king's watchful eye turned upon you and Leanora, my task here will be more easily accomplished. Because of you, Gorham's forces will be divided."

"Then I thank you, friend, and we are in your debt."

"You must succeed," the bard said with the grin of a conspirator. "I have already begun an ode extolling your exploits of daring, and my ballads always have happy endings."

Faran shook his head, feeling far from worthy of being the main character in any tale of adventure. "Keep safe," he said in parting, "and may the Fates find favor with you."

He slipped off toward the old dungeon, hugging close to the mossy stone embankment. Carved from solid rock, the daunting stronghold elicited a feeling of death and doom. At the north wall, a piercing wind sprung to life, and reaching the ponderous wood and iron gates, he gratefully accepted the concealment and shelter.

One door was partially open. He leaned forward to listen, but not a sound did he hear. What he smelled, however, was another matter. He had not thought the air in Lothian could get worse, but he had been wrong. The odor assailing his nostrils was more foul than a bag of dead salamanders.

His eyes burned, and he was afraid to swallow. As he peered harder into the dim passageway, he half expected to see the stench wafting upon the breeze. Loosening the fibula holding his mantle in place, he rearranged the fabric to cover his head and the lower half of his face. Protected by the cloth, he breathed easier and re-pinned the fold of garment into place.

Taking as deep a breath as he dare, he entered the stronghold. The dank chamber did indeed appear deserted, but he must be sure.

The walls were layered with filth and pestilence, and a crawling sensation prickled across his shoulders. Still he advanced into the gloom. The first barred cell housed a pile of moldy straw that seemed to shimmer and waver. He strained forward, his cloth-covered cheeks almost touching the bars through which he peered.

Woden take him, the mound *did* move—with the rats and vermin crawling upon it. But the decomposed body manacled to the wall beside the squirming heap remained motionless. Pressing the mantle closer to his nose and mouth, he gazed intently at what was left of the man in chains. The face of the dead prisoner was frozen forever in a moment of terror, and like a silent scream, a mouse ran out of his open mouth.

"Poor bastard." Warrior or not, guilty or not, each man had the right to die fighting. It was not befitting for even a king to so strip a man of his pride and honor.

He turned away from the sightless, gaping black sockets, and swatting his way through the veil of cobwebs, he advanced deeper into the belly of this beast-like cavern.

Here and there, shafts of dull light forced their way through the cracks in the ceiling. It helped to dispel the darkness and reveal the remains of yet more victims, each one locked away in forgotten agony. Most were contorted in the throes of a torturous death, and the fire of hatred he felt for Gorham burned ever hotter, each corpse a fresh log laid upon the pyre.

The passageway began to slope downward, and

soon the earth beneath his feet became sodden. He heard the sound of water lapping against stone. Now he was up to his ankles in something cold and wet.

So that was why these dungeons had been abandoned. The lake had laid claim to the catacombs, leaving only the dead to dwell in the watery depths.

As if to prove him a liar, a very lively smacking noise and a loud splash echoed out of the darkness. Did the creature of the lake call this home as well? Yesterday, he had escaped the monster by the whim of the gods. He did not wish to test their humor two days running.

Extracting his feet from the sucking mud, he quickly retraced his steps. The feeling something followed in his wake set him near to running, but as he lurched though the main portal and spun around, he found the passageway was empty. There was nothing there but his imagination.

With a shiver, he jerked the mantle back from his head and face and gulped in the miserable air. After the dungeon, it felt almost refreshing. What a comfort to know Leanora was not held prisoner in such a terrible place. But that meant he must breach the heart of Gorham's stronghold and search for her there. A feat easier said than done. The castle lay on the other side of the bailey, and the wide-open expanse loomed before him like the great plains of Hexham.

Wishing there were shadows to conceal his movements, he bent low, keeping to the profile of the outer wall. Time was running out. He must quickly find Leanora and the relics. And they must make good their escape before Romaine arrived to join forces with her brother. No doubt, the royal harlot drew ever closer, and crossing paths again with the Queen of the May was bound to end poorly.

Gaining the western edge of the citadel, he

halted and pressed up against the cold stones. A few paces ahead stood a side entrance to the castle. Voices warned the chamber beyond was occupied. Slipping silently past the entryway, he sought cover in an alcove. A nearby shelf held throwing axes, and the cloaks hanging from the pegs bore the insignia of Gorham. He inched closer and listened to the guards.

"They say she hit him with a battle ax," one man reported.

"I heard she wielded the drinking horn of an enoch," put in another.

"All I know," a third added, "the king has never been so angry. Had she not rendered him unconscious, I believe Gorham would have slain her on the spot."

At their words, Faran's stomach twisted into a knot, then a sharper pain sliced into his right side. He jerked a glance over his shoulder and caught the silhouette of the soldier holding the other end of the spear piercing his flesh. Damn. He raised his hands in a show of surrender. It was still early morning and already his plans were undone. Who would have dreamed adventuring would be this difficult.

Chapter Eighteen

Leanora groaned and struggled to sit upright. Having spent the night on a pallet made of rubies, emeralds, and diamonds, sleep had been an elusive companion. And while it might sound delightful to use a golden coffer as one's pillow, it was most uncomfortable.

Last evening, when Gorham had momentarily reclaimed consciousness, he had ordered her locked away with the rest of his treasure. Now solid bars, as thick as her wrist, encased the doors and windows of the chamber she occupied. In the face of the king's unbridled anger, she was grateful just to be alive.

A crazed expression had enlivened the royal demon's dazed features as he condemned her to the repository. And by his proclamation, she was to remain here until such time as he could again see straight and think clearly enough to personally break her willful spirit. Apparently wealth did not temper a man's cruelty.

To Lord Gorham, she was just another object to be neatly stowed away in a dark chamber, called for when needed and ignored or beaten the rest of the time. So here she sat with the king's other trinkets. His gold, his jewels, his—swords and shields.

Last night, tired and frightened, she had not noticed the armory of stolen weapons. There were hundreds of swords and shields housed here. They hung upon the walls and spilled from open crates. Some lay piled haphazardly in the corners. She scrambled to her feet and wended her way around the trunks and coffers. Surely Faran's relics were here as well. But which ones could they be? If only she had paid more attention to his description of the heirlooms.

Climbing over an obstinate assemblage of chalices and ornate serving trays, she perused the weapons more closely. They all appeared deadly and cumbersome. The ones in the back were far too dusty and tarnished to have been freshly acquired. And the pile of swords to the left all possessed curved blades—those too could be excluded. Faran had said the blade he sought was straight and true.

She lifted and tugged and ferreted through the mound of armaments dragging the most likely prospects to the center of the room. Then dropping to her knees, she scrutinized them carefully hoping to uncover some marking or inscription indicating they were the sword and shield of Beowulf.

Nothing was revealed to her, and in frustration, she rose and paced about the room. Her mindless wandering led her toward a marble bust sitting on the floor. She paused before the work of art and bent to see if she might recognize the rendering. It was Charlemagne, King of the Franks. She had once seen his image upon a gold coin. With a sigh, she turned around and sat on his head.

"You may have a brilliant mind," she said, wiggling upon him in annoyance, "but the rendering of your skull is near insufferable."

In apt dejection, she sat and listened to her stomach issue a remarkably loud complaint. She was near starved, making it difficult to concentrate, and wistfully she recalled the sweet juicy fruit she had hurled at Gorham. As she snuggle her blue tablecloth-cloak a bit closer, hot bitter tears welled in her eyes, and hot bitter thoughts sprung up in the back of her mind. *Where are you Faran,* she lamented? Was he safe? Would he come for her?

During their night at the Gylfi Inn, a special feeling had taken root in her soul, a feeling even deeper than friendship and trust, something she could not name. But the gossamer tether connecting her to Faran was fragile. What if during their separation, it dissolved away to nothing? She should have encouraged his lovemaking. It would have made the bond stronger. Next time—if there were a next time—she would not hesitate. Then one uplifting thought occurred to her. No doubt he would come for the sword and shield.

She glanced absently about the chamber, her gaze coming to rest upon two fur-swaddled articles lying atop a marble dais. Something about how they were stored separately and carefully snagged her attention. Without even seeing them, she knew these were the relics Faran sought.

Hurrying to the parcels, she unwrapped the shield. The craftsmanship was remarkable. Truly, it was no ordinary piece of work. The split-wood and leather buckler was reinforced with a brilliant layer of tinned brass. Silver- and bronze-work emblazoned the center and the image of wild boars, tempered in gold, encircled the edge. As she studied the rendering, Faran's words echoed in her mind. *The shield honors the dwelling of Woden and it is ringed by the symbol of the Geats.* Shimmering with regal beauty, it was even more splendid than she had imagined. Truly the spirit of the Storm Geats was embodied here.

She placed her hand in the center of the shield. The boss felt warm, and an odd sensation pulsed and radiated beneath her fingertips, hinting at a power she did not understand.

Reaching for the second bundle, she bared the sword. The weapon was glorious, a spectacle equal in beauty and strength to the shield. Intricate designs and inscriptions complimented the overall simplicity of the form. The grip was wrapped in wires of gold, the guard and pommel were of solid silver. Above the quillon, the boar's head symbol appeared again beside the mark of Weland.

She grasped the sword, raised it high, and swung the shining steel from side to side. The blade sang through the air. She felt daring and invincible, and for the first time in her life, she feared nothing. No wonder Gorham coveted such a weapon, and no wonder Faran sought to restore it to his people.

Bolstered by the mystical power of the armaments, she hauled the weapon and shield to the barred entryway and sought a means of escape. Built as a treasury, the chamber was designed to keep people out rather than in. This could aid her cause.

Raising high Beowulf's sword, she prepared to attack the hinges of the gate. Then she hesitated. With her luck she would shatter the blade or chink the steel. Faran would never forgive such irreverent use of his prized possession. Setting the weapon beside the buckler, she retrieved a common blade from a nearby pile. Using a levering action and repeated assault, she managed to disengage the top hinge from the wall.

Following her brief skirmish, pain radiated down her arm. Dropping the cumbersome blade, she massaged the muscles of her right shoulder, flexed life back into her fingers, and wondered how a warrior endured a lengthy battle with such weapons.

She was about to further the attack, when the face of a guard appeared on the other side of the barrier. She yelped in surprise. He eyed her suspiciously. She stepped back, struck what she hoped was an innocent pose, and forced her gaze away from the broken hinge dangling beside the man's head just at eyelevel. If he turned but a hair's breadth he would see it.

"I hope you have come to release me," she demanded, trying to distract him. "I am a mass of bruises from your rough treatment and from sleeping in this inhospitable room. There is not one item in here that offered succor to my tender flesh."

Raising the hem of her skirt, she pretended to examine her ankles and calves for grievous injury. The guard fumbled with the ring of keys tied at his waist, his besotted stare fixed upon her legs.

"I just come to bring ya some food and a slop bucket," he said distractedly. She raised the hem an inch higher. Transfixed, he gaped at her like a freshly landed whitefish.

Now what? She had his full attention and no idea what to do with it. He was sure to notice the damaged ironwork as soon as he tried to open the door.

She released her skirts in a huff. "How dare you look upon me thus," she accused, feigning surprise and horror at his gawking. Affecting outrageous indignation, she brandished a weapon and rushed toward the door. "Stay away from me," she screeched and poked the tip of the blade through the bars. "Leave what you have brought and go. I am the king's treasure. You should not even dare to look upon me. I am for his eyes only."

With her free hand she grabbed up a handful of coins, twirled about, and tossed them into the air.

"I am quicker than his silver,
And more brilliant than his gold.
And if you'd like to keep your head,
You will do as you are told."

Following her recital, she added her best imitation of insane laughter.

The man dropped the bucket and tray, never touching the gate. "You be maddish as a sea-witch," he declared and turned to flee.

"And pray do not forget it," she called after him.

Proud beyond belief for having scared away the guard, she congratulated herself for a grand performance of bravery and blatant trickery. How curious—the more oddly she behaved, the more seriously people took her. It would seem she had been doing it wrong all these years, always hiding somewhere safe, never daring to complain or defend herself, never thinking her feelings counted for anything. This approach to life was much more satisfying, and none the more frightening.

Enthusiasm renewed, she hacked away at the lower hinge. The impact of each blow radiated up her arm, but she reveled in the pain, its cause and purpose was by her choice, not another's.

The metal gave way, and she shoved open the gate. Ravenous, she dropped to her knees and crawled about to retrieve the scattered bread and cheese. Brushing off the dirt, she carefully nibbled around the moldy bits. Her mouth was so dry she could barely swallow, but she forced herself to gag down the miserable rations.

The meager fare consumed, she rocked back on her haunches to gather her thoughts and strength. Then she scrambled to her feet. Draping the blue tablecloth around the shield, she knotted the tails of the fabric together and slung the awkward bundle over her shoulder. At first, she swayed beneath its weight, then as it settled firmly against her back, she retrieved the massive sword and struggled down the passageway. Dragging the burdensome relics through the castle was like fleeing with a millstone in tow, yet she could not leave them here.

The shield dug into her back, and laboring under its weight, she felt as if she grew shorter with each step taken. With steadfast determination, she shuffled onward, pleased with her progress until the passageway intersected with another. Which direction should she follow?

Discouraged, eyes downcast, she noticed a trail of red dots on the cobblestones. The spots glistened like a handful of rubies cast haphazardly upon the ground. She bent closer for a better look and grimaced. It was blood, bright and freshly spilled. It led off to the right.

She struck out in the opposite direction, then hesitated and glanced back. *Run-and-save-yourself,* logic screamed in the back of her mind. *To help those in need is the way of the Lord,* echoed the words taught to her by Thomas the monk.

Why should she care about someone else's troubles? She had enough of her own. Besides the person was probably already dead, and she might get caught, and no one had bothered to rescue her, and what if it were blood from a wounded animal, or maybe a hideous beast had dragged an injured person in that direction. The vision of a wolf with glowing yellow eyes and slavering jaws howled through her mind, and she touched the wound on her neck caused by Gorham's bite. Some ungodly creature could be lying in wait. She did not care to be its next victim.

As she prepared to move on, the seedling of courage, so recently sprouted in her soul, fought to take deeper root. It gave no peace of mind nor quarter to cowardice. What if it were Cynric? She had yet to see him since their arrival. What if they had discovered he'd helped her to gain passage to the island?

She gritted her teeth and tightened her grip on the sword. A ripple of strength, mystical in nature, tingled and spiraled straight to the core of her being. Still doubting the wisdom of her decision, she retraced her steps, and crept down the more ominous passageway.

Rodents scurried from her path, their tiny claws

making scratchy noises, their high-pitched squeaks grating on her nerves. Up ahead, a smoky wall torch cast a hazy glow upon the walls. As she stepped into the flickering pool of light, she found more blood on the rough stone floor. Much more. Her stomach quelled. She skirted around the sanguine puddle, and her hopes of finding the injured person alive began to waver.

The next torchlight burned low, and the way up ahead grew dim. With caution and trepidation, she edged forward until something horrible brushed across her face. It clung to her nose and mouth trying to smother her. Recovering her wits she brandished the sword, viciously battling her ethereal attacker.

The gossamer tendrils of a huge cobweb tore loose from the ceiling, and like a shriveled piece of wool yarn, it hung limp from the tip of her blade. Sobbing with relief, she shook it loose and swallowed the slice of fright still lodged in her throat.

She was all right—she was doing just fine. Being brave was new to her, that was all. Fate, or Wyrd, was said to often save an undoomed hero as long as his courage was good and true. Could the choices made and the paths followed bend or change Wyrd? It was a concept she was only beginning to appreciate.

The passageway narrowed, hooked around a sharp corner, and then abruptly ended in a wall fitted with two doors. The one on the left opened easily, leading to yet another corridor. The oaken panel on the right was locked tight. Blood sparkled near the door's threshold. Setting the sword and shield aside, she eased open the viewing port, horrified by the sight revealed.

A rack dominated the center of the room, and close at hand, a table held an array of whips, knives, and other alarming implements. On the hearth, the tips of several pokers nestled grimly in red-hot coals. Manacles and chains broke the monotony of the bare walls, and a dais with seating to accommodate several people completed the gruesome furnishings. Everything appeared unusually clean and well oiled, all ready for immediate and dreadful use.

A movement caught her attention and she peered harder into the far reaches of the chamber. It was a man, strapped upright in a chair-like apparatus. His head was turned away, and although she could not make out his face, she saw the deadly spikes lining the sides of the chair. Nearby, sand trickled from a bag suspended above a bucket. Each time the bucket gained enough weight, it acted as a counterbalance to a ratchet, moving the wheel to the next notch, drawing the sides of the grisly contraption closer and closer.

The wheel clacked, the chair moved, the man cried out.

She bowed her head and closed her eyes, but the sound lived on in her mind. Steeling her nerves, she peeked once more into the room. As if aware of her presence, the prisoner turned his face in her direction.

Chapter Nineteen

"Faran..."

Borne on the wings of disbelief, his whispered name passed her lips. "Faran," she called out more loudly, "can you hear me?" An unintelligible groan was his only reply.

She clawed at the door separating her from the only man she had ever loved, for now she truly did know she loved him with all her heart. Reinforced with bands of iron, the thick panels of oak would not easily be breached.

"Oh, Faran," she sobbed. His head drooped forward, and he no longer responded to her voice.

She closed the viewing window, slid her hands from the rough wood, and glanced around. How was she to reach him? Should she leave him alone to seek help? No, that would never do, besides she could not run about the castle willy-nilly hoping to find Cynric or someone else sympathetic to her cause. The prudent choice would be to hold her position. They had brought her food, would they not feed Faran as well?

Hope replaced wishful thinking as someone came her way. The sound of the person's steps were muffled, but the tinkling of keys rang out more musically than chapel bells.

Seeking a corner, she scrunched down on the ground, and not bothering to uncover the shield, positioned herself behind it. Dampness added to the chill of anticipation already crawling upon her skin, and the weight of the shield forced her back against the jagged rocks in the wall.

As the person drew nearer, she shuffled around to be sure to attract their attention. They took the bait and stood so close she could see a man's leather-clad toes straddling the curve of the shield. His clothes rustled as he leaned toward the buckler. She tensed every muscle of her being, and with the flat of her feet against the inside of the shield, she kicked upward, launching the heavy disk squarely and soundly at the sentinel. The impact felt as if it jammed her ankles up to her knees. The sentry crumpled to the floor.

She rolled to the side, gained her feet, and stood ready to fight. The man's face was bloody—his form unmoving. It was the same guard who had come to the treasury earlier, but now his nose and jaw canted weirdly to one side.

Averting her gaze from his face, she gingerly untied the iron ring from a loop on his leather belt. There were five keys from which to choose but only one was large enough to accommodate the dungeon lock. She ran to the portal. The key slipped into place and turned smooth as silk.

Shoving open the door, she stared longingly at Faran. Then she glanced back at the relics and the indisposed guard. It would not do to just leave them lying about the passageway.

The man was impossible to drag so she rolled him over and over across the hall and into the room. Glancing back, she grimaced. A series of red splotches marked a trail behind her. Each time the guard had rotated full circle, his bloody face had left a telltale imprint on the stones. How could she have done that to another human being? She balled her hands into fists. She had done it for Faran—and she had done it for herself.

She lugged the relics inside, shut the door, and

hurried to Faran's side. Thank the Lord his eyes were open. With a dazed expression, he tried to focus on her face.

Frantically, she wrestled with the leather ties binding his wrists and ankles. Before she could loosen even one binding, the wheel on the contraption turned another notch, forcing a cry from his lips. Her heart quelled.

Afraid to wield the sword lest she injury him, she grabbed a sharp implement from a nearby table and slashed the cord holding the counterweight. It crashed to the floor, spewing sand upon impact, rendering the deadly ratchet immobile. Four more quick strokes severed the bindings, setting Faran free. He grimaced and inhaled sharply as she eased the sides of the chair apart.

Weakly, he smiled up at her. "I've come to save you, Gillyflower," he mumbled, trying to rise.

"Thank you," she said, not knowing whether to laugh or cry. Right now, he appeared too weak to rescue a fly from a cup of broth. "I never doubted you," she added with a slight pang of guilt. Her faith in him had wavered once or twice, but in the future it would not.

Although bruised and pricked in myriad places, none of his wounds seemed severe. He would recover quickly if she could deliver him to safety and clean the superficial cuts. She stepped to the side to assist him to rise, and misgivings colored her hasty assessment. A cloth tied to his lower back was dark red and moist. "You are injured worse than I thought," she said as she touched the stained bandage.

"My cooperation was hard won," he proclaimed, not without pride.

A band of queasiness tightened around her stomach as she recalled the crimson path she had followed all the way to this chamber. It had been painted with Faran's blood.

"I am surprised they tended to you at all," she said. "Compassion does not abound here."

"They only staunched the gash to keep me alive," Faran explained. "A dead prisoner offers little amusement."

"Can you stand?" she asked, not allowing herself to dwell upon the fact he might have bled to death.

Faran nodded and struggled to his feet, and settling one arm across her shoulder, they staggered toward the door. "I see you met the guard," he noted as they stumbled past the man's inert form. "Did he do something to displease you?" he added with a chuckle that turned into a wracking cough.

"Yes," she answered, "he hurt you."

They halted so Faran could catch his breath and as he stared at her, a gentleness softened his features. It warmed his eyes and smoothed away the lines of pain furrowing his brow. He tightened his arm around her shoulder and cupped her chin with his other hand. Drawing her near, he kissed her. It was not a reckless passionate kiss, but a delicate declaration of caring—fragile and elusive like her feelings for him.

She reached to cradle him closer, but he reeled unsteadily and she led him to the door and leaned him up against the oaken panel. He appeared much too wan.

Hoping the sight of the relics might renew his vigor, she pointed to them. "I have a surprise for you," she said. To her alarm, he grew all the more pale. His eyes were wide with wonder as he gazed from the heirlooms to her.

"How in the name of all that is sacred did you liberate the sword and shield?"

"I did not seek the honor," she said, "it was bestowed upon me. We shared residence in Gorham's treasury."

Faran's cheeks grew ruddy, and he refused to look at her. Was he not pleased? She had expected her accomplishment to bring him joy, or at least relief.

"What is wrong?"

"By the Fates," he swore. "You have accomplished what four men could not. Three died in the trying and the fourth stands before you humbled and in your debt. I have been bested by a female, and the crucified Savior who watches over her."

"Who cares if it be by my God's grace or Destiny's design? The relics are restored to you. Is that not enough?"

"Being repeatedly rescued by a mere girl is wearing upon my nerves," Faran muttered.

She bristled at his remark, but at his mournful expression, she realized it was pride talking and not his heart.

"We are partners, remember? We look out for one another."

"Yes," he said softly, "partners to the end."

He closed his eyes and slumped back against the doorframe. Forcing her thoughts to their current situation, she crouched down beside the guard and labored to pull the man's tunic over his head.

"Here," she said, gaining her feet. Faran's eyes fluttered open. "You need clothes," she pointed out and helped to tug the too-small piece of clothing over his head and broad shoulders. As her hands glided across his hard muscled chest, her fingers brushed against his amulet. His arm rings were missing, but somehow his iron heart remained unscathed.

She glanced down at the guard. "I do not think his braies worthy of stealing," she added, wrinkling her nose at the prospect.

Faran's expression appeared more lucid now. "My breechcloth will suffice," he said, "and thankfully they left me my footwear. All that truly matters," he added, "is that you are safe and the relics are recovered."

He had mentioned her first before the heirlooms. That was a step in the right direction.

"I will carry the shield, if you can manage the sword," she said and pressed the weapon into his hands.

He grasped the hilt lovingly, admiring the blade, touching it, and petting it as if it were alive.

She envied the cold hard steel he so cherished and the heat of a blush burned her cheeks. She had never felt such passion and need for anyone. In the past, she had not been successful at stopping her husband from using her body or abusing her spirit, but she had never allowed anyone to break her heart—nor would she—not even Faran. Her heart was ironclad too, protected by the forged metal of self-preservation.

Frustrated by the jumble of feelings tearing through her, she grabbed up the shield still cozened in blue linen, and yanked open the door.

The tunnel was deserted. When she hesitated, unsure which way to proceed, Faran took her hand and the lead. It was tiresome sport sneaking down dark passageways and hiding in the shadowless gloom of Lothian. What she would not give to walk tall in a sun-filled meadow or in a vale full of brightly colored wildflowers.

As they turned a corner, a feeling of familiarity grabbed her attention. They were on the main floor of the castle. She had passed this way while in the cruel grip of the hideous matron who had accosted her when first she had arrived on the island.

"Faran," she whispered, "the butlery is to the right and the main gate lies beyond."

He nodded, turning to follow the direction indicated. As they passed through the storeroom, he grabbed a loaf of bread and a flagon of wine. Then the sound of voices halted their progress and they flattened their backs against the wall.

After a moment, Faran dared to peek through the open doorway, she peered around his shoulder. The main gate was open. And within a few steps of their hiding place, a supply wagon and a team of horses waited in attendance. As the last of the wine butts were unloaded, the driver crawled up onto the seat making ready to depart.

Without preamble, Faran hurried forward, urging her to do the same. She crouched low, her gaze upon the ground as they sneaked between the castle wall and the moving wagon.

Protected from the guards' view on the far side, they escaped through the main portal, and when the wagon bore left toward the docks, they slipped off to the right—bolting into the cover of the gorse and brush bordering the lane. Keeping to the shelter of the forest they trudged overland and headed toward the western shore of the island.

Finally, at her insistence, they halted so she might check Faran's injury. "Why do we head to this side of the island?" she asked, gingerly peeling away the dirty bandage to examine the wound.

"We are to meet Cynric there," he explained and grimaced as she palpated the site. "And when our absence is discovered, Gorham will most likely assume we keep to the south in hopes of securing a ferry back to the city."

"You have seen Cynric? He is unharmed?"

"He fares well. And leaves before dusk with all who wish to follow."

"And we are to go with him?" she asked hopefully.

"Yes. He promised they would wait as long as possible, but they must be away before evening falls."

She gave a worried glance at the sky and

wondered if they could reach their friend in time.

Faran tugged his tunic into place.

"The length of the gash is not worrisome," she reported, "and it does not appear angry. Still it must have been deep to have bled so freely. Open to the air, it should heal well," she reassured, "but you are pale. You should rest."

"In this dismal clime, it's hard not to be pale," he joked.

She took a stubborn stance, hands upon her hips.

With obvious effort, he set his body into motion. "We must keep on the move if we are to reach Cynric in time."

Resigned to the truth, she nodded and retrieved the shield. Yet as quickly as they traveled, it was past eventide when they reached the far shore. Exhausted, Leanora set the shield aside and sagged to the ground beneath a hawthorne tree. Faran placed the sword beside the shield and prowled along the shoreline, gazing intently at the ground. Finally he halted and stood staring out across the water.

Returning to her side, he collapsed at her feet. Again near to starving, she tore off two chunks of bread, handed him one and ate the other. In silence they washed down the meager fare with the wine. Aided by her fatigue, the tangy brew soon made her giddy.

"Where are Cynric and the others," she asked glancing around. "Have we arrived before them?"

"No. We have missed them," Faran casually announced. "I'm glad they are safely away. But it leaves little recourse for the two of us."

The seriousness of their situation had yet to sink in. And growing ever more woozy with wine, she hiccoughed and giggled. "We could swim to Gylfi," she sputtered.

"My thoughts exactly," Faran replied. There was no mirth in his voice, and his gaze was deadly serious.

Leanora extended her hand as if to ward off an evil spirit. "Oh no," she said, "that idea is out of the question."

"It is the only way," he countered.

"It is impossible. You must save yourself, go on without me."

Faran crawled closer. "I will not. What bids you say such a thing?"

She clutched her hands together until her knuckles turned white. "I cannot swim," she admitted.

He stared at her in wonder. "You sailed alone into the North Sea, and sought to live on an island, yet you cannot swim?"

She nodded.

He shook his head. "When we crossed the river, I thought it was only the swiftness of the water that frightened you. You go beyond sound reasoning," he chided and gathered her against his chest.

"I am safe in the boat," she tried to justify. "Then I do not feel the silken hands of the water sliding around me to bear me to my doom."

She gazed at Faran, worried he would think her fears childish. Thankfully, his expression was merely thoughtful. But his caring might change to condemnation when he heard the worst part of her secret? She reached for the skin of wine and took another healthy pull. "Sometimes, near the water," she whispered, "I can still hear him call my name."

"What do you mean?" he asked. "Who calls to you?"

"My husband," she said, clinging to him. "He thought to drown me, you see." Her voice sounded far away, even to her own ears.

"Why would he do such a monstrous thing?"

217

"I was not a good and proper wife."

This time it was Faran who raised the wine skin and swallowed deep. "Go on," he urged, "tell me all."

"Father married me off as a peace-weaver," she explained, "to the man who ruled the neighboring tribe. Our two villages became as one, and much honor and bounty was afforded my new husband. But he was cruel—in ways only a husband can be. Once I tried to run away. But that only earned him unspeakable shame and me the whip."

"That is how you came by the marks upon your back?"

She stiffened in his arms—he knew of her disfigurement.

"I saw them the first morning on your island," he confirmed. "You thought me still asleep, but I watched as you went about your morning ritual."

She winced at the memory of the pain she had endured. "The scars on my mind are even more ugly."

"Nothing about you is ugly." Faran tightened his embrace. "You must never think such a thing."

The compassion in his voice and the warmth of his body gave her encouragement, and like the raging water she so feared, the remainder of her story poured from her lips. "I became a burden to him," she began again, "and although he could not undo the vows already spoken, if I died he would retain all he had gained without me to aggravate his hearth and home.

"He took me to the woods. 'A pleasant outing' he said. I thought he meant to try and mend his ways and start over. We stood on the bank of the river, and following a week of rainy weather, it flowed deep and swift. He grabbed me by the shoulders. 'You will promise to obey me in the future,' he demanded, shaking me until my teeth rattled, 'or I shall drown you like an unwanted pup.'

"I remained silent and glared back at him, thinking he only meant to frighten me into submission. Then he smiled ever so slightly, bid me farewell, and shoved me into the water. I screamed for help but he just laughed. 'It will all be over in a moment,' he said and waved good-bye. The freezing water wrapped around me filling my nose and mouth. It numbed me in body and spirit until I gave in to its cold promise of oblivion. I was happy to be released from what life had become for me."

Faran held his silence, but she thought she heard a roar of rage echoing in his chest.

"My skirt caught upon a tree root growing out of the bank. I clung there with frozen hands and a pounding heart, praying he would not see me. But he had the vision of a hawk, and he ran downstream along the bank, shaking his fist at me and shouting how even in dying I was obstinate."

Overwhelmed by the memory, she buried her head against Faran's shoulder.

He handed her the wine. "Go on," he whispered in her ear.

She gulped down another swallow of courage, knowing she could not stop now even if she wanted to, because as she tore the horrible picture apart in her mind, an aura of calm began to surround her. It was as if giving voice to the gruesome event relieved her of its burden and control. Gazing into Faran's eyes, she dared to finish her story.

"My husband leaned out over the water and kicked at me with his booted foot, but the limb he grasped broke, and he fell in. Fright renewed my strength, and I scrambled up the bank to safety. But he was caught in the current, momentarily saved by a smooth tan boulder jutting up from the roiling water. Eventually, his grip failed, and he cursed me with his dying breath. All that remained was his wet handprint upon the stone, and in the heat of the noonday sun, the mark shrank away to nothing. It disappeared forever and so did my husband." She stopped speaking, but the vision remained vivid in her mind.

"Leanora...Leanora..."

Did he still call her name? She trembled at the thought. But that was not her husband's voice. She fought the haunting recollections, willing them away, and Faran's handsome face came back into focus to comfort her heart and soothe her soul.

He remained silent, but the muscles in his cheek twitched as he clenched his jaw. "You're safe now," he crooned

"But you do not understand." She sniffed. "He could not swim either. I just let him die. I did not try to help him."

"But he thought to kill you." Disbelief edged Faran's words.

"And I thought to kill you once," she reminded him.

"But you did not, nor did you kill your husband. He was responsible for his own death. My brave Leanora, you have suffered much tragedy, yet mercy and goodness still dwells in your heart. Do not chastise yourself for the death of such an evil soul. Besides," he added gruffly, "if the man were not already dead I would have to kill him."

She thought to say more, but he hushed her words, stroked her hair, and rocked her back and forth until she thought to purr like a kitten. Faran had listened to her dreadful tale, without judging or despising, and she felt herself slip more completely under his spell. With him, she felt safe. With him she had rid herself of the past and dared to dream of a future and happier times.

As the world around her came back into focus, her gaze fell upon the black water and the troubles plaguing them. "You see now why I cannot go into the water."

He gave her a comforting hug. "Do not worry. Just rest here beside me." All her fears dissolved away as she melted into his embrace. "We will wait to see what the morning brings," he reassured.

Her heart welled with happiness. He was not going to swim the lake without her. And he was willing to risk staying the night with her here.

She reached up and touched the iron heart. Then she rested her hand upon his chest and felt the beating of his real heart—strong and sure. There lay the true essence of the man who held her in his arms—not the amulet.

Nestling closer, she surrendered to the protection he offered, but worry peeked over her shoulder. She was frightened by the wonder filling her senses. The need to trust and depend upon someone other than herself was seeping into the foundations of the wall that guarded *her* heart. If she gave in to the feelings, it would mean risking all.

Faran held up the wine flagon. "We might as well finish this," he suggested, tempting her to comply. Trading drinks, she curled languidly at his side and watched the dull Lothian sky.

As night leaned closer, Faran smiled and dipped his head to press a wine-flavored kiss upon her lips. It was a simple sharing of affection not threatening nor asking anything in return. Then he relaxed back against the tree.

She licked her lips, savoring the taste of him mingled with the wine.

"That is twice now you have saved my life," he said.

"Three times," she corrected.

"Ah, yes. Three times saved and twice repaid." Faran's brows drew together in a serious scowl, but his eyes, albeit somewhat bleary, were filled with humor. "I should just marry you," he said with a slur. "It would be much simpler. Then we would share everything equally, and no longer have need of keeping such a tally."

At his words, her breath caught in her throat. No doubt it was his loss of blood and the wine talking, yet his declaration set her heart to soaring.

Before she could reply, Faran smiled with innocent charm and passed out.

Chapter Twenty

The wailing of hounds on the hunt drew Faran from a restless sleep. He groaned and raised his head. Stiff from his ordeal at the castle, and chilled by the night air, pain riddled his body. He felt woozy, as if he had overstayed his welcome at the mead bench.

Leanora stirred, and the seriousness of their situation rushed over him full force. The dogs he heard, and the men they led, were searching for him and the girl asleep in his arms.

In the glimmering darkness, he glanced over at the sword and shield. They were safe—wrapped in the blue cloth—just as he had left them. Then he gazed down at Leanora. Although tender and timid, she had won the day and delivered unto him the treasure he sought. And she had reclaimed him from a hideous torture. Recalling the whip marks on her back, and the story she had told of her husband, he decided his Gillyflower was a more stalwart, well-seasoned warrior than he could ever claim to be. She had faced many trials, and was a woman worthy of homage. But now, the temporary asylum she had won for them was being threatened.

Carefully, he slid his arm from beneath her head. She murmured but did not awaken. It was still many hours until dawn, but they could not postpone their departure from the island. His hint at there being another means of escape had been a ruse to ease her worry. They would need to swim for it—

now—in what remained of the night. He prayed Leanora would not become hysterical at the prospect. If worse came to worse, he would render her senseless and take her across. But what to do about the sword and shield?

He rolled sideways and gained his feet. Near the water's edge he spotted a length of half rotted hemp. Retrieving the sodden rope, he tested its strength, and deciding to trust it to the task, he lashed the heirlooms to a stout log.

Grasping the trailing end of the hemp, he nudged the tiny raft away from the shore with his toe. Trepidation rose as he watched the sword and shield floundered and go under. A moment later the listing barge righted itself. Declaring it seaworthy, he secured it back on shore.

As he returned to Leanora's side, the hounds bayed again, hastening his steps.

"Leanora, wake up." He knelt at her side and lightly touched her cheek. She started and gazed up at him. Her sleepy smile melted his heart and hardened his desire. This unsatisfied passion was proving nearly as painful a torment as anything Gorham could devise.

"We must leave, now," he informed her. "We have been found out, and those who search for us draw near."

"But it is still dark," she said groggily and peered around. "Have you found a boat for us to use?"

"There is no boat," he said, hitting her with the undiluted truth. "We must swim across."

Her eyes widened in panic as she gripped his arm and sat bolt upright.

"There is no other way," he explained and smoothed her hair back from her face. "All you must do is believe in me, and we shall prevail." Hastily, he added a silent plea to the gods to keep the sea creature amused elsewhere in the lake.

She shuddered, and with a sob, wrapped her arms around his neck, her face buried against his shoulder. Lost in her embrace, the rest of the world seemed far removed and inconsequential. But as the howl of the master hound echoed like a banshee, he eased her away from his chest.

"Come," he encouraged, "we've no time to spare."

Gaining his feet, he drew her upright at his side. She stood as if frozen in place, tears glistening in her eyes.

"At your word, I will make a stand here," he declared, "and fight for you to the death. But I would rather lead us both to safety. Please, Leanora, I will not play you false."

"Then you shall be the first," she said, barely above a whisper. Grasping one of his hands, she pressed his palm against her chest. Through the gossamer gown she wore, he could feel the wild beating of her heart. "I will follow you, Faran, even if it be to a watery grave."

Her voice was so trusting and innocent. He knew she was terrified of what they proposed to do, and while her faith in him bolstered his flagging energy, it also scared him half to death. This time, should he fail, it meant sure death for the both of them.

She flashed him a smile, half hopeful and half false bravado. "No one can stop the likes of us."

At her words, all his doubts dissolved away. "No one," he agreed and smiled back. Grabbing the free end of the rope attached to the sword and shield, he tied it to his left ankle. Then he stepped into the ebony pool and led Leanora into the black water.

As they moved forward, he tested the footing, making sure they would not drop off into a depth greater than her height. She kept on his heels, clinging to him with the strength of a warrior three times her size. As the water rose to waist level, she panted with fear. Then a strangled cry escaped her, and she twisted in his grasp.

"I can go no farther. Let me go, let me go."

She sounded on the verge of hysteria. With the fist of her free hand she pounded his chest and shoulder, but instead of fighting her, he gathered her close—steadying her, shielding her from the little waves now lapping at her breasts.

She shoved against him, and threw her head back in a scream that near set his ears to bleeding. He clamped a hand over her mouth. "If you carry on thus, the soldiers will need no dogs to track us down. Be silent," he hissed, but his unrelenting grip seemed to drive her panic even higher. She kicked and clawed at the water. Her right foot pressed against his knee. Then her left foot dug into the thigh of his other leg—she was climbing up his body to get above the waterline. As her foot drove into his stomach, he feared she would drown them both.

Wrestling her down to stand before him, he swallowed her protests with deep kisses, replacing her terror with a different need, one just as overwhelming. Her cries turned to whimpers. A savage excitement engulfed Faran as the full length of their bodies swayed together in the ripples of the lake.

She relaxed against him, momentarily distracted. But they could not stay locked in the grip of lust and one another's arms.

"Time has run out," he gasped, "you must do exactly as I say or we are doomed."

****

Yes, Leanora thought as she gripped Faran's shoulders to steady herself. She must listen to the voice of the man who commanded her present, and not to the malicious voice of the dead man who haunted her past.

"Lie back upon the water," Faran whispered.

In one huge leap, her thoughts crossed from good intentions to brutal reality. The brittle eggshell of security surrounding her cracked and fell away, and she was once more a victim of her fears. She could not do this—not even for him.

He gave her a quick nod of encouragement and a tender smile. "I will be at your side every moment."

Stiff as a carp three days dead, she leaned back. The water wrapped around her chest and throat, she gagged and thrashed about until she found her footing. "I'm sorry, I cannot." Ashamed, she hid her face in her hands.

"Try again," he said calmly, as he patted her on the back.

Leonora marveled he did not become impatient or angered by her failure. She wanted him to be proud of her, but truly she was not very brave.

Finally, she willed herself to live or die by her belief in Faran, and thinking only of the magical bond existing between them, she surrendered herself into his keeping. Drifting back upon the water, her legs began to rise of their own accord. Firm and steady, Faran's held her afloat as he cradled her close to his chest.

"Breathe," he ordered.

Unaware she had been holding her breath, she gulped in a lungful of air and concentrated on inhaling and exhaling.

"Now you have it," he praised. "I knew you could do it."

"It's like being a mermaid," she whispered, awed by her accomplishment.

"And I am a seafaring stranger, woefully bewitched by your enchantment." As if mystified by the truth of his playful words, his smile faded.

In the hazy darkness she could just make out Faran's face. He glanced over his shoulder toward the shore, his strong profile marking him bold and daring, but as he returned his gaze to her face, his soulful poet's eyes proclaimed him kind and gentle. The special feeling in her heart for him grew tenfold as she thought how unique a man he was. Clinging to that thought, she fought to keep at bay the dread lurking just below the surface of her mind.

"Now ever so slowly," he instructed, "reach over and place one of your hands upon each of my shoulders. When you are ready, I will float face down over your body, and you must brace yourself stiff-armed against me. Each stroke I take will propel the both of us forward as one."

Carefully, she did as instructed. He slid up and over her in the water, and stretched out on top of her. With his face turned to one side, his cheek hovered against her belly, and the top of his head skimmed her breasts. She bit back a cry of fright as they settled into position. Then she lost herself to the moment.

Drenched in water, her sheer dress melted to a whisper. Faran's loins brushed against her legs, and a wave of excitement rippled through her, obscuring the horror of floating helplessly beneath him. Arms spread wide like the wings of an eagle, he swept them away from the shallows and out into deeper water.

As Faran strained harder to pull them through the thick black liquid, his muscles bunched and the corded sinew of his shoulders tensed. She felt a jerk as the rope tied to his ankle became taut and he dragged the floating log-raft behind them.

Soon he reached full stride, and the cadence of one powerful stroke followed by another, cast a spell upon her. A mere few inches of water separated their bodies, and occasionally his chest and shoulders brushed across her, the repeated contact captivating her senses, arousing a need deep within her.

Then, out of the blue, the precariousness of her position struck her like a physical blow. Her feet drifted downward and her bottom started to sink. She was going under. She thrashed about with her legs and fought to right her position.

"By the gods, stop kicking," Faran gasped, "I've no desire to become a eunuch. Look up at the sky, Leanora," he commanded between the tireless strokes he continued to take. "See how it glides by overhead even as the water glides by beneath us. We are halfway to the shore. Be strong, little flower. We shall make it."

Soothed by his voice she relaxed, and her body once again became buoyant—floating even higher upon the surface of the water. She separated her legs to better accommodate his hips. The top of her thighs unintentionally pressed up against him and the sound of his labored breathing quickened and deepened. She was no longer sure it was from the exertion of swimming

As instructed, she gazed up at the sky. When first stepping into Black Rain Lake, a shock of cold had washed over her. Now, farther from the shore, the water was warm—almost hot. It seeped into every pore of her body, flowing around her, gushing down between her legs like a hot liquid caress. She felt as if she were floating on air rather than water, and she wished she could wrap her arms and legs around Faran and draw him nearer, draw him into her body, draw from him the passion she knew he wished to give to her. As her panic subsided, she dared to hope they might survive this watery ordeal.

Then she felt it...

Something moved in the water beneath them. Faran felt it too, and his stroke faltered. It must be the monster that dwelled in the lake. There it was again. Why did he not speak of it?

Concentrate on something else, her inner voice screamed—quickly. *Think of Faran. Imagine his beautiful body and how it glides above you, back and forth, gentle yet powerful. Feel how it teases you, pleases you, over and over across your thighs, across your breasts. Feel your nipples pucker and harden. Feel the warmth gather between your legs and the wanting that coils in your belly. Think only of him...think only of him.*

Closing her eyes, she let the water seduce her body and inflame her senses. As she drifted to a safer place, one thousand hands caressed her in one thousand places and she imagined the sensation came from his touch. This is what it would feel like to make love to Faran.

Suddenly, they crashed to a halt. Her eyes flew open and the sensuous dream dissolved away. Faran wrapped his arms around her and they rolled out of the water and onto the shore. The momentum of his last stroke had carried them to the edge of a sandy beach, a safe distance from the dock. They sat up at the same time and fell into one another's arms.

"Praise be," she murmured holding him close. "You are daring and stalwart. You swam all that way, encumbered by me and towing the relics."

His chest heaved, and the air rushed in and out of his lungs. He hugged her in return, and a tingle of remembered lust skittered through her. The feeling came to rest deep inside, like a banked coal, where it lay hot and smoldering—ready to be rekindled.

As the wail of disappointed hounds drifted on the breeze, they drew apart and stared across the dark brooding water. On Gorham's island the glow of torches could now be seen. Like confused fireflies, the points of light moved sporadically along the shoreline in the very spot they had occupied only moments before.

"Thank you, Woden. We have done the

impossible," Faran prayed. "We have crossed Black Rain Lake in the dead of night."

Succumbing to happy exhaustion, she sagged against him.

"We should move inland and seek the safety of the forest," he suggested, jostling her awake. Untying the rope from his ankle, he dragged the heirlooms more securely onto the shore.

"Oh please," she begged. "If only I could rest for a moment."

She curled up in a ball, thankful for even the hard ground upon which to lie. Half asleep she heard him rustling about. He was walking through the underbrush, his footsteps growing faint. That could not be right, she was sure he would not leave her. She wanted to raise her head and look for him, but weariness defeated curiosity and she drifted closer to oblivion. Faran would protect her.

Strong arms lifted her from the ground, and wrapped in solid reassurance, she snuggled closer as he carried her so effortlessly. Soon, the sound of a gurgling brook lulled her mind into contentment. He bent over, as if to lower her to the ground, and she waited for the feel of warm earth.

By the saints...her eyes flew open, and she sucked in a breath of surprise. She was back in the water. It could not be. Had she only dreamed they were safely across the lake? Wide-awake now, she reached for Faran as the water in the stream rushed over her legs.

"What are you doing?" she gasped.

Pushing him away, she scrambled to her feet and glared at him, but her words of protest were forgotten as she studied him more closely. At her expression, an ear-to-ear grin split his face. He was covered in black slime, and his white teeth gleamed brightly in contrast.

"Do I look the same?" she asked.

He nodded jovially. She stared down at her hands, turning them first one way and then the other. Grabbing up a hank of hair, she held it out for inspection. It dripped and oozed the same black muck.

Faran retrieved the sword and shield and stashed them nearby. Then without ceremony, he stripped naked and meandered along the bank of the stream. Her eyes widened at the sight of him. "You should do the same," he suggested, unabashed at her ogling. "I assure you, this unholy blackness does not freely relinquish its hold. And it grows more tenacious with time. I found a small pool in yon trees," he added, pointing out the direction. "It is deep and warm." Clothes in hand, he sauntered off.

Not wishing to be left alone, she quickly followed. As she walked, she peeled away her tattered white dress. Fragile as a spider's web, it fluttered forlornly to the ground where it lay like the broken wing of a gray dove.

Reaching the small pool, she sneaked another peek at Faran's naked form and nearly lost her footing. He was magnificent and glorious to behold. Legs braced wide, he stretched and flexed his shoulders as if to ease the muscles no doubt sore and tired from the effort of swimming. Then he ruffled his hands through his hair and leaned over to wash his feet and legs.

Forcing her mind to the task at hand, she eased into the water. But the warm liquid caressed her thighs and hips, rekindling her previous desire. She wanted Faran, desperately.

As she washed her hair, she watched Faran do the same. Finishing first, he stood tall. Droplets of water, fired by the pale moonlight, glistened and ran down the length of his muscled form.

"We made it, Gillyflower," he declared once more. "Although for a moment, I thought the beast would claim us."

"I felt the creature too." She gasped and scrambled to her feet. "Why did you not tell me when it drew near?"

"Would that have eased your concerns?"

"No. But you must admit I did well in the crossing."

"Not bad for a female," he jibed.

"A female." Feeling playful, she put hands together and hurled a scoop of water his way. He laughed and returned the attack. With mock fury, they splashed one another drawing closer and closer, until she was in Faran's arms. His smile faded, replaced by an expression making her weak-kneed at what it inferred. Then, for some reason, she felt unsure of herself. Had he forgotten she was scarred and used goods? She turned in the circle of his arms. Let him see again the ugly marks upon her back— let him see her imperfections. She swept her hair aside and stood ready to be rejected.

As if the marks were not there, he touched her shoulder and grazed his hand down her spine, and encircling her from behind, he drew her firmly up against his chest. The most needful part of him, big and hard, pressed against her backside.

"My beautiful Leanora. I'll not stop this time. I want you more than I've ever wanted anything or anyone."

Again, acting as if the marred and disfigured skin did not exist, he kissed a trail downward and slid to his knees. Cheek braced against her back, he dipped up handfuls of warm water to wash her legs and feet. It was a simple gesture, soothing yet intimate, and it set her to trembling.

She stood in the moonlight, transfixed by this spell of enchantment. Still kneeling at her back, he skimmed one hand upward, touching her breasts and caressing the contours of her body, softly teasing, softly pleasing. The other hand grazed across her stomach, dipping lower, his fingers blazing a path through the triangle of hair crowning the part of her aching for his touch. A moan escaped her. He slid his hand between her thighs, and when he dared to explore the depths of her being, it felt as if warm honey flowed through her veins.

Fists clenched at her sides, she stared up at the sky. For the first time in her life, she did feel beautiful, and truly desired. And although her body was not untouched, her heart and soul were virgin and they soared heavenward on wings of their own. She wanted to love and be loved. She wanted to lose herself to the need pulsing within her—a need only Faran could set free to match his own.

Urges of profound delight ignited and flared into a full-blown conflagration. She was falling, fainting, going out of control. Her knees began to buckle. Faran gained his feet, swept her up into his arms, and in two long strides delivered her to the bank of the little pool. Cushioned by soft moss, and protected from the breeze by a thicket of bracken, he stretched out at her side.

Straining closer, she pressed the length of her body against his, seeking more of the ecstasy recently tasted. His hand raked down her side, coming to rest at her hip.

"So many times I have imagined making love to you," he said. "I want to explore every part of your body, memorize your taste, your smell, your softness."

She opened her mouth to speak, but only a little mewing sound slipped past her lips.

"If you do not wish it," he relented, "I will not lay a hand upon you. Not even a finger," he added solemnly. "Well...perhaps just one finger." He kissed the tip of his right index finger and pressed it to her lips. Then he trailed that one finger downward to the little hollow at the base of her throat, downward across her breasts, first around one nipple, and then the other. She squirmed with delight.

"Look at me, Leanora," he commanded.

As she obeyed, and stared into his eyes, she could not deny she loved Faran with all her heart. "Making love is the most glorious adventure of all," he proclaimed. "It leads one down uncharted paths and must be approached with no less than full enthusiasm."

She clung to her poet-warrior, and freely entrusted her heart and body unto him, even as she had entrusted her life and breath to him in the lake.

He slid his hand lower, tangling one finger in her curls, and she forgot about the past and the future, and from the tiny point where his fingertip made repeated and demanding circles, excitement was born. Like a summer storm about to break, raw desire mounted, pounding in her chest, taking her breath away. This was heaven on earth. She arched against him.

Faster, harder, more, more—she wanted more. A craving took her, obliterating the world, and a silky moan purred in her throat and escaped through her parted lips into the darkness. Brilliant sensations transformed into flashing colors and her body crossed into a realm unknown to her. Faran slid his hand between her legs, his fingers seeking the part of her that had never before known pleasure. Sensual spasms of joy close around him, unstoppable, indescribable. His other arm tightened around her, holding her close as an all-consuming hunger flooded her senses and pulsed through her body.

He kissed her neck and groaned, as if he too experienced the gratification ripping through her body. Gliding back to earth from this whirlwind of passion, she clutched at the man who had given her such unselfish delight. She had not only survived this unknown journey, but felt more alive than ever before. In the blinding light of her happiness, the cruelty and hardships of the world faded. Faran had shown her what coupling should be—a glorious sharing of body and soul, wrapped in delight beyond her wildest imaginings.

"'Tis only the beginning," he whispered in a husky tone. He leaned closer, his erection pressed up against her thigh.

A shiver of starlight sparkled through her.

"Only the very beginning."

****

Faran covered Leanora's body with his. The feel of her naked beneath him was a long awaited dream-come-true.

It had driven him near to madness watching her in the throes of passion, and although he had touched her with but one finger, it had excited him to desperate heights. Now he sought his own fulfillment, and to please her yet again.

Her copper-colored hair spilled around her like the aura of some fabled goddess, and for him she held the world at her command. He hungered for her, wanted to show her his love, wanted to bind her to him with pleasure and joy. He needed to possess her and claim her as his own. Nuzzling her head to one side, he drank in the scent of her. "You are so precious to me."

He explored her mouth with his tongue, silencing any intended reply. Sliding lower, he savored first one nipple and then the other. The blushing peaks taunted him with perfection, and as he flicked his tongue across them, Leanora strained upward offering herself to him. He had bid her trust him and she did, allowing him to do anything he wanted, and for the first time in his life what he wanted most was to please someone other than himself.

Scooting lower, he licked and kissed her belly. She inhaled sharply, but the sound soon turned to sighs of pleasure. Easing her legs apart, he nibbled the inside of her thighs. She was warm and wet and yielding to his demands, and he memorized the essence that made her different from every other woman.

As he consumed this delicate feast, crazy thoughts mixed with his desire. He wanted not only to please Leanora, but to care for her. And not just now, while his blood ran high, but tomorrow and the next day and into the future they could share together.

As carnal need surpassed logical thinking, he roughly kissed a path upward. Face to face, he entered her, fast and fully. Leanora gasped in surprise then moaned, accepting him without hesitation.

Wanting to savor the moment, he moved oh-so-slowly and carefully. Her tiny fingernails cut into his flesh, her body rising and falling beneath his, sweetly accentuating every driving movement he made.

Her stuttering cry of satisfaction sent him over the edge, and wild with needs of his own, he penetrated deeper and harder, unleashing his own long awaited release. The waves of delight within her drew the seed from him, and the blinding satisfaction of his climax exalted every fiber of his being. His heart rejoiced too.

Shaking with exhaustion, he rolled to the side, keeping her close, never breaking their union. An aftershock rippled from his body to hers.

Then a fleeting moment of panic raced through him. Never before had lying with a woman affected him thus. He felt a primitive need to protect and care for Leanora, and he wished her never to leave his side. Here was the emotion he had so successfully avoided and pitied in others. Love had finally warmed his heart where before only the fire of lust and amusement had resided.

Leanora touched his cheek drawing his thoughts back to the present. "Am I really beautiful?" she asked, her eyes round with hope and innocence.

"Oh, yes, Leanora," he said, "that you are." Then afraid he might utter something binding or foolish, he tightened his embrace and avoided her gaze.

That you are indeed, he repeated to himself. *And I am bewitched by your enchantment, and no longer ruled by the iron heart once worn upon my chest with such arrogance and pride.*

Chapter Twenty-One

"Show Her Highness in," Gorham relented.

He was in a roaring bad mood, aggravated by the revolting heap of food his soldiers had prepared to break his fast. His servants were missing from the kitchen, the red-haired girl had escaped with his hard won possessions, and the damn Geat had absconded along with the wench. And now, to thoroughly distress his stomach and pounding head wound, Romaine dared to request an early morning audience.

Unannounced, his dear sister had arrived last evening, just before sunset. Livid because the Storm Geat had escaped, she had insisted upon helping with the search. Unfortunately, her attempts had only added to the general mayhem already running rampant. And in the end, the efforts of her soldiers had been to no avail. He should refuse to see her, but in his misery, her company really would be of some comfort. Of all people, she would sympathize with his frustration.

Swathed in scarlet, Romaine swept into the room—the layers of red silk billowed and trailed along like an angry cloud. There was fire in her eyes and determination in her step. She came to a halt, and the crimson gown swirled to a diaphanous stop a moment later. "Gorham," she spat out his name as if it left a bad taste in her mouth. "It is your fault they have alluded us."

"Be careful how you approach the king in his

realm, dear sister," he warned and stabbed at the food on his trencher.

Her anger faded to a predatory alertness.

"The Geat and his woman first escaped from your little island," he pointed out. "And the two of them could not have known I housed the relics lest they had elicited the information from you." At his accusation, her eyes widened—he had guessed correctly.

"We have both been played for fools," she admitted, adjusting the silk covering her head. "I for one want revenge." At that prospect, the glow returned to her eyes. "Are you with me?" she challenged.

Romaine was an unrelenting, deadly bitch, making him thankful she was on his side. She was also a savagely beautiful woman, making him regret at times she was his sister.

"Without doubt, we stand together." Rising from the table, he strode to her side and stared transfixed at her exposed navel. If he was not mistaken, there was a ruby embedded in it. Despite Romaine's declaration that she now embraced the cross, she remained pagan to the core. As she slid the mantle of veils from her head, his gaze drifted upward and he gasped in surprise. "By the blood of our ancestors, what happened to your hair?"

A large hank of glossy curls was missing on the right side of her head, and a patch of raw skin glowed upon her temple where the hair had once resided. In a newly shaved area, surrounding the livid mark, the face of a snarling wolf had skillfully been tattooed. The unhealed crimson circle formed the animal's blood red mouth, his sharp black teeth glorifying the wound. Had she sported such a symbol last evening? It must have been concealed beneath her war helm.

"I am starting a new fashion," she said dryly.

"Do you like it? I think it lends a certain no-nonsense charm."

"To say the least," he agreed. His sister might be depraved, but one had to admire her audacity.

"Who did this to you?" he asked and peered more closely at the angry scar.

"'Tis the handiwork of the Storm Geat," she railed, "and he will pay dearly for the act."

"He might have slit your throat instead," Gorham pointed out.

"He should have. When I am through with him, he will regret his act of mercy."

"Does your vengeance come served with a plan?" he inquired. "Or shall we each fend for ourselves, gnashing our teeth at will?"

"No doubt you are aware of the trouble in the city," she said, ignoring his sarcasm.

"I have eyes and ears in the opposing camp. We have known for some time of the brewing unrest, just not their exact plan, or who might be their leader. Of course, the arrival of the girl and the Geat was unanticipated." He glanced again at the untouched food upon his table and sighed. "As was the abandonment of the servants in the castle."

A cruel smile twisted Romaine's lips. "The situation is not yet out of our control. With our forces combined we will be unstoppable. We can crush the revolt and snare the warrior and his woman like the wretched little rodents they are."

Romaine prowled about the room, emulating the beast tattooed upon her temple. She seemed eager for the hunt to begin. "With a full-fledged rebellion at hand, they will also attempt to drain the lake," she added.

"Yes, of course. It is no doubt part of their plan. Tomorrow is Alban Elfed, the date father entrapped the spirit beneath the water those many years ago. Still, we have enough time to crush the uprising and destroy their attempt to undermine our authority."

Romaine grazed one hand back and forth across the ruby as she contemplated their situation. "The rebels have lost their fear of us, and have fostered plans more strategic than before."

"I agree. This is not one of their usual petty attempts at overthrowing our rule. They are organized as never before. But without coinage of their own, they cannot have hired mercenary warriors. Their fear will return fast enough when the true fighting begins and they are slaughtered in the streets.

"What about the Storm Geat?" she hissed.

"He travels alone without soldiers," Gorham reminded. "Any attempt at personal retribution would be folly. And now that he has recovered the sword and shield, why would he remain to aid the rebels?"

As she idled about the room, Romaine snatched up a small hand-mirror from a side table. "He most likely makes his escape even as we speak," she brooded. "No doubt the girl is at his side." She stopped to gaze at own reflection. "I do not understand why he bothers with her. She is pale and mousy, and I would see her dead." With that, she hurled the mirror across the room, shattering it against the wall.

"Be careful, Romaine, your fangs are showing." He had rarely seen his sister so distraught. "You must be objective in the pursuit, or the game will outfox you. My men are already posted in battalions throughout Gylfi. At the appointed time, they will converge, tightening the net and trapping all who are disloyal to their king. Then we shall turn our attention to tracking down the Storm Geat and the woman."

He licked his lips. Like his sister, the taste of revenge sat sweet upon his palate. "The two who have humiliated us beyond mere treachery will suffer accordingly. But the girl is mine."

Romaine made to speak, but he raised a hand silencing her protest. "Rest assured," he soothed, "ample payment shall be exacted to slake both our desires for vengeance. And you may do as you wish with the man. He should provide you with several days of entertainment, unless your needs kill him prematurely."

Romaine smiled seductively, as if she took pride in his comment rather than offense. "Yes, I have unparalleled plans for him," she purred, her eyes half shuttered in ecstasy. "His suffering shall be great and my pleasure even greater. I am wet just thinking of what will be."

His sister's unbridled lust and hunger for power set her apart from any woman Gorham had ever known. Again, he rued the realization they could never be lovers, yet what they did share, was even stronger and more important than passion. They shared the bond of blood, the desire to rule this land, and their mutual loathing of the Geats. His sexual needs could be assuaged with any woman, but a trusted ally who matched his craving to rule and dominate, that was rare indeed.

He took his turn pacing about the room, and his mind drifted back in time, visions of long ago harrying his thoughts.

Since Man's beginning and the death of Ymir, Gorham's ancestors had been enemies of the Geats. And he would stop at nothing to see their foe destroyed and their southern lands relegated to his domain. "We must recover the sword and the shield," he stressed, coming to a halt and an immutable conclusion. "With the relics, they wield a special power that fuels the spirit of their people. And, although the sword failed Beowulf when he faced the dragon, it is imbued with his battle courage—the valor and fearlessness that allowed him to destroy dear Grendel and his mother."

Romaine nodded, a worried expression upon her brow.

"If the Storm Geat should dare to join forces with the rebels, this may be our final battle," he worried. "Then the last descendents of Cain will truly be lost forever, and the tribe of Beowulf will survive triumphant."

"We have always lived on borrowed time," she reminded, "ever since father defeated the Spirit of the Mere."

Gorham sat down heavily in the nearest chair. "Recently, I feel my own spirit fading."

"This is all in your mind," Romaine chided. "You do not grow weak, my brother, you are just downhearted due to the momentary victory of the warrior and his woman. If we keep our heads and prevail victorious, we will have many years, nay, decades, ahead of us. All we need do is maintain what father began, and keep that winged whore at the bottom of the lake where she belongs. She's had many years to break the spell and not succeeded. She is no threat to us from there."

Romaine's eyes narrowed to slits, and her voice softened to a menacing calm. "She was so righteous back then—yet just as merciless in her own cause as ever we were accused of being. Father sacrificed much to cast this land under a dark cloud of obedience and to send that fey Amazon to her doom."

"Yes," Gorham agreed and stared out the window. "The cost was high to secure our future. And Father did not long enjoy his victory. Resurrecting the spell of protection possessed by Grendel's mother took the final toll. At times I miss him," he added quietly, "and the sun."

"I rather like Gylfi's dreary clime," Romaine countered. "It keeps my skin milky white and creamy smooth. The night is more to my liking anyway. Who needs blinding sunlight and garish vegetation? Even the Isle of May is oft times too bright. I prefer to be the only dash of color in the realm, which is why I resent those infernal priests with their glittering robes and chalices of silver and gold."

"Do not dismiss them too readily, sister," Gorham cautioned. "It is easy enough to honor our true customs, even as we submit openly to baptism. And having the Church's sanction behind us in our pursuit of war and carnage is an advantage not to be missed. We must use whatever shield is offered for our protection, and this religion condones our actions and absolved our sins as we kill for Christ and fight the Geats and Danes."

"I will always cleave to the covenants of our ancestors," Romaine declared. "They were conceived and worshiped by our forbearers long before the time of this white God. They are the powers to which we owe our thanks and tribute."

Gorham nodded. "We were born of the old ways and have lived by the old ways. And I have a feeling we will die upholding the old ways as well."

"Well aren't you the cheerful little sparrow of doom."

He stared at his sibling in crime. "We dare not fail, Romaine. If the Maiden of the Mere is freed, it will be our undoing." A growl rumbled deep in his chest, and he tried not to remember the curse awaiting them should their plans go awry. "We will suffer the same fate as Father—or worse."

****

Awaiting Faran's return, Leanora sat upon a stump in the forest.

This morning he had awakened her with kisses and caresses, ushering them once more into the arms of passion. Like puppies, they had wrestled and played. Then like full-grown hounds, they had made untamed, uncensored love. She squirmed just remembering the feel of him inside her body.

But now, alone in the woods, her mood alternated between blissful satisfaction and a niggling fear. This newfound joy deliciously enslaved her, making her crave something she should never have tasted in the first place. Oh, who was she kidding? She was glad they had crossed the barrier from friends to lovers.

Faran taught her much in the way of pleasing a man, and he pleased her in kind. And she knew in her heart, if he were here now, she would offer herself up to him without hesitation. A willing sacrifice, she would spread herself beneath him, wanting it as much as he. She lusted after the enchantment he created in her. What did it matter that he did not mention love. He made love *to her*, and no one could take that away. No one could steal the memories they made together.

A cool morning breeze teased across her shoulders. She drew the blue tablecloth-shawl closer and ran her hand across the clean soft fabric. Last night as she slept, Faran had removed it from around the shield and rinsed it free of mud and debris. This morning, when she awakened clothed only in his warm embrace, he had presented her with the dark cloth.

He often did thoughtful things, providing her with little comforts that made the difference between crude existence and enjoyable survival. Even now, he was away in search of food. In turn, she wondered who searched for them. Their escape from Gorham's island would be common knowledge by now. And that horrid black-haired witch, Romaine, was most likely ensconced at the citadel. She prayed Cynric and Kayden were safe. It seemed she and Faran had done little to aid their cause.

"A king's ransom for your thoughts."

She leaped to her feet and spun around. Damnation. For a big man, Faran was quiet as a cat.

She smiled, then glanced away in shyness. "I was thinking what we shared last night and this morning was just a precious dream," she admitted covering her giddiness with talk. "And you did not really exist. This whole adventure must belong to someone else, for I am not brave enough to live out such a fantasy on my own."

Faran eased the bundle he carried to the ground and spanned her waist with his hands. Drawing her near, he pressed his hips close to hers. "Does that feel like a dream?" he said, grinning down at her. "You are not on your own. What started out as my quest and your forced exile has now become our journey. It belongs to the both of us."

"Ours," she repeated. It was a small word to signify so much. It was a soft comforting word, but it did not promise forever.

"I am afraid," she whispered.

"Of what?" At her silence, his eyes widened in surprise. "Of me?"

"Yes."

"But why? You know I will not hurt you."

"Your absence will."

His arms fell slack at his sides. He seemed taken aback by her statement, and she wished she had not voiced her deepest thoughts. Faran had never made any commitment to her, and she had not requested one. Over and over she had been through this in her mind. They would not always be together—she must be prepared for his leaving. She should enjoy the moments as they came, but logic evaporated like morning mist when she thought about life without him.

"It's hard to predict the future," he said.

His words were kind, yet she would always

worry about tomorrow—a tomorrow she would face alone. At least her treasure still awaited, buried on the southbound road on the outskirts of Gylfi. Riches were a girl's most faithful companion. They would not diminish with time, nor disappear when least expected. And when she located her mother and Brother Thomas, they would both be welcome company and stave off the loneliness. Why could she not be happy with that prospect?

Because, the little voice in the back of her mind taunted, *you want this man more than any fortune. He gives you pleasure no cold hard jewel could ever match. And his companionship is a gift of even greater worth.*

In her heart, she knew this was true. Faran urged her to test the boundaries of her world. Boundaries she would only reinforce and build higher with her gold coins. He made her want to tear down the walls restricting her horizons. He made her want to cross the next mountain.

She smiled, and pushed the thoughts aside. It was much too early in the morning for such ponderous thinking. "Did you find any food?" she asked, glancing hopefully at the bundle of provisions. "Poets may be able to live on passion, but my stomach does not heed the notions of a scop." As if on cue, a rumbling coursed through her belly.

Faran chuckled and dropped to one knee beside the packet. "Never fear. We have food aplenty, and I found a tunic for you. Sorry it isn't of a more flattering nature."

He liberated a dull brown heap of material, and held it out for her perusal. With an exclamation of delight, she grabbed the garment, shrugged it over her head, and liberated the blue tablecloth from beneath it.

"A perfect fit," she lied. The over-tunic hung near to the ground, and even belted, her small frame was lost to the folds of fabric. Only with luck, did she make her way to a nearby fallen log without tripping.

An amused expression upon his face, Faran followed, carrying the bread, a wedge of white cheese, dried meat, and a bunch of carrots.

She studied the pale orange spears and watery green tops, wondering if the sustenance contained within them was as diminished as their hue. Who cared? Either way, it would fill her belly. Greedily, she reached for one.

"What is the word from town?" she asked between bites. "Did you see Cynric?"

"Briefly," he replied. "By now he has left Gylfi. Lots were cast for a man to lead the women and children to a place of safety, and Cynric was chosen. Who better than a silver-tongued wandering minstrel to lead a band of frightened souls through a forlorn land? Without a doubt, it will make his best song yet."

"And did you see any of Gorham's soldiers?"

"There were several sniffing around." He met her gaze. "And yes, they search for us," he added. "I overheard them talking. We cannot stay long in this area, or for that matter, in county Lothian. The rebels will drain the lake tomorrow, and during the confusion, I propose to leave Gylfi and journey south."

Leanora's throat went dry, and the lump of bread and cheese sat upon her tongue like a mound of woodchips. He did not say "we" would head south, just "he" would.

"Until the relics are restored to my tribe, I can think of nothing else."

So his quest would continue, but his dalliance with her apparently would not. Dear Lord, she had not thought it would end so soon. She choked down the food and fidgeted with the colorless carrot tops.

Unintentionally, Faran was just as cruel as every other man she had ever known—only he killed her softly and without malice.

"What are your plans?" he asked. His voice was casual, but his eyes narrowed and she thought her response might be important to him.

I intend to follow you, wherever you may lead. Cherishing the ground upon which you tread....I love you, Faran, I love you. The words she yearned to express clawed at the back of her throat and gagged her more than the food. Should she speak the words begging for freedom? He might laugh at her, and his rejection would be more vicious than a physical blow.

"I shall take my wealth and seek another daring exploit," she said with a cheerfulness bred from years of hiding her true feelings. "I think adventuring and I were made for one another." She refused to let Faran see how losing him would leave her hollow and without purpose. "The whole world will be my home." And her world would be a living hell. She would wander aimlessly through it until her death, knowing what heaven on earth could be like—knowing Faran lived and breathed and loved in someone else's arms.

"Adventuring is not what I had dreamed it to be," he confided. "I will be content to return home to my teaching, and to the preservation of the stories of my ancestors."

"And to the women who await you," she blurted, not liking the shrewish tone edging her voice.

"And to the women," he readily agreed. "I might even marry one." He glanced down, then peeked up at her through the black lashes fringing his eyes. He seemed to be waiting for some reaction from her. What did he expect her to do, wish him good fortune in his search for a deserving wife?

"Then again," he added with a sigh, "it might be wiser for me to keep sampling the herd rather than trading away my freedom for just one cow."

What an awful thing to say. He truly was as coldhearted as the amulet hanging around his neck. She rose and turned away, but the voluminous tunic snagged upon the log. It bound her ankles throwing her to the ground at his feet. She scrambled to her hands and knees and ended up staring directly at his crotch, her head and shoulders wedged between his muscled thighs. As the bulge beneath his breechcloth stiffened, the heat from his body warmed her cheeks, and she heard Faran produce a strangled sound—a cross between a laugh and moan.

****

"By the gods, Leanora," he sputtered and placed one hand upon the silken hair haloing her head. He imagined her taking him into her mouth, her wet lips tightening around him, her ministrations drawing the need and seed from him. He could be wrong, but her expression hinted she harbored the same vision.

Was the mutual pleasure they shared the only thing she found interesting? She was the woman he wished to marry. Evidently she was not inclined to settle down. He leaned forward, and the throbbing of his erection intensified. She wanted to see the world, and he wanted her to be his world.

She tilted her head up, and his gaze slid lower. The gaping neckline of the too large tunic displayed her breasts at a most sensual angle. As she parted her lips and stared back at him, a becoming flush crept across her throat. Her blue eyes warmed to smoky violet, and a gentle breeze set her hair in motion. It fluttered about her face and shoulders, and the image of her between his legs set his heart to racing. Why did she not wish to stay with him?

Suddenly, he felt reckless and bold and he wanted to ask for her hand in marriage. As he opened his mouth to speak, a bolt of logic struck him, reminding him marriage was a circumstance he had always avoided. And without permission, he was not allowed to take a wife outside of his tribe, a condition rarely granted. It would be unfair to offer that which he could not deliver. But most of all, until he vindicated his name, he had nothing of value to offer her, nothing except his sorry self.

If only she were not so independent. If only she would remain with him until they reached his home. Just one sign was all he asked—just one sign she needed him.

In a quick fluid motion, Leanora clutched at the front of her tunic, rocked back on her heels, and gained her feet. For a reason he did not understand, the dusky passion faded from her eyes.

What more could he do to win her over?

"I had hoped you might return with me to my village," Faran said, fighting to keep the desperation from his voice. He was not accustomed to begging for the attention of a woman.

Leanora stopped short and stared down at him. "Why should I?"

Did she not covet him in the least? How could she make love to him with such tenderness and enthusiasm yet be devoid of all feelings of oneness? He must give her a reason for going other than his own desire to have her near.

"You are the one who found the shield and sword. My people will no doubt wish to bestow a reward upon you."

"I have my own wealth now and need no reward," she replied stubbornly. Her lower lip protruded slightly in a defiant frown, but her eyes seemed to search his face, beseeching him to come up with what...a better reason. One she could accept more readily. She wasn't making this easy.

"I do not feel I have made restitution for all you

have done for me," he began, unable to think of anything else. "You cannot walk out of my life without giving me the opportunity to repay you."

"Is that what prompts your interest in me?" she asked. Chin raised, she stood proudly before him. "Consider the entertainment of last night and this morning payment in full."

Entertainment? What was she talking about? That had not been what he had meant at all. Now he was into the mire with both feet. "Well, I'm glad you enjoyed the performance," he hollered and gained his feet.

Her cheeks flushed with indignation, and her eyes flashed like the metal of the sword he so prized. Encased in the brown tunic, her arms stiff with anger, she flapped them at her sides like a little bird. He cleared his throat and struggled not to laugh at the curious image she created. Woden help him, he truly did love her. They had to stay together.

"No matter how rich you are," he said, "the world is no place for a woman alone. It is not even a place for a man alone. Stay with me, please, just a little longer." To strengthen his plea, he offered up his best little-boy-lost expression.

Leanora considered his words, but he thought she gazed inward, battling her own will more than his.

She remained silent. What was taking her so long? Many a female had aspired to being his woman. It could not be all that hard of a decision?

"I shall go with you," she declared, "but only because I doubt you can make it back in one piece without me."

Chapter Twenty-Two

As Faran blazed a path through the surrounding woods, Leanora tried her best to keep pace. They were on the move again, cautiously circling through the forest, seeking to monitor the activity in town even as they remained safe from discovery. What cared she that a demon king and the devil's harlot were in pursuit? Unless he bid her do so, she would not leave Faran's side. It was not logical. It was not practical. But it was exciting.

She had given in to Faran because he was just too hard to resist. Being the youngest of seven children, she supposed he had been fawned over and protected all his life. Without doubt, he certainly seemed to expect people and events to naturally go his way. And it was the expectancy and hope in his eyes that had convinced her to go with him. She was not one to crush such feelings, regardless of where she might find them. The elixir of hope had once been her life's blood, and she knew how hard it was to exist without it.

As Faran strode fearlessly through the dense foliage, she memorized the contours of his broad back. The guard's tunic he still wore strained across his shoulders and hugged his trim waist. Her gaze slipped lower. The shirt also rode high, nicely exposing his muscled thighs and legs. He wore no braies, a situation not seeming to disturb him overmuch, and the loincloth, protecting his most vital concerns, accentuated his glorious backside.

Just looking at him gave her twinges in all the right places and she wondered if all the men on the Isle of Gullin were as pleasing to daydream about.

What was the world like from whence he came? The languages he spoke, and the few clothes surviving his shipwreck indicated wealth and learning. Yet, for now, he seemed content with the borrowed clothes upon his back. He remained a mystery to her.

She reached up and touched the small bruise on her breastbone. His iron heart had left its mark. When they made love, their bodies never touched in that one tiny spot. Icy metal, the width of her finger, always separated them from completely joining. Could anyone win the amulet he so favored? Or would the talisman, with its runes and Thor's symbol, always remain a part of this man?

Watching Faran's glorious arse, rather than where she was going, she tripped on a tree root. At full tilt, the ground rushed up to meet her, and the shield flew from her grasp. The heels of her hands scraped along the rough terrain, and a sizable rock took its toll upon her right knee as she skidded to a halt.

Faran spun around and rushed to her side. She propped herself up on one elbow and twisted around to locate his most revered relic. *Woe is me*, she thought, *if any harm comes to his darn heirloom.* "Is the shield damaged?" she asked.

"More importantly"—Faran dragged her to her feet—"are you hurt?"

With a sense of wonder, she noted for the second time he denounced the shield in deference to her.

Setting the sword aside, he manipulated her arms, flexing each joint along the way. Apparently, convinced all was in working order, he raised the hem of her tunic to survey her knees. The memory of how it felt to be a four-year-old with a doting mother flashed through her mind, and she savored the warm remembrance.

"You will feel the bruises tomorrow," he predicted, finishing his inspection, "but I do not think you have broken anything of consequence."

She felt like a clumsy dolt.

"You fall down much too often," Faran said with a twinkle in his eyes, as he pulled dead leaves and twigs from her hair. "It would seem the only safe place for you is in my bed." He leaned closer and swept his hand across her bottom, brushing the dust and debris from the back of the tablecloth mantle she wore over her tunic.

Faran's bed was the last place she would find safety. Even now, his touch caused her breath to catch in her throat, and she recalled how he had looked this morning—naked and wanting.

With his arm in mid-stroke, he froze. Confused, she studied his face, then she heard it too.

A feeling akin to thunder issued around them, only it thrummed in the earth not the sky—the direction indistinct

"Mounted warriors pass nearby," he said. "Our enemies are close at hand."

Retrieving the sword, he hurried to an unencumbered spot in the trail, placed the weapon flat upon the dusty ground, and gave it a twist. As the sword spun around three times and then came to a dead stop, she witnessed firsthand the enchantment of the blade. The tip of the weapon pointed off to the right of the trail. "They come from that direction." He nodded. "Bring the shield," he ordered, scooping up the sword and bundle of food.

At the urgency in Faran's voice, she jumped to do his bidding. They scrambled through the underbrush, briars and brambles snagging her clothing and scratching her legs. Relentlessly, he forged on, and before long the muscles in her legs screamed for a respite, and a sharp pain needled her side. She could hardly breathe.

The unwieldy shield smacked into a low branch. It jostled her sideways, then rebounded off her thigh and sent her into another limb. Taking two steps to each one of Faran's, she was not sure how much longer she could go on. They were still heading in the direction of the town, albeit by a circuitous route. The day was waning, and as she stubbed her booted toe on an unseen rock, she cursed the growing dimness.

Faran abruptly halted, and she plowed into his back.

"You crash through the woods like a boar in season," he complained. "Hold the shield to the side and slightly in front of you, otherwise we may as well call out our position."

Her legs burned and throbbed from myriad scrapes and cuts. Her hand was full of splinters from the wooden backing of his stupid shield, and all he could do was reprimand her for making too much noise.

"Well, I beg your pardon," she said, trying to catch her breath. "I have never received training in the proper method of fleeing through a dense woods while burdened with a weighty shield."

"Well now you have," he shot back at her.

Before she could sputter out a response he hurried on.

Following his instructions she re-positioned the shield and rushed after him. It galled her to admit his suggestion actually helped, but she was still angry at his curtness. Tears stung her eyes, but she blinked them back and kept going. If this was going to be his attitude, once she found her mother, she may not wish to continue on the southbound journey after all.

****

Gaining the backstreets of Gylfi, Faran led her down a dim alleyway, his pace slow and cautious.

When they dared to pause, several veiled figures materialized out of the misty atmosphere. Foggy apparitions, the tattered villagers were swathed in strips of gray material, and their images were blurred and indistinct.

"We are friends of the revolution," Faran declared. "We mean you no harm."

One man, much larger than the others, lumbered forward. Leanora pressed closer to Faran, grateful as he slipped his arm across her shoulder.

The man who faced them wore no gray trappings. He had brown shaggy hair and brown eyes, and clothed in an animal hide, he resembled a bear. Folding his meaty arms across his chest, he tucked hands the size of wine flagons beneath his massive forearms and stared down at them.

"So you mean us no harm," he said. "But do you mean us any help?"

"We have pledged our services to Cynric," Leanora spoke up.

Faran stomped on her foot to silence her.

She glared at him. "Do you think your quest the only one in town?" she muttered under her breath. "We promised to help them."

"That was before."

"Before what?"

"Before Gorham took a personal interest in us. Now, we will be fortunate to help ourselves."

To abandon these people to Gorham's wrath did not sit well with her. She wanted to stand beside them and prove her mettle. "Fighting for the rights of the downtrodden is not something you should do only when it fits your mood," she said. "Honor and valor are where you find them, not where you find time for them." The militant nature of her discourse surprised even her.

"I know that," he said through clenched teeth, "but our presence could lead the king's men right to the peasants, foiling their plans."

"Oh." Well, now she felt properly dimwitted. As usual, Faran was right. She had charged ahead, wrapped in noble ideals and her recently discovered bravado, with no notion of the real scope of what transpired here.

"I am sorry," she said, "your point is well taken." She should have given his honor more credit.

"The lady speaks with heartfelt intent," Faran addressed the brawny man, "but without good sense. Only you can choose whether we stay or not. We are willing to assist your cause, if you are willing to bear the consequences of our help."

The bear-man took a menacing step forward. "Cynric told us you were stouthearted," he said, and slapped Faran on the back. "Your words are spoken wisely and openly, friend. And since Gorham and Romaine now conspire together against us, winning the day will be most difficult. Every man will count. We accept your support, and the risk of associating with the likes of you," he added, with a rumbling laugh.

Leanora's gaze roamed across the determined faces of the rebels. None appeared to be trained warriors, but they seemed brave of heart and courageous of spirit. Still their expressions seemed knowing—as if each man recognized he might soon die in battle.

"How can we help?" Faran asked.

"Tomorrow, at the appointed hour, we rally behind the old monastery. From there we can easily reach the section of dyke where the supporting structures have already been weakened. With small effort, the dam will give way and release the water. Then we must protect any people left in town from the flooding and from the king."

"When do you gather?"

"At the hour of dawn. Once liberated, the Lady of the Mere will be our avenging angel. She will set aright the terrible wrongs we and the land have suffered." To Leonora, it sounded a tall order for one small faerie.

"We shall join you there," Faran said.

"You are welcome to shelter with us for the night," the rebel offered.

Faran seemed thoughtful. "It is safer for all concerned if we do not stay together. The gods be with you friend, as are we."

Nodding, the man rejoined his comrades, and the dusky phantoms faded into the murky night.

When they were alone, Faran stared down at Leonora. "Your eyes are aglow, and your cheeks burn with the anticipation of warring," he muttered. "I have created a monster."

"What do you mean?" she asked, not sure if his words were insult or praise.

"Once you were timid as the wren carved upon your boat. Now you are a hawk, seeking to fight at the least provocation."

"I am still the same bird, but no longer tethered. I only seek to test my wings."

"Be sure you do not fly too high," he warned. There was a sadness in his expression, as if he were hurt or disappointed. She had thought he would be proud of her boldness and independence.

Ever since she had allowed herself to feel and think with her heart, she had discovered a different world, one she wished to conquer rather than hide from. He had changed her. He had forced her to accept freedom. Without him she would still be on her lonely little island.

"If I fly too high," she said, "it will not be the first time I have fallen."

He did not smile at her jest. "Just be sure

someone is there to pick you up."

Considering his words, she reached for the shield, and the front of her "gown" gaped open again. Yanking it closed, she stuffed the overlap within the folds.

"Here," Faran said, "use this." He loosened something attached to the leather band of his heart fetish. In the palm of his hand lay a silver brooch inlaid with amber.

She gasped. "Oh, how beautiful." The finely wrought fibula was fashioned in the shape of a blossom. Was it a gillyflower? "Where did you find this?" she asked. "Was it in your half of the treasure we shared?"

"No. It was in the leather bag that washed ashore with me on your island. It belonged to my mother. She gave it to me for good fortune on my quest. Take it, please."

"Oh, I could not." Why did he offer her such a precious gift? "You may still need its sentiments," she said, not wishing to be in his debt. "Although its powers seem somewhat in question," she teased, "when one considers the hardships you have already endured."

"That is not true, Leanora. It brought me you." He stepped closer, grasped the front of the brown fabric, and slid his hand between the cloth and her bare flesh. "Let it nestle here upon your breast."

As he worked at pinning the edges of her tunic together, his hand lingered, and the heat from his body trickled through her like liquid sunshine. Then he rubbed the back of his knuckles against her skin, and a weakness rippled across her thighs.

Faran lowered his head and slanted his mouth across hers, and enfolding her in a hard embrace, he walked her backward until her shoulders roughly met a stonewall. Shifting his hands to capture her face, he urged her to look up at him, urged her to witness the desire burning in his eyes. The pressure of his hips as he leaned into her, promised more than just a look.

She ran her fingertips along the plane of his cheek, and a warm smile softened the mouth that she enticed with her own. The unyielding stones at her back were cold, but she did not notice the chill as her body flamed with the simple pleasure of feeling him near. Once more, she was swept away to a place of safety. A place where she felt nothing could ever hurt her again.

He spanned her waist and eased her up onto a small ledge. Then he slid his hands down to her thighs. Drawing one leg up, he coaxed her to wrap it around his body as he sought the warmth and softness beneath her shift.

Liberating himself from his breechcloth, full-blown and hard, he teased against the outer recesses of her body—the part she yearned for him to breach and fill.

"Faran...my love." The words slipped out uncensored as he eased into her. Slowly, so slowly, and oh so fully.

He covered her mouth with his, absorbing the moans, accentuating the rush of wanting that sent her reeling. She held on tight, urging him on.

With his hands braced against the wall at her back, he took her—his desperate need equal to her own. As he pinned her against the stonework and groaned in satisfaction, her aching hunger intensified to a wild throbbing explosion.

Chapter Twenty-Three

"Behind you," Leanora shouted.

Three soldiers materialized out of the gloom. Faran jammed his clothes into place and turned to face the attackers. As they closed ranks and advanced, he grabbed up the sword and shield, and maneuvered away from her side.

"Depart here, now, Leanora," he ordered and braced himself for the onslaught. But she had no intentions of leaving.

Frantically, she sought a weapon of her own. The alley, littered with rummage, offered surprisingly little from which to choose. In desperation she picked up a rock and hurled it at one of the soldiers. The stone bounced harmlessly off of the man's thick leather corselet, but it did catch his attention. He drew his dagger, and as the knife whistled passed her ear, she retreated and watched in helpless frustration as a scene of mortal combat unfolded before her.

Faran's arms and legs strained with anticipation and his shoulder muscles flexed, renting the too-small shirt.

He swung the weapon of Beowulf up over his head. "Brother Naegling," he called into the night, "blade born anew. Defend this child of Woden. Protect this Storm Geat—tribesman of your first master."

The blade flashed in the gloomy twilight, cleaving the night air with the sharp-edged voice of vengeance. Coupled with his grim expression, his countenance was fearful to behold. And in the face of his calm daring, the soldiers hesitated.

As if eager to test their mettle, Faran menaced his attackers. He struck the first blow, and the man staggered backwards. Then, in earnest, the clash of weapons echoed through the night.

Although outnumbered, Faran remained in control of the fight. Strong and magnificent, his body seemed made for warring. He fended off sword strike after sword strike, and as blow upon blow rained down upon his shield, he weathered each attack and leaped upon his opponents with agility and cunning.

Awed by his display of prowess, Leanora watched in amazement. Having known the quiet side of this man, it was with wonderment that she witnessed the war-like splendor also a fundamental part of his nature.

The enemy soldiers emitted animal noises and blasphemous curses as they battled for their lives. The first opponent went down. Unyielding, Faran stepped over the man's still form and relentlessly pursued the other two.

Suddenly, the sound of nearby fighting played harmony with the noise before her. They had lingered too long. More of Gorham's soldiers were sure to be drawn to the melee. She peered down the alleyway to make sure no one else approached. Then someone grabbed her by the hair, and viciously yanked her backwards. She reached up over her head, wretched free, and spun around coming nose to nose with Romaine.

"You scrawny bitch," the ebon-haired woman shrieked and slapped her across the face.

In pain and surprise, Leanora staggered sideways. As she peeked out from beneath her raised forearm, she glanced about trying to sort out what was happening.

Romaine snarled and rushed forward. Leanora crouched low and twisted from the path of the depraved woman. With a howl of frustration, the royal harpy turned to face her. Leanora balled her hand into a fist, drew back her arm, and delivered unto the queen a mighty right cross to the jaw.

On impact, Leanora's knuckles cracked, but the startled expression on Romaine's face was worth every bit of the pain. The woman's dark eyes grew wide, then a blank expression replaced her look of surprise and she crumpled to the dirt.

With the toe of her boot, Leanora nudged Romaine. She was out cold. The woman never learned.

Taking stock of her surroundings, Leanora spied the queen's horse. He pawed the ground and sniffed in the direction of the three soldiers now lying dead upon the bloodied ground. She grabbed for the dangling reins, but the frightened animal shied away, and with a wild-eyed snort, he fled down a cobbled footpath.

Faran stood several paces away. His eyes bright with battle courage. "Leanora," he called, "are you unharmed?"

At her nod, his body relaxed. He slid the shield down along his leg and rested the edge on the ground. Holding his arms wide, he beckoned her forward and she ran to his side. With each breath he took, his nostrils flared, as if the heady nectar of victory still coursed through his veins. And with one arm wrapped around her shoulder, he drew her close and buried his face in the curtain of her hair.

For a moment, the sights and sounds around her blurred and faded. Then the cherished quiet was disturbed by the distant echo of chaos growing louder and closer.

They drew apart. Faran grabbed the shield, and hurried her toward a small outbuilding. He kicked open the rickety door and slashed about with his sword, driving back the rats waiting to welcome them. The shed listed to one side, and the rotted planks offered several gaps in the dilapidated wall. A quick peek through one of the openings revealed Gorham as he arrived with a mounted patrol. The contingent of men poured into the alleyway—black specters in the dim atmosphere.

"They will see us if they look closely," she whispered to Faran.

"Not with the help of the shield. Stay behind me." He raised the buckler. She crouched at his back, and peered over his shoulder. She could hear someone speaking.

"At any cost, the Storm Geat and the girl must be found," Gorham's voice rang out, "but pray remember they are not to be unduly harmed. I want them alive."

He reined in his horse directly in front of the shack and the prancing hoofs of the king's steed kicked up clouds of dust. As the billowy puffs drifted about in the sullen air, Leanora had a terrible urge to sneeze. She eased one hand upward, pinched her nostrils together, and leaned her forehead against the solid bulk of Faran's shoulder. After a bit, she cautiously released the grip on her nose. Big mistake.

"Aah-choo..."

The sneeze was out before she could stop it. Gorham nudged his mount a step closer. Faran's body stiffened. He shifted his grip on the sword and readied for the attack. Leaning forward, the king seemed to peer directly at them, but no sign of recognition crossed his features. As he scowled and canted his head to one side, she prayed he would not hear the pounding of her heart.

Romaine's timely groan vied for her brother's attention, breaking his concentration. He turned his mount toward his sister, and Leanora slowly released the breath she had been holding.

"Romaine, Romaine," he clucked as he stared down at her. "You are forever upon your back." There was little sympathy in Gorham's voice.

"Help her up," he commanded. A nearby soldier jumped to do his bidding. "And retrieve her mount."

Romaine gained her feet. "We are but moments behind the Geat," she said with a nod toward the fallen soldiers who littered the ground. "His handiwork lies all around us."

"And the girl, she was with him?" Gorham asked.

The queen rubbed her jaw and wobbled it back and forth, as if checking to see that it still functioned properly. "The wicked tart was here. She is pale of aura and meager of build, but both belie her strength. "

At the last remark, Leanora bristled. Faran pressed back against her, silencing the growl purring in her throat.

"They will not remain free for long," Gorham reassured. "Romaine, you and I will continue searching for the warrior and his woman. The soldiers will seek out the rebels. We have only until morning to foil their plan to drain the lake. Our time is running out."

"You know what to do." He nodded toward the waiting men-at-arms. "You must crush this rebellion even if it means the life of every man, woman, and child in this village. All who oppose me are guilty of treason, and you will deal with them accordingly." Gorham uttered the words with such cold resolution he made hoarfrost sound deliciously warm.

"It would seem," he added, turning back to his sister, "we shall have to spend the evening in town. But with the rebels soon dancing to our tune, there will at least be sufficient entertainment to keep us from boredom."

"Entertainment or not, there is no other way for it." Romaine agreed and leaped upon her mount. "I refuse to traverse that hellish black mere by the dark of night. Wait we must, and return to your stronghold come morning."

Leanora smiled at the crackle of concern in the other woman's voice. It was a comfort to know Romaine was not as fearless as she pretended.

Gorham kicked his horse into a trot. The Queen of the May rushed to catch up. As they disappeared down the dimly lit lane, their final words were lost to the night. The guards and soldiers followed in their wake.

Leanora clung to Faran, listening to the sound of the retreating footsteps and her own rapid breathing. In the ensuing silence, they sneaked from the rickety enclosure. She touched the amber pin Faran had given her just moments before, and a calming strength seemed to issue forth from it.

"Gorham is crazed with bloodlust," Faran said. "He means to spare no one. We must warn our friends."

"Yes." She nodded. "And his soldiers are equally devoid of mercy or conscience. Thank the Lord, the women and children have already been taken from the city. Gorham did not appear to be aware of that."

She inched Faran's shirt up. He grinned and reached for her. "Are you never satisfied, woman?"

"I wish only to check the wound on your side." She grinned. "And yes, I am very satisfied," she added. "Your wound fares well, it has not opened." She tugged his tunic back into place and retrieved the shield.

Faran drew closer. "Thank you again for traveling with me. With you at my side, I feel all things are possible."

What did one say in the face of such unexpected

accolades? She studied his face—a face she had come to love and cherish. "You're welcome, Faran. Despite the mayhem and hardships, these last few days have been the happiest of my life."

He opened his mouth as if to say more, then just smiled, took her hand, and led down the dark passageway to the street.

At the corner, they paused and scurried into the entryway of a merchant's shop. The town was a deserted battlefield. Broken pottery lay in pieces on the ground. Carts and barrels were crushed and overturned. The shutters on several cottages hung at odd angles, nearly ripped from their hinges. In other parts of the city, smoke from burning thatch poured into the air, adding to the dismal clime.

Like carnivorous beasts, the guards lingered in wait, but there was no more prey. No rebellious villagers were in sight, only the dead, who laid motionless upon the cobbles. In the face of this bleak reality, Leanora's enthusiasm for fighting quickly waned. Her shoulders drooped, and hope trembled a little more tenuously in her chest. As she surveyed the carnage at her feet, her dream of a valorous battle was transformed into a nightmare.

"This way." Faran slipped his hand into hers.

"Where are we going?" she whispered as he tugged her along.

"Into the thick of it, most likely."

At the sound of foot soldiers approaching, they made tracks for the village square and the fishmonger's stall. Bones crunched beneath her boots, and she skidded sideways on the guts of today's catch. Faran grabbed her around the waist keeping her upright. She gagged at the stench, not daring to look down.

The group of enemy soldiers passed harmlessly by, but before they were out of sight, something clamped down around Leanora's ankle. Pain shot up her leg. She bit back a scream and struggled in vain against the iron grip holding her captive.

"Faran," she squeaked, "help me."

Visions of the monster living in the lake flashed through her mind. Had the beast crawled upon the shore to vindicate its scaly friends who daily met their fate here? Faran swung his sword to cut her free, but at the last moment he held back and she glanced down to see what stayed his intentions.

It was a human hand holding her, not the slaver jaws of some fearsome beast. The grip on her leg eased, and her gaze jumped to the face belonging to the hand. It was the bear-man, and he was gravely injured.

Faran shoved aside the chopping block beside which the man lay. She knelt at his shoulder. The fire of life flickered weakly in his eyes and the ground near him was dark with blood. As if gaining life from the very people who died fighting for its liberation, the cadaverous Lothian soil greedily sucked up the sticky substance.

"The rebels have been overrun and routed," the man forced out through clenched teeth. "Few if any survive to drain Black Rain Lake." He pointed a bloody finger at Faran. "You must see that it is done."

Without hesitation, and in a show of fealty, Faran reached out and clasped the man's forearm.

"And make sure the bastards get not my arm rings," the big man added with what seemed his last bit of strength.

"We shall not fail you," Faran promised.

Leanora retrieved a small battle-ax lying in the dirt and slipped it into the hand of the wounded man. A smile hovered on his lips and he grasped the weapon, then he exhaled slow and long. As he surrendered himself into the keeping of his god, the weapon fell from his slackened grip.

Fingers shaking with cold and dread, Leanora closed his unseeing eyes. As bidden, Faran tugged the gold and silver war circlets from the bear-man's arms.

As if in a daze she gained her feet. "What now?" she asked.

"It's simple," he said as he slid on the arm rings replacing the ones stolen from him by the guards at Gorham's citadel. "We drain the lake."

But she knew it would not be simple, and like weasels 'round a mulberry bush, one worry after another chased 'round in her mind.

****

They hurried toward the dyke. In the distance stood the deserted chapel where all survivors were to meet come the dawn. The small prayer house was in dire disrepair. Cracks and fissures scarred the sides of the once white walls, and the broken windows offered a forlorn expression devoid of welcoming warmth. Cold and unfriendly, it seemed to glower at them.

As they followed an overgrown walkway, dead leaves brazenly danced around her legs, and the wind sang through the monuments in the graveyard. Slowing to a more respectful pace, they crept between ancient markers listing like drunken old men around a gaming table.

Evening mist curled languidly through the burial ground, and haunting moans seemed to scurry about on the cold breeze. A collapsed berm spilled forth a jumble of skeletons and a foul green fog, and dry-heaving, for once she was thankful for an empty stomach.

At the towpath, they circled the dyke and bore to the left. Ducking beneath the branches of a sprawling oak, they halted within the welcome concealment. "The weakened area is most likely close by," Faran said. "By the lay of the land it is the logical site. We can keep searching for it tonight, or stop now and rest until the morning. What do you wish to do?"

"I say we wait until morning." Her muscles ached, and her body yearned for sleep. "There is little more we can do tonight. And mayhap the bear-man was wrong. More rebels may have survived than he realized. A united front come morning is our best hope for success."

Faran studied her face. "Why is the plight of these people so important to you?" he asked.

"I understand their desire to be free," she explained. "I thought I was free on my island, but I was wrong. I had only found a sanctuary purchased at the cost of the liberty I sought to preserve. You helped me to see that, and you gave me the courage to overcome my fears. You gave me the will to fight back, Faran, and I would now help others to do the same."

"Freedom always demands a price," he cautioned. "This time it is the lives of the rebels and the angering of a king."

"The lives already lost must not be in vain. And as for Gorham, it is his nature to be angry. For all he has gained as king, he is not a happy man."

"It would be my pleasure to end his sorrow, permanently," Faran offered. There was a flinty hardness about his voice. He still sought justice for his people. Leanora understood this need, but for the one who wielded the sword, vengeance could vanquish as well as satisfy. If nurtured, it outgrew the seeking of justice, then it corrupted as well as vindicated.

"Let us take things one step at a time," she urged, and touched his arm.

He covered her hand with his, and the lines harrying the corners of his mouth gentled. "Yes," he agreed, "one step at a time."

They circled around to the front of the dilapidated holy house, and crept inside. In Gorham's kingdom, the Christian faith had not been met with full open arms. She wondered what had befallen the priest or monk who had tried to bring religion to a land where none was wanted.

Faran sank to the ground. She dropped down at his side. Tugging open the bag of provisions, she doled out the last of the bread and cheese.

Finished with the paltry repast, Leanora nestled beside Faran. As he skimmed his fingers up and down her arm, an aching replaced exhaustion. It spilled lower, tantalizing the part of her now belonging to him.

Faran drew her atop his body. "Dear Gillyflower." He sighed, and hugged her against his chest. "You drive the weariness from my bones, and the heaviness from my heart." He gently bucked his hips upward, his intentions obvious.

"Faran." She laughed. "Not here. Not in a chapel."

"Why not," he countered, nipping and kissing at her neck. "No one's god should condemn the sharing of love."

Chapter Twenty-Four

"While the Lord does encourage us to love one another, we need show respect in the house of our Father."

As the unexpected voice rang out, Leanora reared back in surprise. Then she flattened herself against Faran, seeking the protective circle of his arms. Her gaze leaped from corner to corner of the dim structure. Who had spoken in this ghostly chapel?

Faran pushed her aside and scrambled to his feet. "Show yourself," he challenged, sword in hand.

From out of the shadows stepped a man of small stature. He was dressed in the garb of a monk, and he appeared to be without a weapon.

"Be you Saxon or Dane, you are welcome to shelter here," the man said, "as long as you behave yourself."

A sigh of annoyance escaped Faran. "I am Storm Geat, not Dane. And I shelter where I please." He raised the tip of his sword level with the holy man's throat.

Leanora struggled to her feet. "Faran," she said, and peered around his shoulder, "I doubt this old monk means us any harm."

"Stay back, Leanora," Faran cautioned, "in this curious realm danger comes in many forms."

"Leanora?"

Silence hung in the air. All three people stood motionless and stared at one another.

"Leanora, it is I, Brother Thomas."

"Brother Thomas? But how can this be?" She eased around Faran to see the man more clearly. Then she ran forward into the arms of the monk.

"How is it you are here? What of mother? Is she well? Is she with you?"

The monk laughed and eased her away from his chest. "Calm yourself, child," he advised. "And I shall tell you all that has transpired."

Faran snared her arm and drew her back. "Who is this man that you go to him so readily?"

"'Tis Brother Thomas, Faran. When I fled for my life, he risked much to see me safely to my little island. He is a friend to my people and a wise man."

Faran did not appear overly convinced. He held his position, a dark expression shadowing his features. As she stood between the two men, an insightful revelation washed over her. Both men had come to her unbidden, and both had rendered immense changes in her life. One had rescued her by sending her *to* her island sanctuary, and the other had rescued her by leading her *from* it. A *Bodiend* and a *Mundiend*—a mentor and a protector. She was thankful God had seen fit to send two good men her way, to counterbalance the evil ones.

"This is Tyne Faran Kilbraun," she said by way of introduction.

The monk's brows shot up in surprise. "*Tyne* Faran Kilbraun?" he repeated as if had not heard correctly.

"Faran will suffice," her warrior sharply advised.

"As you wish," Brother Thomas acquiesced with a slight bow.

The monk's reaction seemed curious, and it niggled at the back of her mind, but there were more urgent matters to address.

"Where is Mother," she asked for the second

time, hope quickening in her heart.

A look of sorrow captured the monk's features. Something was wrong. The news was not good. He took her hand and led her to one of the benches lining the wall. Alert and silent, Faran stood at the ready.

"Much has changed in the short time you have been gone," the monk began as he sat at her side. "Following your husband's demise, his tribe claimed his death as a reason to break the peace covenants. They would not listen to logic, and attacked soon after your departure. Death took a mighty toll on both sides. But your people, being outnumbered, suffered the worst of it. Your father and brothers fought valiantly. They always did enjoy a good battle," he said with a wry smile. "They died as warriors."

"And my mother?" she asked, already knowing the answer.

"Many people fled to the hills, but she remained in the village to help the wounded—as the wife of a chieftain is wont to do. Then she was wounded herself, and very nearly captured. I found her in the woods. She entrusted me with the clan's war chest, its bounty to be used to help the women and children. And although she too fought with valor, she died the next morning beneath the big oak tree standing on the mound west of your village. Now she rests there in peace, and in the hands of the Lord."

A painful knot constricted her chest, stifling her breath, turning her world black. Covering her face with her hands she cried, and one heart-wrenching sob after another tore at her body. Gone—they were all gone. Her father and brothers had died as they lived, sword in hand, warring in their souls. And her mother had died as she lived too, compassion and mercy in her heart.

"It is my fault," she whispered, horrified at the

chain of events she had set in motion. "If Ivar had lived, none of this would have happened. Even in death, the man I once called husband causes grief and pain."

"Nay, child, it is not your fault. Had you died rather than Ivar, or had they captured you and taken your life in payment for his death, it would have changed nothing—except to bring more sorrow to your mother. Helping you to escape to your island was an adventure she cherished and spoke of often— a secret smile upon her lips.

"You warned your people many times that Ivar intended to play them false. If not in retribution for his death, his tribe would have concocted another reason for warring. Or at your death, your father would have been honor-bound to declare war upon your husband's tribe. You must not blame yourself."

She wanted to believe the monk, but she had been given into marriage as a peace-weaver, and only now did she fully grasp the enormity of that responsibility. At the time, she had thought only of herself and what trials and tribulations it heaped upon her. Stubborn and willful, she had fought Ivar every step of the way. Was it too late to make amends? As the only living member of the tribal king, did she not have an obligation to lead her kin to battle to recover their land and demand restitution for those who had died?

She balled her hands into fists. "I must return home and rally those remaining."

"The village is burned, Leonora, the warriors dead and gone. And I have secured a place of safety for the women and children with the Saxons south of the Wear. They are content where they be. There is no one left to lead or be concerned about." He became silent and glanced between her and Faran. "Besides, it would seem you have a different path to follow."

"Your words ring true and wise," she admitted. "But I should have been there." Now she knew how Faran felt, not standing with his people as they fought for their lives.

With pride, she thought of her mother, and how she had helped the wounded and secured money for the women and children. And although she could no longer help her own people, or change what had happened, she could follow that example and still aid the rebels here. Faran placed a hand upon her shoulder, his touch strong and reassuring. She smiled at him through her tears. He did not return the smile, but rather he studied her with an expression of thoughtfulness.

She turned once more to Brother Thomas. "I am thankful you were with my mother at the end. She found comfort in your preaching and your counsel. You taught us much."

"There is still much left to discover in this world, little one. You must always keep learning."

"At present," Faran said, "to keep living is a more pressing need."

"Yes," Thomas admitted, "danger and treachery abounds here."

"How is it you are in this northern clime?" she asked.

"After your mother's passing, I went in search of you. I feared eventually you would seek to return home—unaware only death awaited. When I discovered you had abandoned the island, I put to sea intending to return to the mainland. But a storm blew me off course and I was fortuitously rescued by none other then King Aelfred himself."

Faran appeared surprised. "So, the man who claims to be king of all the Saxons now takes to the sea as well."

"You have heard of him then?"

"Indeed. After his exile in Athelney, my tribe

278

gave shelter to him and his thanes. We taught them of ship building."

"That was very generous of your people," Thomas commended.

"He fights the Danes," Faran said with a shrug. "And although it was not always true, now we fight the Scyldings too. Their treachery has touched many. In every pot tended by the Danes, trouble brews to bubbling over."

"Time can wreak unthinkable change," Thomas agreed. "And when friends become foes, it is a sad business—painful to the heart as well as the mind."

"It seems change is the only constant upon which one can rely."

Thomas nodded in agreement. "Did you have an opportunity to speak personally with Aelfred?"

Faran gave a snort of amusement. "Not talk, but listen. At night, around the campfires, we all heard his tales of great expectations. It would seem he desires to rule not just the West Saxons, but all of England. Yet according to rumor, while hiding in the swamps, he could not even be relied upon to keep fennel cakes from burning."

Thomas chuckled. "That tale will no doubt haunt him beyond his grave. But he is quite a remarkable person. And a pious man."

"Pious to the point of near obsession," Faran countered. "Being a word-weaver, I enjoyed the recounting of his many travels abroad. But I dare say his attempt to convert the entire Isle of Gullin tarnished his welcome a bit. It was also completely ineffectual. Pagans we are, and pagans we shall be."

"The Geats have remained true to their history longer than most," Thomas acknowledged. "It is good to remember the past and to learn from it."

"And how is it you know so much about my people, monk?"

"The knowing of languages is my special

passion. Therefore, I have taken quite an interest in those who inhabit this realm and the islands surrounding it. Your people have quite a remarkable history. And ensconced upon the Isle of Gullin, Tyne Faran, you have been more successful than most in remaining true to the old ways."

"You speak in riddles, holy man, like the rune-counselors in my tribe. And as I told you before, I prefer you simply call me Faran."

"I beg your pardon. It will not happen again. I understand your caution as you travel far from home and without kinsmen. By the way, what is your purpose here? Have you come, like your predecessor Beowulf, to help a people in need?"

"I have come to right a wrong. Helping the local rebels was Leanora's idea. She is too softhearted. No doubt your doing."

Lost in thought, Leanora did not respond to the conversation whirring around her. Rather, she recalled the unlimited wealth she had attained and realized it had come too late. Sadly, there would be no safe shelter or life of comfort for her dear mother, dead and gone forever. By the saints, now she was an orphan as well as a widow. How pitiful a feeling to be all alone in the world.

She glanced at Faran. In a heartbeat, his place in her life had become even more important. And in a heartbeat, he could just as easily disappear from it. A feeling of panic gripped her. No matter what deity one believed in, all remained at the mercy of unseen hands. Tears spilled from her eyes. She was glad now she had agreed to follow Faran to the south. But to what ends? Perhaps to no end—but rather to an unexpected beginning. At least Brother Thomas was once more at her side. That was a saving grace.

"You have not told us why you are in this dark northern region," she said to the holy man.

"It is due to King Aelfred's pious intentions." Brother Thomas threw a glance in Faran's direction. "After fishing me from the sea, he bid me come to Lothian to locate the previous monk who dwelled here, and to continue spreading the word of God. As I owe him my life, refusing was out of the question. But I am beginning to think it will take more than one or two lowly monks to stem the tide of evil dwelling within this realm."

She nodded and leaned her head upon her old teacher's shoulder. "I am so weary of all the chaos and sorrow surrounding us of late. Maybe I shall return to my island."

"You would not be safe even there," Thomas said. "Unimaginable wars are in the offing. And soon all men—and women—will have to choose between the past and the future."

Chapter Twenty-Five

The sky remained dark, but Faran reckoned it must be near dawn.

He leaned over and kissed the tip of Leanora's nose. She sighed, but showed no sign of awakening. Even under dire circumstances, rising early was not her specialty—in truth, it left her rather cross. But her other qualities made up for her morning petulance.

"Leanora," he whispered and traced a lazy pattern upon her shoulder. She murmured but still did not open her eyes.

He watched her sleep, and memories of the love they had shared the evening before blazed across his mind. Desperate for privacy, they had wandered a short distance from the chapel and Brother Thomas' eyes and ears. Their burning passion for one another was unquenchable, and regardless of time or place, it would not be denied. Each day it overwhelmed him anew, and he grew ever more accustomed to having her near at hand.

As he stared at her, he recalled the enlightening conversation she'd shared with the monk. Because she was a peace-weaver, he had assumed her family was of some stature, but he had not realized she was the daughter of the tribe's leader. Would this help his cause when he returned home and petitioned the king of the Geats on her behalf? It could not hurt.

He glanced again at the chapel window. The predawn light now truly struggled to be born.

Levering up on one elbow, he shook Leanora with more determination.

"I am awake," she mumbled. "You need not jostle me to the point of scrambling my brains." She sat up, and gave him a playful push. When she yawned and stretched her arms over her head, he caught her around the waist and wrestled her back to the ground. The morning offered no time for a proper bout of loving making, but he couldn't resist a small taste.

He kissed her, and growling like a tiger, nuzzled her neck. She giggled and wiggled, and it took much effort to turn away from the path she led him down.

"It is very near daybreak," Brother Thomas called, his voice ringing out from the other side of the small chapel.

Their secret pleasure interrupted, Leanora quickly withdrew her hands, and the blissful touching came to a painfully abrupt halt. "We are awake, holy man," he grumbled, and adjusted his breechcloth.

Gaining his feet, he helped Leanora to hers.

The monk set out brown bread and mugs of ale.

"Where found you this unexpected fare," Faran asked in surprise.

"Last eventide, while the two of you were *occupied elsewhere*, I sought more edifying purpose and discovered the larder. Lord Gorham may not have believed in the one true God, but apparently he felt obliged to feed the priest who lived here. The man dined moderately well before he was driven from the land."

"Well done, monk." Faran reached for the bread. "You are proving to be worth the trouble of listening to your religious prattle."

"Thank you, I think. Shall we say grace before we partake?"

Faran sighed and stilled the handful of food

already halfway to his mouth. When it came to food, a warrior ate first and prayed later. Who knew when the next meal might come? While the gods were always there and ready to listen.

"...Amen," the monk finally concluded.

"And praise Freya as well," Faran threw in. He would not be out-prayed any more readily than he would be out-fought.

"Come," Faran said, downing the last of the ale. "We've no time to waste. The appointed hour draws near, and we must make sure there are no villagers upon the lake when we set free the water."

"We are on our own then?" she asked.

"I am not hopeful that others will be joining us," he admitted

"And what of the guards?" Leanora asked.

"With the rebels routed or dead, they will most likely think trouble has been averted. I do not believe they will be expecting us."

****

As the pale sun worried the far ridge, Faran stood beside the dyke. From this angle, the wall appeared near vertical with few if any handholds.

Leanora's expression reflected his trepidation. Then she smiled, tightened the lacings on her boots, squared her shoulders, and stood at his side ready to risk all. Again, he admired the pluck and courage housed in so small and gentle a frame.

"I could make the climb more swiftly alone," he suggested. Besides," he added at her crestfallen expression, "someone must remain here with the sword and shield. Other than you, I trust no one to that task."

Her brow remained furrowed with concern. "With Cynric guarding the women and children, and no other rebels in sight, you will be on your own should things go awry," she pointed out.

"I still have you," he said. "Keep the sword close

at hand. When I am sure it is safe to drain the lake, I will return to destroy the last brace holding back the dyke." He studied the row of wooden buttresses and cross pieces already hewn to near the breaking point. When the final strut was eliminated the fortification would collapse. The south wall would crumble near the top, and the water would be set free.

She rested a hand upon his chest. "You must signal down to me if there is anything I can do to help from here."

"I will." He cradled her hand, raised it to his lips, and kissed her fingertips. Then he forced himself from her side to begin the ascent.

The jagged rocks scoured his hands and knees, and as he pressed against the craggy wall, his heart amulet dug into his chest. The climb was more arduous than he had anticipated, and he was glad Leanora had stayed behind, safely awaiting his return. How wonderful it would be if she would always be waiting for him, no matter where they wandered or where they sheltered.

He glanced over his shoulder. She nodded encouragement. His brave, sweet Gillyflower. Sometimes he could not bear to admit what she meant to him. He had begun this woeful quest devoid of hope and happiness. But with her help, the relics were recovered and his future held promise. Once he returned home, the gods willing, he was determined to win back the favor of the king, vanquish the dishonor he had brought upon himself and his family, and claim Leanora as his woman.

The dirt beneath his right foot gave way. Woden's teeth, he should be thinking about his next handhold to the top, not about holding hands with his lover. Backsliding, he grabbed a bush. The prickly scrub, full of thorns, bit into his hand. But he held tight and labored his way upward. By sheer will and determination he finally hoisted himself to the top of the dam. Gasping for breath, he collapsed against the earthen wall, and heart pounding, he cautiously peered up over the embankment.

Out upon the black water, the ferryboat careened its way across the lake toward the citadel. A maelstrom of wind assaulted the pitiful craft, and as the fury of air turn in his direction, it conveyed the words spoken by those onboard.

"I told you it was folly to venture out before full sunup," the stooped old ferryman chastised. "We be goin' down," he cried in high-pitched panic and boldly shook a fist at Gorham.

"Stop jabbering. It is nearly dawn," the king growled back. "And it is not the creature who threatens our passage." Disengaging Romaine's arms from around his neck, Gorham foisted his terrified sister onto a guard. "It's the anniversary of my father defeating the water spirit," he snarled. "That is what disturbs the mere."

Gorham was correct. Today, as if in anticipated of what was to come, the water seemed alive with discontent. The small boat pitched and rolled, skidding down one swell only to hit the next surge broadside.

Faran smiled. If good fortune were his, as the lake was drained, Gorham and Romaine would meet their doom. It seemed a proper ending for the bloodthirsty pair and their henchmen. But it must be done without delay, lest the malevolent pair reach shelter on the island toward which they headed.

He scrunched down out of sight, and cupping his hands to his mouth, called down to Leanora. "All is well. I am coming down now."

"What?" she called and hurried to the foot of the dam.

The weather had worsened, and although he could hear the voices on the lake, his own words were torn asunder. Pronouncing each word slowly, he repeated them.

"All is well. I'll climb down now."

Why did she look so confused?

****

All is well. The time is now? But shouldn't she wait until Faran was clear of the wall. Had dawn broken and time run out? The sky did appear somewhat less dreary. She wrung her hands. What should she do? Brother Thomas had gone to reconnoiter in the city, and to search for help and watch for soldiers. There was no one else to aid her in the decision or the deed. It was up to her, she must free the water.

Misgivings churned in her mind and stomach. She could barely swallow around the fear lodged in her throat. Then mercifully, a heady feeling of excitement devoured the panic. The future of Lothian lay in her hands. She must not, would not, fail.

She took stock of the lay of the land to determine which way was best to run when the wall gave way. Then she positioned herself before the last sturdy beam holding back the water. All she had to do was hack her way through one main log, no matter it just happened to be twice as big around as her waist. Good Lord, the task could take her half the morning, and make enough noise to turn lemmings from their path.

She glanced at Faran. He waved his arms frantically, his words captured and swallowed by the wind. She smiled and waved back. He seemed most anxious for her to begin.

With Beowulf's cherished blade in hand, she braced her legs and took a deep breath. Her hand tingled. Then the feeling intensified, spreading up her arm and into her chest. A ripple of daring flowed through her body. Faran had said if the weapon was

287

wielded by a warrior who truly believed, it could hew a full-grown tree with one stroke. But a warrior who believe in what, or in whom? Woden, Freya, Beowulf? Maybe you had only to believe in yourself, or in one other person who believed in you. One other person for whom you would die.

She raised the blade over her head. "For you, Tyne Faran Kilbraun," she cried, and struck downward with all her might. The sword hewed the timber with the ease of a hot dagger upon honeycomb.

In mute surprise she stared at the severed timber. The pieces tumbled sideways to the ground. Above the cry of the wind, she heard the groan of wood as it twisted beneath a ponderous weight. The ground shook and heaved beneath her feet, and the sound of impending disaster goaded her into action.

She turned and ran, scrambling up the nearby hill to where the shield was hidden. Then as she watched, a mountain of black water burst through the weakened bastion.

****

What was she doing?

Before Faran could think of a logical answer, the earth disappeared beneath his feet and the lake rushed at him from behind. Instinctively he drew his knees up to his chest and wrapped his arms around them. Jaws clenched tight, he took a deep breath and squinted his eyes shut as he hurtled passed the rocks and logs once forming the edge of the dyke.

Breaking free of the downward drag of the water, he sailed through the air faster than a shooting star and farther than a well-thrown pike. This he must see—even if he were going to die. He opened his eyes, and his mouth followed suit as the thrill of defying nature surged through him. For an instant, he hung suspended over the lip of the excavated wall, and the world around him appeared frozen in time. He saw the tops of trees and small hillocks and the winding path of mud formed by the escaping water. A strange breathlessness drummed in his chest, and with his heart in his throat, he glided like a hawk. Then he dropped like a rock.

Blurry images of the sky and the earth alternately flashed before him. He spiraled toward the ground, and saw Leanora floundering through the mud.

****

A wave of water swept Leanora off her feet. She tumbled sideways, and hit her head on the ground. Spitting dirt from her mouth, she wondered why Faran had insisted she free the water when he was still atop the dyke.

As if beckoned by her question, her warrior dropped from the sky. He landed in a patch of mud-covered brush, bounced off the cushiony foliage, and careened straight toward her at an alarming rate. His arm caught her around the knees, and she hit the ground for a second time. Grabbing onto his shoulders, she clung to him with a death grip. They slithered along in the river of mud and finally ground to a halt. Tugging her arm free from beneath him, she sat up beside his still form, and her heart skipped a beat. He did not move nor breathe.

Lightheaded with fear, she knelt at his side. Seeing him prostrate upon the ground reminded her of finding him on the shore of her island. Back then she had wished him dead with every fiber of her being—now she would give anything to ensure his survival.

"No," she screamed. "You cannot die." As if he were to blame, she hit his chest with her fist. "Please, God," she begged. "Spare him. He is more kind than most, and a good and honest man."

Trying to wake him, trying to make him breathe, she pushed on his ribs and pulled on his shoulders. Suddenly his chest heaved, and he gasped and coughed his way to consciousness.

"Faran," she cried, tears of relief blurring her vision. "I thought you dead at best."

With a groan he opened his eyes then laughed. "I have flown like the birds," he exclaimed, "and lived to tell the tale. Not even one of my brothers has ever done such a thing." He grinned at her as if he had just invented the wheel, and struggling to sit upright, he leaned forward and kissed her muddy cheek with his muddy lips.

"Are you injured?" Frantically she ran her hands over his shoulders and arms.

"The balm of victory soothes my aches and pains," he crowed. "At least it did," he gasped as she hugged him soundly and nearly tumbled him backward onto the ground.

"Why did you tell me to set the water free while you were still upon the dyke?" she asked.

"I didn't. You misunderstood my words."

"But you could have been killed, and it would have been my fault." She hid her face in her hands, and her stomach heaved at the thought of what could have happened.

He patted her shoulder as if she were a child with a broken toy. "All is well, Gillyflower," he said, "You wielded the sword as bravely as any Geat warrior."

There was pride in his voice. She peeked at him from between her splayed fingers, and then lowered her hands. "I did rather enjoy it." She laughed.

They basked in their success, until a commotion coming from the lakebed caught their attention. "What is that?" she asked, and grabbed his arm. "Is it the creature that lives in the lake?"

"Most likely it is Gorham and Romaine." The spark of anger burned in his eyes. "They were upon the lake when you severed the last timber. I thought they would be consumed by the cataclysm, but by the sound of it, they have survived." A muscle along his jaw twitched. "We had best see what they are up to." Shakily, they helped one another to stand.

He made sure the sword and shield were untouched, and then led her toward the incline. The slope was at less of an angle now and the going was easier. At the top Leanora peeked over what was left of the ridge, transfixed by the sight offered.

The lakebed was a glistening plain of black slime, and there sat the stranded ferry, mired in the muck. The wind was calm, and although Leanora could not hear the words uttered, the angry tones and gestures of Gorham and Romaine assured her they were far from happy with their plight.

Then a slithering motion drew her attention, and she cringed. The monster *had* endured. He thrust his scaly tail out of the ooze and slapped it down with a resounding smack. Mud splattered halfway across the lake, pelting the group of castaways.

The King of Lothian and the Queen of the May ran to the far end of the ferry. The guards ran the other way. Unbalanced, the craft foundered. Everyone save for Gorham and Romaine were delegated to the slime. The hungry quagmire swallowed the treacherous soldiers. Only the little ferryman was spared as he clung to a barrel trapped in the ooze. The royal twosome battled one another as they clung to the slim portion of boat remaining above the muck.

She watched in expectation until a crack of thunder turned her attention. The sound split the heavens, and the wind again wailed across the land. She shivered and flattened herself against the ground, thankful Faran drew close to shield her body with his. So mournful was the sound of the wind, it was as if a multitude of weeping women descended upon them.

The air crackled with anticipation, and thunder echoed around the lake. The hair on the nape of her neck stood on end, and she curled her fingers into the earth and held on for dear life.

As if hurled by the hand of Thor, a formidable bolt of lightning speared down from the sky. It struck the lakebed on the west side spewing dirt and rocks in every direction. Burned clean by the fiery blast, a cavern was revealed. The cave gleamed with an inner radiance, and Leanora's eyes widened in wonder as she saw the silver sarcophagus lying nestled within the grotto. The effigy upon the deathbed wavered as if it pulsed with life, and it quivered faster and faster as the wailing intensified.

Something grand was about to happen. The earth trembled, and she could taste a freshness in the air. Her body kept pace with the primordial throbbing rhythm. Then her anticipation turned to concern as her chest grew painful and she felt as if she were being torn apart. Heaven and earth seemed about to collide, and thoughts of never seeing Faran again screamed through her brain. Just as she feared she could bear no more, a comforting sense of relief blanketed her. Released from the spell of chaos, she sagged to the ground.

The image within the cave was now infused with color. Life flooded into the reclining figure and it began to move in earnest. The wailing ceased. The wind stopped. The transformation was complete. The Spirit of the Mere of Sleeping Misery had been re-awakened.

Unable to realize the beauty of the entity emerging from the cavern, Leanora glanced away. Then bound by curiosity, she dared once more to gaze upon dazzling display and her mouth opened in wonder.

The people of Gylfi had referred to their

guardian as a fearie creature. But what stood before them was not some sprightly figure conjured from long forgotten lore. This was a Warrior Maiden—glorious, resplendent, and fierce.

Although lithe in form, she possessed height uncommon even in a man, and her beautiful war rings encircled arms indicating strength beyond the normal female. Her hair, pure white and abundant, fluttered in wild disarray, while the spark of life flashed in eyes of deep lavender ringed by thick dark lashes. A corset of chain mail girded her from chest to hips, and the underlying garment shimmered in ever changing hues as if it were woven of threads made from seashells and pearls.

Standing tall, the Enchantress of the Lake unfurled her gossamer wings. Gleaming black spikes of iron sprung forth along the ruffled edges, and ready for battle, she held a deadly looking spear adorned with raven feathers and bells of gold.

Faran eased Leanora back from the edge of the dyke, trying to keep them hidden. But the splendid Amazonian apparition had already noted their presence.

She smiled at them, then spun around as if exuberant with her newfound freedom. Silver dust sparkled in the air, but where she tread no mark was left upon the wet earth. Then, with one hand upon her hip and the other grasping tight her spear, the Spirit Maiden surveyed the land and the empty lake. A look of sorrow crushed the joy from her face, and anger thinned her lips into a determined line. During her long years of banishment, her beloved land had become a place of darkness and suffering.

Lifting her arms, she chanted in a language unused since ancient times. A warm breeze danced across the countryside and sunlight burst through the hazy sky. Leanora squinted against the return of light, then she sighed and turned her face toward the warmth. Faran held out his hand, nudged her shoulder, and nodded toward the shadow it cast.

The enchantress rapped the blunt end of her spear upon the ground and a rainbow sprang forth spanning the lakebed. Droplets fell from the colorful arch, filling the empty black hole with vivid swirling liquid. The water reflected every shade in the spectrum and as it rose higher and higher, it closed the gaping breach in the wall of the dyke and sealed off the cavern where she had laid those many years in mute captivity.

The Spirit Warrior commanded the rainbow to grow larger, and soon it encompassed the land from horizon to horizon. The pale-leafed trees glowed effervescent green and the dull gray flowers dotting the countryside turned scarlet, blue, and yellow. For as far as the eye could see, the ether was clear and the clouds were absorbed into a canopy as blue as ever a sky could be.

The land had been delivered from darkness, and the people of Gylfi had been set free. Lothian no longer held its breath. It gasped in a lungful of life and energy, and exhaled laughter and joy.

As the scaly tail of the monster broke the surface of the beautiful lake, Leanora's optimism wavered. The beast bellowed and leaped about as if it found the pure clean water painful. When next it breached, the stalwart maiden tossed a handful of silver ash over him. In a twinkling, the ugly creature was transformed into nine white swans. Like a child amused by her own antics, the mail-clad spirit laughed and clapped her hands

Then Gorham's angry voice shattered the calm, and the brightness of the realm flickered. He and Romaine had gained the protection of the island. They were the only two inhabitants to be seen, and with no means of escape, they prowled along the shoreline cursing their predicament.

"The wretches still live," Faran growled and clamored to his feet. "It cannot be so. I will see justice done." He stepped forward, intent upon entering the water to swim to the island.

"Wait," Leanora cried and scrambled upright at his side. "Vengeance belongs to the Lord."

"Then tell your God I await His pleasure most impatiently. And if He does not accommodate me quickly, I will lend Him my services—requested or not."

It was madness for Faran to single-handedly challenge Gorham and Romaine. She clung to his arm, desperately trying to think of some way to convince him not to risk his life to take theirs.

"Warrior," the enchantress challenged, "stand fast. Those two are mine. Your quest may be worthy, and your need for revenge hard earned, but I shall deliver their punishment. I have waited many years, in unending darkness and mind shattering silence, thoughts of this moment my only succor. Watch now, mortals, and learn the ways of a time long forgotten."

Her eyes blazed, turning from sweet lavender to piercing lilac. Faran took a step backward.

"Gorham and Romaine." Her commanding voice echoed across the lake—the king and queen froze in their tracks. "Your covenant with Cain and the evil roaming the netherworld has been broken. Your power and protection no longer exist. The sins of the father shall be visited upon the children, and you shall fulfill the curse of your ancestors. Like wolves in human form you ravaged this land and the people. Now live as the beast in all respects." She raised her spear in a sweeping arc and transformed the imperial siblings into two black wolves. "And so shall you remain until the end of time."

The pair was trapped upon the desolate isle, with only grubs and rodents to eat, and no company to keep other than one another's. Gnashing their teeth, they howled and wailed, pitiful in their torment.

The Spirit of the Land turned her gaze upon Faran. "Warrior, has justice been served to your satisfaction?"

Faran nodded and gave a bow of respect. "'Tis more fitting and lingering then a quick thrust of the sword. I am content."

"Then all is well." She ascended a rocky pinnacle near the shore, and surveyed the countryside. The sky grew ever brighter, and the nine swans paddled toward her, honking and clamoring in homage to their mistress.

Since seeing was believing, Leanora could not deny all that had just transpired. And she would not in the future doubt there were mysteries in the world that refuted logic and rational thinking. God worked in mysterious ways—and through even more unlikely emissaries, and she hoped the enchantment of days-gone-by would forever flourish in this northern clime.

A feeling of contentment was in the air, and a warm rain began to fall. It washed Leanora clean of the black mire and revitalized her with a tingling sensation. Laughter and music bubbled up from the village. In the distance Cynric could be seen leading the women and children back from the hills. A dog barked playfully, and the cry of a baby split the air, lusty and full of vigor.

Faran encircled her with his arms, and as he tightened his embrace, she leaned against him, reassured by the solidness of his form. The sun warmed her body, and his kiss warmed her heart, and she had never felt so at peace.

Releasing her, he took her hand and they half slid, half scurried down the slope of the dyke—back to the sword and shield—back to solid ground and reality.

Suddenly, an empty feeling overshadowed her mood, and even the sun did not dispel the cold gripping her soul. She should be happy, but she felt sad and uncertain, as if something precious had been stolen from her. And she felt off balance, as if she stood upon a precipice between the past and future.

It was over—the heart-thumping excitement and rush of daring-do—gone, all gone. Their adventure was at an end.

Chapter Twenty-Six

Merriment, like sparks from the bonfire, spiraled through the night air, and the stars shone bright in the velvety black sky.

"There will be much dancing and celebrating this eventide," Cynric said as he gave Kayden a twirl. "We owe you much, Storm Geat."

"In truth," Faran admitted, "it was Leanora who set free the water." He hugged her, pride flavoring his words.

"Then we are in your debt as well." Cynric gave her a smile and a bow. Then his expression sobered. "There are many faces missing from the circle tonight," he added.

"They died bravely and not in vain," Faran reassured. "The Spirit of the Mere will see them justly rewarded in the Summerland."

"And I shall pray for them," Brother Thomas promised as he strolled forward to join them.

Cynric patted the harp slung across his back. "Their memory and deeds will also live on in song. By the way, Faran, I've nearly finished your story." He added thoughtfully, "But, I don't know how it ends."

Faran felt a twinge of discomfort. How his story was to end was a mystery indeed. It was a long journey back to his home. And even after recovering the sword and shield, the need of forgiveness for his original trespass hung over him like an unwanted shadow.

"Will you be staying with us a while?" Cynric asked. "We would be glad for your company."

"No," he replied, thinking he would miss Cynric and the brave people of Gylfi. "I must soon take my leave."

"And your woman goes with you?"

He studied Leanora's face. His woman... He liked the sound of those words. How easily she had become a vital part of his life. Would that he could bind her to his side for all time. He touched the iron fetish at his neck. The love he felt for her was stronger than any he had ever known.

"She goes where she will," he said softly. Leanora's gaze held his as if she hoped he would say more—and this time he did. "But I would welcome her companionship on the long journey south. What say you, Gillyflower?"

She hesitated and glanced at Brother Thomas.

"I've received a missive from Aelfred," the monk put in. "He bids me meet with him in Athelney. Something about building a monastery there. I could travel with you at least part of the way."

Faran understood Leanora's reluctance to leave her teacher, so recently reunited. And to his good fortune, it seemed the monk encouraged her to go.

"Rumor has it," she said, eyes wide and innocent, "there is treasure to be had at Sutton Hoo. That lies to the south, does it not?"

In her usual roundabout manner, she was saying yes. His heart soared. "So, it is just another adventure you seek." He shook his head with feigned disappointment. "I'm afraid that destination is completely out of the question. Sutton Hoo lies within Danelaw. And remember, I am..."

"Yes, we know," declared Leanora, Brother Thomas, and Cynric in unison. "You're a Geat, not a Dane."

****

Come the morning, they were off to a late start. This was due mainly to the fact that it had been a late evening—a very late evening—with much feasting and much imbibing. Even Brother Thomas walked with caution, as if each step was an agony setting his head to throbbing.

After reluctantly parting company with Cynric and Kayden, they discussed their mode of travel.

"We have two choices," Faran advised as they readied to move on. "Find a boat, and travel well out upon the whale-road where the Danes will not see us. Or head farther inland on foot or horseback, facing terrain near as inhospitable as the Danes."

Both Leanora and the monk petitioned to go inland. To Faran the sea was a longtime companion, but to them it seemed an enemy. "Traveling overland will be time consuming and most uncomfortable," he added in hopes they might recant their choice. "Sleeping on the cold hard ground, game scarce, outlaws and cut-throats of every ilk lying in wait."

When the hardships he mentioned did not elicit a favorable response, nor lessen the green tinge highlighting their complexions, he realized travel by sea was not an option.

"We had best procure three sturdy mounts," he suggested, giving in to their determined faces, "and more serviceable clothing."

****

Reaching the outskirts of town, they uncovered the cache beneath the small pine and retrieved their treasure trove and Leanora's little boxes. Then they headed south at a leisurely pace.

Leanora rode a small gray mare, Brother Thomas a mischievous brown pony. Faran masterfully sat a large black gelding. The sun shone with an appreciated brightness, the sky was true blue, and the flowers along the edge of the woods were reassuring in their array of colors.

To Leanora, all seemed right with the world.

As usual, Faran took the lead. But it no longer disturbed her when he assumed command. She realized now he did so out of a desire to protect rather than govern her. And he had asked that she remain at his side, at least for the journey to his home. She felt content and—happy. Yes, she was happy. So happy it was frightening. What if when she grew accustomed to such contentment it was snatched from her grasp? Oh, for heaven's sake, now she feared having nothing to fear.

You're in love with him, a voice whispered in the back of her mind. *That is something worthy of your fear.* It was true. Never in her life had she felt such love. It was worth more than the treasure strapped to her horse's backside. It was worth dying for. And it was also worth living for. She should enjoy the glorious sensation to the fullest. Love Faran—make love to him—for as long as he would have her. A secret smile confirmed the logic of that idea.

"Brother Thomas," she called as they ambled along three abreast. "Tell us more regarding your mission to Athelney."

The old monk jerked to attention, then smiled sheepishly at having been caught nodding off in the comfort of the sun. "Athelney? Oh yes. Quite the honor," he murmured, "quite the honor." He sat up straighter and adjusted his worn woolen robe. "During the previous winter, when King Aelfred took shelter in the swamps near Athelney, there was little food to be had and only the most primitive of shelter. Before long, his soldiers were near mutinous. Turning to the Lord for help, Aelfred promised should he survive this hardship and drive the Danes from Wessex, he would build a church on the very spot where he knelt to pray.

"As the Danes are now generally contained

along the eastern border, he returns to fulfill that promise—which is apparently where I come in. I am to oversee the project, but I doubt Aelfred will remain there long. There is much he is destined to accomplish besides building churches." As he pondered this thought, the monk glowed with admiration. "Already, many consider him not only king of the West Saxons, but king of all England, and I daresay someday he will be."

Faran issued a sound of discontent. "Don't forget, the Geats took him in that same winter when he left the swamp and reached the coast."

"Yes, I remember. How very Christian of you." Brother Thomas chuckled.

"Maybe Aelfred will build a church for you as well," Leanora put in, adding to the ribbing Faran was receiving.

"We need no white God's house," he grumbled. "I am just saying, it seems that particular part of the story is always left out. Yet perhaps it is for the best. We are a small tribe and seek to be left in peace on our island."

"Peace seems an elusive quality," Thomas mused. "With Gorham and his sister no longer a threat, do you believe warring will be a thing of your past?"

"No," Faran admitted. "I think warring will forever plague mankind. Only whom we fight has changed. The Danes, once our brothers in the time of Beowulf, now side with the Swedes. Unlike their ancestors, they have forgotten blood-sworn treaties. No longer do they honor the promises of long ago. Times change and friends become enemies." He glanced at the two of them. "And sometimes strangers become...friends." Then as if he feared he had said too much, he clucked his horse into a trot and went on ahead.

"He seems a good man," Brother Thomas

observed, "even if he is a pagan."

"There are worse things a man can claim to be," she defended. "And he is thoughtful regarding the ways of nature. When I lay in his arms at night, he tells me wondrous stories of how the world came to be, and he shows me the images hiding in the pattern of the stars. There is wisdom in the tales he carries. And although he would be loath to admit to it, Faran has a poetic streak rare in a man so obviously a warrior."

"You are in love with him, I take it."

"Yes," she admitted. "But our ways and beliefs are more different then alike. I see no future for us."

"You were born to be a peace-weaver, Leonora. A person to bridge such differences. You may still fulfill that destiny."

"I am also the daughter of a chieftain," she reminded, "born to marry the son of a leader. Of course, that hardly seems important anymore as my clan is scattered beyond existence."

"When you introduced me to Faran, you gave his name as Tyne Faran Kilbraun, did you not?"

"Yes," she confirmed, recalling how he had called himself such on the day they had triumphantly crossed the river.

"Did you note he clearly wished me to call him only Faran, not Tyne Faran?"

"Again, yes. But what does that matter?"

"In his language, Leonora, Tyne means prince. He is the son of their king."

Chapter Twenty-Seven

The third day upon the road, Faran felt the need to put as many leagues behind them as possible. He urged his horse onward and studied Leanora as she kept pace at his side. Ever since yesterday, she seemed unusually quiet. Of course, he supposed she could barely get a word in edgewise as all he had done lately was talk about going home.

Why did she not share his enthusiasm? Their quest was at an end. With the sword and shield recovered, he harbored grand hopes his life might soon return to normal and everything would go back to the way it was before.

****

Nothing, Leanora lamented, would ever be the same again.

During their escapade, the closeness she had shared with Faran had been born of danger and mutual need. He had praised her daring and resourcefulness—traits prompted by necessity. But now they were out of danger, there was no further need for those qualities. The exciting past they shared had lived a bright and glorious life. She could only pray their mundane future would not die a silent, painful death.

What a surprise to discover Faran was the son of a king. Had he kept the information a secret for his own protection? When first they had met, fearing he would hold her for ransom, she had done the same regarding her own status. Later, she had simply forgotten to tell him, and now it no longer mattered. Her tribe was no more. And while she now possessed money to be used as a war chest, no warriors stood at her command in sworn allegiance, either to herself or an ally. So much had changed— in her circumstance as well as how she viewed the world.

With enlightened insight, she studied Tyne Faran Kilbraun, Prince of Geats. Relaxed and confident, he rode in communion with his mount. And as he gripped the prancing steed with his bare thighs, their sculpted musculatures blended as one.

He seemed larger than life, yet was also observant of the smallest of God's creations. This morning, while they bathed, he had presented her with a tiny pink blossom. A gillyflower, or so he claimed. His strong hand cradled the delicate bit of color with tenderness and care—the same way he touched her. But that hand could also wield a sword in deadly fashion or thrust a spear with cold accuracy to the heart of an enemy. What was it like to be made of two such opposing forces? Did a battle rage within him? A warrior would always seek to go to war. Did a wordsmith feel equally compelled to fight for the life of a poem or a good story? She was enamored of the tales and fables he told. A man like no other, he appeared well suited to either circumstance.

And what of Faran, the Iron Heart? He practiced the art of pleasing women like other men practiced the art of combat. A grand sport, mastered to perfection, one he plied frequently with enthusiasm and gusto. He never spoke of the previous women who had shared his bed, but no doubt he would find another partner if she were not available. She was convenient—and determined to keep herself so. Her life was better now than ever it had been, and she would remain by this man's side for as long as he would have her.

Rocking along on the mare, a sensuous and irrepressible aching seized her and spread inward. She squirmed and recalled all the times she and Faran had made love. But it was not only this physical delight she coveted. They shared thoughts, as well as their bodies. Other than Brother Thomas, no one had ever taken the time to listen to the reflections of her mind. This was a different and rare pleasure.

She touched the amber brooch adorning the shoulder of her new heather gray cloak. Faran was generous too. He had refused to take back the gift. And even more curious, he had stated his mother would want her to have the beautifully fashioned fibula.

What would she be like, the woman who had borne Faran and six other male children? She must be stalwart indeed to keep up with seven sons, especially if they were all as winsome and trying as Faran. Was she a white-haired, dignified old lady with a shy smile and a gentle hand, or a hardy robust female, full bosomed and rotund?

Thoughts of Faran's family and his village made her wistful. Seeing him surrounded by his kin would resurrect her own loss and loneliness. And if, as he told her, he planned to marry—she could not even contemplate such a vision. Yet, he had casually mentioned words to that effect, and seeing him in the arms of another woman would truly break her heart. All the more reason to enjoy him while she could.

The heat of guilt warmed her cheeks. Brother Thomas continued to reprimand them for coupling without sacred union, but his scolding was less frequent and tempered by his fondness for the both of them. Often times he made himself scarce at night, knowing nothing and no one was likely to impede the path of two lovers. Besides there would be time aplenty for repenting and regretting and saving her soul once they had all gone their separate ways.

Faran glanced at her as if divining her thoughts. The one-dimple smile, able to melt her resolve, stole across his face, and his pale green eyes brightened as she smiled in return.

He was a most difficult man to resist.

****

Traveling inland, they chanced upon a ford granting calm passage across the wild and oft dangerous river Wharfe. Then, not slackening their pace, they moved on.

By midday, Leanora was provoked to boredom. She missed the rush of exhilaration adventuring brought. It was a fleeting thrill, warranting no promises or long-term commitment. And it demanded only her immediate participation devoid of prior worry or consideration. What a surprise to discover this intrepid aspect of her personality. But again the credit must go to Faran. He had released her from the bonds of her self-imposed limitations. She would always love him for that. He had given her the world, or at least the ability to face it.

But what should she do once they reached the Isle of Gullin? Traveling on to Athelney with Brother Thomas seemed the most commonsensical choice. There were many things she yearned to see. But she also yearned to share those discoveries with someone special at her side.

They entered a stand of cottonwood. The golden rays of the setting sun slanted down through the branches, and the heavenly radiance illuminated faerie-like wisps of cottonseed floating on the breeze.

"Could we stop here for the night?" she asked, captivated by the enchanted hollow. A pond, complete with croaking frogs, lay but a few strides away.

"I don't see why not," Faran agreed and dismounted. "Although it is still a bit early, we have made excellent progress today,"

"It seems a peaceful place," she added.

"Yes, and I for one could do with a good long night's rest." Faran's words were innocent, but his heated gaze indicated intentions of something more than sleep.

Pretending to ignore his bold stare, she slid to the ground and ambled over to admire the white and blue flowers growing along the water's edge. Brother Thomas dismounted and helped Faran picket and rub down the animals.

Rummaging around in the packs, Faran retrieved two heavy blankets and spread them beneath a natural bower of yew branches. Leanora's pulse quickened, knowing what they would do there later when darkness fell.

****

Gathered close around the small campfire, the three weary travelers ate in companionable silence.

"This is the last of the food," Faran said, breaking the quiet. "Come morning, I'll go hunting, and hopefully procure enough game to keep us from starving until we reach a town of suitable proportions."

"When next we purchase supplies," Brother Thomas put in, "I have a few coins to contribute." He searched his robes for his small leather pouch. "You were so kind to buy that fine pony for me, it is the least I can do."

Leanora gazed at the monk and tears pricked at her eyes. This gentle old man had come to mean a great deal to her. He was more a father than ever she had known, and they shared a history, which counted for much in this world of uncertainty. And now, here he was, offering them money he could not spare. His sandals were worn, and although clean, his coarse-spun clothes were threadbare.

"Save your money for the poor, holy man," Faran said a bit gruffly. "Your prayers for our safe journey would be of more value to us than your coin."

The monk smiled and nodded. "That I can do."

****

The fire burned down to red-hot coals and the sky turned inky black. Brother Thomas wandered off to pray, and with her heart pounding, Leonora watched as Faran retired to the blankets they would share.

Without a word, he took off all his clothes, stretched out upon the little bed, and opened his arms to her. God above, he was so handsome and self-assured, yet he wanted to share his passion not inflict it upon her. She wanted it too.

"Come here," he commanded.

This was one request she obeyed with out rancor or resistance. She shrugged free of her cloak and walked toward him. Standing at his feet, she unpinned her tunic and let the garment flutter to the ground. She wore nothing beneath it and was pleased when Faran's gaze intensified and he grew full and hard just at the sight of her. Straddling his legs, she edged forward, not halting the advance until her feet rested one on either side of his thighs.

His body was as if sculpted in marble, and he was so full of life. "You are like the sun. You dazzle my eyes as well as my mind.

He sat up, gripped her bare bottom with both hands, and nuzzled her—his shadow of a beard tickling and exciting the soft skin of her belly. Tugging gently, he drew her down to her knees. "And you are the moon," he breathed. "Ever changing, yet a comforting warmth, even on the darkest of nights.

She felt him ready and waiting beneath her, and

with a moan, accepted the full length of him. He shuddered and arched upward.

With her hands braced against his muscled chest, she gazed up at the sky and the orb to which he compared her, and a primitive sensation enveloped her. Making love outside felt so natural, offering a kinship with the entire universe.

Without hesitation, Faran trailed his hands up and down her back, the scarred and less-than-beautiful back. Then he moved slowly inside of her, seemingly content to let her to set the pace, and given free rein, she explored what felt best. Riding a rippling wave, she rose and fell on an ocean of delight, and when Faran's movements gathered strength, a tidal wave of pleasure flooded her body. It drowned out proper thought and reason, and she felt as if she floated higher, spiraling across the heavens—near close enough to touch the constellations that watched them from up above. Filled with wild abandon, she cascaded down a raging river with only Faran to hold on to. He bucked beneath her, holding her close, grinding against the space between her thighs that ached for and found release. Finally, she remembered to breathe, then she collapsed atop him.

Each time they made love, he took her beyond what she had experienced before. Each time they made love, she surrendered another part of her being to a man who could never be hers. It was madness, it was sinful, and it was all she wanted in the world.

As she lay in Faran's arms, little twinges of lingering pleasure lapped at her body while unbidden twinges of reality, nibbled at the back of her mind.

****

In the middle of the night, Leanora awakened to find the blanket beside her cold and empty. Where was Faran? Confused by sleep, she sat up and peered around. The moon was down, the countryside dark. She glanced at the horses. Their mounts seemed contented enough. "Faran," she called softly. Her tongue stuck to the roof of her mouth, and she tried to lick her lips.

"I am here," he replied, and stepped from the shadows. He took his place beside her and gathered her in his arms. His skin was cool, as if he had been standing for a long while in the evening chill, but his mouth were warm as it teased against her neck.

"I thought you gone," she murmured.

"I dreamed we were pursued by faces unknown to me." A gasp, then a groan, cut short his explanation as she stroked the part of him wedged up against her belly. "I feared someone hovered nearby," he managed to add as he slid one hand between her thighs.

As renewed pleasure conquered logic, the seriousness of his words was lost to the starry night.

Chapter Twenty-Eight

The next morning, the nearby pond proved not only beautiful but also fruitful. A few unlucky fish met their doom, and they all enjoyed a hearty breakfast. Then while Faran hunted for larger game, Leanora and Brother Thomas cleaned up camp and readied the horses.

"If we keep to this pace," she quietly observed, "we should reach Faran's home in but a few days."

"You do not sound pleased with the actuality," the monk noted.

She shrugged. "Why should it matter to me one way or another?"

"I think," he boldly pointed out, "your feelings for this man run deep and you have surrendered your heart to him, as well as your other attributes."

"Yes," she freely admitted. "Although I fear it is to no avail."

"But you are a widow now, Leanora. You may seek another as your husband."

"If Faran ever did decide to keep constant with only one woman, no doubt his family would wish it to be with someone other than me."

"I do not see why they would." Thomas frowned. "You are a good person, fair of face, and most times of a gentle disposition. And when you try, you are a good Christian."

"In this instance, I do not think being a Christian will weigh in my favor. His father and mother will not welcome me with open arms."

"It might be wise to meet these people before judging them too harshly. You may be surprised as to what the Lord has in store for you."

"'Tis possible," she admitted. "But surprises have rarely improved my lot in life."

A noise in the brush halted their conversation. Faran sprinted toward camp—his spear in one hand and today's catch in the other.

"Take cover by the pond," he ordered, dropping the brace of cony beside the cold fire pit. You, monk, bring the sword and shield."

"What is wrong?" she asked.

He didn't answer, but rather grabbed her by the arm and hustled her toward the large boulders ringing the little mere. "Riders approach," he explained. "In my haste to return, I could not see them clearly. But they head in this direction."

Struggling under the weight of the armaments, Brother Thomas stumbled over to them. Leanora reached for the shield. Faran shoved his spear into the hands of the holy man and took up the sword. "Get down, remain quiet, and stay put."

Silently he slipped away into the surrounding trees. She reached out, yearning to go with him. But the tone in which he issued his orders bade her do as she was told.

The clatter of horses was now easily heard, and their own three mounts pricked up their ears and snorted. If those who approached bore them ill intent, they did so with riotous anticipation. Heart pounding, she crouched low and peeked around the little rock fortress.

At her side, Brother Thomas gripped the spear with brave intent. A grim smile tightened her lips, and she positioned the shield a bit closer. They seemed a woefully meek defense in the face of the noise issuing forth from the woods.

Branches snapped and the thunder of hooves

drew louder. She wished Faran were at her side. If they were going to die, she willed it would be together.

"Faran. Leanora." The impending hoard called out their names—this was a different approach to warring.

Two riders broke through the ring of trees, and careened to a halt near the pond. It was Cynric and Kayden. No others followed.

Faran stepped forward. "You were crashing through the forest with such fury," he accused, "I thought the hounds of hell came our way."

Cynric leaped from his horse. With joyous backslapping, the two men clasped one another in friendship. As Leanora and Brother Thomas rose and followed suit, Kayden smiled and waved and slid to the ground.

"What do you here?" Faran asked once the female laughter and hugging played out.

"Soon after your departure from Gylfi," Cynric began, "three strangers skulked about the city seeking information regarding Leanora. We knew not from which tribe they hailed so offered no assistance. Eventually, they left town. Or so we thought. Then one night, while spying upon us, they heard me sing of your brave deeds. They waylaid and questioned me—thoroughly and none too gently I might add. I told them you had both gone to join the Danes."

Faran growled and clenched his fists.

"I know, I know." Cynric raised his hand to stem the flow of words they all knew were coming. "I figured it was the last place they would ever find you."

Faran nodded and relaxed his stance.

"When they headed southeast, Kayden and I rode southwest to let you know you were being hunted."

"You were not followed?" Faran asked, concern troubling his brow.

"We did our best to ensure such. We traveled fast, never looking back. Already you had several days head start on us."

"Who were these strangers?" Faran asked.

"I do not know. But they were well armed, and dark in disposition."

"You risked much in coming to warn us," Faran acknowledged. "Now they hunt you as well."

"What else could we do?" Cynric shrugged. "It is poor advertisement for a scop to have unfinished songs in his inventory. And by the look of those who pursue you, your adventure has not reached its end. Besides, Kayden and I wanted to go someplace for our honeymoon."

"The two of you are married!" Leanora squealed in delight. Faran shook his head in wonder and the hugging started again. Brother Thomas made the sign of the cross and offered a quick blessing.

"This riotous trip is not exactly what I had in mind." Kayden laughed. "But anyplace we are together is the place I wish to be."

Leanora suffered a pang of envy. She felt the same way about Faran. His gaze was upon her, and she hoped similar thoughts crossed his mind. "I'm so happy for you," she said and meant it. "You have gone through many remarkable changes recently."

"All of them good ones, I assure you," the girl said and cuddled closer to Cynric.

He put his arm around her. "After Kayden was released from the spell of County Lothian, she was like a child, wanting to see and feel and experience everything around her. Who would have suspected my wife harbored such a penchant for wanderlust."

"Speaking of wandering," Faran said, curtailing their idle chatter, "we had best be on our way. Do you truly wish to travel with us?" he asked, giving the couple one more chance to disassociate themselves from what could be a dangerous journey.

Kayden gave a nod of affirmation. "Can't think of anyplace we'd rather be," Cynric assured them.

****

In two days time, they reached Winchester.

While the men stabled the horses and secured lodging, Leanora and Kayden ambled down a cobbled street lined with shops. The town, a center of activity since Roman times, offered a large bounty of trade goods. At one stall, Leanora purchased a nightrail while Kayden admired a red woolen shawl. Her hand lovingly lingered upon what she could not afford, then she sighed and walked on. Lagging behind, Leanora bought the shawl and hid it beneath her cape. It would make the perfect wedding gift for her friend.

These last few days, having Kayden as a traveling companion had been an unexpected pleasure. Sharing sisterly secrets and womanly concerns was a joy she had never thought to experience.

"Come," Kayden called. "Dusk is nearly upon us. We had best make for the inn before darkness falls."

****

Ubba the Underling lumbered into the stable—nearly dragging his beleaguered horse behind him.

Two ominous looking companions followed close at his back. He tossed the reins to the frightened stable boy. "Sees these horses be rubbed down and fed up, you little bag of weasel piss, or I'll have your hide."

He stalked over to the mounts already penned securely in the stalls along the back wall. Those he sought were here. He had only seen them from afar, but he recognized the four horses and one pony. He sniffed at the blankets stacked nearby, and grunted in satisfaction. He could almost smell her—his dear, murdering sister-in-law.

It hadn't taken long to realize the bard had led them astray, and they had quickly made up for the time lost. Soon he would have his revenge, starting with the look on Leanora's face when she saw him. Then, after he'd plowed her field a time or two, she would pay with her life for the death of his brother.

Ivar had always been the chosen one, had always gotten the good-looking wenches. And until now, Ubba had lived in his older brother's shadow. When he returned home triumphant, with plunder and the girl, they would not call him the Underling anymore. He would be Ubba the Overlord, and he would have everything he had always wanted.

But first, a good meal and a tankard of mead were in order. No use letting blood and swiving the bitch on an empty stomach.

Chapter Twenty-Nine

Leanora turned in the circle of Faran's arms and snuggled closer.

There had been only two rooms available at the inn. They shared this one with Brother Thomas, and the newlyweds had been granted the privacy of the other. Faran had seemed disappointed, but she didn't mind. She savored simply lying beside him, cosseted in pure contentedness, no amorous intentions obscuring the moment. Sheltered by his broad shoulders and well-muscled arms, she felt so blessedly safe. Besides, they were all so road-weary and tipsy with mead, anything more strenuous would have seemed somewhat unlikely.

Drifting back to sleep, a noise outside in the passageway caught her attention. Then splinters of wood flew across the room as the door was kicked in.

Leanora screamed, scrambled off the bed, and crouched down beside it.

With a most unholy expletive, Brother Thomas rolled from his pallet and staggered to his feet, only to be laid low by a fist to the face.

Faran hit the floorboards ready for battle, but three burly men armed with clubs descended upon him, soon crushing any hope of his taking command of the situation. The invaders beat him savagely, and when he fell to the floor, they tied his ankles together and his wrists behind his back.

Rendered helpless, Faran lay unmoving. The tallest of the brutes kicked him in the ribs. Then the towering man turned in her direction. A fragment of light from the hallway illuminated his face, and for the first time in her life, Leanora thought she might faint. It was Ubba, her husband's brother.

He threw back his head and laughed. "Surprised to see me, Leanora?" he snarled with a cruel twist of his mouth. "You didn't think you could kill Ivar and not pay the price did you?"

"It was an accident, Ubba. I never meant for Ivar to die."

"Dead is dead," he proclaimed as he reached down and hauled her to her feet.

She glanced at Faran, he was still unconscious. Brother Thomas was awake but seemingly in a daze. How could this be happening? She recognized the other two men now. Both were friends of Ubba, and both had always encouraged his mad schemes and underhanded dealings.

"I will not go back with you," she said with a defiant tilt of her chin.

"I see you've learned insolence, as well as how to screw a Dane."

An involuntary smile pulled at her lips and she almost corrected him for assuming Faran was a Scylding. Ubba grabbed her by the hair, forcing her face to within inches of his.

"You find this amusing, you worthless cow?"

"No." She winced. Anger and desperation joined forces, surging through her body, urging her to fight, urging her to spit in the face of the man who sought to end her life just when she had found a reason to live. But she must cooperate, not resist, and lead Ubba from the room before he injured Faran even more. Or worse yet killed him.

"Lord Ubba," the old monk said, "do you not recognize me? It is I, Brother Thomas. Could we not talk this over like civilized men?" With a bruise already darkening his cheek, the old man bravely stepped forward, only to be confronted by Ubba's raised fist.

"Stay out of this, you righteous bastard. Once before, you helped her to run away. Try again and you will meet your beloved Maker sooner than you thought."

"Do not hurt him," she pleaded. "I will go with you."

Footsteps sounded in the hallway. "Faran, Leanora—what goes on here?" It was Cynric's voice.

Realizing he was drawing a crowd, her brother-in-law dragged her toward the door, his henchmen following at his heels. He shoved Cynric aside. Kayden wisely scurried back to her room. With his arm around her waist, he propelled her down the hall, her bare feet barely touching the ground. More people poked their heads out of their rooms, but one look at Ubba and the two horrors with him, and they quickly retreated behind closed doors.

Outside, he tossed her to the ground. The cold predawn air seeped beneath her thin nightclothes. She shivered, and tears bit at the back of her eyes, but she willed them away, refusing to cry in front of her brother-in-law. Struggling to her feet, hands clenched into fists, she turned to face him down. Dear Lord, he seemed even more imposing then she remembered. He was an ogre from a nightmare, and every bit as cruel as his brother. It all came rushing back to her—the pain, the humiliation. But she could not go back. She would die first.

****

Faran struggled to sit up.

"Be still my friend," Cynric suggested, "we nearly have these bindings loose."

"Where is Leanora?" Faran demanded.

"The men who beat you unconscious took her," Brother Thomas answered.

Faran glanced over at the holy man, and one

look at his battered face stemmed the words of recrimination hovering in his throat. Having been taken by surprise, none of them could have fended off such an attack.

Freed from the ropes, he sat up and spit blood and part of one tooth from his mouth, then thankfully drank the water Kayden offered. By the gods, he felt worse than when he had washed ashore on Leanora's island. Leanora—he had failed to protect her, failed to keep the promise that had coaxed her from that sanctuary.

He held his throbbing head in his hands. "Who would do this," he asked of no one unparticular.

"It was her dead husband's brother, and two of his men," the monk informed them. "His name is Ubba the Underling. Now he rules his tribe and has outgrown his name."

The room fell to stunned silence.

The dread in Faran's heart increased ten fold while rage stood fast beside it. For just one moment, he had defied the gods and dared to be happy, and now he paid the price. But Leanora was innocent of wrongdoing. He recalled the story of her husband's death. Or had she lied? No, he would not believe it to be so.

He struggled to his feet, stumbled over to the bed, and eased down onto the edge. "What do you know of this, Brother Thomas?"

"I told you before," the monk began, "the death of Ivar, her husband, was an accident. I swear it upon all I hold sacred. But his tribe does not want the truth. Without mercy, they declared war on Leanora's clan. And they still seek more blood, more violence."

Faran was familiar with revenge, a cause he championed of late. It was a potent drink, able to drive those who imbibed too freely to either unexpected acts of courage or unimaginable acts of degradation.

His head continued to throb unmercifully. He could hardly think straight. But he had enough sense to know they must follow these men immediately, lest they lose the trail, and Leanora become lost to him forever.

He dropped to his knees beside the sleeping-pallet and retrieved the sword and shield from beneath it. Then he prayed to Beowulf for strength of body, and he petitioned the gods that they might grant him victory in righting this injustice.

Kayden and Brother Thomas tore strips of linen from the sheets. He staggered to his feet and they wrapped the pieces around and around his chest to support his cracked ribs. As he submitted to their ministrations, his other injuries seemed to fade in seriousness. But his anger increased in leaps and bounds, and he wanted roar in fury and frustration.

He waved his friends aside, and even in the dim light, the bear-man's war rings glittered on his arms. He drew battle-courage and strength from the memory of the warrior, and tearing loose the leather thong holding back his lion's mane, he shook free his hair. Stepping across the room, he grazed the tips of his fingers through the soot that coated the inside of a candle lantern. With a few quick strokes, he painted two black stripes across each cheek and one across his forehead. Raw energy surged through his body, and with sword in hand, he wheeled around to face the others.

They fell back in unison, mouths agape.

"Who is with me?" he demanded, his weapon raised on high.

They all swallowed hard and stepped forward.

"Then dress with haste," he instructed, "I make for the stables." He retrieved the red shawl lying on a chair and tossed it to Kayden. "She thought to give you this as a wedding gift," he explained. "Wear it now to keep her close in mind and heart."

He touched the amulet at his neck, grabbed the shield, and made for the door.

****

Wide-eyed and quaking, the stable boy stared up at Faran. "Yes, master," he answered. "Three men and one lady left just a short while ago. They was in a terrible hurry, and the one man was none too kind." The boy rubbed his shoulder and arm as if it may have recently been twisted.

"Which direction did they head, lad?" Faran asked.

"They took off that way."

The boy pointed toward Hyde Street, the north road. Of course Winchester was a large city, and once out of sight, they could have easily changed directions to confuse the issue.

"Give me a hand with the horses," he requested. "When my friends arrive, tell them the direction to follow."

As he rode out, he tossed the boy a sliver of silver to insure his cooperation, and to compensate for the trouble that had followed them to his town.

By the time he reached the north edge of the city, the sun had crested the horizon. There was a vendor selling apples, and dismounting he bought several. Biting into one, he wished there was time for a meal of more substance to break his fast. The old man viewed him warily and quickly conducted his business.

"Did four others pass this way?" Faran asked between mouthfuls. "Three men and a russet-haired woman."

"Indeed, indeed. Not long ago. They met up with several others in yon meadow."

That did not bode well. Faran surveyed the land. As far as the eye could see, nothing untoward caught his attention. The road at his back was empty as well. Where were Cynric and the others? His horse danced to one side, anxious to be on its way. He felt the same. He decided to go on ahead and scout out the trail, then double back for his friends. With that plan in mind, he mounted up and laid heels to the horse.

Owing to the fact that Ubba had brought reinforcements, rescuing Leanora would be more difficult than first anticipated—difficult but not impossible. All she must do was stay strong until he could reach her. A smile pulled at his mouth. She had escaped Gorham's clutches in Lothian, saving his ass in the bargain. Leanora had changed much since her brother-in-law had last seen her. Then the thought of another man touching her caused his jaw to clench and his teeth to grind. The smile faded. Leanora was his woman now, his refuge, his future. Somehow, he would find her.

He approached the meadow with caution. No one lingered, but the grass was well trampled, and the remnants of discarded food indicated several men had spent several hours biding time there. The trail led northward. He supposed that made sense. They had recovered what they sought, and now headed back to their realm. But why had Ubba brought so many men? Surely not just to retrieve one small woman.

As the woods grew thicker, he heard a noise off to the left. Shield raised and sword ready, he gripped the horse with his thighs. Unless they had posted a rearguard, it was unlikely to be the contingent he followed.

The forest came alive with foot soldiers. Armed with spear and ax, they were dressed in typical Saxon garb. Some wore the insignia of royalty. He traversed the open space, assessing their intentions, planning his attack should the need arise. But soon he was surrounded and overwhelmingly outnumbered. Sword lowered to show compliancy he held his ground. One figure, more commanding than the rest, rode forward. The man possessed the keen eye and bearing of a sovereign. With relief, he recognized Aelfred, King of Wessex.

"Surrender your weapons, Dane," the king ordered.

Faran bristled. "I am Tyne Faran Kilbraun," he declared, "friend to the King of Wessex, and I am Geat not Dane."

"A convenient story," the king replied. "I know of no Geat who robs and pillages the likes of what we have seen from here to Derby."

"Neither my companions nor I would be involved in such mischief," Faran defended. "We pay for what we need or desire." As he waited, he mulled over the words of the king. Was the destruction observed by Aelfred the work of Ubba and his men? Had they wreaked havoc along the way, only to blame it on the Danes? It was an old trick, similar to the machinations Gorham and Romaine had used.

"You appear ready enough for battle," Aelfred pointed out.

Faran shook his hair back from his face. No doubt his image did seem far from innocent.

The king motioned a few of his men closer, the others stood ready to fight. Faran resented this needless delay, and he surly must not be taken prisoner. Then he remembered Thomas the monk was under Aelfred's command. "I travel with Brother Thomas," he said.

The king raised a hand, indicating his men should stand fast.

"He calls me friend and I carry this for him." Rummaging around in the small pouch at his waist, Faran fished out the aestel the monk had entrusted to his safekeeping.

Alarm rather than relief transformed the king's

expression. "Brother Thomas would never part with the gift I gave him. How would you even know such a man, let alone keep his company?"

"The reason we travel together is our business." Faran retorted, annoyed at the king's insinuations. "And it was not by force this came into my hands."

The king and the warrior measured one another's mettle. Faran was not intimidated. It was not the first time he had been scrutinized or questioned by a sovereign. Of course it was usually his father, ruler of the Geats who raked him over the coals, not a stranger. But Aelfred was not truly a stranger.

"Once, on the Isle of Gullin, you sheltered with my tribe," Faran reminded. "Lord Aris, my father, introduced me to you. It was only one year ago. You have a short memory for those who offered aid to your men and support to your cause."

The king's expression turned thoughtful. Still he did not signal his soldiers to stand down. Then, in a cloud of dust, Cynric and Kayden came tearing along the road at breakneck speed. Leanora's riderless horse was in tow, laden with their personal items. The monk, upon his stout little pony, was not far behind.

To Faran's wonderment, the king took note, dismounted, and stood waiting for the monk's arrival. The old holy man commanded much consideration. Aelfred motioned for two soldiers to assist the man to the ground, then the king hugged him affectionately.

"Well Brother Thomas, what have you gotten yourself into this time? On land or sea you seem to flirt with danger. Do you know this man?" he added with a nod toward Faran. "I feared the worst when I saw he carried the gift I bestowed upon you when last we met."

The monk bowed, his expression grave. "Yes, my

lord. I know him. We all travel together. And as these are uncertain times, he keeps your gift safe for me."

"Then I stand corrected, warrior," the king graciously admitted as he remounted his horse. "And I thank you for protecting my friend's property."

"My lord," Thomas made bold to speak, "we search for a young woman in grave danger. She is the same girl I sought when you rescued me at sea. She is a Christian, and now in the hands of a terrible man, one who intends her much harm."

"And who is this man?" Aelfred asked

The monk hesitated. "He is her brother-by-law, my lord."

"And why does he seek to do her harm."

"She is falsely accused of her husband's demise."

"They are from Wessex?" Aelfred hedged.

"No my lord, from the North Country."

"It is most unusual for a king to come between family members in a tribal dispute."

"It is more a matter of coming between a woman and the devil," Thomas prompted.

This seemed to grab the king's attention and satisfy his previous qualms.

Aelfred perused the odd assortment of people surrounding him. Then he studied Faran. "What do you propose, warrior?"

Chapter Thirty

Leanora rode double with the man who would see her in his bed and shortly thereafter dead.

Trapped in Ubba's iron grip, and pressed unyielding up against his chest, she felt smothered by his nearness. He smelled foul, and his disposition was equally as bad. Thank the Lord, they had been obliged to quickly take to the road before he could do more than roughly kiss her and paw her breasts.

She squirmed and dared a glance backward—hoping yet not hoping to see Faran upon the trail. Ubba had too many men. It would mean certain death if Faran tried to rescue her.

"Eyes front," her brother-in-law growled. "He ain't coming for the likes of you. You ain't worth the trouble."

A short while ago, she would have hung her head in defeat, and believed every vicious word aimed in her direction. But not now, and never again. Such words were merely weapons designed to keep her in a state of hopelessness—dependent and compliant. But her love for Faran was a shield against such verbal armament. Ubba's hands might bruise her flesh, but his words would not wound her soul.

She sat straighter and smiled. At least he had not gotten his hands upon her fortune. Should she tell him what he had foolishly left behind? Would he go back for it, delivering her closer to Faran rather than farther from his side? Most likely he would not believe her. If only she could do something—anything—to disrupt his plans and slow their progress. In her heart, she knew Ubba was wrong. Faran *would* come for her, and dismissing that possibility would be the biggest mistake of her brother-in-law's life.

****

Aelfred and the main contingent of men followed the renegades. Faran, and several of the sovereign's best, swung west in an effort to outflank them.

Trying to determine the enemy's exact position and how far they had traveled, Faran called a halt. He slid from his horse, laid the sword on the ground, and gave it a twist. The blade spun around three times then came to a halt. The king's mounted soldiers gave the sign to ward off evil. Cynric dismounted and peered over his shoulder.

"The men we follow are directly to the east," Faran said. "And if the terrain is friendly, and we do not tarry, we can quickly outdistance them and double-back, blocking their progress upon the trail."

"Just as we planned," Cynric encouraged. "With the king and his foot soldiers following close behind, the interlopers will be trapped between the two forces."

Faran retrieved the precious sword, but made no move to take to his horse.

"What troubles you?" Cynric asked.

Every fiber of Faran's being ached to answer the call to battle, but his heart ached with a different need. The need to protect, the need to bend toward caution. "Leanora could easily be crushed in the rush," he said quietly, "like the gillyflower for which I named her."

"There is no other way for it," Cynric reassured. "To do nothing would be worse."

"Aye, I realize this. Yet it does not lessen the danger or my worry."

"She will be ready and watching for us," the bard assured him.

"Do you think so? The Valkyrie take me, I love her, and I'll let no person and no reason keep us apart."

"You will tell her this yourself," Cynric urged, "but not if we stand her talking."

Faran nodded, hurried to his horse, and leaped astride. "Keep ready the signal horn," he advised the king's man on his right. "And at all cost," he directed the entire group of the men, "protect the red-haired woman. No harm must come to her or you answer to me."

He wheeled his mount and cantered into the woods seeking the path of least resistance and least noise. Ubba's men were a sorry lot, but they were battle-tested. They would not be easily beaten.

****

Brother Thomas rode beside Aelfred, the foot soldiers surrounding them.

"Tell me more of this pagan warrior whom we go to help," the king commanded, as he labored to keep his horse in check. The beast smelled excitement and fought for free rein.

"Tyne Faran, prince of Geats," Thomas began with a flourish. "He is a curious man, my lord. One whom I think you could respect and possibly call friend. He is easy to hold cheer with, and although he follows the old ways, he was quite instrumental in vanquishing the evil dwelling in Lothian." He paused and sneaked a glance at the king. The sovereign did not seem overly impressed. "Had this man not aided the rebels," he added, "Lord Gorham and his sister Romaine would still rule there. And the young priest hiding in the mountains would not have returned to Gylfi. The cross would not have been restored to the people.

"And you would not now be riding to battle," the

330

king put in.

"We all battle for what we believe in, do we not?"

"Yes, Thomas. However, the bruises upon your face would indicate words are more your weapon of choice than swords and shields." Taken aback, Thomas was reduced to silence. "That was not meant to be criticism," the king soothed. "The good Lord knows there are enough warriors in the world. It is men of learning who are rare, and I highly regard them. That is why I wish you to remain safe and accompany me when I go to Athelney."

"As before, I am honored to serve you in any capacity," he replied. "And it is commendable you fulfill your commitment to build a chapel there."

"A man must honor his promises, and stand by his word. At times it is all we have upon which to rely. I recall now this warrior," the king admitted. "His father, Lord Aris, seemed a generous and well principled sort. But the man had so many sons it was hard to keep them straight. With this one's face painted, I did not recognize him. He looks as untamed as a Pict. You gave the aestel to him," he added in tones akin to accusing.

"Only for safekeeping," Thomas quickly reassured. "The times are treacherous, and I am wont to misplace things. I prize your gift most highly, and will put it to good and frequent use in Athelney. Tyne Faran is a man to be trusted, my lord. And if I may humbly add, it is benevolent of you to lend your men-at-arms to his cause. He has a good heart, even for a pagan."

"We shall soon see," the king replied and gestured toward the scout returning to the main compliment of men.

"My lord," the man recounted, "those we seek are around the next bend. And based upon the bounty they carry, I believe they are the troublemakers who wreaked the destruction noted on our southbound journey."

"Excellent," the king replied. "Bringing them to task shall then serve two purposes. Close the distance slightly and keep pace. Be prepared to answer back the call to battle and to charge forward. Pass the word."

Thomas maneuvered his pony closer to the king. "We must remember the girl is with them. Could she not be hurt in the melee?"

"If, as you say, she is a true Christian, God will protect her."

Thomas stifled his words of concern, and instead offered a prayer for Leanora's safekeeping. The king placed many burdens upon the Lord's shoulders, burdens that could oftentimes be alleviated by commonsense. But it was hard to reason with a king, especially one who so fervently believed in the will of God.

****

Lulled by the euphoria of success, Ubba and his men now traveled at a leisurely pace. Then the sound of a horn wailing through the forest took them by surprise. As the equally unexpected response echoed from behind, Ubba's horse reared.

Grasping the opportunity, Leanora wrenched free and tumbled to the ground. Intent upon escape, she gained her feet, but Ubba leaned down and struck a glancing blow to the head. Reeling sideways, she landed in the dirt.

"To me," Ubba commanded his men. He brandished his sword and swung his shield into position. "Form a circle."

The men gathered around to make a stand. Dust rose from the trampled ground. Vision obscured by the cloud of dirt, she tried to avoid the flailing hooves, dodging first one way then the next. They were under attack. But who were the assailants, friend or foe? Spears sang through the air, and the sound of metal upon metal rang out as swords clashed and axes found their mark.

Men shouted, horses screamed, yet over it all she thought she heard someone calling her name. She stumbled toward the voice, hoping it was Faran, knowing it was Faran. It would not be Ubba. He would have worried about himself first, and looked for her later amongst the dead and dying.

Saxon foot soldiers reached for her, but they did her no harm. Quickly, but not unkindly, they passed her from one to another, delivering her to the perimeter of the battlefield. She fled toward the safety of the trees—the stench of blood already hung in the air.

Before long, an uneasy silence blanketed the area, and the dust drifted away on a welcoming breeze. The men dressed with royal markings had taken the field. Wounded and surrounded, Ubba's small party of men was at the disadvantage. From the corner of her eye she spied a scarlet blur. It was Kayden. She scurried to her side. Kayden hugged her close and wrapped the red shawl around the both of them.

"Lay down your weapons," the command rang out.

"Who is that man," Leanora whispered. "What is happening?"

"'Tis King Aelfred himself," Kayden whispered. "Brother Thomas enlisted his aid in rescuing you."

Leanora watched in stunned silence as the enemy rabble did as they were bidden. Then she spotted Ubba. Sword still in hand, he charged back and forth voicing his anger. "What right have you to attack a man from Bernicia. A man who is simply traveling the realm?"

"I have it on good authority you have taken this woman by force," the king said with a glance in her direction.

"She is my sister-in-law, accused of murdering my brother. I have the right to return her to my tribe."

The king did not respond. Leonora began to tremble. Ubba told the truth, as far as it went. Was she to simply be handed back over to this brute?

"I also see your horses carry many unusual trade goods," the king pointed out. "Some appear quite similar to items reported stolen by the people through whose towns we did pass."

"We traded for them fair and square and you've no proof we didn't," Ubba railed. "Besides, what concern be it of yours?"

"I am Aelfred, their king."

This at least gave Ubba pause—but not for long. In the North Country, where they had grown up, kings and kingdoms changed hands frequently. And although most people in England had heard of Aelfred, she was not sure Ubba realized the scope of the king's power and the breadth of the land he ruled.

"We will leave the trade goods if you like, but the woman goes with me," her brother-in-law insisted.

Again, Aelfred hesitated. In truth she was not his royal concern, and interfering in family affairs was a rare occurrence even for a king. Lightheaded at the thought of being once more under Ubba's control, she gripped Kayden's arm. Then Faran was at her side. With his hair unbound and his face lined with black markings, he gave her a start. Then he smiled, and her heart was at ease. Somehow Faran would make everything all right.

He stepped in front of her, his sword and shield at the ready. "I demand the right to face this man in personal combat," he declared. "He and two of his men attacked me as I slept, granting me no chance to defend myself, my honor, or my woman."

Despite the noonday sun and the shawl still snuggled about her shoulders, a chill now crawled down her spine. This was not what she'd had in mind. Faran was more than capable of besting Ubba in a fair battle. But what of the wounds he had sustained? She had not missed the fresh bruises on his face or the wrapping around his ribs. And the hand on his shield arm was badly swollen.

As if he welcomed the challenge, Ubba dismounted with a flourish and a laugh.

Even the king seemed to warm to the idea. "Fall back," Aelfred instructed his thanes, "form a circle. Divine providence shall determine who is right and who is wrong."

Faran strode forward into the arena formed by men and anticipation. Ubba held his ground and cocked his head to one side. It was the shield. He was confounded by what he saw, and she remembered the shield had the power to momentarily obscure the vision of one's opponent. Evidently the others saw it too as whispers of disbelief rippled wave-like around the circle. Her brother-in-law opened his mouth as if to protest.

"You may begin," the king announced curtailing any hope Ubba may have had for a delay.

With a bloodcurdling war cry, Faran rushed forward. Ubba responded in kind, and like two forces of nature conceived in human form, warrior met warrior. The curiosity of Faran's shield faded. Now true skill would determine the outcome.

As they circled one another, Faran drew close to one of Ubba's men. Lacking all sense of honor, the bastard stuck out his foot and tripped Faran. Her heart quelled as the man she loved rolled to the side, leaving his back vulnerable. Ubba seized the opportunity, but managed only a glancing blow to Faran's ribs. Growling with pain, the injury appeared to enliven Faran rather than lessen his abilities. He scrambled to his feet, and the man who had dared to interfere garnered several blows from the king's soldiers.

Mouth dry and heart pounding, Leanora watched in awe and fear. Faran was in his element, and the well-muscled body she had felt respond with tenderness, now emanated the unbending strength and power of the jungle cat he so resembled. He surged forward, hunting down his opponent, giving no ground as he harried his prey

To her surprise, Ubba already showed signs of weakening. After destroying her tribe, he must have rested too long upon his laurels. The girth of his belly showed more time spent eating well, rather than training hard. Faran's next barrage left Ubba's shield in pieces, and for her brother-in-law, the smell of defeat hovered near.

"Do you yield and give freedom to the girl?" Faran asked not going in for the kill. It was undeserved mercy, for Ubba warranted no quarter. But unfamiliar with the king's rules, she suspected Faran forced himself to the side of caution. He dare not overstep the boundaries recognized in such combat.

"Never," Ubba snarled. And true to his dishonorable nature, he snared a nearby spear and sent it hurtling in Faran's direction.

Using his shield, Faran deflected the lance and maintained the advantage. "Do you yield," he asked for the second time.

Ubba retreated, only to find himself in the arms of the king's men. Sword at the ready, Faran advanced. The crowd closed ranks and rushed forward, propelling Ubba back into the fray. The space separating the two men was small, and Ubba was swiftly impaled upon Faran's blade. No sound was heard, and all stood frozen in wonder. Faran wrenched the sword of Beowulf free from the other

336

man's body. Ubba remained standing, a questioning look upon his face. Then he crumpled to his knees, fell forward, and lay unmoving.

Eyes wide, Leanora stared in disbelief. The lifeblood pooled and spread around the enemy of her people. He would not rise again. A sob escaped her, and her breath came in fits and gasps. It was truly over.

"God have mercy upon his soul," Aelfred said piously, as he stared down at Ubba. Brother Thomas bowed his head in prayer. Then the king turned his gaze upon her. "The charges against you have been duly revoked. You may now leave with whomever you chose."

Chapter Thirty-One

"Halt," the sentry demanded, his tone unfriendly. "What dealings have you in our city?" He barred their passage, his expression one of no nonsense.

Leanora sneaked a sideways glance at Faran. Why did he not speak? Why did he merely sit idle, with a placid look upon his face?

The guard perused them more closely, and a flicker of recognition widened his eyes. He bent down upon one knee and bowed in homage. "Welcome home, son of Aris. The people have long awaited your return."

"It is good to be home, Duncan," Faran replied, "the time away has been long for me as well."

As if expecting more riders, the man craned his neck and studied the road at their backs.

"They are not coming," Faran said his voice thick with sadness. "The ship and the others were lost to a storm, a maelstrom that could only have been created by the wrath of the gods. They died bravely, Duncan, and will be remembered thus. Arise now," he gently ordered, "and open the gates that stay me from my beloved hearth and home."

Suddenly, the day seemed a little less bright, the sun a little less warm. She had forgotten Faran's homecoming brought sad tidings as well as good. As she offered a quick prayer for the souls of his three shipmates, thoughts of Brother Thomas came to mind. He would have known the appropriate words to say, but as requested by king Aelfred, he had remained behind at Winchester. The monk promised they would meet again. She hoped it would be true.

The guard gained his feet, opened the gate, and issued orders to a curly haired lad. With a small brown dog yipping at his heels, the boy ran ahead to alert the townspeople of their approach. She urged her mount to follow Faran's through the rampart. Cynric and Kayden were close behind.

The sentinel saluted, and the notion Faran was a prince again took her by surprise, although thanks to Brother Thomas' urging, she and Faran had finally discussed the revelation that they were both children of tribal leaders.

Near the center of town, a joyful crowd descended upon them. She sat taller and brushed the trail-dust from her cloak. Prior to crossing the small path of water to the Isle of Gullin, they had thankfully sheltered overnight in Lymington. The respite had refreshed her spirit and granted time to don proper attire. She did not wish to be found lacking when she met Faran's parents.

The jubilation was near deafening, but the voices turned hushed with reverence as Faran held the sword and shield aloft for all to see. The evening before, he had gently and thoroughly cleansed the grime, dust, and blood from the heirlooms. Now the cherished items flashed glorious in the morning sun, and the adoration the people held for the relics thrummed in the air.

"The land will be restored," Faran declared, "and all will be as it once was."

A hearty cheer erupted, and the festive mob surged forward surrounding them. Frightened by the clamor, Leanora's horse turned skittish, and as the villagers rejoiced and leaped about, Faran ebbed farther and farther from her side. Happiness beamed from his face as he returned their battle cries and shouts of victory. In the excitement he seemed to have forgotten her.

As the enthusiasm of the town's people roared in her ears, six strapping men—remarkably similar in form and face to Faran—grabbed him from his horse. Together with the sword and shield, they hoisted him to their shoulders and paraded him along the thoroughfare. Desperately trying to keep up, Leanora prodded her mount to follow, but again the horse shied away from the noise and confusion.

Twisting around, Faran appeared to search the crowd. Then his gaze came to rest upon her. He reached out, and she saw his lips move, but his words were lost to the din echoing all around them.

Shoulders slumped, heaviness filling her heart, and she gave up trying to reach him. The image of Faran grew smaller and smaller as he was borne away by the love of his people—a trailing veil of pretty young girls danced in his wake. The high-spirited females squealed and giggled and called out his name. How many of the comely wenches had felt the touch of his hands and the kiss of his lips?

Laughing and gasping for breath, Kayden and Cynric rode up beside her.

"We lost track of you in the crowd," the girl said, "the entire town is awash with a joyful madness. Where is Faran?"

Leanora nodded toward the royal avenue. Their gazes followed her indication. "And now," she said to the scop, "you have the ending to the ballad of *Tyne Faran, the Iron Heart.*"

"I have a feeling this story is far from over." Cynric smiled.

Oh, if only that were true. Yet for her, the tale seemed at an end. Following Ubba's death, Faran had readily claimed her, still she felt out of place here.

An inhospitable wind curled along the dusty

lane, ruffling the edge of her cloak. She pulled the gray wool tighter, and her fingers brushed the amber pin. It felt warm to the touch, as if in coming home had restored it with life, just as the sword and shield restored the land and the people.

She really should return the brooch to Faran's mother. It was probably a cherished keepsake. After all, it was not the woman's fault her son went about casually handing out the family treasures as he bounded through life like an unruly pup. And it was not his mother's fault he left a trail of broken hearts in his path. Besides, she needed no man-made memento to remind her of Faran. Her heart stored enough recollections to forever keep him fresh in her mind.

"Come," Cynric suggested, "let us make our way to the palace. After the great Tyne Faran Kilbraun has had his moment in the sun, he will search out the friends who stood by his side and saved his hide a time or two on this journey. We shared the pain, why not the glory?"

Why not? She had known all along the time would come when Faran would return to his old way of life and she to her new one—one that might not include him. But circumstance did not preclude making the best of the here and now. "You are correct, Cynric," she said, her spirits rising. "Lead on. Let us find the Prince of Geats, and remind him and all who will listen, how I rescued him in Lothian and how you fought at his side in the forest of Wessex."

****

Faran stood before his parents in the formal greeting hall, and reduced to feeling like a twelve-year-old, he fidgeted and cast his eyes downward.

His mother gripped the arms of her chair as if to prevent herself from rushing to his side and taking him in her arms. His father sat unmoving, his expression cold and noncommittal. The return of the lost heirlooms was evidently not enough to bring joy to his countenance or forgiveness to his heart.

It was foolish to imagine so irresponsible a transgression would be so easily pardoned. But he had left home ashamed and repentant, and had returned humbled by his experiences and appreciative of what it meant to be the son of a king and the protector of his tribe's history. Could his father not perceive these worthwhile changes?

"The sword and shield have been restored." He pointed out the obvious, anything to shatter the unbearable silence.

"Yes, Faran, and we are thankful. That they needed to be recovered in the first place, however, is still a concern. It is my understanding your ship and three friends were lost on this voyage."

The hand of sorrow gripped him hard, and his cheeks grew ruddy with pain and regret. Apparently the grim tidings as well as the good had preceded him to the royal citadel. "Yes," he admitted barely above a whisper.

"Tell me all that transpired," the king ordered.

Faran stood tall, and related in detail, the saga of his first journey out into the world. He held back nothing, not even his feelings and intentions for Leanora. By the end, he was tired and hungry and his muscles ached from standing so long inactive.

"What am I to do with you?" his father said, not without compassion. "By neglect you lost the sword and shield, yet by your courage regained them. You also removed from our midst Gorham and Romaine, a blessing duly noted—although regrettably, Lothian now be a Christian realm. Still, your original dereliction of duty demands punishment.

"Like any of my soldiers, you are subject to penalty. And what of the loss of your three friends? I know you grieve their passing, and although their deaths were determined by the will of the gods, it was a journey of your necessity that facilitated their demise. Had your boat-companions died in battle, we could at least demand blood or coinage. Now their parents must be satisfied with only the memory of their bravery and your words of apology."

Each syllable spoken pricked him deeper until the wound felt cavernous. It was all he could do not to drop to his knees and weep with sorrow—his burden to carry for all time. His three friends had insisted he not leave without them. He should have insisted harder that they stay behind. They had found honor and glory, but was it truly worth the ultimate price—a price that would always be too high in the eyes of their mothers and fathers.

"The usual punishment for such an offense is twenty lashes," his father pointed out. His mother inhaled sharply and made to rise from her chair. His father shot her a look that stilled her movements.

A public whipping... He supposed his father had little choice, for to do nothing would be unforgivable favoritism. And to go without punishment would also lessen Faran's standing as a leader in the eyes of the tribe. He could only hope the physical pain would be a balm of distraction to the torment in his soul. Still, even the most stalwart of men found the prospect of twenty lashes a frightful thought. Then he recalled the healed whip marks on Leanora's back. He would think of her as the whip fell. Knowing she had also once endured such, would bind them closer, another shared experience to chip away at their differences.

He glanced at his mother. Tears glistened in her eyes, yet her expression remained stoic.

"I regret, Father, I have forced you to such an impasse. I honor and respect your decision."

"There is, of course," Aris pointed out, "the other penalty which you may choose. It is rightfully offered to any man facing twenty lashes. Few have chosen this option. Those who did were not successful."

"Aris, no," his mother cried.

Faran had forgotten the alternative to the whip. If he survived, it would prove his worth unquestionably—even make him a hero. A whipping merely tested the strength of a man's body. The other tested a man's heart and soul, as well as his good standing with the gods.

"I choose the cavern of the gods," he said quickly before he could change his mind.

His mother covered her face with her hands and sobbed. Aris appeared surprised, yet proud of the choice.

"So be it," he declared. "At dawn tomorrow, clad only in breechcloth and prayer, you will be taken to the caves. There you will remain for three days and three nights, with no food, knife, sword, or ax.

"Make your amends and peace tonight, my son, with those you love."

****

Leanora, Cynric, and Kayden wended their way through the frolicking mob. Unchecked, the rippling crowd ebbed and flowed like a body of water, and it was just as impervious to crossing. Then two soldiers appeared, and the sea of faces parted. The men drew near, their expressions respectful yet serious.

"Lord Aris and his lady request the presence of you and your companions," one man stated, staring up at her. "You may leave your mounts here. They will be well cared for."

As if noncompliance was not an option, the other man collected the reins of all three animals. The first soldier helped Leanora to dismount, while Cynric assisted Kayden.

At the thought of appearing before Faran's royal mother and father, old feelings of insecurity hit her full force. Then she thought of all the unimaginable obstacles she had recently faced—faced and conquered, with Faran's help. Could this be any worse than the Tower of Ella or a raging river? The flame of raw courage licked at her heels, and the excitement she had experienced while adventuring slid over her like a well-made glove. She was a lady of substance now. She would cower before no man, and there was only one King whose judgment she feared, and she prayed He would give her strength yet one more time.

"The red-haired woman is to be shown in first," the escort explained as he ushered them along inside the small palace. Kayden and Cynric remained behind, giving her encouraging nods as she followed on the heels of the guard.

Rich tapestries lined the walls, and clean rushes covered the floor. Yet for all its grandeur, the hall emanated a relaxed and happy atmosphere. Head held high and shoulders back, she strode forward and realized this was where Faran had grown up. Where he had played as a child—his laughter and mischievous antics echoing through the halls. And this is what he had left behind when he had gone out into the world to recover the life-spark of his people. This is what was denied him until he reclaimed his honor and his rightful place in the tribe.

They halted before a set of ornate oaken doors, and her musing fled. The guard opened one of the portals. Before he could announce or squire her forward, she entered and marched up to the dais dwarfing the far end of the room.

On the verge of impudence, her hands clenched at her sides, she stared up at the man who occupied the throne. Then she glanced at the women beside him. The queen was not at all what she had expected. The woman seemed ageless, not young, not old. And she was very beautiful. Her hair was as golden as a sunset, shot through with shimmering strands of silver. Her eyes were light green, like Faran's.

The queen's gaze momentarily locked onto the amber brooch, and an approving smile played upon her lips. Unmoved by the woman's manner, Leanora remained impassive.

Aris, the king of the Geats, peered down at her as if he inspected a joint of beef to be judged suitable for tonight's dinner. "You are Leanora Wrenn?" he questioned.

She jumped at his words. He knew her name. Faran must have already had an audience with his parents. Was he near at hand? She wished he were here at her side.

"Yes," she replied. "I am Leanora Wrenn, formerly of Bernicia, and traveling companion to King Aelfred." It never hurt to do a little name-dropping in these situations. "I am honored to stand in the hall of the Storm Geats," she hastened to add with a quick curtsy. It never hurt to be polite either.

The stillness of the room became oppressive, and to keep from fidgeting, she clasped her hands together at waist level. "Why have you summoned me here?" she demanded.

The king gave a little snort of amusement, and lounged back more comfortably in his chair. "It has come to my attention," he said gruffly, "you were involved in the recovery of the sword and shield. Is this true?"

His choice of words made her somewhat leery, *involved in the recovery* made it sound like she had committed a crime. "Yes, it is true," she answered holding her chin a little higher.

"Why?" He threw the question at her like a dagger, taking her by surprise.

She had done it for Faran, because she loved him, but that was no concern of this man's. Aris might be Faran's father, and ruler of the Storm Geats, but it mattered not to her if he was sovereign of the known world. She did not intend to publicly reveal how she had risked her life for the love of a man, a man who had promised her nothing yet taught her so much.

"My motives are my own," she replied firmly but quietly.

His eyes narrowed. "By your attitude, I see you are not lacking in courage."

"I am sorry, your highness," she countered, not giving ground, "but my reasons are personal, and I would prefer they remain so. Is it not enough the relics have been restored to your realm?"

"That is indeed of supreme importance," he assured her. "What might I grant you in return for the service you have performed for my people?"

What indeed? She had wealth, so it seemed avaricious to ask for more riches. The only thing she wanted he could not grant her. She wanted...needed...Faran.

"I wish only to depart this town after returning this to its rightful owner." As she spoke, Leanora unfastened the pin from her tunic and held it out in the palm of her hand.

The queen gracefully rose from her throne and descended the steps of the raised platform. Pausing before Leanora, she retrieved the fibula and studied it carefully. Then she studied Leanora.

"Do you believe in the Fates, my dear?" she asked, not unkindly.

"I believe in the cross," Leanora replied. Concern shadowed the older woman's expression, and Leanora wondered why the queen would care what religious path she chose to follow. She also noticed the queen's eyes seemed reddened as if she had recently been crying.

"Do you harbor ill will toward those who do not

honor your God?"

Another odd question. Carefully, Leanora contemplated her answer. She had never categorized people according to their beliefs. When driven to judge another, it was always much safer to rely upon the truth of their actions.

"I believe a man or a woman must honor whatever deity makes them the best person they can be. If kindness and brotherly love stands sentry upon their path, then it is the right one for them and it will eventually lead to the one God."

"And what of children born of an uncommon union?" the queen asked, with a veiled expression.

Leanora did not appreciate being interrogated, and she was about to refuse to answer the query. But it seemed truly important to the woman who stood before her, and like fragile flowers, she carefully gathered her words.

"I would raise such a child with the knowledge of both religions, and when he or she were old enough to reason well, I would let them choose their own course."

The queen glanced up at her husband. He gave the smallest of nods. With a sweet and kindly smile, the older woman placed the brooch back in Leanora's hand and folded her fingers around the pin. "I wish you to keep this," she said. "As did my son."

As *did* her son? The woman spoke as if Faran had gone away or was dead. Darkness settled over her heart.

Tears now sparkled in the other woman's eyes. "If he lives," she said softly, "you may wed."

Chapter Thirty-Two

If he lives, you may wed...

The words screamed through Leanora's brain, making it hard for her to think. The words stabbed at her heart, making it difficult to breathe.

The locked room, to which she had been escorted—or rather dragged—seemed to grow smaller and smaller as she paced about in anger and dread. Dear heavenly Father, what was the meaning of all this? Why had Faran not come to her? They promised he would. Yet the evening had arrived long ago, and the slice of sky visible through the barred window was as dark as the worries plaguing her mind.

When she had insisted upon seeing Faran immediately, which had precipitated her present condition, she had been told she must learn the virtue of waiting with calm. How could they intimate Faran—their own son—was in mortal danger, and then sit idly by.

A knock sounded at the locked door. She rushed to the portal, ear pressed against the smooth expanse of wood.

"Who is there? Please let me out."

"It is I, Faran. May I come in, Gillyflower?"

"Yes, yes, of course. Hurry..."

The door was unbarred from the outside, and as it swung open, she threw herself into Faran's arms and fell sobbing against his chest.

"Where have you been? I thought you gone or

worse."

She leaned away from him and gazed into his eyes. They were pensive. The usual mirth, present in even the most dire of situations, was lacking from his expression.

"Forgive me for not coming sooner." He closed the door and ushered her across the room. Sitting upon the edge of the bed, he tugged her down to sit at his side. "I needed time to spend with the parents of my three ship-companions. To watch their faces was heart-wrenching. I felt so helpless. It is impossible to comfort the inconsolable. The death of my hearth-mates will be a burden I shall always carry, saved only by the fact that their friendship and loyalty will stand beside the grief."

She did not know what to say. He seemed faraway and lost in thought, so she sat silently and waited for him to continue. "Also," he added with the slightest of smiles, "I needed time to make sure I was doing the right and honorable thing where you are concerned."

She reached up and framed his face between her hands. The face of a man she trusted and loved. What could be so complicated, so important that he hesitated to speak of it?

Faran captured her hands and held them in his. "I wish to ask you to marry me, Leanora."

Her senses reeled. She could not speak, could barely swallow. Now the questions his mother had asked began to make sense. "But I am no longer pagan, and not of your people."

"Nor is my mother a Geat," he reassured. "She is of the tribe of the Wulfingas. In days of old, they were our only true allies. And father realizes if our tribe is to prosper and live in harmony with other clans and philosophies, the sword can no longer be the only weapon in his arsenal. He sees you as a peace-weaver," he added with a grin.

"Not again," she groaned.

"I did not point out to him it is not a perfect concept."

"What if they had not granted you their permission?"

"It would have made no difference. I will always choose you over all else in this world. You must remember that, no matter what happens."

At his last words, the happiness rushing at her from all sides made an abrupt halt and dissolved away. "What wretched information awaits to destroy the most joyous moment of my life?" she demanded. At his hesitation, she knew the answer would not be short or sweet.

"When the sword and shield were stolen due to my neglect, dishonor fell upon my father as well as upon me. For a king, this is a most grievous offense. In the eyes of our people, his judgment and wisdom became questionable. And as a sovereign, he lost face and power with other groups, friend and foe alike. I too am now viewed as less of a man and less of a prince. And although I have recovered the antiquities, I cannot just return home without reprisal."

"What is your punishment to be? Are you to be banished or imprisoned? I will go with you. I will wait for you. What is it, God's teeth, what is it?" The last words came out between anguished sobs as she imagined what must be endured before they could finally be together forever.

"Tomorrow," Faran explained, "I go to a place on the isle known as the cavern of the gods. Fasting and praying, I will stay there for three days and nights."

This did not sound like a terrible fate. Many monks performed such rituals, and in doing so, found peace and enlightenment.

"If it is the will of the gods," he added, "I will be given a vision and perchance even speak with my ancestors. The purpose of my life will be revealed before I travel the path back to this world. And assuming I live to tell the tale, I will have battle glory never before witnessed by men in this age."

He told her this so casually. Then the words of his mother came rushing back to her—*If he lives, you may wed.*

"What do you mean, never before witnessed by men in this age? How many others have survived this...this...ordeal?"

"None in recent time. But do you not see?" he explained over her protests. "Beowulf did not turn his back on the challenge from Brecca. Nor did he run like the others when gazing upon the face of Grendel or the monster's mother. Neither can I turn away from what lies before me. Some of my people may have forgiven me, but the deities ruling my life are not so easily mollified. Recovering the sword and shield was a task pitting man against man. Now I must face the judgment of the gods."

"I still do not understand the need for this challenge. You may only provoke the gods, and I remember they do not take kindly to amusement not of their own making."

"You once told me my dream of the stag was meant to lead me away from the battle to save my life. Now a dream must tell me why I was spared. Why I alone survived a doomed journey that took the lives of three others and brought me to your shore."

"But can you not have the dream here, in the comfort of your bed?"

"I must show courage, and risk the life that was spared. And I seek the cup from the dragon's lair to stand beside the sword, shield, and scabbard."

A sacred cup? It sounded like Arthur's search for the grail. That venture had not turned out so well. "You never spoke of this when you told me the story of Beowulf?" she accused, trying once again to turn him from a perilous path. "What proof have you this ancient cup even exists?"

"Only the story handed down by my mother's people. The cup would bear witness to the claim."

"But it could all be a lie for which you risk your life. How would her people come by such an item?"

"When Beowulf became king of the Geats, he was unmarried, and he grew old thus. But unbeknownst to all, he loved one woman. She was an outsider, and like my mother, of the tribe of the Wulfingas. At that time, such a union was strictly forbidden. But their love, as ours, was strong and would not be denied.

"She was younger than Beowulf, and was with child when he died. All were unaware of this, and his kingdom was left to another. She raised the child alone, never marrying, never forgetting the man she loved, or that the blood of such an honored warrior ran through the veins of her daughter.

"Before his final battle, when he went to destroy the hoary worm terrorizing his domain, he bestowed upon his lover the cup stolen by the slave from the dragon's tower. The theft of that chalice had set all in motion, and although he fought the winged monster and was victorious, Beowulf returned upon his shield. The cup that caused his demise became his last gift to her."

Tears streamed down Leanora's cheeks, and she wept for that woman of long ago, and for all women who loved men who were called to greatness. Visionary men, who could see a time beyond today. Bold and courageous men, who could see a world beyond their shield and sword.

"In the years following the death of Beowulf," he continued, "the winters grew harsh, our tribe grew smaller, and the Danes were no longer our allies. Our nearest neighbors, the treacherous Swedes, overran the territory. The Danes did not offer aid, and the Geats had no choice but to leave their homeland far across the sea. We settled here on the Isle of Gullin. An island named for Gullinbursti, Golden Mane, the beloved boar of Freyr. My ancestors arrived here safely enough, but with little coinage left to run a kingdom.

"At the same time, our old neighbors, the Wulfingas were also overrun by these enemies. They bore the curse of having only girl children, which left them with a heavy war chest and few soldiers. For the salvation of both tribes, the rule of marriage was changed to include these outsiders, and the joining of the two people became permitted by law. The Wulfingas have always claimed the cup as heritage. But it disappeared when Beowulf's lover was no more."

"There may be good reason the cup is gone," she pointed out. "To change history is not always a good thing."

"If I survive the caves, it is possible we shall know the answer."

Dear Lord, there was that word again, *survive*. "Faran, you can not risk your life on an ancient story and a dusty relic."

He shook his head and smiled. "Do you not believe a man was crucified, buried, and rose from the dead? And would you not seek to recover for mankind his holy chalice?"

"I see your conversations with Brother Thomas were more than playful badgering. But it changes nothing. Arthur's knights were not invincible, nor was Beowulf. He was slain by the dragon. Please do not do this thing."

"Beowulf was old. His time had come. Besides there are no dragons in the carven of the gods."

Heavenly Father, what could she say? There was no changing a man's mind when he fought for honor, reputation, and fame. The need to be remembered in glory blinded men to reason.

She studied the face of the man she loved. His expression held determination not fear. Faran seemed almost happy to be facing this travail. Was his guilt for the death of his friends and his unintended lapse of duty so profound that risking his own life was the only way to bring peace to his soul? She suspected he would never be whole if he did not conquer his demons. But the pagan gods were not always forgiving or generous.

He captured her in a gentle embrace. "Let us speak no more of what is to come," he whispered against her cheek.

Cupping her breasts, he teased her nipples to hard peaks, transforming cold fear to hot desperate wanting. They fell back upon the bed, and driven by a need more powerful than either had ever experienced before, they tore at one another's clothes. Lips met, hard and sure. Arms held tight to dreams, as well as flesh and blood. Wet with sweat and desire, their bodies joined as one—this might be the last time they would ever make love.

****

The morning came too soon.

Leanora stood on the edge of town, Kayden and Cynric at her side. The Isle of Gullin was not especially large, and part of it was hidden in mist— the part that spoke of old ways and old legends. Without being told, she knew that was where they would take Faran.

He stood a short distance away, his father and mother looking on. The two soldiers assigned to escort him to his destiny stripped him of all clothing save his breechcloth. The scars and wounds of his beautiful body were revealed to all, declaring battles won and other dangers faced. He was allowed no sword, no shield, no dagger. They even took his arm rings. When one of the guards reached for the iron heart hanging around his neck, Faran knocked the man's hand aside. He removed the fetish himself, and receiving a nod of consent from his father, he strode to her side.

As he placed the cherished item in her hands, the expression in his eyes gave voice to the words he dare not utter.

"I shall keep it safe until your return," she promised.

"I'll not ask for it back, Gillyflower. Whatever the future holds for me, it belongs to you now."

Before she could reply, the beating of a drum and a primeval chanting began. Flanked by the soldiers, Faran proudly walked beyond the gates of the city, and finally beyond her field of vision. If he did not return on the morning of the fourth day, he would be assumed dead. No one would be allowed to search for him. All were forbidden, without permission from the king, to enter the area he now crossed into.

She clasped the iron heart to her chest, and tried to be as brave as Faran. When tears pricked at the back of her eyes, she gritted her teeth and inhaled through her nose, refusing to show weakness. Then she stared at his precious amulet. Once she had held the man, but could not touch his heart. Now she had won his heart, but could not reach the man.

Chapter Thirty-Three

The cavern of the gods was a mystical realm.

On the first day, Faran wandered about examining the lush foliage and extraordinary rock formations. The sacred area was ringed by thick fog, yet the center, open to the sky, was as bright as any place on the isle. Tucked away within the mounds of hulking stone, stood several delicate grottos, brilliant crystals were imbedded in their walls. The sparkling gems glimmered in the sunlight. And now, as evening fell, they glowed by the light of the moon.

Inside one of the smaller caves, he sat down, his back against the cold jagged surface. Water ran down the wall. As allowed by the rules, he captured a handful, wetting his lips and using the remainder to wash away the day's grime from his face. He thought of the water-skins Leanora had suggested they bury with his friends, and he prayed his hearth-mates were happy and looking down from the Summerland with good intent. Would he be joining them soon?

Contemplating his fate, he curled up onto his side and tried to get comfortable. His stomach growled, long and loud. Then hunger of another kind set in, and he pictured Leanora. She was the last thing on his mind as he fell asleep.

****

Awake at the crack of dawn, Faran scratched a second mark on the wall to denote the beginning of day two. Then he sat on a log in the sun, and using a stick, drew random symbols and figures in the dust.

What would this day bring? Had he earned an adequate amount of success and fame to grant him entrance to Asgärd? Had he fought with enough courage and daring to honor the gods? To die in battle was the best way to insure a place in the hallowed mead hall. But in today's world, peace was sought after more than war, and the chances for gaining honor were much less than before. It seemed the laws governing his beliefs did not allow for the changing times.

Then he was struck by a terrible thought. What if this truly was the end? Not just of his life, but of the memory of his tribe's existence. It was his duty to preserve the stories and pass them on to the next generation. If he died within the next few days, all would be lost. What if the Geats no longer existed in a future he could not even begin to imagine?

His mind was rife with questions. They swirled about like birds on the wing. He had never before thought so hard about such quandaries. Teasing women with words of delight, and inspiring men with tales of glory, had been his only concerns. He realized now there was more to be cherished in the world—things outside of himself.

He sat as if in a trance and tried to recall all the stories he had been told. Not only the tale of Beowulf, but ones commemorating the important dates and places of his people. The names of the elders who had passed away. Sorrow Hill and the battles won and lost. Their journey here to the island. The legends roared through his mind, then shattered into disjointed phrases, all mixed up in a boiling soup of memories. Was he losing his mind?

****

On day three, he awoke with a feeling of nausea. How could an empty stomach feel so troubled? He was weak and irritable, but he'd had no visions. The gods were ignoring him. Apparently he was of no consequence, not even worth killing. And to live without even one word from the deities would be worse than dying.

Angry, he picked up a large stone. It was different from the rest, and as he struck the side of the cave to mark the beginning of day three, sparks flew out from where rock met wall. He dropped the stone and took a step backward. Then he gave a small sheepish laugh. It was just a firestone. In the dim cave, it had seemed more impressive, almost magical.

Like a cold breath, a shiver licked across his bare shoulders. He glanced around, bothered by the feeling that someone was watching. Unable to shake the mood, he stepped outside and sought the warmth of the sun. There was something different about today.

Bleary-eyed with hunger, he wandered over to the pond and stared down at his own reflection. The water was pure and clear, glowing with an inner light even as it reflected the bright blue sky above. He stood transfixed, for how long he did not know.

A rumbling overhead split the silence and gained his attention. He glanced up. The sky had grown dark. Clouds, thick as porridge, collided and merged into a canopy of gray forewarning. He shifted his gaze back to the pool. Bright and inviting, it seemed not affected by the machinations of the world around it.

As if pushed by unseen hands, he stepped closer to the water's edge. Then he recalled Black Rain Lake in County Lothian and the monster dwelling within its murky depths. Still he moved forward. The water lapped at his knees. He was being pulled in two directions—logic told him to stay his actions—an unknown force urged him onward. In truth, he held no fear of the water, only of what living thing might call it home.

His desire to know what was at the bottom of the pond became overwhelming. As a fork of lightning speared across the heavens, and thunder shook the earth beneath his feet, he took a deep breath and plunged headfirst into the pool.

The horror of his foolish act hit him full force as he swam like a demon toward the lights below. This was madness. Or was it his Wyrd, spun by the Fates?

Fragments of color flashed across his downward path, but the light at the end seemed to grow no closer. His lungs felt near to busting, he couldn't go on, then he recalled the tale of Beowulf and how he had fought his way to the bottom of the dark mere to fight Grendel's mother. Inspired once again by the man whom he had always tried to emulate, he felt a burst of energy.

He touched bottom and followed the light spilling forth from an opening in an underwater cave. As he passed through the entrance, the water diminished, replaced by cool clean air. He rolled to a halt, dripping wet and gasping for breath. Easing up onto his hands and knees, he hung his head and waited for his heart to calm and his senses to return. Then he heard movement in the stony chamber. He scrambled upright, reaching for the dagger he forgot he did not carry. Crouched and ready to do battle, he glanced around, stunned at the sight meeting his gaze. He was in a magnificent feasting hall, and all those present returned his stare—their expressions more amused than amazed.

"Welcome Faran Kilbraun, Prince of Geats," said the man on dais. He wore a crown, and on his right sat a woman of regal bearing.

Faran studied his surroundings in more detail. "Is this Asgärd?" he dared to ask.

"Not quite," the same man answered with a

chuckle. "Do not wish yourself so recklessly to a place of no return. I am Hygelac, ancient king of the Geats and this, of course, is Hygd my queen."

Faran passed his hand before his eyes, then peered once more at the splendor surrounding him. This was the vision for which he had prayed.

"Come join us," Hygd offered. With a graceful sweep of her hand, she indicated he should take his place at the mead-bench among the other men.

Only one position was vacant. It was situated at the far end of the long table, a bit more secluded than the rest, a bit more dimly lit. With as much dignity as a near naked man can muster, he strode forward and took his place beside the warrior who was the largest and most formidable of all the men present—including the king. This had to be Beowulf. His hero. His forefather.

Music, soft and lyrical, filled the hall. Several beautiful girls stepped forward to dance. With his attention focused upon the man at his side, he barely noticed them, not even when one drew near and set a mug of mead before him.

"You are Beowulf," he blurted. His voice near cracked with emotion. "I am honored to be in your presence."

"Thank you." Beowulf nodded. "And you are the one who keeps my story alive. I am grateful to you."

Beowulf—grateful to him. At the very concept, Faran's mind went blank. But he must find his tongue, and shake loose at least one intelligible sentence from his word-hoard. "It is my privilege," he declared. "I am also keeper of your sacred relics."

"Yes. I heard Weland had restored my sword. That is good. I also heard you lost it along with my shield."

Faran cringed. Even in the netherworld, bad news traveled fast. "It was quickly recovered. And both shall be watched more carefully in the future."

"Do not worry overmuch," Beowulf graciously forgave the incident. "That is how adventures are born. It all worked out well in the end, and every man must have his own story to tell."

"Regarding the recounting of legends," Faran said, grabbing this rare opportunity to discuss a subject that worried his thoughts, "according to my mother, the story I tell of you is not the whole tale as it truly happened."

"I know." There was a far away look in Beowulf's eyes, and his gaze settled upon a beautiful woman sitting somewhat separate from all the others. She held an intricately crafted golden cup, and she returned Beowulf's smile with an expression of pure love.

"It has to do with the dragon's cup," Faran dared to add.

"The cup and the woman are a private matter," the big warrior growled.

So, Beowulf intended to keep the relic and the existence of his woman a secret from the outside world. Faran remained silent, fearing to pry further. Surprisingly, Beowulf granted an explanation. "During my life on earth, I was forbidden to acknowledge this woman—the one person dear to my heart. I will not share her now."

Faran appreciated this sentiment, and it was a comfort to know even Beowulf could be tamed and tormented by a female's touch.

"It is more worthy," the revered man continued, "to change the story to fit what dwells in the hearts of men, rather then changing men's hearts to fit your story. Truth is a strange thing. It is akin to looking through a crystal, like those lining the caves above. The image seen is shaped and wrought depending upon who is looking and from which side."

"I don't understand," Faran admitted.

"She was my one weakness," Beowulf confessed.

"To reveal this now, might lead others to feel free to break the rules that govern us all. And if you were given the cup to take back, knowledge of its whereabouts would spread far and wide. Many would seek it for the wrong reasons, and many would seek it mistaking it for another. It would bring war and sorrow to your people, not honor and glory. It takes more faith to believe in something you do not see, than to worship something held in ones hands. You will carry the knowledge of its existence. That will be enough."

"So it shall stand," Faran said, "Your tale will remain as it is. But I do most heartily regret the story beginning with praise for the Danes. This too worries me. They are no longer our allies."

"Times change, people change, allies change. That is one truth that should not be left out. Let your stories remind Man of the importance of loyalty and honor as it once was. These qualities are fading fast. The world is of a much different nature now than when I was young. Men will always seek accolades for evil purposes as well as good, but fame is in the doing, and not so much the reward in your lifetime but in the next. Again, the story is best left as it is"

The next life... "What is it like in Valhalla," he asked in hushed tones.

"It is all you have heard and more," the warrior promised.

Faran felt a presence hovering near. He glanced up, it was Beowulf's consort. He had neither seen nor heard her cross the room, but she was there at his side—and she was magnificent. More beautiful than any mortal woman. Her gaze spellbinding as she spoke to him.

"Tell your mother I am very proud she has risen to be queen—an honor denied to me. And I am pleased the blood of the Wulfingas flows in one such as you. Tell her you have gazed upon the cup. She will understand why it is mine to keep and cherish."

"As you command, lady," Faran murmured.

The big man at his side smiled contentedly. "There is one thing I would ask."

"Anything. Say the word and it is done."

"Be there someone you might trust to scribe the glorious tales of the Storm Geats?"

"Yes," Faran replied, as Brother Thomas came to mind. "A holy man. He is very learned, and although a bit too keen on promoting his God over ours, he is good at heart."

Beowulf nodded his head in amusement. "Even in my time there were such men. Make sure he does not record the legends of our people in that Latin gibberish. It is a dying language. And always remember, Tyne Faran, the days on earth for every one of us are numbered. He who may should win renown before his death. That is a warrior's best memorial when he has departed from this world. It would be a reassurance and a comfort for me to know this concept has been recorded for all time."

"Again, it shall be done," Faran promised.

As a sign of fealty, Beowulf raised his cup.

Faran reached for his own mead, but Beowulf's woman stayed his hand. "You may drink from this," she offered holding forth the golden chalice.

Stunned by such an honor, he took but one sip and the room began to spin. Mead on an empty stomach—not a good combination. Then the room grew dark, and he realized the reaction was more then the effects of a heady brew. He felt Beowulf's strong arm around his shoulders, cushioning the fall as he collapsed to the floor.

****

He lay sprawled beside the pond, sunlight warming his wet body, and he remembered lying thus on the shore of Leanora's island.

Dazed and unsure of all that had transpired, he struggled to sit upright. He recalled diving into the pond, but not returning to the surface. Was it all a dream? As he shifted to a more comfortable position, his hand grazed against something. It was a cup. Had Beowulf given him the dragon's chalice after all? No, this one was of silver, but as artfully inscribed, and it gave credence to the vision granted by the gods.

With great effort, he gained his feet and noted the sun was about to set on this his third day. Unbearably tired, he stumbled toward the caves. He felt as if he could sleep for a week.

****

Leanora stood on the edge of the village. It was the morning of day five, and still Faran had not returned. All the others had given up hope. Even his parents no longer came to stand watch. They had returned to the palisade, his mother in tears, his father walking proudly yet with a hesitation to his step.

But she would not leave. She would remain standing beneath the same tree until they bore her away by force. Cynric and Kayden brought her food, but she could not eat. In truth, food made her rather ill in the morning, and she had missed her monthly fluxes.

She hugged Faran's iron heart to her chest, and thought of the burgeoning life growing in her belly. He must return. If the babe was anything like the father, chaos would reign unchecked without a man strong as Faran to oversee their household. She recalled the tale of Beowulf's woman. Bravely, she had raised her child alone, but Leanora did not relish a similar fate.

As the day grew long, she prayed to her God and she prayed to his. She made bargains and promises to all the entities—promises she would never be able

365

to keep. Then she prayed for forgiveness for making such oaths.

It could not end like this.

She sent Faran her love, her strength, her need of him. She saw him in her mind's eye—and then with eyes wide open.

As soon as Faran crossed the line cordoning off the sacred area, she ran to him and they collapsed to the ground side by side, laughing and crying in one another's arms. She kissed him repeatedly, tears of joy wetting her cheeks.

"Thank you for waiting for me," he whispered his voice weak and hoarse. "You are the only one who did not give up hope."

"We knew your courage would not frail."

"We..." He looked around the abandoned area, his brows knitted in puzzlement.

She took his hand and placed it upon her belly. As the light of understanding brightened his expression, he gave a joyous laugh and gathered her close. "If it be a girl, please let my mother teach her how to cook."

"And if it be a boy," she returned, and held up the iron heart, "he'll not wear this."

"No, he will not, Gillyflower. Now and forever, it belongs to you."

Epilogue

The Isle of Gullin, one year later

"It is complete," Faran said with a sigh of relief. "I feared never to see this day."

He clapped Brother Thomas on the back, indicating a job well done and nearly sending the old monk toppling off his stool. Brother Thomas righted himself, then gathered up quill and ink and carefully set them aside.

"Once Leanora has deciphered your chicken scratching," Faran added, "and she assures me all is well and good, we shall celebrate with an unprecedented feast."

The monk beamed with pride. "She is an outstanding pupil, and has done remarkably well learning this written Saxon language."

"And you, holy man, are an outstanding teacher."

"Thank you. Now if only I could teach you to trust I have not altered your words to suit my causes. Your attitude is most hurtful to my integrity."

"It is not your integrity in question, but your enthusiasm. You and I both know there are instances where you have embellished these manuscripts with your unflagging Christian tendencies. It is second nature to you, and beyond your control."

"That is true," the monk conceded, "and I will

not apologize for it."

"You need not. We are most grateful to you for undertaking this labor. And we are grateful to King Aelfred for allowing you to do so."

"Had he been aware you had so many tales to tell, he might not have been so generous with my time. I, on the other hand, am glad to be away from Athelney for whatever reason." The monk shook his head in frustration. "I have misplaced the aestel Aelfred gave to me, and I dread what will happen should he discover it is missing. I am old, and too forgetful and preoccupied with prayer to have such a valuable item in my keeping."

"If he realizes the loss, tell him I am at fault and it went missing when we were fighting in the forest of Wessex. A king is less likely to hang a prince than a priest."

"I might do that." Brother Thomas chuckled. "I will search for it again when I return to Athelney. It has to be there somewhere. Hopefully not beneath the foundation of the church he builds."

Faran gained his feet and picked up the newly completed manuscript. Together he and Brother Thomas left the citadel and strolled toward the trees growing along the banks of the river. Leanora, Kayden, and Cynric took shelter there from the noonday sun, and as he approached, Faran smiled. The very sight of his Gillyflower still quickened his heart.

Always the scop, Cynric leaned against a nearby oak, plucking periodically at his harp as he entertained the ladies with song. Leanora and Kayden sat upon the ground in the shade. Between them, two squirming babies wriggled upon a woolen mat. The girl baby, belonging to Cynric and Kayden, happily gurgled away as she played with her toes. The boy child, belonging to him and Leanora, growled like a bear cub and waved a willow reed about as if it were a sword. His son would no doubt be a renowned warrior.

"We have accomplished the impossible," Faran said as he carefully placed the manuscript aside and dropped to the ground beside his wife, his lover, his best friend. Much had happened since his return from the cavern of the gods. His transgressions had been forgiven, his place in the tribal community restored, and best of all he had gained a wife and child.

He reached out with his little finger to test the grip of his son. Leanora smiled and leaned against his shoulder.

"I am so proud of your achievement," she said. "Now the history of your people will live on forever in renown and reputation."

He slipped his arm around her shoulders. "You and the monk have made it possible. However, there is one more tale that must be rendered to the velum."

"I don't believe you," Leanora laughed. "After all these months of labor, what could you possibly have forgotten to record?"

"It is the most important legend of them all," he said with a grin. "The story begins with a bold adventure, and tells of the undying love between a brave warrior and the most beautiful woman known to any realm." Predictably, her smile dimmed, for he knew she did not wish for him to even momentarily envision another woman's charms.

"Who are these people of whom you speak?" she demanded.

Faran kissed her long and sweet, then loosed his grip and stared into her eyes. "It's our story, Leanora. And the gods willing, it shall be long in the telling."

A word from the author:

Who wrote Beowulf—the saga of a pagan Geat warrior written in Anglo-Saxon with Christian overtones? Perhaps it is best we never know, therein keeping alive the wonder of the ancient manuscript and the dreaming of romantic speculations such as this story.

****

During the reign of Aelfred (Alfred), the Isle of Britain was fraught with chaos, fueled by wars between indigenous tribes and invaders alike.

Instrumental in uniting the land, he was the first king to consider himself ruler of all England, and the only English king to earn the epithet "the Great." The story of Alfred burning the fennel cakes is apparently true, and he did invent a candle ingeniously marked so as to calculate the hour of the day.

An aestel like the one Brother Thomas lost in my story was found near Athelney in 1693. Known as the Alfred Jewel, it now resides at Oxford's Ashmolean Museum and is thought to be a book pointer. It remains a mystery as to how it came to be in Athelney.

St. Swithun, the Saxon Bishop and patron saint of Winchester Cathedral, was Alfred's tutor and traveling companion to Rome. He gave orders to be buried in "a vile and unworthy place" outside the church. Years later, in 971 A.D., when his body was re-interred in the cathedral, it rained for forty days, giving rise to the childhood ditty used somewhat anachronistically in this story.

My serpent tower of Ella is a derivation of King Aelle's Northumbrian pit of vipers, where the Viking Ragnar Lodbrok truly did meet his death. Conger eels still roam the Sargasso Sea—huge and terrifying, they are the fodder for nightmares.

The gillyflower plant existed in 798 A.D.; however the name did not become fashionable until years later.

The word scop is an Anglo/Saxon term for a poet or bard. The pronunciation seems debatable—shope, shop, or skop. Whatever you chose to use, you couldn't go wrong.

And finally, may I offer my heartfelt apologies to wolves everywhere. Your magnificence was much maligned in this story.

****

In the background of my beautiful cover, there is a tantalizing glimpse of page one of the original Beowulf Manuscript.

Thank you for purchasing
this Wild Rose Press publication.
For other wonderful stories of romance,
please visit our on-line bookstore at
www.thewildrosepress.com.

For questions or more information
contact us at
info@thewildrosepress.com.

The Wild Rose Press
www.TheWildRosePress.com

www.ingramcontent.com/pod-product-compliance
Lightning Source LLC
Chambersburg PA
CBHW071647260626
47170CB00001B/272